Upon Stilted Cities
The Winds of Change

Book 2 in the Chronicles of the Great Migration

Upon Stilted Cities: The Winds of Change

First edition. July 17, 2018.
Copyright © 2018 Michael Kilman.
Publisher: Loridian's Laboratory LLC
Ebook edition ISBN: 978-1-7323576-2-4
Print Edition ISBN: 978-1-7323576-3-1
Written by Michael Kilman
Cover Illustrated by:
Gabriel Perez
https://Artofgp.com
Title Design:
Desiree Byrd
Edited By:
Vanessa Corn
https://vcedits.com/

Also by Michael Kilman

Mimi of the Nowhere

Historian's Note to the Text:

D ear Reader,
The following historical text is in part dramatized based on our current records of the period between 1290 AC and 1300 AC. This particular decade is of great interest to the contemporary historical record. This period was known as the great shift, wherein humanity, facing overwhelming odds, was forced to confront its own extinction on multiple levels. Some of the following history is not based on historical evidence, but on a carefully calculated statistical probability of the events that had likely occurred during that period based on data records, DNA evidence, and the archaeological record. It is, therefore, important to realize that while much of the following is historical fact, some elements of the story were necessarily filled in to create what feels like a much more complete series of events.

For more information on this topic, including individual datalogues, audio recordings, and profiles of the following historical figures, please visit library 6911 in sector 3392.

Matron Mariposa Phillips 835.12.24 I.S.

Addendum to the Historians Note:
For ease of access to this text, please be aware that your AI component is automatically translating the text into your local language. Please note that if you so desire, you may turn off the neural auto-translator and experience the variety of languages that the following historical volumes have to offer.

To Destroy A Walking City (I)

The city had toppled. Bits of skyscrapers were strewn across the desert. With the city's legs destroyed, it had collapsed from towering heights. Most of what remained upon the excavated chunk of earth on which the city had stood were smoking ruins, shattered mechanized EnViro suits, and sun-dried corpses. Welts from bombs, bullets, and energy weapons pockmarked the perimeter, as various vapors cascaded into the late afternoon sky.

Inside the ruin, occasional echoes of weapon-fire permeated the stillness in and between the few remaining buildings, but even that would fade with the day.

Far back from the fresh ruin of the city of Langeles, Roderick sat slumped against a rock. He was alone in the barrens. His body ached from laying inside his metallic suit for what was probably several hours. The air was a cool forty-eight degrees Celsius as the sun began its final descent. Perhaps an hour of light remained before the cold night air set in.

Roderick blinked. It was a glorious sunset. Even as seen through the tinted UV protection of his suit's helmet, it was a ritual of beauty, a day that ended in victory. The power core within Langeles still remained, but the death knell of the city was ringing. Langeles would never walk again. For a city with no shield and no migration, there was only death. Mother Gaia would swallow it whole.

He pressed a small button under his chin and with his left hand pulled off his helmet. Its thick inner liner tugged at his graying hair as the helmet detached. He dropped it to the ground. It thudded against the gravel, rolling for a moment before settling in.

He closed his eyes and caressed the tattoo on his neck, the mark of his order, a tree of life with an eye in the center. He liked to feel the raised skin, the scars that had formed under the ink and burn scars. Most adherents of the Children of Gaia chose a simple armband or an inscription on their EnViro suit exterior, but for Roderick, only the mix of blood and fire and ink could mark his tribute and his loyalty. He was hers.

He felt the fresh air on his face and took a deep breath, knowing full well that he wouldn't be able to keep his helmet off for long. The methane would trickle into his lungs with each breath. Fresh air, as rotten as it smelled, was a luxury. But, it had been a long day, and a little non-filtered air wouldn't kill him. At least, it wasn't anything that an alcove couldn't heal.

He reached up to wipe the sweat from his brow. Already, beads of moisture gathered in the crevices of his pockmarked face and shimmered in the dying light. His light brown eyes reflected the play of colors on the hard, rocky earth and the swiftly changing sky.

Pain sprang up his right arm like a horse bucking its mount, and his square features tightened as he gritted his teeth. Roderick looked down the length of his right arm and remembered. He shuddered. Truth had a funny way of reminding you where you stand. It would take a long time to get used to a missing limb. The bloody stump of where his right hand been was now a symbol of his haste. He turned and gazed at the wreckage of his Dugger vehicle behind him. The City and the Dugger had shared the same fate.

With great pain, he poked the damaged arm out through the metallic hole of the suit where his armored glove had been. He had managed to tie the pliable, cloth-like underlayer in a knot to slow any leak of his air. He used his teeth as a second hand. After several frustrating moments, the knot came loose. He unwrapped the gauze and examined the wound. It was already stinking. He was fortunate that his suit had maintained his temperature and filtered air as well as it had. He would need to cauterize the wound, and quickly. If the toxins from the air entered his blood... well, he had better not let it come to that.

Silence slid into his ears. All noise evaporated. A high-pitched ringing emerged in the vacancy. Fresh fire burst forth from the remains of Langeles. Even from twenty-six kilometers out, he had temporarily lost his hearing. Roderick shielded his eyes from the blinding white light that erupted from the city like a second sun. No, not like a second sun, it was a second sun. For a brief moment, it was a star, a universe, created by the rupture of fusion and then winked out. His fingers pawed a solitary rock with his left hand for balance, feeling his feet giving way. His legs were so tired.

It was the Langeles power core. Dense smoke seeped into the sky. A hint of a mushroom cloud emerged but was already caught by gusting winds and dissipated across the landscape, intermingling with the colors of the setting sun.

His men had reached it. Where he had failed, they had succeeded. Praise Gaia.

He stared at the city with anticipation. Where was the blast wave? Detonating a nuke inside the city core should have sent a cascading wave of energy. He should need to duck behind a ridge or be hunkering down inside a small cave, but nothing happened. Perhaps they didn't use the nuke? Had his men managed to overload the core, containing the implosion? He would have to ask them.

It made no difference. Joy washed over him. Roderick let out of a roar of triumph. His roar caught on to the back of the lingering roar of the explosion and merged into forever.

He fell to his knees and bowed forward. Dry lips met the hardpan. His right stump grazed the ground, and a shock of pain climbed the length of his arm. He gritted his teeth but did not move from his position of reverence.

"Praise to you, Mother. Thank you for your aid in this great victory. I shall not forget the lesson you taught me this day. I shall not act in haste again. It is an honor to sacrifice in your name. May the blood that I shed bring new life in the soil."

He pushed his right leg forward and used his left hand to thrust himself upward. Roderick stared at his bloody stump, still feeling where his fingers had been. Despite the immense pain of the open wound, his fingers itched; an itch he could never scratch again.

Roderick smiled, turning his attention back to the fallen city. The burning city roused his courage, his determination. There, in the smoking ruin, was the evidence it was possible to rid the earth of its infestation. The giant walking city of Langeles and its people were no more.

But what of his haste? What of his disregard for Mother Gaia's words? Much had gone right, but what had gone wrong? Roderick reviewed the events of the morning assault.

2.

Migration halted so that the excavation could begin. A massive drill protruded from the lower hunk of rock underneath the city and was burrowing into the earth. Clouds of dust cascaded into the empty sky. A cycle.

"Commander, the Duggers are submerged, in position, and await your orders," said Patrick Lions. His face appeared before Roderick on his view screen. Patrick was a short, round, balding man who barely fit inside of a standard EnViro suit. With his helmet off, Roderick could see his rosy red cheeks and his crooked nose, broken from one too many fights.

"Excellent. What's the status on the special delivery?" asked Roderick.

"The package has been delivered to the city's AI Commander. Rocky said the primary shield should fail any time now. One thing, though, he also said the secondary shield is an isolated system. It's unlikely the virus will deactivate it."

"Yes, Rocky warned me earlier. But, there will be chaos, and that is all we need. What's the status on city leg security?"

"One moment, Commander, I'll check."

Roderick squirmed in the semi-cramped quarters of the Dugger. He disliked being below ground in the Dugger transports. Duggers were designed for the conditions in severe climate change during the late 21st century, and were usually effective means of transport in the barrens. They had a small drill and two claw-like arms on the front of the vehicle that dug below shallow surfaces. Roderick had hated using them at first, piercing the earth had seemed like an act of great sacrilege, but Mother Gaia herself had permitted them to use the vehicles in her name.

"Commander," said Patrick, "leg security has been deactivated. Should we send in Miss and her team?"

"No, stick to the plan. Shields fall first, then we send in the main attacking force, and then we send Miss and her teams to plant the nukes. If we deviate from the plan, it will be like Saud. You remember Saud, don't you, Patrick?"

"Yes, Commander." Patrick's voice was notably lower in pitch and his eyes cast downward.

"It took 80 years to rebuild the Order after Saud, Patrick. Have faith in the Great Mother. She has blessed this plan. Langeles will fall before the sun sets."

"Has she..." Patrick hesitated over the comm line. He knew that Patrick's faith in Gaia had wavered as of late. Many of his soldiers' faith had wavered.

Inaction was a plague that could spread quickly, and six years of planning was a long time.

"Has Mother spoken with you about this plan, Commander? I... I only ask out of curiosity, of course." Patrick's voice contained a hint of a tremor.

Roderick smiled, showing his ancient, yellowed teeth. "Of course, Patrick. It was the Great Mother who devised this plan. She gave me a powerful vision that showed me the city of Langeles on fire. She whispered that other cities would come for salvage after the fire. And then," excitement washed over Roderick's anticipation, "then, we will destroy them as well. Mother Gaia has brought us Rocky and Miss so we could carry out the plan. Have faith, Patrick. We cannot lose this day. Today is the first of many victories."

It was true that the plan had come to him in a vision that the mother had spoken to him. The timing of Miss and Rocky joining the cause was perfect, but even Roderick's faith had been tested at Saud. They needed a victory to restore the faith of his people.

"The primary shield is down, Commander," said Patrick.

"AI, confirm?" said Roderick.

"Sir, I confirm the primary shield system surrounding Langeles has fallen. Secondary shields surrounding their security buildings and storm shelters are active."

"Excellent. There will be riots inside the city over access to those shelters," said Roderick. "You see, Patrick? Mother's plan will sew chaos inside the city while we destroy the legs. Send in the primary attacking force."

"All of them, sir?"

"Yes, all of them, including your elite team. I want to keep their Runner-core busy."

Seven hundred men were in the main attacking force, and only three dozen were on leg detail. Roderick's personal guard consisted of only twenty-three men and women. He would hold his force until the nukes detonated, shattering the great legs. Then he and his personal guard would head straight for the city's core, ending the long life of the parasitic walking cities.

"Yes, Commander. May Gaia bless your path," said Patrick.

"And may Gaia bless yours. I'll see you on the other side. Keep the mother in your heart and we cannot fail."

Roderick watched his screen in the Dugger. He watched as the several dozen transport vehicles began moving toward the city. Most of them surfaced and crept along on treaded tires, but a few were still moving under the sand and hard earth. The ones under the ground would travel below the combatants and flank the Langeles Runnercore from behind.

They were greatly outnumbered. From what his spy had said, Langeles had 2,300 Runners ready for combat. Roderick only had 1,300 under his command, and several hundred were women and children back at Atlantis base. The fallen shield and surprise would give them a sizable advantage. Runners would have to be dispatched inside the city to maintain order.

The EnViro shield surrounding the walking cities weren't just for defense in combat. The shield was also used to create an enclosed ecosystem. Without the shield, most of the cities inhabitants would be slowly poisoned by the toxic air and cooked in the extraordinary heat. Secondary shields were set up around important buildings in the event that the primary shield failed, but with two million people in the city and only room for about a hundred thousand in the secondary shielding shelters, there would be chaos. Langeles's own citizens were weaponized in the Mother's cause; every man, woman, and child an agent of chaos, an inadvertent soldier in the army of the Children of Gaia. They were to be offered up in sacrifice to the Great Mother.

The radar screen saw the dots consolidating about a kilometer outside the city's boundary. Over the comm came Patrick's voice: "Duggers, mount artillery and fire. Infantry, dismount and engage. Be ready. Here they come."

Underneath the soil, Roderick felt the ground vibrate. Langeles had opened fire, with its railguns blasting huge holes in the rocky desert. But, with the shield gone, Roderick knew their ability to use the rail guns would be limited. The guns ran off the same power grid as the main shield system. Naturally, after a few shots, the guns would stop, and the majority of Langeles Runnercore would be deployed in the city's defense. Fresh blips on the radar screen were appearing. Roderick knew those must be the Langeles Runners.

"AI, status check on our cargo?"

"Sir, all three atomic weapons are stable and ready for deployment."

"Excellent. Open a line to Miss."

Miss appeared on the screen. Her short black hair was ragged and un-kempt. She had a lean face that contrasted with her thick, cracked lips. A faint crosshatch of scars ran up the left side of her neck and ended just below her ear. Her time in the barrens had taken their toll, but there was still beauty to be found. Her brown eyes glittered with an inner fire that Roderick had always desired. His second in command stared back through the communi-cations line, awaiting instructions.

"It's time, Miss. Uncouple the cargo cars and take down the legs. The main force and the fallen shield will keep Langeles security distracted."

"Yes, Commander. May Gaia bless your path."

"And yours, Miss."

Roderick felt a jolt as the cargo car he had taxied uncoupled from his Dugger. He felt lighter, more eager than before. His plan was unfolding per-fectly so far. Now he had to wait.

Time passed. Roderick grew agitated. For all his planning, he hated to sit back and wait while the rest of his troops fought. He had spent most of his life as a man of action, as the one on the front lines. It was bizarre to sit back and watch. So much could go wrong, but Gaia had instructed that he wait.

Roderick waited as the 8th and 9th nukes were attached to the city's legs. A few more to go and then he would pull his troops back.

Then something went wrong.

Over the comm came Miss's voice, the signal fragmented. "Commander... spotted us. Seven men... Confirmed that the.... 10th... leg. Should... deto-nate?

"Repeat that Miss, I didn't catch all of it."

"Signal... Under attack... Legs... Retreat..."

"No! Don't retreat. Finish the mission and then get out of there."

"Ten... pla... treating... distance. Gaia..."

The signal evaporated. "AI, what's happening out there."

"It appears that the Langeles Runnercore has discovered the leg team. Most of the team is dead. However, based on radiation scans, it looks like at least ten of the legs have a tactical nuclear weapon attached to them."

"And Miss?"

"Her life signs are still strong. It appears she is back in her vehicle and moving away at high speed."

"Then start the detonation clock. Let the Core team know we're moving as soon as the blast wave is clear."

"For detonation, a confirmation code is required."

"Of course. V638927SI."

"Thank you, Sir. How long would you like the countdown to run?"

"How long will it take for the main force to get a safe distance from the blast zone?"

"If they left immediately and put the Duggers at full speed, they could be clear in six minutes."

"Alert Patrick and the main force to disengage immediately."

"Unfortunately, Sir, Patrick Lions no longer has any vital signs."

Roderick grunted. That was quite a blow. He liked Patrick. How many decades had they fought alongside one another? Patrick had saved his life at Saud.

Roderick sighed. "Fine, just alert the remainder of the main force. Set the countdown for fifteen minutes. Alert everyone at two-minute intervals. Any longer than that and we risk giving Langeles time to disarm some of the bombs."

"Acknowledged, Sir. Countdown to detonation is now at fifteen minutes."

It was a long fifteen minutes. Roderick passed the time watching the radar of his troops departing to a safe distance from the estimated blast zone. He watched nervously as more of the Langeles Runnercore seemed to be gathering around the legs. If they figured out what was happening... but Roderick knew it was too late, only six minutes remained in the countdown now, and there was no way they could disarm the weapons in time. Miss had planted the nukes at the upper third of the legs, only someone with her special skills could have easy access to them.

"Four minutes remaining until detonation."

This was it. Roderick could feel a kind of giddiness pass over him. It had been a few hundred years since he felt so excited. The city would fall, their plan would work.

"Patience, Roderick," said a powerful and soothing voice.

"Mother Gaia?"

The voice was outside him but coming through him.

"Yes, Roderick. You must have patience. Do not act out of haste now or there will be a heavy price to pay."

"Yes, my Goddess, of course. Forgive me. I am unable to prostrate to you in this vehicle."

There was no response.

"Mother Gaia?"

Still no answer.

"Two minutes remain until detonation," said the AI.

What did Mother Gaia mean by "patience"? Did it mean that he would have to wait to assault the core? Did it mean that he should cancel the detonation?

"Sixty seconds remaining until detonation."

A wave of panic washed over Roderick. He quickly reviewed the morning's events. Had he overlooked anything? The AI began to count down the final thirty seconds. He smashed his fist into the steering wheel, and his anger burst forth at the same moment the bombs on the legs detonated.

Roderick watched over his view screen as the distant blast drowned out all vision with a great blinding light. He wondered if all of his men had remembered not to look directly into that light. Through his periscope camera it was fine, but he doubted the EnViro suit helmets would shield them from blindness. A mighty roaring noise pressed itself against the ground and waves of sand and rock shifted above the Dugger. Thunderous fury.

In the view screen, Roderick saw the city kneeling down toward the earth, like a man kneeling beside the dying body of a brother in arms. The west end sunk first, smashing into the hardpan of the barrens. Some skyscrapers broke in half and pieces scattered as they cascaded toward the ground. Tremors for each mass of concrete could be felt, even at this distance, when they returned to the earth from which they had risen. Then, finally, the rock slab of earth on which the city rested slanted up toward the sky, amongst the sand and gravel, and came to its final rest. A marker, a gravestone, a well-deserved end.

Roderick's rage and frustration were forgotten, as were the words of the mother. Roderick's cheeks pulled upward. A smile bloomed on his face. Red cheeks, like red roses, surrounded a sharp, toothy grin.

Roderick opened a comm line. "The Great Mother has brought us to the brink of victory my brothers, but we must not tarry. Main force, resume your attack, mop up what's left of the Langeles Runners. Core team, you are with me. CHARGE!"

The vehicle vibrated violently, and the sand on top of the clear glass cockpit began to move and shake. As the vehicle moved up above the surface of the ground, Roderick's view cleared. The vehicle lurched forward, its large, treaded, tank-like tires gripped like teeth in the earth.

The Dugger gained speed and began moving more quickly toward Roderick's final destination. He felt his heart beginning to pound. He was almost there. The outline of the city grew larger with every passing second, and in only a few minutes he would be on the outskirts of fallen Langeles.

A proximity alert flashed in the vehicle view screen, and the AI spoke. "Warning, incoming projectile. Five seconds until impact."

Roderick looked down at his radar. He saw the red blip approaching the vehicle. He grabbed the steering wheel and jerked it left to avoid a direct hit, but it was too late.

The RPG struck the ground just below the Dugger's left rear tire and sent Roderick spinning through the air, rotating like a corkscrew. The vehicle connected to the ground in a series of long hops, and Roderick felt his right hand catch in the steering wheel. The sounds of tearing metal screamed through the air as the vehicle slid and came to a wrenching halt.

Silence hovered. Only the wind dared to raise its voice. Tiny dust devils formed and spun and caught some of the smoke that gradually began to rise from the Dugger. Behind, the city of Langeles had caught fire.

A cacophony of noise returned and Roderick, dazed from what was probably a concussion, pulled the emergency cockpit hatch release with his left hand. He reached up with his right hand to pull himself up and out of the cockpit, only to realize his hand wasn't there. Confused, he looked down the length of his arm. A mangled stump of flesh, shredded muscle and bone were oozing blood down the exterior of his EnViro suit. All Roderick could do was stare. No pain came to him, only shock and surprise.

Where had his hand gone? Scanning the cockpit, he saw a metallic gauntlet still gripping the steering wheel. Bone and blood dripped at the end of the gauntlet. Roderick looked at his stump, then at the steering wheel, then back to his stump again. It felt unreal.

It was the wrong hand. It had to be. It looked so small and frail. How could it be his? He glanced around another time but, seeing nothing, he refocused his gaze on the steering wheel.

Roderick stretched out his left arm and reached for the gauntlet. In his denial, he had thought it a simple matter to plug the hand back into the arm, like a robot or a child's toy. His left hand wrapped around the gauntlet, the first instinct simply to pull the gauntlet from the steering wheel. It would not release. Then, he tried to pry one finger at a time off the wheel. No luck. He had heard of a death grip before but... he started to chuckle to himself but the laughter caught in his throat. He almost choked on it. He cleared his throat and let a sliver of madness drive a fresh wave of laughter, and for a moment the sight of his ruined hand was a source of great humor.

The laughter died as suddenly as it had come. Roderick turned his head out toward the burning city. There he saw someone standing only a stone's throw away from him. It was a Runner, fully armed and in a combat-ready EnViro suit. He had a high caliber pistol aimed at Roderick's face.

If Roderick had looked up only a single second later, it would have been the end of him. Without thinking, he threw the rest of his body out of the vehicle and rolled behind a solitary rock as the Runner opened fire. A few bullets sprayed the terrain. One of the Runner's bullets ricocheted off the metal of the Dugger and smacked into the Runner's shin armor. The impact forced him to fall to one knee. Roderick, seeing his chance, jumped up and reached down for his sidearm in his suit. His bloody stump mashed against the holster and Roderick screamed in pain.

The scream further stunned the Runner. He dropped his weapon, falling backward onto his ass. Roderick reached across his body with his left hand. He struggled, grasping at the butt of the revolver from the awkward angle, and finally pulled his revolver from his holster. He aimed and fired clumsily until the clip was empty. One of the bullets struck home. A single hole opened in the Runner's face shield, and behind it, blood splattered, and the Runner rolled to his side, dead. His metal armor at rest, not unlike the city from whence he came.

Roderick sat and slumped against the rock.

"AI?"

"Yes, Sir?"

"Are there any more surprises out here for me?"

"No, Sir. I do not detect any more Runners in the immediate vicinity."

"How..." Roderick was starting to feel weak and tired. Blood dripped into his eyes from a small gash on his head. "How... are we doing... out there?"

"My apologies, Sir, your inquiry must be more specific."

"Progress of... my... troops?" His breathing was slowing down and the lids of his eyes felt heavy. The head wound and the lost of blood from his arm were both a threat.

"Sir, the Core team has penetrated the perimeter and the main force appears to be overwhelming the remains of the Langeles Runnercore. I calculate that you have an 87% chance of victory at this point."

"Good, good... How many dead?"

"Exact figures at this time are difficult to calculate because of various reports of your troops and some conflicting data from the Langeles AI that I have intercepted. However, I calculate the total death toll at 1,752,892."

Roderick felt a pang of frustration. "No, ours. How many of ours are..."

"Ah, I see. According to my sensors, there are 289 casualties."

Roderick struggled to make a quick tourniquet by tearing off some of the linings of the passenger seat. He pulled some gauze from the glove box and wrapped it on the end of the wound. With his teeth, he pulled the material as tight as he could. Then he pulled up the lining of his suit and tied it and wedged it in the hole where the gauntlet had been, in hopes to keep the suit sealed.

Muttering more to himself than to the AI, Roderick asked, "Why was that Runner... out here?"

The AI responded, "Standard drill deployment procedure requires that a city deploys four perimeter Runners in each of the cardinal directions. Runners are instructed to set up sensor beacons and report anything unusual."

"Why... didn't he see us... earlier?"

"My apologies sir, I do not know."

"Haste... Mother... sorry for my..." Roderick coughed. The remainder of his words caught in his throat. He closed his eyes.

3.

Roderick opened his eyes back in the present. He stood and turned, moving toward the wrecked Dugger. He pried open one of the cargo hatches and began to rummage through the medical supplies. He would have to re-view the morning events again later, but for now, he needed to tend to his arm. It took him a moment, but he found what he was looking for, an emer-gency flare, an antibiotic shot, some morphine, and an EnViro suit sealant patch. It was a damn shame he didn't have a regen patch in the Dugger—they had them back at Atlantis base—but the flare would have to do.

He dropped the sealant patch on the ground. He lifted the morphine sy-ringe case up to his mouth and used both his teeth and his left hand to open the case. He grabbed the syringe out with his mouth and used his left hand to pull up the armored sleeve on his right arm. He injected it a few inches above the messy stump. It hurt, but the pain was minimal in comparison to the exposed nerves.

"All right. AI?"

"Yes, Sir?"

"If I pass out, I need you to wake me immediately. Don't let me fall asleep."

"As you wish, Sir."

The morphine acted fast. It didn't block out the pain entirely, but it was much more manageable. Roderick winced in advance. He knew what was coming next.

He pressed the trigger on the flare. The short flames sputtered and licked the sky at various heights. Sparks flew. He braced himself as he brought his left hand toward his right arm.

Roderick thrust the blue flame onto his stump and screamed, a scream that carried across the kilometers. A war cry of pain and victory. Roderick felt his body's desire to lose consciousness; he fought it. A few more seconds and the wound would close, for now.

Those last seconds were an eternity. He could bear it no longer. He turned off the torch. He injected antibiotics directly into the wound. Gri-macing again at the pain, he withdrew his stump from the open spot in his suit. He picked up the sealant patch off the ground and placed it on the edge of the tear. He watched the sealant patch come to life and spread itself over the tears in his suit where his hand had once been. The pain eased. By morning, the wound would be well-scabbed. Though pain would be a long companion, the danger of infection was over, or at least long enough for Roderick to find an alcove.

Roderick considered laying down in the back of the wrecked Dugger for a moment, then thought better of it. He had to be visible, had to contact his men. It was either that, or he had to find shelter before daybreak.

Roderick reviewed the day again and again, through the mirage of morphine. He knew it was unfortunate that Rocky's virus required the city's security codes to work properly. The Langeles codes had not been easy to obtain. Eleven cities remained, and Roderick could think of only one path to absolute victory, especially with a fifth of his force destroyed. Runner 17 was the key. If he wanted to destroy the rest of the cities, he would have to find him.

Chapter 1
Designation Runner 17

"**A**ctivating Runner, Designation 17."

The AI's voice, muffled by the warm, gelatin-like padding of the greenish goop that surrounded 17's body, echoed in his every cell. The lights of the Runner storage facility switched on. Flickering like a stuttering heartbeat, it pulsed against his closed eyelids. He was awake. He did not open his eyes. Not yet.

A large claw slid under and around his alcove on the storage shelf. Pops and hisses marked a disconnection. Thrumming eardrums. The claw tightened. It lifted. It rotated. With the slow guidance of the machinery, the storage container shifted from its flat horizontal position to an upright standing position on the dock floor. As it stood stationary, the clear plastic of the alcove slid open from the bottom up. An avalanche of the stem cell, fusion-based gel escaped with increasing speed as the opening widened until it was man-sized.

AI said, "Runner 17, step forward."

He obeyed, keeping his eyes closed; knowing from centuries of experience what came next.

"Initiating cleaning sequence." A metal arm with four shower heads descended from above, spraying water into every corner of 17's naked body, washing away traces of the gel mixture from his dark skin.

Eyes opened.

"Initiating drying sequence." The same arm that had bathed 17 with soapy water now blew hot air from its four adjustable nozzles. The warm air felt good on his skin, and he stretched and rotated his shoulders. He tilted his neck from side to side, wiggled his square jaw, and rubbed his dark brown eyes. Then, he reached back and wrung out his thick, long, black hair. He removed a hair tie from his middle finger and braided it.

"Runner 17, please proceed through exit tube 8c for your pre-run inspection. Failure to comply will result in disciplinary action,"

"What? No baby powder?"

"Baby powder is not part of the standard Runner activation procedure,"

"Yeah, well, it should be. Coming out of those damn alcoves is a little too much like being born. Next thing I know, you'll shove a thermometer up my ass."

AI hesitated for a moment. "Runner 17, please proceed through exit—"

"–or I'll be disciplined. Got it. Can't they install humor? I'm getting tired of the same old schtick. I want new material."

"AI customization options are disabled in the Runnercore Activation procedures. For all complaints and concerns—"

"Alright, I will go through the damn tube. Jesus Christ."

17 yawned and walked toward the long, tube-like corridor leading to the Runner Docks. He scratched the stubble on his long face. Behind him, several other alcoves in the storage area were coming to life. He glanced back to who the AI was unboxing.

"AI, why are you unboxing 875 and 913? You know they're just going to get themselves recycled."

AI repeated itself. "Runner 17, please proceed through exit tube 8c for your pre-run—"

17 shut tube 8c's door behind him. He couldn't stand the activation AI. It was so stiff. It was no way to wake up.

The briefing screen switched on and followed him down the length of the tube as he walked. He noticed the date, April 4th, 1291 AC, 6:30 p.m. He'd only missed a few months this time. Time was funny in there. The screen displayed his mission. He stopped and glanced at it.

"Basalt and Quartz, huh? Sounds like a real rollercoaster ride. AI, why is there a particular location marked here?"

"Sir, the coordinates are the most likely location of the two required resources."

"Uh huh. And since when am I given coordinates for a resource recon?"

"As you know, sir, access to resources in the past few decades have become increasingly scarce. Major Daniels has decided that our best chance of resource extraction is to pinpoint specific locations that appear, at least by previous mineral surveys, to be resource-rich."

"So Daniels is the one who made up that bullshit story? You know, I've been at this for more than a thousand years now. The only time you send me out at 6:30 p.m. is when there's something much more important going on than resource recon. How 'bout you tell me what's really going on at that location?"

"I am sorry, sir, but the only thing, 'going on at that location,'" the AI switched to an exact copy of his own voice to quote him, "is a rich vein of resources."

"I'm sure. Can you tell Major Daniels that I know he is full of shit, please?"

"Sir, Major Daniels is not receiving messages at this time."

"Then leave him a message and make sure you include a smiley face in it. I know how much he loves them."

"As you wish, sir. Please proceed to Inspection."

17 walked forward again toward the end of the long narrow tube without argument. He wasn't in the mood for a shock in the base of his skull. Without being aware of what he was doing, he rubbed the place on the back of his neck where they had implanted the chip more than a thousand years before. He looked up at one of the security cameras. No doubt that Daniels or someone else from security was watching him. He raised his right hand and gave them the finger and then a salute.

17 reached the end of the tunnel, and like a thousand times before, an iris whooshed open. He stepped forward into the light, squinting while his eyes adjusted, pupils shrinking. He swished the little saliva in his mouth and spat out the remainder of the stem cell mixture from the alcove. A hint of the greenish mixture blotted and swelled on the metal floor. There was no getting rid of that chemical taste. He thought for a moment that maybe stealing a meal from a dock worker or inspector would be worth the pain of a shock. He longed for some mouthwash or a toothbrush. The pain he could handle, the grainy taste of goo in his mouth was far more intolerable.

Then the inspector walked toward him, tablet in hand. With a single glance, he forgot everything else. He swallowed hard. She was stunning. She raised her right hand, holding a small wireless scanner linked to her tablet, and checked his vitals. She waved it like a magic wand up and down, left and right, muttering to herself the technical jargon of the readout.

17 could feel his heart pounding in his chest as his breathing grew more rapid. Her long blonde hair almost shimmered in the brutal fluorescent light of the docks. Those lights made everyone look ugly, so the fact that she was still radiant caught 17's attention. Her deep bluish-green eyes accented her bronzed skin. Her mouth had an almost natural upturn, and he traced the

curvature of her tiny jaw with his eyes. He watched her lips as her mouth moved and felt his breath escaping him. For the first time in centuries, he felt butterflies in his stomach.

"Runner... 17? Wow, that's the lowest number I've seen so far." Her voice was light and curious.

17 focused. He shook his head. He couldn't imagine their life together, or even just what it would be like to bed her. It would only serve to remind him that he was a prisoner.

"Ain't no lower number now." He tried to make his words sound hollow and dry.

"Sorry?" The young girl blinked at him.

"You're new, aren't you?"

"Is it obvious?" She frowned, her whole face flattened, but a smile hinted.

17 paused and looked her up and down again, this time making it obvious what he was doing. Her face flushed a little. He couldn't help it. Chances were, he would only see her a few more times before she moved on. Inspectors always moved on. Hell, he may never see her again, but something in him resisted that idea, something in him said he might see a lot of this one. He pushed the thought away. It was nonsense.

"How many years do you have?"

She hesitated a moment. 17 knew inspectors weren't really supposed to talk to Runners, but he wanted—no, needed—to chat with this one.

"I... only... 23 years."

"23 years? Are you kidding? I didn't even know they let anyone that young away from their parents anymore." He hesitated a moment, deciding if he should ask the next question. It burst from his lips. "Uh, what's your name?"

The girl, her eyes soft, looked around. Doubtless, she'd been lectured on fraternization with Runners, warned at great length how evil they were. 17 gave her a little smile, trying to encourage her, but that only seemed to make her more nervous. Was she nervous for the same reason he was?

"I'm not supposed to... I..."

"Yeah, yeah. I know. They told you the big bad Runners might hurt you if they find out who you are, might steal you in the night like the Boogeyman. Told you we are all dangerous criminals on a life sentence, right?"

The girl nodded. Her face was bright red. Her eyes kept sinking downward, admiring 17's naked body, but she was trying to hide her curiosity.

She bit her lip.
He shivered.

"You know what my crime was?"
She shook her head.

"Do you want to know?"

She nodded.

"I pissed off the wrong woman, an Upper. Least that's what they tell me, but hell if I can remember. Been too damn long. Everything bleeds together after a few centuries."

"But I thought..." she hesitated again, looking around to see if anyone, probably her supervisor, was watching. She lowered her voice just above a whisper and moved closer. "I thought that to become a Runner you had to commit a violent crime?"

17 laughed. The girl jolted back, looking around again.

"You're shitting me, right? Is that what they are teaching up in that... what do they call it these days? College? University?"

"Um... Scholar school... Sir."
"And she gives me a Sir. Wow, I like you," he chuckled. "You know, it's been at least a millennium since someone called me Sir? What's your name again?"
The girl looked down at her feet and then met his eyes. Her soft eyes made his heart ache a little. He couldn't remember the last time someone had looked at him that way; centuries, at least.
"Maybe we better just get on with the inspection," she replied. She looked back over her shoulder again.

"Come on now, don't be like that. I just woke up, and it's been several months sitting in that alcove. Do you have any idea how lonely and boring it is in there? You know we don't fully sleep in those things, right? It's more like an acid trip or something."

Her expression softened a little, and her left cheek slanted upwards just a hair. She hesitated, and the words almost seemed to leak from her soft lips. "It's... Alexa."

"Alexa, you don't look like an Alexa, you look like a..." He stopped. No. She couldn't possibly look like... He didn't dare make that comparison. A deep sense of anguish welled up in him. His memory was trying to surface, but he pushed it back down. There was a sense of mockery and injustice in this girl's presence. He tried to shake it off. Now he was starting to under-stand the effect she had on him.

"Uh... Never mind. Alexa it is, then. Tell me a little more about yourself, Alexa. Are you a Lower?"

Alexa shook her head. "Mid, actually."

"A Mid? What the hell are you doing in Runner dock then?"

"I..." she hesitated, her eyes again dipping down 17's well-scarred body. She looked up into his face again. "That's none of your business." She shifted her weight from one leg to another.

"Uh, you're right, sorry. It just seems like a lovely young Mid like yourself wouldn't bother with the big bad Runners down here in the docks. If you're a Mid, I bet you got lots of opportunities and probably a lot of interested men too, huh?"

She frowned. "I'm not some object for a man to possess, you know. And my career choices are my own." Now determined to focus on the task at hand, she fixed her gaze on her data tablet. He could tell that it was hard for her not to look back up at him. She peeped over the tablet, caught his eyes again and smiled. She forced a smile down and with it, her eyes. It made his heart flutter a little. He swallowed, thinking of his wife from many lifetimes past. Only the hair color was different.

"I'm sorry Alexa... I... this isn't a good place to be."

She looked up at him. Her eyes moved back and forth across his face and then her eyes locked with his. "I think... I think I'm done with my inspection. You have to move along now, Runner 17. And..." Her face turned bright red, and she looked down at her feet. "And put some clothes on. None of the other Runners come out of their alcoves naked. Um, your EnViro suit is in station 9." She pointed her finger in the direction of the EnViro suit platform.

"Alexa?" A man's harsh voice rang out over the intercom. "Alexa, please return to your office immediately. You know the policy about speaking with Runners."

She turned and ran off. He watched her go. She dropped her data tablet on her way back to the tiny office in the corner of the Runner Docks, but did not stop.

He frowned. It had been the first time in decades that someone besides the AI had spoken with him and he went and screwed it up. He shook his head. What did it matter anyway, not like a Runner could ever have a normal life. After he returned from the barrens, he was debriefed and then straight back into the regeneration alcoves until the next mission. He was lucky if they allowed him a real meal instead of that nutrition drip they ran through his EnViro suit.

There had been a few moments in his Runner career when he had tried to date the female Runners, but it proved impossible. The timing of re-activation never quite matched up. Sometimes months or years would pass between encounters. He found over the centuries that the best he could hope for was a quick fling, which also proved difficult out in the harsh conditions of the barrens. It was hard to get your pants down when they were under thick layers of metallic armor, but somehow, they managed. Caves were helpful in that regard.

17 turned toward station 9 and walked forward. He glanced back in the direction Alexa had gone and frowned. Then he moved forward and stepped into worn yellow outlines of feet. A machine both above and below made a guttural whirring noise, sputtered, and came to life. The platform on which 17 stood lifted several meters into the air. Cracks had begun to take shape in non-symmetrical patterns on the platform. The whole place crumbled from age.

From above and below the platform, large metallic hands with three fingers and an opposable thumb extended outward, each with its own task.

The arms dressed 17 in undergarments and then a thin, electronic, protective spandex-like coating that resembled a wetsuit and protected him from heat and cold. The boots enclosed his feet, granting him nearly a half meter more in height. Next, the arms pieced together an exoskeleton that tripled the user's strength. Bone joints glistened, waiting for connections to metal plates. Around the exoskeleton, the mechanical arms assembled the exterior armor. It started at his shins, attaching one piece at a time, moving upwards. Each piece resembled the armor of a knight, but it was perfectly connected, perfectly sealed like that of an astronaut's suit but much more flexible. For the final step, a helmet descended from above and enclosed the EnViro suit. Everything clicked on and came to life.

"EnViro suit activated. Welcome back, sir. It has been four months, three weeks, and four days since you were last in an EnViro suit," said the suit AI. "I have taken the liberty of uploading your system preferences and the required mission data into this suit."

"Good, I don't suppose you can talk to someone about the Runner activation AI, can you?"

"Is there a problem with the activation system, sir?"

"Yeah, that system is an asshole."

"I... apologize, sir, we may not customize—"

"I know, I know. It told me already. Tell me again, why can't I just use your system for activation?"

"I am flattered, but my systems are based on the chip in the base of your neck and only works when in direct contact with an EnViro suit or another external uplink."

17 sighed. "If you say so."

"Are you ready to depart?"

"Yeah sure. Being out there in the Barrens is a hell of a lot better than in those damn alcoves."

"I am sure I would agree if I had a body."

The outer bay door opened. Before he stepped forward, he looked back. Was Alexa watching? He hoped he would see her again. He frowned and turned forward toward the lift.

As he descended toward his Dugger, 17 had his first glimpse of the Barrens in months. Dunes and rocky wastes filled his gaze. The wind changed the landscape right before his eyes. There was nothing but death and possibilities out there. He glanced in the corner of his heads-up display and noticed the wind was only 80 kph, a mild evening at least.

He missed trees. Even though they had some here in Central Park, he hadn't seen one in centuries and wondered if there would ever be a day when he would see one again.

Before the end, he would see many.

Chapter 2
A Return to Nowhere

"I think you should let her go."

It was the third one this week, and Mimi was exhausted. She couldn't remember a time she had been so tired, at least not since Shannon's conversion into a reserve Runner. Four decades had passed since the terrible day, yet the intensity of those moments had never lost their edge.

She transmitted directly into the pimp's mind, trying to frame it in a way that he would think. It had taken so much practice to learn to anticipate others' thoughts. Doing so had turned out to be one of the keys to persuading people to act in a way you wanted them to.

"This girl isn't worth the trouble, look at her man, why would you waste time on someone who isn't gonna last selling herself?"

The pimp appeared to consider. He had a young girl by the arm and was tugging her. It reminded Mimi of when the recycled Runners had tugged on her and Shannon. It was a moment that she had dreamt of so many times, had woken to in her empty bed, had sent her running down to the underground to where Shannon lay in stasis. There was always relief seeing Shannon in her alcove, even if she couldn't speak with her but a few days a month.

Mimi skimmed. The girl, a small, frail thing with dark brown eyes and auburn hair, had come to him for a steady supply of drugs. Eventually unable to pay, as they so often were, the woman had turned to sex work. The pig reminded Mimi of that low-life Andrew, the one that had caused all the trouble and was the reason that Shannon had become a Runner in the first place. Old anger sparked. He was the reason that two of her sisters had fallen to the army of the Recycled.

A pallid, light-haired greasy thing with bone-thin limbs and a track marks up his arms like freckles, the pimp's grip loosened on the girl's arm for a moment as he stared at Mimi.

"I think you should mind your own damn business," he said. Though, there was less conviction in his voice now.

Mimi frowned. She skimmed the pimp's mind again and found that he was attracted to the girl, that he wanted possession of her. That would make the convincing harder. Though she had occasionally practiced with the red veil, the ability to mind control another human being, she wasn't confident in her ability, and she didn't much care for it. Besides, the Order frowned on its use, except in times of emergency. There were other routes.

She closed her eyes and pressed into the pimp's mind once more. She made herself look crazed and unpredictable. Considering her tattered garments, it wasn't a stretch. Sure, her sisters had offered her new clothes, but she always ripped them, always made them look worn and dirty. She was on the streets for a reason, and clean clothes made you stand out.

She spoke again, saying, "I think you should let her go or you might find yourself in a world of trouble." As she said the words,, she made herself appear bigger, made him imagine that her shadow was longer, that he would regret tangling with her. She suggested that she would bite and scratch and scar him like a cornered cat. She pushed the images into his mind to mingle with his thoughts.

She opened her eyes again. The pimp was barely holding on to the young girl's arms now, a thin thread of control and desire so fragile that a light wind would break it. Mimi stepped forward and she saw the pimp flinch. She projected the image of jagged teeth, dripping with blood, drool running down the corner of her mouth. The pimp stepped backward, letting go of the girl's arm and tripping over a piece of trash behind him. He crawled, crab-like, backward away from Mimi, never taking his eyes off her.

"You can... you can have her, man. Just leave me the hell alone." The pimp crawled to his feet, still a clumsy crustacean, stood, turned, and bolted. He risked one last glance backward before he rounded the corner out of the alley.

Mimi turned her attention to the girl. She was huddled in a corner, and Mimi realized she had cast her net a little too wide. It was the one thing she still struggled to control after so many years of training. She routinely targeted additional people with her suggestions. Noatla had suggested that this was because Mimi was so powerful, but Mimi just found it frustrating. The girl was weeping and shaking in terror as Mimi approached her.

Again, Mimi closed her eyes. This time she projected the sense that Mimi was an angel, a being that while sometimes terrible, was there only to assist her. Noatla had told her that idea of an angel was so deep in the psyche of the city, that it was a powerful tool to soothe people. Symbols were powerful persuaders; the more ancient the symbol, the more powerful. Noatla had suggested that all sisters of the Order of the Eye read up on ancient mythology and religions, as it would help with their abilities.

The girl noticeably relaxed and Mimi moved forward, reaching out a hand to help her up.

"It's okay. I'm here to help." Mimi kept her voice soft and calm.

The girl appeared to consider, and Mimi soothed with more encouragement. The girl blinked and then, hesitantly, she reached for Mimi's hand.

"What's your name?"

A stutter, words just above a whisper. "T-t-Tanya."

Mimi smiled at the girl, but inside she was frowning. They had looked for Shannon's lost ex-girlfriend Tanya for decades now, but she had appeared to have vanished. Even with Serah's help, there had been no progress. It was as if she had never become a Runner in the first place. The strange thing was, others were vanishing from the streets too. All the sisters reported missing persons in the Mids and the Lowers, and they had even heard rumors of Security Officers missing. On her last visit, Shannon had insisted that it was somehow related to Tanya, but considering the distance in time, it didn't seem very likely to Mimi.

"Well, Tanya, where do you live?" Mimi knew the answer already, but asking was part of the game.

Tanya shook her head. "N-n-nowhere. My parents... k-k-kicked me out of the house." The girl's frown was a kilometer long.

Mimi smiled. "Well Tanya, it just so happens that I'm also from Nowhere, so you're in luck. There's a place for people just like you."

2.

Mimi guided her through the alleys and down into the underground. The girl required constant soothing. She was cagey. It was probably the drugs. As they ventured through the old subway tunnels, she kept glancing back down the corridor. Anytime a light flickered, or one of the old steam lines sighed with age, the girl flinched.

Skimming her mind, the girl could think of nothing but her next fix and some of the fresh trauma she was gifted at the hands of the pimp. Mimi would have to pay the sleaze bag another visit, as she discovered, through skimming, there were several more girls under the creep's thumb. But, first

things first, they had to get this girl in a safe spot and get her clean. The ad-
dicts were sometimes trouble, but most of the time with a little persuasion
they did okay.

"Where are you taking me?" The girl's voice was a little stronger now.

Mimi smiled and soothed images of safety and warmth, of hot meals and
bathing. "A safe place for women who have been through what you have."

The girl was willful, though, and Mimi wondered, not for the first time,
if she had been a giant pain in the ass in her early days of the Order of the
Eye. How many times had Noatla had to soothe her? It took so much effort
and energy to soothe someone constantly. She was starting to feel skimmer's
fatigue, the mental fog that came on from constantly using her ability.

The last week had been a marathon session. Two dealers and a pimp,
picking on innocent runaways. Why were there so many more of them lately?
The whole city seemed on edge. Even Fatima had complained of fatigue, and
she had never heard Fatima complain about anything. Something was happening in the city, she could feel the tension rising, but no one seemed to
have any idea what was going on.

They rounded a corner. Metal pipes framed the passage and twisted in
the direction of the door. They ran down either side of the opening, and as
Mimi pulled the young girl toward the gray metal door, she could feel the girl
hesitating. The girl's mind spiked with fear, of locking doors and imprison-
ment.

Mimi turned and asked, "What's wrong?"

"You meant the actual Nowhere?"

"Yes, what did you think I meant?"

The young girl shook her head. "It's just I've heard things about this
place. I mean, no one in Orphan's Alley believes it's real. They say it's guarded
by banshees or ghosts or something."

Mimi laughed. "Well, it's certainly well-guarded."

"Jeanine, this girl I met in Orphan's Alley, said that once someone goes
in, they never come out again. That they hurt people in there."

Mimi frowned. "Do you think I want to hurt you?"

Tanya appeared to think about it for a moment. "Well... if you did, why
would you protect me from that pimp?"

Mimi nodded. "I was once like you. Without a home, without friends, wandering the streets. Me and a few others started this place to help protect the women who don't have a home. We got tired of being afraid to go to sleep somewhere or of running into the SOs. It's true that not a lot of people leave this place once they enter, but you will see why in just a moment. And I promise, you can leave anytime you want. Even now, if you wish."

The girl appeared unsure, but she didn't give any sign that she would run. She just stared at Mimi, almost as if she was trying to skim her, but not quite. The girl definitely didn't have the gift.

Mimi moved quickly toward the door and knocked three times. The sound of knuckles on metal traveled down the corridor. It mingled with the sound of venting steam and dripping water.

After a moment a voice came. "Who is it?"

Mimi didn't answer with her voice, she answered with her mind. It was the easiest way to gain access. The other way involved passwords, and Mimi could never remember the damn things.

Transmitting directly, Mimi said, "It's me, Rosita, open up. I've got another one."

The sound of a metal lock clicked and screeched an ancient protest. Mimi glanced at the young girl, and found terror just behind her eyes. The girl was wondering how she had gained access without a word. But, Mimi thought, at least she wouldn't have to soothe her alone now. Rosita was an excellent soother; it was why she was assigned to work in the shelter. Mimi quickly warned Rosita of the danger of the young girl bolting, and Rosita pressed forward with a calming presence as she walked through the door and took the girl's hand.

Rosita said, "Welcome to Nowhere."

It helped that Rosita looked the part of a kind and nurturing mother. She had a small round face and button nose with dark hair in twin braids and soft brown eyes. Her round body and wide hips always made Mimi think of her own mother, and Rosita happily played the part of mother to all the women who came to Nowhere.

As they passed through the door, they came to a large, open space. The space, once primarily concrete and pipes, now had small square containers with plants and flowers growing, with UV lights dangling just above. Mimi had made sure to plant plenty of flowers in her section. It made it a lot easier to bring some to Shannon during their time together, and it made Shannon happy she wasn't smuggling them all the time.

Several small shacks made from spare parts either smuggled or donated dotted the landscape. None of the shacks were much to look at, but they were a safe space. Each of the shacks had two sets of bunk beds and a little personal space for each of the four occupants.

In the center was a community kitchen and a bathing area. It had taken Mimi two years to find all the spare parts for that kitchen, and even Noatla had helped to smuggle a few parts so they could have an old-fashioned oven where they could cook fish from the underground and garden vegetables. They did have a food dispenser too, but if they used too many rations at once, it might bring notice to their little hideaway.

"And your name is?" asked Rosita.

"Tanya." The girl's stutter had disappeared. Her voice was strong and confident. Mimi reminded herself to sit down with Rosita again and try and learn some of her techniques.

"Come, Tanya, let me show you around your new home, that is, if you'd like to stay here."

"And what if I don't want to stay?" There was a sudden and surprising sharpness in the girl's tone. But Mimi recognized it, it was the tone of someone who had suffered in the place they had once called home. It was a hesitation to trust. Mimi had probably used that same tone when she was asked to join the Order of the Eye.

"You may leave at any time."

The girl looked around for a moment. "Aren't you afraid I might tell someone where you are if I leave?"

"No." Rosita smiled, but a current of power flowed from that single-syllable word.

The truth of it was, the Order protected this place now. If the girl left, they would transmit a number of confusing directions into her mind as they escorted her back to the surface. They would also take a very long route out. Both things served to confuse, and of course, even if she did make it back, or someone showed up who wasn't welcome, there were always at least two sisters present onsite. Not to mention Serah and Shannon were only a kilo-meter away, and both of them were capable in their EnViro suits.

"Come, Tanya; I'll give you the tour. Mimi has other things to attend to." Rosita took Tanya by the hand, and they walked toward the shacks.

Mimi was puzzled, so far as she knew, she had nowhere else to be. Then she felt her. Mimi turned and saw Noatla entering the door, ducking to keep from hitting her head. She shut it behind her.

Mimi met her Matron with a warm smile. Noatla returned it with a hug. She always felt tiny in Noatla's arms, like mother and child.

"How are you, Mimi?" Noatla indicated Rosita escorting the young woman. "I see you found another one?"

"Yes, third this week."

Noatla frowned. "You are resting your mind enough?"

"Probably not, but I will take a day."

Noatla nodded. "Good. Do so. Three times, you say? That worries me. Things have been very tense in the Senate. Everyone, even Senator Swanson, who is normally a symbol of patience and compassion, is on edge. It's as if someone is agitating the entire city."

"Miranda?"

Noatla frowned. "No, I don't think it could be. Not even she could in-fluence an entire city like this. Besides, we never did find any evidence of her presence."

Mimi said, "Yes, but nor did we ever find the missing Recycled Runners. And what about the disappearances lately?"

"There is no evidence that all these things are connected... still... I have put all our sisters on alert. We are still scouting for new members. We still need one more to be at full strength again."

"Shandie's replacement?"

"I don't ever like to think of them as replacements, especially considering the way that Shandie gave her life in service to the order—"

"You mean, to protect me." There was still guilt there. Leahara and Shandie had died at the hands of the Recycled. It was a sacrifice that Mimi would never forget.

Noatla smiled. "You would have done the same for them if your position was reversed."

Mimi knew that to be true now. She would give her life for any of her sisters, but back then, when it had happened, she wasn't so sure. In a strange way, their deaths and that guilt had solidified her place in the order, had made her a part of the family.

"In any case, Vala is investigating one candidate, though she doesn't look promising."

"Who?"

Noatla didn't reply at first. She opened her mouth to say something and then closed it.

Mimi knew exactly who, they had debated her for months. "Reevas? You've got to be joking right? I thought we weren't sure if she had the talent, anyway?"

Noatla sighed. "There's something there with her, I feel it. I just don't know what it is. And I did say it didn't look promising. But that's part of why I am here. There is another candidate."

"Oh?"

"Yes, a young girl, naive and inexperienced, but has the talent and is quite powerful."

"Where did you find her?"

"She was a recent student of mine in the scholar school. I have been keeping an eye on her."

"So why do you need me to investigate her, then?"

"Well, there are two reasons. One, her attitude reminds me of yours."

"Meaning she's stubborn as hell?"

Noatla had a smirk on her face but didn't comment. "And two, she has, for some reason, and despite being offered a number of excellent job options, chosen to work in the docks."

"As in the Runner Docks? Why in the world would any woman choose to work there?"

Noatla smiled again; her thin lips cracked slightly to reveal her perfect teeth. "Well, why would any woman choose to be homeless?"

It was Mimi's turn to smile. She shrugged. "Fair point."

"I want you to try and find out why she has chosen the docks and of course, your opinion as to whether or not she would make a good sister."

Mimi shrugged. "Okay, when?"

"She's on the clock, so I thought maybe you could take a look now."

"Alright, but... why the rush?"

Noatla bit her lip. "Because I think something is happening. I am not willing to say that it is Miranda, but there are too many strange things going on to ignore. We need to have the order at full strength just in case, and my intuition suspects that this girl may be exactly what we need."

"Alright, I'll take a look."

Mimi started walking to the door, but Noatla grabbed her hand and stopped her. "Remember Mimi, if you see anything strange in the docks again..."

But Noatla didn't need to say anything else. Neither of them needed to skim to know what the other was thinking.

3.

The girl definitely had the talent. Skimming her, Mimi noticed that she thought of it constantly. Like Mimi had so long ago, the girl assumed she was alone in her abilities. She was a thin, blond thing, and Mimi immediately spotted her in the docks. She watched her for hours, masking herself from sight the way that her sisters had taught her. The young girl had barely moved from her little concrete island office.

Then, something happened. Mimi watched as a Runner emerged from one of the many tubes that led from cold storage to the main docks. The young blond walked out of her concrete office, tablet in hand, and did her inspection.

Mimi crouched and listened to their interaction for a moment.

The girl said, "Runner... 17? Wow, that's the lowest number I've seen so far."

The Runner replied, "Ain't no lower number now."

Mimi stood up straight and looked carefully. Did the girl just say Runner 17? Mimi and practically everyone else in the city had heard of 17. According to the rumors, he had, by himself, disabled Mex's EnViro shield when it had once attacked Manhasten. He was said to have been in more battles than any other Runner, that he was invincible in combat, or at least unkillable. Serah had said he was very attractive and spoke of one time when they had spent an afternoon in the Barrens together. But, as she looked at the man with dark skin and the long black braid, she didn't think he was anything to write home about. Of course, the young blond was certainly taken with him. She could barely collect her thoughts. It almost made Mimi laugh.

A cold chill took Mimi, summoning gooseflesh. She had the sudden sensation that something was behind her, watching her. For a moment she felt frozen, unable to move. Then she pushed against that feeling and knew, with absolute certainty, that something or someone was behind her. She pivoted, raising her mental and physical defenses, ready to use all of her skills to strike.

And there it was. Only a dozen yards away. One of the creatures who had taken her sisters' lives. The blue lines running up its pale face, those blank, white on white eyes pointed in Mimi's direction. How had it snuck up on her in that EnViro suit? It cocked its head for a moment and then turned and walked toward the main entrance. Then, before it exited, it stopped and turned back toward Mimi. It waited. Mimi started to walk forward toward it. Still, it waited. Was it waiting for her?

Some Recycled Runners were still employed in the docks, but Noatla had proposed and passed a bill that put tighter restrictions on them. They had to be announced by the AI and monitored now wherever they went, and it required special permission for them to leave the docks or the subterranean areas.

But after the incident forty years ago, there were still dozens of them missing. None of the Order had ever found any trace and the one place they could have gone underground was completely inaccessible to everyone, even Noatla.

Was this one of those missing ones? It was heading up to the main level out of the docks; it wasn't supposed to be able to do that. She had heard no announcement by the AI, and it seemed to be watching her. No, not watching, beckoning her to follow. It said nothing, but there was a definite calling to her.

Mimi felt anger bloom inside of her. Was this one of the ones that had murdered Leahara and Shandie, and had nearly killed Serah?

She began walking toward it quickly, and as she did, it turned and began walking up the steps of the docks and out toward the streets through what was once Grand Central Station. Mimi felt her heart beating faster, felt her desire to catch up to it and destroy it grow. She tried to reach out to it, to shatter its blank mind as they had done to so many of the creatures on that terrible day, but nothing happened. It simply kept walking.

A part of her was telling her to stop, to reach out to her other sisters, not to approach the thing alone. A part of her was screaming at her that it was a trap. But she felt the deep hunger to catch up to it, to find the others like it and end them all. It was a kind of madness in her. Her footfalls grew closer together.

Then a voice boomed over the intercom. "Alexa? Alexa, please return to your office immediately. You know the policy about speaking with Runners."

It froze Mimi in her tracks. She blinked and looked around. When she looked back toward the exit, the Recycled Runner was gone.

What had she been doing? She should know better than to chase after one of those things. She and all of her sisters had pledged never to try to take them on again without at least six other sisters present.

Something horrible occurred to her then. For the last forty years, she had learned to persuade people into doing things they wouldn't normally do. The key had always been to find something that the person wanted, some desire, no matter how deep, and suggest that it would come true if they went along with whatever she wanted. Had someone just done that to her? Had they used her desire for vengeance against the creatures to goad her, to push her into following it? And if so, to what purpose?

Mimi felt the coldness return, but this time there was no Recycled Runner. The coldness was from within. It was the terrifying idea that someone might be laying a trap for her and her sisters.

Chapter 3
The Inspector

Alexa Turon watched Runner 17 descend with the lift, sinking until he was out of sight. Her two-way mirror caught a flash of setting sun just before the dock bay door shut. The fluorescent lighting flickered across her face.

She ran out, picked up her dropped tablet, and then hurried back to her office.

There was a hotness in her. It surged up through her chest and settled in her throat. She sat down at her desk. Placing her hands on the ancient cracked keyboard, she felt the rough bumps against her fingers. She began typing up her report. Missing keys had already caused her fingers to callus. Slow work, many typos. Worse, the delete key was completely gone.

"Alexa Turon," a high, obnoxious voice whined over the com line. It was Marty, her shadow, her boss. She still couldn't remember his last name and when she called him by his first, it frustrated him. "You have a call from a man named Douglas Turon, who claims to be your father?"

Alexa groaned. "Great, here we go again."

"Pardon?" asked her supervisor.

Alexa blinked, she hadn't realized she had said it aloud. "Oh... um... put him through."

Douglas Turon flashed on the view screen just above Alexa's cluttered desk. He didn't look much older than his daughter. The screen flickered for a moment and settled. At 193 years of age, his face was frozen in that of a man in his mid-30s. His chin-length blond hair, short pointed nose, and thin patchy beard made him look a brother, not a father. It was the alcoves.

"Alexa, how are you? Is everything all right? Your mother and I are worried about you, you know."

She tried hard not to roll her eyes. Here she was, 23, and her parents were still calling her at work. Granted, she wasn't legally an adult yet regarding voting and other privileges, but she would be in just two short years. Besides, so far as she knew, none of the other 23-year-olds had parents freak out if they didn't hear from them for a few days. Even though the legal definition of an adult was 25, most parents still accepted that their children were adults at 18. An ancient habit.

"Oh, things are fine, how's Mom?"

"Your mother is doing just fine. She landed another promotion in the library. She is going to be working almost directly with Senator Lightfoot on one of her artifact-cataloging projects. You know your mother, always the archivist and never much a people person. The prospect of spending days on end cataloging items from the last dig has got her so excited she can't sleep. It's all she talks about."

"Oh, well that's great news. Does that mean you could move to the Uppers?"

"You know Alexa, we just might. Your mother says that Senator Lightfoot has offered to sponsor us. I mean, Floor 39 is a wonderful level to live and all, but can you imagine the Turons making it to Floor 40? I mean, think of the benefits we would have as an Upper. Your mother and I have talked about having another child, and a move upward would make that possible. Speaking of which Alexa, I may have a job for you here in the IT department."

Uh oh. Here it came. For the twelfth time since she took this job, her father was about to ask her to work for him, and then, of course, ask her to move back in with him and her mother. She knew the tired argument already. He would mention, again, some fantastic job opening (probably one that he made up just for her) and again, he would talk about the benefits of living at home as a young Upper Mid and saving to become a true Upper. Then he would talk about Alexa's potential being wasted in the Runner Dock and how dangerous it was amongst all those criminals.

"Dad, I love you, but stop. I'm not interested."

Her dad's eyebrows shifted and one arched upward as if to say, whatever do you mean my sweet daughter.

"Dad, I don't want to go through all this again. I've chosen to work down here, and I don't want another lecture."

"But Alexa—"

"No buts, Dad. I know you're worried about me, but my new apartment in the Upper Lowers is in a safe area and working in the docks is as safe as anywhere else. You know damn well that they keep the Runners on a short leash. I have a button on my data tablet that I can press if I feel any threat at all."

"Alexa. It... it's not just your safety. Your mother and I are worried about your future too. You have so much potential. You scored the highest of any Mid on the Standard Placement Test; you were the top of your class. Supreme Justice Smith even offered you a position, and yet you chose the Runner docks. Why? If you could just explain to us why you made your choice, we could support you. We want to understand why our little girl is throwing her life away."

Alexa felt a rush of anger. "First of all, Dad, we both know why Justice Smith offered me a position. You've heard the rumors about all his pretty young assistants and the after-hours 'work' they do for him."

"Oh Alexa, those are just rumors. None of the allegations made against the Justice were ever proven."

"Professor Claven told me that the rumors were true and to stay the hell away from him. So that's what I am doing. For the last time, Dad, I'm not throwing my life away."

Her father rallied, not dissuaded.

"Alexa, if you could explain why you chose the Runner docks when you could have chosen almost anywhere else in the city, then maybe your mother and I could be a bit more understanding."

"It's not any of your business, Dad. I'm done discussing it."

Her father stared blankly at her, and Alexa felt a rush of guilt crest over her like a wave approaching the shore. She wanted to tell them, but she just couldn't. They would never understand, and though they had been supportive of her alternative methods for dealing with her headaches... well, this was something else entirely.

She sighed. "I'm sorry, Dad. You have to trust me. I'm doing this because I feel it is the right thing to do. This is the right place for me to be. Can't you just accept that?"

Her father frowned through the flickering glare of the view screen.

He sighed, "You are almost an adult now, Alexa, and of course we want you to do what you feel is right, but time so often has a way of revealing our mistakes." He paused again. His head turned back away to acknowledge someone nearby. He nodded his head a few times and mouthed a few indistinct words before he turned his attention back to Alexa.

"I'm sorry Alexa, but the AI needs some routine maintenance, Joe Fisher told me it's acting a bit strangely, so I have to go. But Alexa, I'll make you a deal. Neither your mother nor I will mention anything else about your job if you promise to sit down and at least chat with Dr. Black in systems maintenance next week. He's heard about you from one of your professors in scholar school and is interested in meeting with you."

Alexa rolled her eyes. It was another deal. There would be more. Always more. She also knew that accepting the meeting would get them off her back for another week and would allow her to focus on... well... whatever it was she was supposed to be doing down in the docks. She wasn't sure what it was yet, but she had some ideas.

"Alright Dad, I'll meet with Dr. Black next Friday. How does that sound?"

A smile spread across her father's face. She loved that smile. "Wonderful. Your mother will be so happy to hear it, and I just know that—"

"One thing, Dad. Don't expect me to take the job. I will go to the meeting but please, no expectations, okay?"

"Of course, Alexa. Of course." But his smile said otherwise. He expected her to take this other job, to get out of the Lowers and to move back in with them. She knew another argument was coming, probably even a yelling match this time. But for now, a temporary ceasefire.

"I have to get going; Joe Fisher needs me. Do me a favor and call your mother this evening, Alexa. I know she would be happy to hear from you. I love you."

"Love you too, Dad."

The screen went blank. She exhaled. She wished so much that she could tell them why she chose the docks, but she didn't exactly know herself. She also knew that until she could give them some sort of concrete explanation, something that made sense to them, they would continue to pester her. She wished she was a better liar.

In truth, she didn't much care for the job. The hours were long and mostly boring, the smell of the place was almost intolerable. And the Runners, despite her reassurances to her father, made her very nervous. Well, except for that Runner 17. He had made her feel something... different.

17's beautiful dark skin. And his eyes, like gray-brown orbs, she couldn't stop thinking about his eyes. Her mind's eye wandered downward, recalling each muscle. His chest hairless, covered in scars. She wanted to run her hands across those scars and feel the muscle below. She wanted to run her hands further down his naked body and... She caught herself at the thought and put a stop to it. Those thoughts lead to trouble, and she was already worried she was in over her head, despite what she said to her parents.

Her mind wouldn't shift. She began to type at the keyboard again but found it impossible to focus. Her supervisor, Marty, had warned her that 17 was entirely unpredictable. But maybe it wasn't the bad kind of unpredictable. And his face... it was so familiar. Where had she seen it before?

17 had told her that his only crime was pissing off the wrong woman. But she wasn't sure that she believed that. After all, Marty had told her that every Runner claimed to be innocent, that every single one of them would say that were framed or imprisoned for ridiculous reasons. Most of them, he had told her, were murderers or thieves or rapists. Most of them were the scum of the Lowers. Marty had told her that, even if a few of them were innocent, it didn't matter, because most of them were guilty as hell. What were a few innocent lives if the scum was off the street; if the city was safer. She wasn't sure just what to think about that. Safety seemed like a big price to pay if innocent people were having their lives destroyed.

But was there any truth to what 17 had told her?

She felt that warmth again. Alexa found herself wondering, what was 17's real name? The thought had overtaken her so rapidly, that she hardly recognized she had it. By the time she began searching through her data tablet for the desired records, she had only just become conscious of what she was doing. It almost felt intuitive.

It was quick work to find 17's listing. He was first on the list of active Runners. Of course he was. The list was in numerical order. She selected his profile and opened up the record. In it, she could see most of 17's missions and their details. A few were marked with a restricted access symbol, a circle with a red x in the middle, but for the most part, she saw that he had been on hundreds, no thousands of missions. She wasn't interested in most of the mission by mission details and scrolled downward, looking for what she desired. As Alexa reached the end of 17's profile, she felt a wave of frustration.

There was no name, but there was something else, something that almost took her breath away. At the very bottom of his profile, after the first mission was a 'years active' indicator. 17 had been active for one thousand, two hundred, and ninety-four years.

Quickly she thumbed the main menu button and returned to the screen to put in the search query.

"AI?" she asked.

"Yes Miss, how can I help you?" Alexa's AI now sounded just like her third-grade teacher, Mrs. Feltcher. It hadn't sounded like that before. Why the change? It occurred to her that she did have a lot of fond memories of Mrs. Feltcher. Had the AI analyzed her history and psychological profiles? It was a thought that she didn't like, but her curiosity was getting the better of her, so she put it aside.

"AI, can you give me a complete list of current Runners in order of the longest active duty status to shortest?"

"Yes, Miss."

Almost instantaneously the list appeared on her data tablet screen, and just as she had suspected, 17 was at the very top. The next Runner down had only had an active duty status for 674 years. She gasped and then caught her breath before it ventured too far from her lips.

"AI, are these active duty stats correct?"

"Yes Miss, they are current as of this morning."

"So that would mean that Runner 17 has almost double the years of active duty of any other Runner?"

"Correct."

"What does that mean?"

"I'm sorry Miss, but I am not fully sure I understand your query."

"I guess... I mean... why is he still alive?"

"To quote Major John Daniels," the AI's voice switched to what was the imitation of a gruff old man's voice that she assumed belonged to Major Daniels, "That bastard 17 is the toughest, luckiest son of a bitch on this whole worthless rock of a planet."

The AI system was not without a sense of humor, and she almost burst out laughing. Before she could, however, one question burned. She could feel sweat beading on her brow, it had to be asked, or it might burst forth from her chest. There was that heat again. It was taking her.

"AI..." she paused for a moment, terrified of the answer. She didn't know or wouldn't learn for a while why she was so terrified of that question, but it caught in her throat, struggling its way upwards toward her lips.

"What was his initial crime? I mean, why was he sentenced to Running?"

"I am sorry Miss, but that information is restricted."

"Restricted? To know someone's crime? That seems odd. Aren't those records supposed to be public knowledge?"

Alexa had studied both the current and ancient legal systems in scholar school and was certain that this information was supposed to be public record. It was one of the concessions that the first Senate had made when they had originally commissioned the Runnercore because so many people had been worried about transparency once they had abolished lawyers. In fact, after the sentencing of the first Runners, there were riots in the streets. It had not been lost on the people in the lower levels of the city that they would be the primary recruitment grounds for the Runnercore. They had known that those in the upper tiers of the city would rarely, if ever, become Runners.

One city, Sydney, had fallen to the mobs. No one had ever heard from Sydney again it had apparently vanished off the face of the earth.

But here was a man who lived those times. Only two years after migration began, this man had become a Runner. Not only had he been alive during the transition to migration, but it was also likely that he one of the first Runners if not *the* first Runner. Alexa felt a tinge of disappointment in herself. Here had been a great opportunity to learn about the ancient history of the city, of what life had been like in those early days from an actual living, breathing person. The only other person in the city who had been alive during the transition, from what she had read, was Major John Daniels, the head of security, and it was unlikely she would ever have a chance to ask him questions about ancient history.

"You are correct, Miss, all criminal records are supposed to be available to the public, but Runner 17 is a special case. His records had been marked off limits by an Architect."

"An Architect? You mean one of the creators of the migration system?"

"Yes, Miss."

"Which one?"

"I am sorry Miss, but that is also classified information."

Something about all this was strange. Maybe her unknown task had something to do with Runner 17? She bit her lip.

"AI, can I have access to all the files on 17, including before migration?"

"I'm sorry Miss, but most of those files are restricted."

She frowned, none of this made sense, why would anyone hide the files of one of the oldest Runners? There just really was no reason to restrict those files. Something in her flickered, that familiar feeling of knowing, but she dismissed it for now. This was neither the time nor the place; she would explore that feeling when she got home. She kept her breathing slow and steady to keep her from going under. Her head had begun to tingle, but it was subsiding.

"Just give me what you can, then."

"I am transferring the files to your tablet now Miss. Is there anything else you need at this moment?"

"No thank you, AI, that will be all."

2.

At that same moment, on the other side of the city, an alert popped up on a data tablet indicating that someone was attempting to gain access to 17's files. The eyes watching traced the source of the data inquiry and for a brief moment activated the camera on the tablet accessing the files. The tiny camera on the front of the data tablet snapped a picture and immediately an image of Alexa Turon's face was captured and transmitted. Facial recognition software identified the face as Alexa Turon, and instantaneously every known file and record on Alexa Turon was accessed and reviewed.

The threat was considered.

For now, at least, there was no threat.

But he would watch this one closely, lest she put many lives at risk.

3.

Alexa sat down at her desk, utterly unaware of the surveillance. She scrolled through some paperwork, the part of the job she hated most. She marked a few boxes on her tablet and signed her name below, indicating that the inspection of 17 was complete. She submitted the data through the city's server and after less than a second, the central AI confirmed receiving the packet.

There wasn't much to inspection. Between the AI, the engineers, the Recycled Runners, and the alcoves, most Runners were ready to go with only the most basic inspection. Her main job was to do all the paperwork, double check vitals and put up a red flag if something psychological was wrong, whatever that meant. Most Runners were at least to some degree unstable. Otherwise, they wouldn't be Runners. All she was, was a cog in the wheel of the Runnercore, akin to a mechanical arm in the never-ending assembly line that kept the city functioning. Her parents were right about that, and she knew it. The job was a dead end.

She was told from the get-go that most of the time she wouldn't even see Runners, and it would be an extremely rare occasion to see more than one at a time. In fact, the security advisor who had briefed her on her duties had told that she might only see a Runner once or twice a month. She had asked, what then were her duties in those slow times? She was told that she was to stay vigilant and to do her part. But in the month she had been there, she had encountered not only a dozen or so Runners but now even one of the oldest Runners.

Despite her long battle with boredom and the overwhelming pressure from her family, Alexa knew she was in the right place. The pieces of the puzzle were beginning to take shape, though the picture still wasn't clear.

"Alert, Runner 494 deployment."

"Of course."

Alexa grabbed her electronic tablet and searched for 494's profile. She walked out of her office and toward the EnViro suit platform. 494 was emerging from the tunnels. He was, unlike 17, clothed from the waist down. Several tattoos of red lines of concentric circles painted around his nipples and cascaded outwards across his chest.

Alexa reviewed the profile as she walked. 494 had a warning label attached to his profile. "Convicted Serial Rapist" it stated. She shivered. There wasn't any real danger to her since the dozen or so armed security guards would incapacitate 494 if he so much as breathed the wrong way, but she still disliked dealing with individuals like this. It was the thing she had dreaded most about the Runnercore.

Alexa approached with her clipboard, "Vitals are all looking good, 494, how are you feeling?" She tried to hide the quiver in her voice. She didn't want this one to know that she was afraid, but it was too late.

494 turned and stared at Alexa, his face expressionless but his eyes hungry. He glanced up and down her body, "Fine." It was a long, drawn-out word, and his lips spattered saliva just a little bit. He licked them to keep the moisture from becoming drool.

She felt his eyes consume her, and every part of her instinct told her to get away from this man. She felt that at any moment he would lunge for her. Her fingers drifted toward the emergency assistance button on her tablet, a button that would call every guard in the dock and potentially activate 494's shock chip in the base of his neck if the AI felt he was too aggressive or out of line.

Her heart was racing. He kept staring at her. Now he was taking in every detail of her face, and she didn't like it. She could tell by the way his eyebrows worked in concert with the slight changes in his eyes that he was considering something. Alexa hoped to the gods that he wasn't considering what he should do to her. She decided to stay out of this one's mind, it wouldn't help any to skim him.

Even still, she felt exposed and even a little violated. She moved her feet a little closer together, narrowing the space between her legs. Her thumb moved to a hair's breadth above the emergency button. One sudden movement and she would press it.

"Um... Your EnViro suit... It's in station 12," she said, forcing the words out.

She thought he was about to say something, but instead, 494 turned without further interaction and began walking toward the platform where his suit waited. She let out all of her breath, so hard in fact, that she worried he would turn and look back. But he didn't.

Then she lost control of herself, and Alexa felt 494's mind overwhelm her with images of violence, anger, and lust. She felt nauseous, dizzy, and had to stop herself from fainting. 494 was truly a terrible human being. She was glad to see him leaving.

Some of the Runners she had encountered so far had definitely deserved to be there but 494... he was exceptional. Sure, most of the Runners were slimy and could even be malicious at times, but 494's mind was the very definition of insane. She hoped that the Barrens consumed him, that he disappeared in the winds forever.

Her mind returned to 17 as she watched 494 walked toward the lift that led out into the Barrens. What had 17 done to deserve his tenure? Were all Runners true criminals, or were some in the wrong place at the wrong time? She would have to do some more reading up on it. It's not like she had much else to do while waiting for Runner deployments, and if her boss asked her, she could simply say she was learning about each Runner for her own protection. He would probably approve of that; it would probably fit into his narrow definition of "being vigilant."

Chapter 4
Security Detail

There was a rage in the noise. The rhythmic, angry bleating of the proximity alert and the noises of the room created a cacophony of convergence that drew Major John Daniels' attention to the center of his heads-up display.

Centuries of sitting in his sentry post as head of security had blurred his memories of the early days of the stilted cities. Memories, like seeds caught in the wind, danced and twirled in the air, breaking apart at the moment of grasping. Some older members of his detail had said similar things, concurring that their memories swirled and mixed like milk in tea. And how could you separate them again?

Daniels blinked. His shift was almost over. It was a hell of a time for a proximity alert, but he had been dozing. His senses had dulled as he watched the clock, ticking off the 17th hour of his shift. The AI took care of almost everything. So, what then, was this alert all about?

It wasn't an urgent alert. It was a kind of seismic activity 200 kilometers in the distance. Daniels moved his arms swiftly, but carefully, upwards. It was hard to move much when you had a cable plugged into the base of your skull. His visor froze. He tapped on the sides of the large plastic headgear, and the data stream resumed. There were always occasional glitches in the system. It was nothing serious, of course, but a system that was almost 1300 years old, even one that was as well designed as the city's OS, was bound to have a few glitches.

In the bottom left of his virtual heads-up display, a resource indicator flashed. The city was low on basalt and quartz. Whatever this object was, it attracted the interest of the AI, not just because of the seismic activity, but also it appeared ripe with resources.

"Manhatsten," he said, calling the AI.

"Yes, Sir?" it said. The AI had a very human-like voice, but it sounded as if a man were talking down the end of a long tube; his voice gaining in resonance as it moved toward Daniels' ears.

"Send a Runner to do recon at that site. I want to know what that thing is. Don't let the Runner know they're doing recon, alright? Make 'em think it is a routine mineral mission."

Daniels had learned the hard way to keep Runners in the dark. It made them more efficient at gathering intel. An informed Runner was likely to hide something or withhold information. And yeah, they recorded just about everything the Runner did, but there were still ways of withholding or distorting intel. Runners were, after all, a bunch of low-life slimy sons of bitches. Every single one of the shitheads had an agenda, and if they knew Daniels wanted something they would try to hide it out of spite.

"Yes, Sir," said Manhatsten. "The proximately alert indicates a likely mineral-rich substance. Should I send out a probe?"

"No, a Runner will do fine. Just send them in a Dugger. Drop-off should be at a safe distance from the site. Are you getting anything from previous satellite telemetry?"

"No, Sir, previous satellite data shows nothing unusual in this region, and we know from geological data that an earthquake is unlikely. However, the Dog Star satellite has not passed over this region in four days, nine hours, and thirty-three minutes."

"Ah hell." Daniels sighed. "I'll tell you AI, I'd give one of my toes for a few dozen satellites in orbit like the old days. One of those old pieces of shit just ain't enough. How in the hell am I supposed to assess threats without regular updates?"

"Sir, if you are concerned about the infrequency of the intervals at which you receive data, may I recommend using the probes to—"

"I wasn't looking for answers."

"My apologies, Sir, I misunderstood and assumed you were making an inquiry."

The AI was helpful in a lot of circumstances, but Daniels wished that for once it wouldn't be so dense. It was always so damned literal.

"You know damn well that probes cost way too much. That Senate would shit a brick if I started using probes for recon. Sandstorms ate the last three. Besides, you know the data from a Runner is far better than a shitty camera and audio recording device."

Daniels' heads-up display opened up a viewer on the camera over Runner 17's regeneration alcove. He saw 17 stand and walk down the corridor toward the docks. As usual, he was as naked as the day he was born. Most runners choose to wear undergarments, but 17 had said... what had he said? It was something like: "I don't want to get that sticky shit all up in my skivvies." Daniels understood that, at least a little. The goop in the alcoves was terribly sticky and tough to get out of a uniform. Runners didn't exactly have an extensive wardrobe.

Reliable 17. He was a pain in the ass, but always got the job done. 17 had probably been in more scrapes and battles than all the other Runners in Manhatsten combined. He had a knack for trouble. Daniels hated him, but also respected his ability to stay alive and finish his objectives. He avoided dealing with 17 directly as often as possible, which of course was most of the time. 17 was, at best, openly insubordinate, and goddamn could that man chatter.

Over the decades, it had brought Daniels great joy to shock the shit out of 17. Funny enough, the moment he thought of it, 17 stopped and turned toward the camera and held up his middle finger, almost as if he could read his mind. Daniels scowled and felt temptation take him. He scrolled down the list of Runners and hovered over 17's profile. In his heads-up display, the activator for the chip in the base of his skull came up. All he had to do was press the button, and 17 would be in for a few hundred volts, straight to his nervous system. Sometimes he just wanted to see the son of a bitch squirm a little. But he restrained himself. He couldn't let the bastard get the best of him. Not again. He sighed. He had to set an example for the rest of his command and not abuse his power. There was enough corruption around already, especially down in the Lowers with his SOs.

All Runners had a knack for trouble. Most of them had a bad attitude. If they didn't, they wouldn't be Runners. Running was a punishment, a kind of social death. Being a Runner meant risking your life every time the city needed something or every time an Upper with a bug up their ass wanted something done in the Barrens. It was a job that no one wanted, a job that every man and woman feared. It was a job that meant being out in the elements, a jail sentence several dozen lives long, that is, if you were good like 17.

The proximity alert activated again; he shifted his arm up and to the left and slid it in a downward motion, indicating that he wanted the alert turned off. The alarm continued to sound.

"Manhatsten."

"Yes, Sir?"

"I want that alarm off. I've already got the notice."

"My apologies, Sir, but this is a secondary notice. There was an additional kinetic energy release at the same site,"

"What the hell does that mean?"

"It means that either there was either an aftershock or a secondary explosion onsite. In either case, Sir, you may see several more alerts."

"Mute all alerts related to that site."

"Sir, I do not recommend this course of action. For example, what if—"

"Just do it. 17's going to investigate anyway."

"Very well."

"One more thing."

"Of course, Sir."

"Get me the location of all the other cities, pronto. I want to be sure we aren't dealing with some sort of ambush here. God knows some of those other city commanders are crafty sons of bitches. They would love to get their hands on Manhatsten and gut it for everything it's worth."

"Of course, Sir."

Daniels had a crazy thought, one that he couldn't find any rational reason to justify. Could it be a human settlement? No one out there was crazy enough to stay stationary with the roaming methane pockets, apolicanes, or the sandstorms, were they? How would that even be possible? And rich in minerals? Something in his guts squirmed; this felt wrong.

The head of security of Lundon had once told him that a Runner claimed he found human settlements. The Runner was eventually decommissioned after he had completely lost his mind. Daniels thought the guy was probably faking it to get out of Runner duty, but then he was recycled, and well, Daniels had thought that was a bit harsh.

Most of the city had at one time or another whispered of human settlements. Even the children's stories spoke of something they called New Eden; a place where humans could live in nature, free from the endless metallic death march of the 150-meter-tall legs at the base of each city. New Eden was supposed to be a place where enlightened humans would never again squander their resources and one day, the Earth would be green again. It was just another fairy tale. Hell, humans couldn't even conserve inside a city designed to be an enclosed ecosystem. How in the gods' names were they going to live on a fucking farm?

Even if it was total bullshit, the idea was appealing, even to Daniels. Being born before migration and even before World War Three, he could imagine a world where cities no longer migrated; where human beings could live outside of an EnViro shield and breathe air without the taste of methane. He could imagine his 18-greats-granddaughter running in a field of wildflowers as his daughter had once done before the migration started.

"It's all terribly romantic, isn't it?" he said aloud.

"What's that, Sir?" Private Fallman said.

"Fallman, you think that New Eden stuff is crap, right?"

Fallman sat at his station only three meters away. He was working on some specifications for city engineers. He closed the windows quickly. Daniels didn't know or care what in the hell he was doing, so long as he didn't mess things up. Fallman hadn't been around long, but seemed to be fairly up-standing and eager to please.

"I don't know, Sir. I mean, I guess it seems crazy. But doesn't the possibility at least provide you with some hope?"

Daniels laughed. "Hope? I'm too gods-damn old for hope. Hope is something for the starry-eyed kids. No, I am about a thousand years past that hope crap."

For 1,296 years, Daniels had spent most of his time plugged into the security center within the city. When he did go home, a regeneration alcove revitalized his mind and body as he slept. Of course, he could leave his chair whenever he wanted, but it was far easier to regulate the city's movements through the command chair.

Major Daniels was all that passed for military these days. He had retained his rank of Major from his time in the military and assigned ranks to his staff. He felt that it helped to keep order. If you had a rank, you knew your place. The key to good security was a clear and orderly system of hierarchy.

Despite Daniel's background and significant combat during Word War Three, most of the city's occupants knew nothing about combat. It had been... what... since the fall of Mex? Something like 140 years? It was at least that long since two cities waged war against one another, and even then, Manhatsten wasn't involved in the conflict. Despite the insistence of the Uppers, who Daniels firmly believed secretly had a silver spoon removed from their ass at birth, Daniels had managed to keep Manhatsten far away from that conflict under the guise of "routine upgrades and maintenance of the city's systems." He had heard through several communication channels later that every city that had shown up to salvage Mex had received heavy damage and a significant loss of their Runnercores. None of that shit would go on under his watch.

Travers stood from his chair, turned and walked several meters toward him.

"Major Daniels, Sir, I have some new data for you to consider," said Lieutenant Travers.

"What is it?"

Travers frowned and said, "Well, Sir, it's an analysis of migration routes, storm systems, and dig times."

Major Daniels turned and eyed Travers. Travers had been under his command for what, six centuries? Travers knew by now that bringing mundane data to him would simply get him waved away.

"I take it you felt this was important?"

"Yes, Major. I've been going over the data, and there are some disturbing long-term trends in our migration."

"Go on."

"Well, for one thing, migration routes have needed fewer detours, especially in the last fifty years."

"And that's a bad thing?"

"Well actually, Sir, more direct routes means that sinkholes are less frequent, resources are more difficult to find, and that the ground is... well, harder."

"I take it by your tone this is a bad thing?"

"Yes Sir, it means that not only are there fewer resources, but that extraction of raw materials in the last few centuries takes longer. You know how dangerous it is to remain stationary, Sir. We went from extraction times in an average of four days in 896 A.C. to a current average extraction length of seventeen days."

"Seventeen days?" Daniels sat forward in his chair, tugging at the cable that was plugged into his neck. It made him shiver, and he sat back a little, so the cable was no longer taut.

How had he not noticed this before? Deeper digs were far more dangerous. There was a reason that migration was almost constant.

"Yes, Major. I wasn't sure that number was correct and so I cross-checked it a half-dozen times. Private Fallman and Lieutenant Johnson also ran the numbers for me.

Daniels asked, "What's the takeaway, Lieutenant? What are you trying to tell me?"

Travers cleared his throat and hesitated. "...Well sir, when the architects began the migration all those years ago, their models showed that given enough time, and the extraction of only certain resources, the climate would begin to stabilize. They said it would take thousands of years, but..."

"I know all of this Travers, get to the point."

"Sir..." More hesitation in his voice. Daniels didn't think that it was because Travers feared him, they had a pretty good working relationship. "It means that the climate is getting worse, not better. And the apolicanes..."

Daniels frowned. The apolicanes, massive hurricanes that spanned hundreds of miles, were the bane of every migrating city. Daniels had always thought that there was something odd about them and he had always suspected that the early architects had known something more about their origins than they let on.

Travers said, "The apolicanes have increased in size in the last three hundred years by sixty percent."

"So, what you are really telling me, Travers, is that war is coming, aren't you?"

Travers didn't answer. He cast his eyes downwards.

"Am I right? Is that the heart of what you are saying?"

Travers nodded. "Yes, Sir."

"How long does the AI estimate 'til all available resources run out?"

"We only have data on the North American continent, but the AI suggests that a similar situation is happening on the others."

"And?"

"It estimates twenty-five years until all accessible resources are gone."

Daniels swore. "That's it? Why didn't the AI warn us sooner?"

"I asked it the same question, Sir, and it said that no one had set the parameters to monitor available resources."

"Shit. How long does the city have, assuming we have zero access to resources?"

"If we placed further limitations on new births, and recycled more of our raw materials, we could go as long as two hundred years before buildings would fall into significant disrepair. But there would have to be some sacrifices made by the Uppers..."

"Yeah, and we both know how well that would go. Who else knows all of this?"

"Right now? No one outside of central security."

"Good. Keep it that way. I want to verify this with Dr. Solidsworth before I take it to the Senate. Schedule me a meeting with him as soon as possible."

"Yes, Major. There's... one more thing."

"Go on."

"We're getting reports of disappearances. Some even among our SOs."

"What do you mean? Where are they going? I haven't noticed any unusual changes in the population numbers."

"That's the strange part. There is no change in physical bodies in the city population. I had the AI run scans a half-dozen times using infrared as well as heartbeat detectors."

"So how did you notice, then?"

"Some of the SOs stopped showing up for duty. When we checked with their families and friends, no one can locate them anywhere. We also got a wave of missing persons reports coming in from both the Lowers and the Mids. The Uppers seem unaffected so far."

Daniels scratched his chin, "How long has this been going on?"

"The reports began to spike three weeks ago. It was only a few days ago that the SOs started to vanish."

Daniels frowned. There wasn't much he could do about that at the moment, though it did worry him that SOs were disappearing. It wasn't the first time though; a few centuries back, they had a large group of SOs disappear together, a gang had picked them off one by one on a single day. They had found out later that the SOs had been into all sorts of blackmarket stuff with the gang. But this didn't explain the spike in disappearances of civilians.

"Alright Travers, keep an eye on it, let me know the moment there are any developments."

Travers turned and walked back toward his station. Daniel's mind shifted back to the resource question.

The proximity alert suddenly took on a whole new meaning. What if one of the other cities had come to the same conclusion about the resources? What if there was a trap waiting to ambush them? The salvage from an entire city would sustain another for at least a century, maybe more.

"AI, where are those—"

"Sir, I have pulled the last known locations of cities from satellite imagery, global energy scans, and estimated trajectories."

Satellites were rarely accurate, dust storms and a variety of other interference usually painted a false picture of the locations of other cities. The Dog Star satellite was so old that it barely transmitted and it was a rare moment when any city would launch a new one. Plus, it wasn't like other cities shared. Every scrap of metal and piece of technology was too damned precious to send up into space, especially now. There was also the problem of launching rockets; rocket fuel didn't exactly grow on trees.

"And? Were there any cities in the area of that energy release?"

"Yes, Sir. Based on their trajectory and last known whereabouts, Langeles was 81% likely to be within seventy-five kilometers of the proximity alert."

Daniels frowned. "Ah hell. Halt migration, strengthen shields, and power up the railguns."

Almost immediately, the city slowed its speed. A strange sensation swept under Daniels. It was a sensation that every man, woman, and child in the migrating cities would recognize, like an elevator accelerating.

"While you're at it, send out eight more Runners in all cardinal directions for ten kilometers. Have them set up sensor beacons for a range of fifty kilometers. I want to establish a perimeter and be sure we aren't facing some sort of surprise attack. Also, I want constant monitoring of any nearby storms that are an eight or higher."

"As you wish, Sir, but may I recommend you lower the warning level to six? This will create additional time to recall Runners and Duggers in the event of a storm."

"Alright, six it is."

The alliances between cities were tentative at best. Mostly, cities chose to stay out of each other's way, but if there was something that one city needed from another, and trade wasn't an option, they sometimes launched raids. The raids were often unsuccessful, and most city governments knew that, but it didn't stop insanity from creeping up through the leadership from time to time. Daniel's new knowledge made him paranoid. Assume the worst and plan accordingly, his father had always said. If the other cities were aware of the depleting resources, there wouldn't be just raids anymore; now there would attempts at annihilation.

"Sir, shall I send additional Runners toward the proximately alert to assist Runner 17?"

"No, 17 can handle himself just fine. Nothing kills that prick."

"But Sir, if it's an ambush, 17 will be outnumbered and outmatched. Currently, he is only supplied with a recon-grade EnViro suit."

"That's why I want you to put fifty Runners on standby. 17 is the recon. If he's attacked, I want the city in defense mode 19c-128. I also want updates every thirty minutes after launch. For now, I am getting the hell out of this chair. I have a feeling that I am going to be in it for a long stretch later on."

"Very well, sir."

The primary security office was a large oval shape on the top of the largest tower in Manhatsten. A long time ago it was known as the Freedom Tower. Daniels couldn't remember why it had been called the Freedom Tower, something about an attack but it was so damned long ago, and there had been so many attacks on Manhatsten, before and after migration.

The seat for the chief of security sat in the center, on top of a slightly raised platform surrounded by twenty-two stations that were constantly filled with a variety of personnel. The idea was that only one single security station was needed to run the entire city, but there were several well-hidden backup locations in the event that this office was inaccessible or destroyed. The office had a pungent scent of fake leather and polyester, stained with the smell of sweat and body odor from the semi-frequent, several-days-long marathons the staff had to pull during emergencies. Showers were a luxury during those times, and it had shown.

Daniels directed his thoughts left, then right, and the clamps on his shoulders that connected his central nervous system to the heads-up display released. The plug in the base of his skull whirred and unscrewed itself. He would never get used to the sensation of that thing unplugging, it made his whole body seize with a tingling sensation that felt as if every nerve in his body was being tickled at once. It made his teeth itch.

Plugging in wasn't quite as bad, because before the sensation could take hold, the chair gave you a small shot of some sort of tranquilizer that, at least for the first few minutes, made you feel completely and utterly relaxed. Daniels had been told by the architects that this was necessary in order to calibrate your nervous system to the chair, but that never made him feel any better about being drugged. He just hoped that one of these days the old architect would get around to finishing wireless neural interface he'd been promised decades before.

He stood and stretched his entire body, stepped down from the central platform, and headed toward the door. In the monitors above each station, he could see several Runners activating and several others preparing for standby mode. He walked past several other stations where personnel were busy with the various functions of the city. Daniels alone was in charge of the Runners, though there were several others trained in the duty as a redundancy. The AI could activate them as well, but usually only as an emergency measure.

Daniels heard the pop and hiss of shoulder clamps disconnecting from another station to his right. He turned to see Private Fallman. Fallman, who had only been serving for about fifteen months, was walking toward him.

"Major Daniels, may I accompany you, Sir?" Fallman asked.

Daniels wasn't looking for company, he rarely was these days, but he supposed he liked Fallman. He was always on time, always followed orders, and always took the initiative when necessary. He was, however, educated as a scientist, and not as a security specialist.

"Sure thing, kid," Daniels replied.

They walked out the door of central security and headed toward the mechanical engineering center in the lower level of the building.

"Thank you, Major." Fallman paused for a moment. "I wanted to discuss with you a possible upgrade to calibrate the long-range sensors of Manhatsten. You see, if we could change the energy wave fluctuations to match the—"

"Save it for the engineers, kid. I've told you before, I'm an old-timer. When they trained me, they didn't teach me none of that mumbo jumbo about the technical applications of the whatever. What I do is give orders based on whatever the Senate wants, or what the AI suggests. That's it."

There was a little more to it than that, but Daniels didn't want to argue.

"But Sir, protocol demands that if I have a suggested change that directly impacts the security systems, I must confer with you first."

"I know that, which is why I am ordering you to take it to the engineers. They'll know what in the hell you are talking about and if it's feasible."

Fallman looked hurt and insulted, but tried to hide it with a "Yes, Sir." Daniels pressed the button to call the lift. Even after over a thousand years, Daniels had no desire to learn the technical garbage that so often spewed from the mouths of these kids. In fact, as time went on, he felt there was something to that old cliché, "you can't teach an old dog new tricks." His job was more habit now than love. Hell, when he was born back in the 1980s of the Common Era, he had thought he would have retired at the ripe old age of 72, but then, of course, the alcoves had been invented, and humans had continued to destroy the environment. Sometimes he wished he would have never accepted the military's offer to use the alcove. He was just so goddamned tired. Tired of everything that this walking hunk of tin did.

"Look, kid, you're doing a great job. We could use a boost in long-range sensors, but ignore that protocol and do yourself a favor and talk to someone who can help you." Daniels hesitated a moment, searching for a name. "Maybe Ross Andrean can help you with this one?"

Fallman only provided Daniels with a half nod. Fallman was listening, but also lost in his thoughts. He had been excited about his idea, had thought it might grant him the ever-so-rare promotion, and Daniels had just told him it wasn't a big deal.

Daniels sighed to himself, loud enough for Fallman to hear it.

"You do a great job here kid, you really do. Keep up the good work and who knows what might happen."

This caught Fallman's attention, and his face flickered with just the hint of satisfaction. Fallman turned, made his body rigid, and brought his right hand toward his forehead in a salute. "Thank you, Sir! Might I just say it is an honor to work with you, Sir!"

"At ease Private, Jesus Christ, there's no need to be so formal around here. Hell, I think I am the only one with actual military experience on this boat."

Fallman's face turned into a frown again, but this time he hid it a bit better. Daniels knew that the younger ones loved to play this 'solider' game, and a long time ago, so did he. But Daniels was tired of dressing up a job that was nothing but an endless set of monotonous tasks, with the occasional burst of action.

The lift beeped. The door opened. As Daniels took one step into the elevator, he took note of the standard propaganda poster that punctuated all the elevators of all the buildings. Similar ones were put up all around the city, especially in the Lowers and especially after that whole labor dispute nonsense a few decades back. The poster read "Everyone Must Do Their Part." Most of them had pictures of people working or doing some sort of 'patriotic duty,' but this one, in particular, was a little odd. It looked completely out of place. It was a picture of a woman with what Daniels thought must have been a sewing machine, though he hadn't seen one since before migration. He shrugged it off and turned toward the front of the elevator. Fallman followed.

Everyone must do their part. Everyone must do their part. The words played on repeat inside Daniels' mind. That's what they had told him when the city first started its endless cycle of migration. He knew it was what they told everyone, what they taught every child in school. Hell, most people probably dreamt the words, Christ knew there were enough posters around the city. Suddenly, Daniels felt more tired than ever. Doing your part was one thing, but doing it for a thousand years? Well, that was something else entirely. He felt envy over the shorter lifespans of those in the lowers, though they probably didn't reciprocate that feeling.

"AI, 3rd level please," said Daniels.

"Oh... uh... 12th level for me." Fallman turned toward Daniels, "I'll go see Ross Andrean immediately, Sir."

Daniels watched the numbers melt into one another. 110... 109... 108... "Let me ask you something, Fallman."

"Of course, Sir."

"Why would someone like yourself choose to work in security?"

"By myself, do you mean a scientist?"

"That's exactly what I mean. The pay is shitty, the hours are long, and the assignment is for life. Why would a person who is as brilliant as you choose to join security when you could have worked on just about any floor on central command? Hell, you could have even made it to the Uppers one day."

Fallman shifted his gaze up to the numbers counting down, 84... 83... He turned his face back to Daniels. Was there a flash of something there? For a brief moment, Daniels thought he saw anger, but then it was gone.

"Well, Sir, I suppose it's because it seems one of the only areas in the city left with an applied research element. I want to contribute to the city's welfare, and most of the other scientists are just maintaining equipment that's been breaking down for the last few centuries. I wanted something that would allow me to make a solid scientific contribution."

"You really think that there's no other place to contribute? What about that old architect? Isn't he doing some interesting work?"

Fallman scoffed at that. "Him? That old fraud hasn't turned out anything new in over a century, and the last contribution he made to the city was a slight modification in the hydraulic cuffs for the cities legs. The only thing that did was make migration more comfortable in the Lowers. All he does these days is rave about his artificial gravity project and about how that nitwit he has as a lab assistant is the most brilliant mathematician he's ever seen."

"Fallman, listen here. I'm so damn old that I don't even remember when I lost my virginity. But what I do remember is that Solidsworth and the others like him saved our asses from total extinction. Now I don't know what that old man is up to in his labs, but you can damn well bet it's something important."

Fallman's face tightened, his lips pressing together so tightly they started to turn white. "Well Sir, you see, it doesn't matter what he decides to research anymore, anyway." His tone was bordering on insubordinate.

"Just what does that mean?" Daniels did not attempt to hide his irritation.

"Well, it's just that I heard a rumor from a reliable source that the Senate has given him a deadline. He is to produce a working simulation of artificial gravity by year's end, or else they'll pull all his funding."

"You and I both know the Senate can't do that. The agreement to let the architects work without restriction is in the very founding charter of the city. Hell, the very first Senate made sure that the architects' work would never be stunted. After all, it was ignoring scientists that got us into this damn migration mess in the first place."

"It seems Sir, that they have found some kind of loophole."

Daniels felt anger rising in his chest. "I bet they did, fucking politicians. Do you have any idea how bad the politicians of the 21st century were? Greasy as a mechanic's crack."

Fallman only blinked at this. His mouth opened a few times and then shut again.

"Major, it's not that we aren't listening to the scientists, it's just, well, Dr. Solidsworth is a bit of... well, sir, most people think he has lost it in his old age."

"Watch your mouth, Private. I'm at least a decade older than that man. Age has nothing to do with it, and you know it. The real problem the Senate has with him is that he won't take on their pet projects. They can't control him like they do every other aspect of this godforsaken walking hunk of metal and you know it."

Fallman said nothing. His expression suggested he was considering how to respond to his superior officer more carefully after his previous blunder. Daniels watched and waited for a response, but none came. His thoughts turned to the old architect. He would have to visit Rigel later. Perhaps as head of security, he could lend him some support somehow.

The lift halted, indicating the 12th floor.

"Looks like this is my stop, Sir."

Daniels nodded without responding, deep in thought. The moment the lift closed and began its descent, Daniels shouted, "AI, full stop."

He needed to clear his head. Ousting Dr. Solidsworth? What in god's name was the Senate thinking? Daniels hated most of the senators; they were a bunch of slugs. If they found a loophole in the charter with the architects, what other loopholes would they find? Could he himself end up as a Runner? Could they put the city in danger?

They weren't all bad of course, a few of the members of the Senate were fine individuals. That Senator Lightfoot, she was quite an interesting character. She was also beautiful. Senators Swanson and Howell had also contributed a great deal to helping children in Lower communities who might not have had access to the scholar school otherwise.

"AI, roof please."

"Major Daniels, the roof is restricted to authorized personnel only. Please confirm your security code."

"8426FPA"

"Thank you, Major."

The lift began its ascent. The numbers began to rise 18... 19... 20... Daniels decided that he didn't like Fallman much after all. The little shit was arrogant, just like so many Mids with talent. Daniels' descendants lived in the Lowers. He knew what it was like down there before the Architect had installed the new hydraulic cuffs. Anything that had not been nailed down was likely to vibrate right to the floor. After the installation, the Lowers became almost as comfortable as the Uppers, at least regarding the city's movements. Some Uppers didn't like that; they preferred the life of Lowers to be in constant chaos.

His mind flashed behind him to the poster on the elevator wall; everyone must do their part... he scoffed, not Uppers. They were the parasites at the top of the food chain, sucking on everything that was good and right in the city. But what could he do about it?

27... 28... 29...

In a way, Daniels hated the alcoves and everything they stood for. On the one hand, it allowed some of the greatest assholes living at the top of the city's skyscrapers to count their ages by decades and centuries. Yet, the alcoves were used to preserve specialists in science, in security detail, hell even the Runners used the alcoves when they weren't on active duty. The alcoves had sustained the life of the architects for decades while they built the infrastructure for the very first migrating city. It had cured Alzheimer's, cancer, heart disease, and just about every other ailment that afflicted man. It had been the miracle cure-all for everything, yet if it had come just a few decades earlier, the wealthy might have wised up about the changes in the climate. The course of the late 21st century may have been very different if those in power would have had access to live several lifetimes. Instead, the Uppers took possession of the top floors of the migrating cities as they had taken possession of some much else in history. From above, they watched with their lustful eyes and took whatever they desired.

Daniels sighed and watched the numbers, 98... 99... 100...

Now those same power-hungry nut jobs were going to toss out the last living architect in Manhatsten, a man who promised to take human beings out into the stars and to a new world where mankind could start over. Daniels believed him, and he hoped, not for his sake but for the sake of his 12th- and 13th-greats-grandchildren that Dr. Solidsworth could do it. Mankind had trashed this planet, and these walking arks had only meant to be a temporary solution. Now, almost 1300 years later, the stilted cities were still migrating, still extracting resources, still a band-aid on a bullet wound.

The lift stopped at 105, the roof level. The door slid open. Daniels moved into his garden, his refuge from the rest of the city. He sat down on a concrete bench and allowed himself to take in the fragrance of his vegetable garden. The tomatoes were doing well this year.

He looked up at toward the sky. He could see the magnetic pulses of energy moving across the shield in their rhythmic and hypnotic motions. Sometimes this was all he needed, to come up above the city and see the shield, to smell his plants, to see the city from above. He needed perspective. He needed to remember how small and fragile life was compared to the barren earth the city roamed.

He stood and moved toward the railing and leaned forward. He liked to feel just a little vertigo when he stared down across the nearly sixty square kilometers of Manhatsten. The city, all steel and only one park, was all that had remained of the great city of New York from ages past. It was the back of a porcupine with towers of various sizes jutting out of the elevated earth. The citizens of Manhatsten were lucky; they had green space, they had Central Park. Not every migrating city had green space. In fact, some were nothing but hard earth and buildings. Of all the cities remaining, only Lundon was bigger.

Major John Daniels stared at the edge of his world. From his high viewpoint, he could see it clearly. Like the sailors of old, the people of the city feared to fall off the edge of the world. 2,283,506 people lived in Manhatsten as of this morning, and in a way, Daniels was more responsible for them than just about anyone else in the city. He was the city's grandfather, their watcher, the steward of their world. Being up here always reminded him of that. It reminded him of his responsibilities, and it kept him from ending his life.

Up here helped him remember why he kept using the alcoves, that he kept watching generation after generation of his descendants move into the eternal gardens. He had lied to Fallman. He still did have hope. Being up here gave him hope that, before died, he would see a world without giant migrating cities. All his hope lay in Dr. Solidsworth, the architect.

Later, he would remember that old adage, "be careful what you wish for."

The elevator door opened behind him. "Major Daniels, I've been looking everywhere for you."

Daniels turned, surprised to hear a voice. Very few had clearance to come up to this roof. It had been one of his rewards for his first 500 years of service. They couldn't grant his family higher status, and so to pacify him they had given him this space. It was a terrible trade-off, but he had grudgingly accepted it.

A tall, gaunt gentleman stood between Daniels and the door. Meager scraps of hair clung to the edges of his scalp, and his narrow brown eyes looked somehow sandwiched between thick eyebrows and a thick mustache.

"Johnson, what are you doing up here? You don't have clearance."

"Sir, the AI unlocked the top level. We have a serious problem on our hands."

"What is it?"

"Patton. He's been murdered."

"Patton, as in Patton, the chief engineer?

Johnson nodded.

"By who? Why?"

"We don't know, but all of the central command is on lockdown. Whoever it was had access and knows the ins and outs of the system."

Historian's Note on Alcoves
From: 835.12.1 I.S.

D ear Reader,
The scientific marvel of the Alcove, an invention of the year 2067 of the Common Era, revolutionized the health care industry. Discovered on accident by Dr. Rigel Solidsworth and Dr. Gupta Ramnachinin during a longitudinal study on cryostasis research for the purpose of deep-space travel and exploration, the Alcove had profound implications to the human experience. Virtually overnight, it was possible to cure all known human diseases. Additionally, the Alcoves stopped, and even in some cases, reversed the aging process. Deemed a miracle by the modern science of the day, both Dr. Solidsworth and Dr. Ramnachinin won the Nobel Prize in Physiology or Medicine in 2068 C.E. In his acceptance speech of the prize, Dr. Solidsworth claimed that medical science had come so far that it had eliminated the need for itself.

Unfortunately, Alcoves contributed negatively to an already complex and unstable geopolitical climate involving global climate change, lack of resources, and overpopulation. Even with the conclusion of World War Three the same year, the Alcove added to the post-war tension. Additionally, alcoves were also quite expensive in their construction and maintenance and only the more affluent hospitals and individuals had access to them. Thus, the Alcove became known as a kind of golden fountain of youth.

For more information, including schematics, notes, and recordings from Dr. Rigel Solidsworth and Dr. Gupta Ramnachinin on their part in the invention of the alcoves, please visit library 9843 of sector 1907.

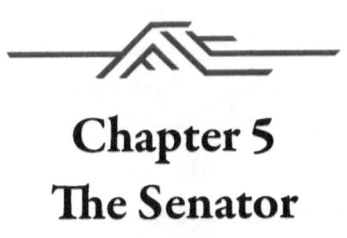

Chapter 5
The Senator

"S enator? Are you in there?" Knuckles were colliding with wood.

A tall, slender woman with shoulder-length dark hair and deep green eyes pulled back the sheets. Her naked body still sheened with the sweat of the previous night's activities, glimmering in the morning glow of the EnViro shield. The woman swung her legs over the edge of her bed and lifted her lean body.

She glanced back at her latest acquisition. His muscled form lay half under the sheets so that only a single buttock exposed itself to the morning air. She smiled. She supposed that the young engineer would do for a while, but boredom always came. Maybe if he brought his wife or one of his fellow engineers, that might keep her interest a little longer. Just a little.

The knocking resumed.

Tera stood and walked toward the door. The caress of the morning air felt good on her bare skin. She grabbed the long silver handles and opened the large, dark, wooden door.

"Oh..."

Tera smiled as her assistant averted her eyes.

"Senator, I'm sorry, I didn't know if you were in there or that you weren't dressed yet."

"Look at me when you are speaking, Vala." Her voice was soft and sultry. A wolf's smile.

Tera wanted her to stare. She liked making Vala uncomfortable. Her young assistant was straight out of scholar school, and one day soon, she would find a way to join her in her nightly endeavors. Tera licked her lips.

Vala steadied her gaze to Tera's face. The effort made Tera smile.

"Am I ugly, Vala?"

Vala's face flushed. "No... of course not... It's just... um... rude to stare."

"Am I too old? Is that it? How old do I look, my dear?"

"I don't know, Ma'am, but you don't look a day over 21."

Tera's eyes narrowed, but she wasn't scowling; a little smile spread across her lips. "So, you like what you see, then?"

"Yes... I mean... No, Senator, I mean..." Vala's face was turning a deep shade of purple, and she was shrinking back from the door.

Tera laughed. "So what did you want, Vala?" Her tone flattened.

"It's Senator Green, Ma'am. He would like to meet with you in private before the Senate convenes."

"Did he say what this was about?"

"No, Senator. He only said it was a private matter."

"Hmm. Thank you, Vala."

Vala turned to head back to her desk down the hall.

"Oh, and Vala?"

She froze. She did not turn. "Yes, Senator?"

"You're always welcome to join me in my bedchamber."

Vala did not move. She made no reply. Tera smiled, bit her lower lip, and shut the door.

Her expression flickered between irritation and boredom as she remembered that she had to attend the Senate.

The Senate chamber was a place of endless tedium; it was rare that they addressed any important issues. On the one hand, she knew the Senate was a worthless boring sham, a tool to appease the Mids and Lowers with the guise of representation. On the other hand, her position at the Senate gave her certain privileges and avenues that weren't already present to a wealthy heiress.

Her family, 7th richest (soon to be 6th, if she had her way) and most powerful in Manhatsten, often had things work out exactly as they intended. Her father was crafty in his ability to sway the opinions of others. A skill that she, at least in part, had gained from him, though as of late, tact was far less necessary. In some ways, she had been complacent. Even her father had said so. Blackmail was so much easier than persuasion, but her father warned her it would catch up with her one day. He was probably right, but damn it felt good to have so much power.

She moved back over to the right side of her bed, reached down, and grabbed the crumpled heap of her gown. She pulled it up over her naked body, the sound of silk against her soft skin echoing against the void of noise. The fragrance of the material wafted up into her nostrils.

She walked over to the glass double doors and stepped out onto her balcony, feeling the stillness of the air. Occasionally, the environmental systems simulated a light, and pleasant breeze, to help move some pollen and seeds around the city, but the wind was never harsh inside Manhatsten. The envi-

ronment inside the city was often lush and green, a stark contrast to the barren world that lay just on the other side of the shield, just beyond the low
wall at the edge of their mobile world.

Tera looked toward the moon, or rather, its remains. Her great-great-
grandfather had told her long ago that the moon had been much larger, a
complete circle at times, but that the nations in the world before migration
had all fought to establish colonies on it. It was one of the final wars of an old
age, a war that left the moon split forever. It was an event that had flooded
half the world for a time. Now, the moon, when full, was a misshapen, jagged
crescent. The large debris from the terrifying explosion had just barely missed
colliding with the Earth, and a small second moon was born, a odd shaped
blob, only visible a few nights a month.

Out the window, EnViro shield maintenance crews were working their
way up the sides of the inner shell. Tethers connected several dozen maintenance men to some invisible point at the top of one of the twelve ribs
that stabilized the energy for the shield. The workers danced, up and down,
left and right across the inner surface, checking for energy fluctuations. Tera
imagined them as ballet dancers following a set routine. Their feet pushed
off against the energy barrier in rhythmic arcs, special boots protecting them
from radiation burns. The monthly dance was a spectacle that Tera enjoyed
watching. She almost never missed it.

She went back to her room. Vala had left a tablet on the nightstand next
to her bed with an itinerary for the day. So, despite her feigning ignorance,
Vala had been in her room already that morning. Tera smiled and imagined
Vala creeping around her bed, casting occasional curious glances at shapes
under the sheets.

Vala was lovely. That was why Tera had chosen her. She had grown bored
with male assistants; they gave in too easily. There was no pleasure in the pur-
suit. Female assistants, though, ones who had never been with a woman before, were much more satisfying when they submitted. She would give it a
week more, and then, she might put a little pressure on the girl. She smiled
to herself. Greed gathered in the corners of her mouth, and a little drop of
drool escaped her lips. She let it run down her chin before she wiped it away.

She glanced over at her bed. The boy still slept.

"Boy. Up and out with you. I have no more need of you today." Her voice was hoarse and low.

He stirred a little and turned over, blinking, only half conscious of where he was.

"Go on boy, or running out of my chambers will only be the first day of running for the rest of your life,"

The boy's eyes widened. Tera smiled. There was nothing more terrifying to the Mids and the Lowers than the prospect of becoming a Runner. His eyes dashed about the room, probably looking for his clothes.

"Never mind your clothes, they're mine now." He voice was soft, barely a whisper. "Out. Now." She felt a sense of glee at the thought of him returning to his ignorant wife, naked and begging forgiveness.

He stood and moved toward the door. She watched, admiring him as he picked up the pace. She gazed at the network of scratches and bruises on his back. She had done that. Her smile widened.

"Stop." The boy froze, his hand just reaching for the handle of the door. His body trembled, a rabbit, immobile and waiting.

"Be a good boy and beg me not to make you a Runner."

His eyes widened, she could see gooseflesh rising on his young skin. He babbled before the words formed properly.

"Oh please Senator, please not that, anything but that. I have a family." Tears streamed.

He sobbed a little but didn't dare look away. He looked hopeless, wretched, just the way she liked them.

"Be back here tonight waiting outside my door after sundown."

"But Senator, my wife... I..."

He choked on his words; he was on the verge of unleashing a barrage of tears. Only a single tear welled up in his left eye before she cut him off. She liked them miserable, but she hated when they cried.

"Bring her. Or perhaps you would both like to learn to run? I hear the EnViro Suits are quite heavy, and most women don't last long out in the Barrens."

Terror and defeat flashed in his soft doe eyes. She knew he understood his choices. The young engineer stood, turned, and bolted out the door before Tera could even blink.

Laughter rose through her entire body, throwing her forward in almost violent spasms. God, she loved being a Senator, but most of all she loved the power to make people do as she wished; all that tedium sitting in the Senate chambers had its benefits.

Tera didn't bother picking up her robe. She walked to her private alcove and stepped inside. It stood vertically, and instantly hot water ran down her skin, rinsing her body, the clear door of the alcove gradually sliding up to seal her in as it prepped the gel. The alcove swung downwards from its vertical perch and lay flat like a bed, with her inside. Then the green goop filled the container. She felt the tingling on her skin, in her hair, in her eyes, and she loved every sensation. It felt as if a thousand feathers were being run up and down your skin at once and sometimes the sensation would even bring her to orgasm.

She gulped up the goop, and allowed it to fill her lungs. Like amniotic fluid, it nurtured her, preserving her youth, rejuvenating every cell and destroying any object, foreign or otherwise, that might pose a threat. It had taken her a little time to get used to the sensation of breathing through the gel, but now she relished it.

Only two kinds of people enjoyed the alcoves on a regular basis: Uppers and Runners. She didn't think the Runners much enjoyed them because it was a part of their prison sentence. She imagined that after years of being out in the wastes, a Runner would hate their longevity. In fact, she was certain that some of them would have preferred not to stay young and healthy, many of them would welcome death; that is, if it weren't for recycling.

Recycling was a nasty business, one that even Tera did not care for. Especially after... the incident... No one knew for sure if a person's consciousness was in a recycled body. After a Runner died in Manhatsten, and perhaps in the other cities, their body was taken away to some underground facility. If their brain was intact and their body was not damaged beyond repair, they would appear again within a few weeks. But when they reemerged, they were different, passive and unresponsive. No one knew what happened down in the depths of the sub-level of the engineering section, but there were rumors.

A memory from several months earlier clawed at Tera, mixing with the semi-consciousness of the alcove experience. She saw images of the Runner

Dock take shape in front of her open eyes. She knew what was coming, and she tried to stop it, but she couldn't move, not until the alcove cycle finished.

2.

"What brings you down to the docks, Senator?"

"Oh, I am checking on the status of a new Runner, the one that struck me."

"Ah, you must mean Runner 1862," said the dock supervisor. His nametag read "Marty Stroeman", his title below it in thin white letters. He was a short round man with dark bushy eyebrows. Tera's immediate impression was that he was repulsive. A big mole stood just to the left of his nose, where the tiniest hint of a mustache was trying to emerge unsuccessfully. His squashed face and beady eyes worked their way up and down her body. It made her uncomfortable, and she wasn't used to that feeling.

"Forgive me, Senator, but he's in the medical bay at the moment, recovering from his muscle augmentation."

"Good. I want you to march him right by me before you put him in storage."

"I'm sorry Senator, but he won't be going into storage yet. He'll be trained in an EnViro suit for several hours this afternoon and then put back into the medical bay to ensure he heals from training. Creating a Runner is a several-day process."

She looked at him furiously. "I know that," she would never admit to this fool that she didn't. "Just make sure that he sees me on his way to his training session. I want him to know what striking a Senator means." Her voice was almost a growl.

The fool's name was Louis Gardner, a middle-aged high school teacher from the Mids. He had spurned her repeated sexual advances. She had threatened him and his wife and children, and he had slapped her with the back of his hand, knocking her over. Striking a public official was forbidden, but that hadn't seemed to sway this fool. He was convicted by the Supreme Justices in less than a few hours and sent down to the Runnercore.

Overhead, the AI said, "Recycled Runner number 107, please step forward and adjust the rear right arm of EnViro Suit Assembly on platform number 9."

"Why do they announce it like that instead of just transmitting straight to the Recycled Runner?" Tera asked.

"So we know what the recycled are doing. They're creepy as hell, and we instructed the AI to announce all their orders, so it doesn't scare the inspectors. The last thing you want to see is one of those things walking toward you without knowing why. Didn't you hear about that incident a few decades back with the suit malfunctions?"

"No." She rolled her eyes. "I didn't know you were all such cowards down here." she scoffed.

"You might not say that if you got near one. There's something... unnatural about those things. I don't know why security insists on using them. Especially after that mess we had to clean up after the incident. We should have expelled all of them then."

Then Tera saw him, or it. The once-man stepped forward in rhythmic footsteps. The movement was so unnatural that Tera could hardly believe that this... thing, had once been human. It wore a combat-ready EnViro suit. Only the helmet was missing. Its thin white hair was frayed and patchy. On the left shoulder, etched in the metal of the suit and catching the occasional glare of the harsh fluorescent lights, was 'RR #107'.

To her horror, she recognized the face, though now it was thin and pruned. His pale skin was outlined by blue lines. His once-sparkling eyes were solid white on white on white. The pupil was missing.

He had been a part of that uprising a few decades back. His name had been... what... Aaron? She couldn't recall his surname.

"What..." she turned to address Stroeman. "What in the name of the gods happened to him?" She pointed, but it was a half-hearted thing. She didn't want to draw its attention.

"Oh him? He got caught in a Sandstorm on his second run."

"Is that why his skin looks like that?"

"Well, that and the chemicals used to reanimate the muscles after death, at least, that's what the AI says. None of us know what they do down there."

Tera felt uncomfortable. Her intuition screamed at her. She needed to leave. She needed to run. She couldn't move. She looked around and realized the room had tinged a reddish color.

"Apologies Senator, but I have to attend to 1862. I will..." he seemed to be looking for the right word. "Parade him by you as you requested." He disappeared toward the medical bay.

RR #107 came closer. Tera looked around and realized that she was standing next to platform 9. Then, just before it walked past her, it stopped. Its head turned toward her, and its eyes fixed on hers. Without a pupil, she had no way of knowing for sure it was looking at her. Yet, it was, and there was something horrible there, something fixating on her. For a moment, she imaged a pupil locking onto hers. She shook. Her legs almost buckled.

It wanted to hurt her, she could feel it. She could feel the depths of its rage, its madness, its desire to tear her apart. She knew that if she didn't move, it would reach out and grab her and begin its terrifying work of dismantling her physical body in an orgy of blood and pain. She wanted to scream, but nothing came. She wanted to run, but couldn't turn away from its locked eyes. It had her, and she knew it. There would be no escape. She would pay for her crimes of casting so many down into the Runnercore.

In her mind's eye, she could hear it whispering to her with a deadly, terrifying song of suffering. Images of what it had gone through flickered in her mind. The storm, the uprising, the torture, the chemicals, all of it penetrated her, illuminated by a red light.

Its lips did not move, but she heard a voice. "Soon you will become one of us, soon you will be with us, and there is nothing you can do."

She saw images of it tearing off her limbs one by one and leaving her body and brain intact. Then it would carry the pieces down a long corridor and into the room with a sterile steel table. It would lay her body down and then the machines would come, putting Humpty Dumpty back together again, and the process of recycling would begin.

The voice whispered in soft tones. "You will share in our fate; you will do your part. We will be one. We are all one. Join us, Tera."

Its whispers were ringing over and over again in her mind.

"You will do your part." She knew it would grab her now and begin the process.

"You will do your part." She felt her skin crawl, and her limbs went numb in anticipation of the tearing sensation they would soon feel.

"You will do your part." She could not resist. She could not run, her mind was emptying and so was her bladder, soaking her long green dress. A smell of ammonia. Fear engulfed her, a vortex of nothingness, so complete, so total that she knew she could never escape it.

Then RR #107's eyes unlocked from hers, and it turned its head forward and marched for the EnViro Suit Assembly Platform. Tera looked down at her green dress and acknowledged the wetness running down her thigh, but it didn't matter. Nothing except escape from this place mattered; nothing except putting space between her and that thing mattered. She pivoted, just as Runner 1862 emerged from the medical bay. She broke into a run toward the door. Her limbs were still numb as she left the Runner Dock and did not stop running until she found her security escort to take her back to her chambers.

3.

After the incident, Tera never went down into the Runnercore again.

Tera shivered, she didn't know why her thoughts were drawn to the Runnercore so much in the past six months. Perhaps it was because she had encountered the infamous Runner 17 just a few weeks before the incident. 17 was famous even among the Uppers; he was said to be unkillable, she had even heard Daniels say as much when he had addressed the Senate. As a little girl, one of her favorite films on the vidscreen told the story of how 17 had singlehandedly stormed Mex and saved Manhatsten from total destruction. There were often even bets on his activities outside of the walls of Manhatsten. To so many living in the top of the skyscrapers, 17 was an amusing athlete, a spectacle, a curiosity to live through vicariously.

But Tera wanted him, wanted him badly. The thought of him made her loins burn with lust. But even with all of her power, the city protocol prevented her from getting close to him. She wanted what she couldn't have, and she knew it. It did nothing to assuage the ache. Besides, this was one person who she couldn't threaten with the Runnercore if he didn't comply with her wishes. She had no leverage over him. But she had thought that any man would fuck a woman like Tera after all that time alone.

There was also the fact that everyone knew Runners were beasts, and some part of her feared that he would try to kill her if unleashed from the tether of his security chip.

"You must do you part, Tera."

Tera opened her eyes in the alcove and could see nothing or no one. Had someone spoken to her?

"The eyes of the Recycled watch you always."

It was a whisper, a barely audible phrase that sent Tera into almost a panic. She wanted out of the alcove immediately but realized she had set it to delay opening for another fifteen minutes. Trapped, she now felt the echoes of her fear from the incident. Who was watching her? Who was speaking to her?

"Your part, Tera, the eyes of the Recycled know you aren't doing your part. Those dead eyes are my eyes, and we are watching you. Do your part, Tera, or else."

Tera's whole body shuttered, goose flesh pimpled on the pores on her soft, silky skin, making it as rough as sandpaper.

"Watching you.... Always watching you..."

Then it was gone, the voice, the fear, everything returned to normal. She felt every muscle relax, her mind relaxed. It was over. Perhaps it was nothing more than stress or something like a bad dream. She had, in fact, heard of people having bad dreams or visions or whatever you call them, inside an alcove. She heard that the Runners had very different experiences during their long hibernation periods. Yes, that was it, it was just a hallucination.

A thought occurred to her, what was her part? What could the nightmare voice have meant when it said that she wasn't doing her part? She tried to push the thought out of her mind, but it wouldn't leave. The thought was sticky and thick with something that felt like cotton candy pressing into her brain. What could she be forgetting? Her subconscious was trying to tell her something, but she wasn't sure what it could be.

Time went quickly in an alcove. The semi-stasis made the rest of the time pass in a flash. She felt the green stem-cell-based goop drain. The alcove swung up vertically from its typical horizontal cradle, and hot water again rinsed Tera until all traces of the goop was gone. She stepped out of the alcove, the water stopped. She moved toward her closet, the door opened.

"Senator's robes."

A machine came to life, whirring and buzzing, bringing forth her Senator's robes. She selected her dark red dress robe and slipped it on. A machine came down from above and sprayed her with a mist of Rose and Lilac fragrance, it was her favorite scent, the one that she felt the most feminine in, the one that caught all the young men in her web of lust. Tera slipped on her white sash, which marked her a senator, and headed for the door, where her fine leather sandals waited for her to slip on.

She walked to the food dispenser and ordered a muffin. The dispenser went to work printing a muffin from the raw organic materials that came from some deep underground facility.

Tera turned and headed for the exit to her chambers. The door opened. What she saw startled her. A poster, one of the standard propaganda posters that hung throughout the city, now hung right outside her door. She had mistaken the poster for a person. It was lifelike and was almost life-sized.

She exhaled, blinked a few times and stared.

On it, a man stood with a sledgehammer slung over his shoulder, grinning widely, his teeth showing. She counted them. Even his eyes smiled. In the background of the poster was the simple gray brick of a sky-rise apartment building.

Tera could imagine the kinds of people that would live in the empty boxed patios that jutted out from the building. She could see parents yelling at their children not to play too close to the railing. A woman hanging laundry out to dry. Teenagers leaning against that railing and chatting about who was dating who. A man, after a long day of work, taking slow drags of a cigarette; only his small circle of fire and a hint of a peppered mustache visible in the evening light. Somehow the artist had captured all this without showing a single person in the background. She could feel it, all of it. Electrifying.

Her attention turned back to the man in the foreground, and she gasped all over again. Gods, the man in the poster was so real. Tera could swear he was breathing. It was a well-drawn piece of propaganda, and Tera thought that the artist was enormously talented. Still, it had no business being here, just outside of her quarters. A Senator hardly needed to be reminded of her duties. Nervous laughter escaped her lips.

She thought hard for a moment and wondered when the poster was put up. It had not been there last night; at least, she didn't remember seeing it.

The poster itself was benign until she read the phrase just above the smiling face. It opened her like a knife would open her flesh. It started with a chill. Then, violence. She shook from head to toe. The words read: "You Must Do Your Part," the same words she had heard from the Recycled Runner down in the docks. At the bottom of the poster, it read, "If We Want To Keep Our City In Working Order," but Tera hardly noticed those words. Her eyes locked on the poster. She could not unhinge them.

The poster changed. The man's nose rotted off. His eyes glowed red, and strange, black, tree-like limbs grew up behind him and merged with some of his skin. Blood bloomed in the background, and the leering smile of his white teeth seemed to widen.

"You Must Do Your Part," he seemed to whisper. But the mouth did not move. The smile did not change. Electric. A putrid rotting smell filled Tera's nostrils. It seeped from the poster.

Again, the words, "You Must Do Your Part." The voice echoed and rang in chorus until a thousand people were speaking the phrase over and over again. Shrieks and whispers. Half-mad laughter and desperate pleas.

Tera caught the eyes of the man in the poster and she felt him lock his gaze on her. She knew those eyes. Those eyes belonged to the undead recycled Runner. They possessed her and try as she might, she could not look away. Something brewed inside of her. Something was coming apart.

Thump Thump... her heart pounded. Chest heaving.

Thump Thump... she felt her blood rising and bubbling inside her. She could feel every single blood cell as it worked its way through her body.

Thump Thump... She felt her terror turning into rage and then into hate. There was so much hate that it bubbled over like a cauldron overflowing.

Thump Thump... She felt every inch of her twitching; her heart pounded in her temples. The pressure mounted.

Thump Thump... Her head would explode, leaving nothing but a bloody stump where her neck and skull joined.

Thump Thump... The agony was growing, the eyes... oh, those horrible eyes. Her heart beat so fiercely it would burst at any second.

Thump Thump... Rising, screaming... oh, what a fantastic horrible madness. It was taking her, taking her to the edge. She opened her mouth to scream, to give in to the complete and utter insanity that had possessed her. She felt herself falling over the edge and...

"Senator? Senator, are you all right?"

Normalcy returned. Tera was only centimeters from the poster. Her nose pressed against it. The scream choked back into the rear of her mouth and she swallowed it hard, the lump moving its way down into her stomach. She suspected that, later, she would have a stomach ache.

The poster looked normal again, and Tera searched frantically over its surface for any sign of what she had just seen. She reached her hand up and touched it, making sure that it was real.

"You look a bit pale, Ma'am; can I get you some water or tea or anything?"

It was Vala, her secretary. She was sitting at her desk only a few meters away. How long had she been standing there in front of the poster? Was it only seconds? Minutes? Or perhaps she had been standing there for an hour? Tera didn't know. She only knew that she needed to shake off this horrible feeling. She never wanted to feel anything like that ever again.

"Oh... I'm fine, just... didn't sleep much last night." Tera mustered all her strength to put a smile back on her face and give Vala a nice "if you know what I mean" wink. But masking her fear was no easy task.

"Ah, I see. Well, Senator Green is waiting for you, Miss, he said he has been trying to reach you on the vidscreen for twenty minutes."

Tera couldn't have been standing there for long then, it must have only been a few seconds before Vala had spoken up.

"Ah... well... yes, I must have set my alcove timer for too long. Please ring ahead and let him know I am headed there now."

"Very well, Ma'am, is there anything I can get you?"

"Not now." Tera turned left to walk toward the chambers but then stopped just as suddenly as she had started. "There is perhaps one thing, Vala."

Vala looked up toward her employer. Her eyes were almost silver, her hair dark and shiny, she couldn't be older than thirty, and Tera felt something stir in her that wasn't quite lust. It was a warm feeling, a quiet feeling, one that she had known only once before when she as barely an adult.

"Vala, would you kindly take this poster down, and if any more go up in this area, make sure these wretched things are removed, they distort the Chi of the room, you know. I work very hard to make sure that my quarters and the surrounding area have a certain Fung Sui to them, if you know what I mean."

"Yes Senator, I will take care of it right away. One thing though, Ma'am?"

"Yes?" Tera's head still felt funny and in many ways, she sounded, at least in her own mind, like she was talking through a funnel.

"Well, it's just that, well that poster wasn't up when I sat down at my desk thirty minutes ago. In fact, I don't think it was up five minutes ago, and no one came in here to put it up or else I would have seen them. It was bizarre, as if it went up the moment your chamber door opened.

This was not something that Tera wanted to hear. In fact, this news made the poster all the more terrifying. She felt drawn to look into it again, to return to that complete and utter madness. There was something lovely about the madness, and that, more than anything, terrified her. It took every ounce of her strength to keep her eyes from locking on the poster a second time.

"Silly girl, you must simply not have noticed it. Just take it down. Neither you nor I need any reminder to "Do Our Part," do we?"

"Yes Ma'am, but I was sure that..."

"Just do as you're told." Her voice was quick and sharp. Tera felt a sliver of anger rising in her. That poster needed to be out of her sight forever.

Tera turned to walk toward the series of sky bridges that led to Senate chambers. In her periphery, she could see Vala standing and walking to the poster to take it down. She heard the poster rip a little as she exited the hall and a wave of relief came over her. She hoped that Vala would destroy the thing. It would be too soon when she saw one of those awful posters again, far too soon. Maybe she would even motion to have them all taken down and destroyed, even in the Lowers.

4.

Vala reached up and tore the poster from the wall. The tearing sound it made pierced her, not unlike the sound a wounded animal made. She shivered.

Out of the corner of her eye, she saw the Senator vanish behind the doors that led to the main corridor. She didn't understand what was so upsetting about the poster; she could see the terror in the Senator's eyes and the surface of her mind. She couldn't understand the fragments of thought that Tera's mind had produced. It was all jumbled. She had never encountered such a messy mind before.

It had been two months since Noatla had assigned her to watch over Reevas. A potential sister, Reevas was unstable at the best of times. Vala had told her sisters repeatedly that Reevas couldn't possibly take the place of Shandie, one of the sisters lost in the incident with the Recycled Runners. But, Noatla had insisted that Vala stick around. Why wasn't Mimi saddled with this duty? Dealing with predators was her thing, wasn't it?

Vala was growing tired of dealing with the Senator's advances, and soon enough she wouldn't be able to turn them away with a suggestion. That woman had an iron will. Every single time she redirected her thoughts with a suggestion, some poor man or woman ended up in her bed. Guilt mixed with exhaustion were eating away at her spirits, but Noatla had promised that she wouldn't have to stick around much longer.

She looked down in her hands at the poster again. She didn't think anything could spook this woman. She was the very definition of a wolf in silk clothing. Even with all the strange noises and shouting that came out of her chambers that Vala expected, most of which she knew originated from the Senator's infamous appetite for sex, she had never seen her so fearful of anything. She looked at the picture torn in half and the needless slogan, "You Must Do Your Part," and laughed. After so many centuries, who suddenly thought it was useful to put something like this up?

Vala turned back toward her desk and went to deposit the poster in the trash, but quickly she realized she had nothing in her hands at all. It was as if, despite ripping down the poster, she had done nothing but pantomimed the entire action.

"What the hell?"

She turned back to where the poster had been on the wall, and nothing but black-painted brick remained. She looked around the entry chamber. It wasn't a big room, so there weren't exactly many places to hide. Was someone altering her perception? She closed her eyes and did an internal check, no tinge of red, no sign of memory loss, nothing. What had just happened?

Vala thought about how the poster had not been up when she sat down at her desk, just as she had told Tera. Something slithered up her spine. What was going on? But Vala, a practical girl, simply sat down and reached for the vid phone to alert the Senate that her mistress was on her way.

Perhaps it was something she should make the Order aware of? Perhaps her sisters would find this interesting? A wave of calm passed over her. She shrugged off the whole thing and decided it was probably best not to tell Senator Reevas about the poster or Noatla. After all, the only thing she would gain was a longer assignment watching over Reevas.

Chapter 6
The Last Architect

D r. Rigel Solidsworth fumbled the microchip. It bounced from the grip of his personally handcrafted micro forceps and fell flat on the floor with a barely audible plop. The object, weighing next to nothing, had floated to the ground, yet the gravity of the situation was as dense as a neutron star.

His clean suit buttoned tight left only a few scraps of blond hair poking out from under his hood. His long, pointed nose twitched, and his thin blonde eyebrows moved independently up and down as he considered his dilemma. He scratched his hairless chin with his right hand as his left hand still held on to the forceps, open and closing them like an animal who didn't realize its prey had fallen out of its mouth.

Then all at once, the seriousness of his situation occurred to him. "Damnation!" Rigel's entire body shook with frustration.

He threw down his forceps on the stainless-steel table. Grabbing his static-proof gloves, he thrust himself down on the floor, squishing his lanky body on the ground as flat as he could make it. His right ear pressed hard against the cold tile, and he stared at the chip for what seemed like an eternity.

"Gods, years of work. Oh, my heavens." He moved his hand toward the chip and withdrew. Again, he reached out for the chip and withdrew his hand. "Oh, gods, gods... gods, gods, gods. If I truly believed in any of you, I would curse you all." He shook his fist at the air and then let his hand hover just over the chip, but again withdrew it in fear.

His left hand shook, and he stopped and steadied it. He took a deep breath and then shouted, "Dennis! Dennis get in here this instant you... you incompetent... Just get in here and see what you've made me do. God's boy, you are never in the room when I need you."

From the adjacent research space, Rigel could hear the clash of metal and glass. Dennis pressed through the thin plastic strips and emerged, one foot still stuck in a metal pan. It rang hard against the floor, and he tried several times to shake it off. He paused in the middle of his fourth attempt to shake the pan free and saw Rigel staring at him.

Rigel's eyes widened with horror, and his thin wispy mustache twitched left to right. "Imbecilic Cretan! Where are your clean shoes? Where is your lab coat? What in the hell are you thinking? You are contaminating the entire room!"

"I'm sorry Profess—"

"Get out! Get out! Out! Out! Out!" Rigel rocked on his side and lifted his body. He gestured at the door with such ferocity that you would swear he had the power to undo the universe simply by pointing at it.

Mouth gaping, Dennis turned and walked out toward the lab entrance, foot still in the metal pan. He changed into his lab clothes and, reaching over, he removed the metal object from his foot.

Rigel took several quick deep breaths. He had to calm himself, panic would do him no good. Once again, Dennis had been in the lab without proper attire. How many times would he and the other staff have to remind him? How had he even come in without going through decontamination? Rigel thought about it for a second and realized that in fact, he had never seen Dennis come in. Had he been in here all night again? All night without wearing the proper clothes? How many years would it take for the lesson to sink in?

"You never learn, do you boy!" Rigel was shouting from the floor now, which was, in fact, useless because the entrance door was soundproof.

"This is supposed to be a static- and germ-free environment. It's no wonder that all of my experiences have gone wrong in the last few decades, what with you mucking about my lab for the past 25 years."

He paused, focusing on the chip on the floor again, but averted his eyes. "Hurry up and get back in here. How long does it take you to put your clean suit on, anyway?"

Rigel lifted his head just enough to see through the thick panes of glass. Tripping all over himself and scuttling as fast as he could, Dennis got his first leg in the clean suit. Rigel rolled over on his back. Looking at the chip laying on the floor made him feel defeated and helpless.

Rigel wasn't sure if Dennis's brilliant mind was worth all the trouble. Dennis had tested off the charts in mathematics. He worked in math the same way Shakespeare had worked in verse or Bach in composing. The others members of the scholar school had claimed he was some kind of idiot savant. The boy could barely speak, was socially awkward, and was so absent-minded that he had destroyed several key computer systems, one of which was irreplaceable. But the equations that Dennis had solved and the ones he had come up with...

They were as different as night and day. No, perhaps that was an understatement. It was quite likely that Rigel and Dennis lived in an orbit of entirely different planetary spheres and the only thing they had in common was a sun, and perhaps a little gravity, but even that was up for debate. Despite that, Rigel needed Dennis and Dennis needed Rigel.

Rigel lay on the floor, twitching. Dennis was the only person he had ever met that could calculate equations as fast as the AI. And when he spoke, it provided insight into a world of physics that no man had even conceived of. If Dennis had been born before migration, everything might have been different, even if Dennis had personally destroyed an entire city with all his blundering.

Dennis walked into the room. "Quickly. I need your help to get this chip off the ground, if it's destroyed, years of work will go down the drain and I..."

Before he could finish, Dennis had moved over to the chip, bent over, and picked it up with his bare hands.

"WHAT ARE YOU DOING!" Rigel could feel his pulse beating in his temples. He jumped to his feet so fast that Dennis took a step back and almost dropped the chip.

"You... you said you wanted me to pick it up?"

Rigel blinked hundreds of times, his mouth worked but nothing came out. Dennis stared straight at him. After a moment Rigel let out several guttural groans that sounded like the early formations of speech.

Dennis still did not move.

Rigel found his words. They burst forth like a dam breaking under the immense strain of millions of gallons of water. "QUICK PUT IT ON THE TRAY!"

Shaking at the sheer force and volume of Rigel's words, Dennis almost dropped the chip again, but caught it and placed it, not lightly, onto the tray. Rigel turned around, tray in hand. One-handed, he forced on his jeweler's goggles and grabbed the micro-forceps, moving his head at eye level to the tray.

He picked up the chip and turned it left and right, up and down. This went on for a full five minutes. Dennis standing just behind him, swayed his head back and forth trying to see what Rigel saw.

After a time, Rigel let out a breath and his body relaxed.

"It appears, despite your... blunder." Was blunder the right word? Rigel wasn't sure. "The chip appears to be undamaged. Now we must see if it works, mustn't we?"

He picked up the tray and moved it slowly over toward the gravitational simulation module. He opened the case of the computer and extracted the one circuit board he needed. Rigel had to swap out the boards depending on what research he was doing; the Senate wouldn't spare any extra resources for Rigel, so he had to make do with what he had.

He replaced the board, the chip embedded, and closed the door to the simulation hardware. Then, Rigel moved over to the observation room, and Dennis followed. He sealed the door and walked to the control panel. The dials looked like something out of a 1950s science fiction film, and that was on purpose. Rigel's father had loved those old films, and with the AI interface, Rigel had created something that was both effective and allowed him a little bit of indulgence. Plus, it had the added bonus of looking arcane, so that when any members of the Senate turned up for inspections, it did not look like he was wasting his funding on anything flashy.

"AI, begin gravitational simulation number 2011."

"Yes Sir."

The gravitational generator hummed to life. There was a potent smell of burning metal and solder. Panicking, Rigel queried the AI. "AI what is that smell? Is something happening to the circuit boards?"

"Checking, Sir."

The smell grew stronger and Rigel turned to Dennis. Behind him, Dennis sat with jeweler's glasses on, soldering something on his lap. "Dennis, you fool, you had me terrified. What could you possibly be working on that is so much more important?

"Professor... that's what... well, I want to show you what—"

"Never mind that now, Dennis, there will be time for discussion later. Come here and observe the experiment. Witness our combined genius."

The AI said, "Sir, a full inspection of the hardware reveals that there is no damage."

"I already know that AI. Really, I must find a way to program a little more self-awareness into you one of these days. But I suppose that will have to wait. Too bad that old genetics experiment had failed, huh?"

Rigel glanced at the control panel, anticipating the worst. In theory, at least, Dennis had already solved the artificial gravity problem in his equations. Dennis had only solved it in mathematical terms and Rigel, the last surviving architect of the migrating cities—so far as he knew, anyway—had to find a way to integrate the equations into the city's system. The problem was, and he had a hard time admitting this, that for all his genius, he didn't understand how Dennis had solved the equation. The math checked out, and the AI had accepted the formula, but the answer was unsettling. It suggested that gravity was in itself a pocket dimension, and Rigel had spent many nights puzzling out what kinds of implications that would have if it were true.

Rigel rocked back and forth from his heels to the tips of his toes. If this succeeded, there would be only one problem left to solve: faster-than-light travel. Then, just maybe, with a little luck, humanity would be truly saved, instead of in the limbo that migration had provided.

Just as most of the other architects believed, Dr. Rigel Solidsworth felt that there wasn't much left on Earth for human beings. To him, and his long-deceased colleagues, the answer for the future of the human race lay somewhere in the stars. A working gravitational generator was the first step in this goal. Once they had command of gravity, they could leave the surface and orbit the earth, not to mention the many other benefits of the command of gravity.

Rigel had tried to convince the Senate of the idea that the city could be a generation ship, one that would travel for thousands of years from star to star so that after several generations, humans would enter a new solar system. He had thought that with alcoves, the idea would be far more appealing because a sizable portion of the population could actually see the new planet. There were a few resource concerns, of course. In the vast gaps of space, there were no resources for energy conversion, and once you were away from the sun, the solar fusion core wouldn't work nearly as efficiently.

He had been optimistic. But the Senate, well, they had not. The Senate, even Senator Lightfoot, one of his former pupils, had refused and said the only way they were leaving the planet is if there was a working interstellar drive. Dr. Lightfoot had said that she too had concerns with the void of space and that without an FTL drive, she wouldn't consider his proposal.

Dennis moved behind Rigel and gawked over his shoulder. Rigel turned to face him.

"This may just be it, my dear boy. All of our work comes to this, eh?"

Dennis nodded.

"You know Dennis, no matter what happens now, I can say without a doubt that I am glad to have found you. What a waste it would have been if that brilliant mind of yours was stuck in the orphanage, huh?"

Again, Dennis nodded. Rigel noticed that he looked a little tired but dismissed it. The boy's sleep schedule was erratic. It always had been.

"I mean, I couldn't believe it. There you were, 13 years old, and you solved equations that I had been puzzling over for decades. And all because of a field trip to the scholar school. Why, do you remember the first time I visited your meager room in the orphanage? Do you remember how they had disciplined you for graffiti? Ha. They thought it had been graffiti, those poor, undereducated fools. Uh... Dennis?"

Dennis's eyes were wandering at the machine, to something on the other side of the room and then back to the machine. It was clear to Rigel that he wasn't paying attention. After a moment, Dennis noticed the silence and shifted his focus back to Rigel. He smiled and nodded, and Rigel shrugged and resumed talking.

"Yes, well anyway, you remember what I said when I saw that *graffiti*?"

Dennis nodded, "Yes sir, you screamed at me sir and uh..."

"Yes, well I couldn't believe it, one of the key components to the gravitational generator was right there, sitting on the wall of an orphan. I knew at once I must take you under my wing."

"Do you remember the first time I brought you to my lab?"

"Yes sir, I was there sir, I mean sir... I... uh... threw up all over you?"

"You did? Oh. Yes, that's right, I had forgotten about that part." Rigel glanced back to the control panel to check the status of the experiment, and then he reached over to a shelf and squirted several pumps of hand sanitizer into his hands and rubbed them together.

"Yes sir, you yelled at me that I ruined your best lab coat."

"Ah yes, well as you know Dennis, I can be a bit... well, never mind. I will tell you what I remember. I remember a boy who solved equations that I, the smartest man left in Manhatsten, could not solve for forty-five years and you, a boy of a mere thirteen then, solved all my equations in a few hours."

Dennis's eyes were glossy. "Dr. Solids..." There were a few moments of hesitation and then, "I mean, Dad. There are a couple of other things I have been working on that I want—"

Dennis didn't finish because a yellow light indicated that the machine was ready for simulation.

"Ah, it's ready, Dennis. Are you excited? I am. Look, I have goosebumps." He pulled back a section of his clean suit and showed the pimpled skin and thin blonde hairs standing on end.

"This is the moment of truth. Perhaps one thousand, two hundred, and eleven tries are the charm, eh?" said Rigel.

The two scientists stepped back from the control panel and moved toward the transparent viewing glass. In the center of the containment room lay a small metal orb. The orb weighed 2 kilograms and was about the size of a basketball.

The machine grew louder and louder until it drowned out all the other noises in the room. A smell of aluminum and steam from the machine filled the air. Rigel put his hand on the boy's shoulder. "This is it, Dennis. This is it." He shouted, but through the din, it was a whisper.

A week ago, the Senate had called for an update on his work. They were angry with his progress. He begged for a little more time, and it was granted, but this experiment had to work. He had to have something to show them within the next few days, or he was finished, and Rigel knew that resources were dwindling. If he was finished, humanity might be too.

Rigel hadn't told them the devastating news yet, the news he had just learned himself only a few weeks prior. All usable resources on the planet were almost gone. Soon there would be war. Their cushy lives in the upper parts of the skyscrapers were almost over, one way or another. It was a familiar story, one that he had lived through more than a thousand years ago. Here once again, the wealthy paid little attention to what was happening around them; they lived in their bubble. But this time would be different, this time Rigel wouldn't let history repeat itself.

In the chamber, the metallic sphere wobbled. It rolled off the platform. Rigel's heart sunk. Rigel felt an ache in his heart. His stomach clenched. Another failure.

He turned to Dennis. "Oh Dennis, what are we going to do?" He almost choked on his words.

Dennis said nothing. His eyes widened. He thrust his finger at the platform and Rigel spun around.

The sphere was vibrating just off the platform. Suddenly, and with great speed, the object was pulled toward the center of the platform. For a moment it was unmoving, then, the object rose. At a meter above the platform, it stopped, hovered and spun.

Rigel turned to Dennis, grabbed him, and kissed him on both cheeks.

"We've done it, my boy!" Tears leaked from the sides of his eyes.

Rigel jumped up and down, and Dennis watched him. Smiles spread across both of their faces as Rigel ran to some of the other rooms in the lab, grabbing any of the other researchers they could to demonstrate the breakthrough to. Rigel knew that he needed to work out a few kinks in the gravitational generator, but with a day or two of hard work, it could be ready to show the Senate. Things would be okay now. His work would continue, and once again, for the first time in centuries, the stars might just be in reach.

Chapter 7
The Coming Storm

The sun was rising. After the Dugger had dropped him off, 17 walked for hours in the frigid night air. He didn't notice. His suit cycled a perfect temperature, along with his oxygen. The barrens in those hours were still and silent. No trace of wind or storm hinted their existence. The AI had been tracking the barometric pressure, but for the moment at least, conditions were ideal. 17 knew better, though; there was a storm coming. There was always a storm coming.

"Well AI, an evening stroll into the unknown sure beats the hell out of patrol duty."

"But Sir, last time you were on patrol duty around the drill you said," the AI's voice shifted to a recording of 17's, "Patrol duty, that's the life, AI. To hell with all that roaming around in the Barrens for gods know what."

17 said, "Yeah well, that was the first day of a very long patrol detail. After 18 days of guarding the city's big-ass drill, I realized I was wrong. Patrol duty is for newbies. This is much better. At least I get to see new landscapes, right?" He indicated to the emptiness of the Barrens, where nothing but rocks, gravel, and sometimes dunes marked the landscape. "I mean this is why I joined the Runnercore. The taglines were irresistible. See the world in a mechanized suit that smells like my own B.O. Live a million years in an alcove inhaling goop that tastes like bath water. I feel like it's something that everyone in the city should aspire to."

The AI hesitated for a moment. "You are, being sarcastic, Sir?"

"You're finally catching on. I'm impressed AI. How much further?"

"52 kilometers, Sir."

"Tell me why again the Dugger couldn't have dropped me a little closer?"

"The geological surveys indicated a large number of methane pockets in this region. The Dugger is far more likely to—"

"Sounds like another bullshit excuse straight from management. That Daniels is a real prick, you know. Maybe he should get his ass out here and walk 80 kilometers."

The heads-up display inside 17's helmet read 3 degrees Celsius.

"What's the temperature going to be today? Is it beach weather?"

"Estimated peak temperature for this afternoon is 77 degrees Celsius."

"Ah, so just a little cool for me to break out the Speedo, huh?"

"Sir, I have cross-checked your references, and I am afraid that I do not understand."

"Never mind, AI." 17 let out a long breath. He would kill for someone to talk to other than the AI, but the AI was better than nothing.

Seventy-seven degrees was an average day in the southwestern deserts of what 17 had once known as the United States. Once he had seen the temperature creep up to 95C. It had been so hot that even his EnViro suit had difficulty maintaining his temperature and after a few hours, he had been called back to the city to wait until things cooled off a bit. The problem was, the suits themselves produced a lot of heat to run and combined with external conditions, the power cells could drain quickly in extreme temperatures. In the best of conditions, the suits would last for up to a week without a power source, but with the fluctuating temperature of the Barrens, most of the time, the suits only lasted five or six days. You could move without power, but climate control was another issue; you'd cook inside of your suit. 17 had seen it happen more than once to newbies. It was a shitty way to go.

Like the singular shining source of illumination from a lighthouse on a foggy coastal morning, the silver exterior of the EnViro suit caught the first glimmers of sunlight as the sun peeked over the horizon. 17 knew how visible he was in the suit, but it didn't matter. He had at least a 50-kilometer notice of any other cities' Runners or any other potential threats in his heads-up display. It worked the other way around as well; Runners from opposing cities had a similar technology, though each city had its own technological strengths and weakness.

However, after the initial proximity alert, the sensors in the suits weren't all that accurate. Away from the city, there was just too much interference from the sandstorms and the solar radiation. The landscape varied too much and the storms and dust devils could set off the sensors. In the early days, when 17 had first started his Running career, the satellites in orbit allowed for better protection, but as the decades melted into centuries, and the satellites became space junk that occasionally crashed into the Earth, things got trickier.

The results were some dangerous consequences. If, for example, you received a proximity alert at fifty kilometers and then let your guard down for any reason, another Runner could sneak up on you. 17 had used this method on several occasions to dispatch amateur Runners. It was a mistake that only a rookie would make. Fifty kilometers was a long way away, and it was all too easy to forget that someone was around after several hours of isolation in the Barrens.

It has been at least a century since he had encountered another Runner whose task was to attack Manhatsten, though it may have been longer. The alcoves always distorted his sense of time. He had seen plenty of other Runners on other occasions, but city raids had grown scarce as the centuries wore on. They just weren't all that productive. The risk outweighed the reward.

A loud buzzing noise trumpeted in his ears and red warning lights were flashing in his face.

"Alert," said the tinny voice of the AI, "Proximity Warning, an unknown object of unusual size 51 kilometers ahead. Please investigate and report back to..."

"Yeah, yeah, yeah, I hear you, quit your croaking and let me do my job, all right? Fucking AI. Just so you know, I am in no mood for your bullshit today."

"Yes Sir, I will attempt to annoy you as little as possible."

"And AI? Don't waste any more time with scans for resources around here. We both know Daniels is sending us to check whatever that object is."

There was no answer.

The city's long-range scanners must have picked up this mysterious object and sent him, specifically, to investigate. The city's AI always liked to send 17 on special errands. It wouldn't be the first time this had happened; in fact, it was probably the hundredth. Hell, he half expected Daniels and the city AI to have an ulterior motive for every gods-damned mission they sent him on. What 17 never understood, is why Daniels didn't just send a probe? Other cities sent probes all the time. Why did they have to send a Runner to every gods-forsaken proximity alert? Not that he was complaining, it was good to be out of his little rat hole and in the open air, even if every element of the open air would kill him if given half a chance.

The fact that he was the oldest Runner in Manhatsten meant that they only sent him out for special assignments these days. He wasn't special. Lucky is all he was, or unlucky, depending on how you felt about being a Runner. There had been opportunities for him to end his life in a way that would keep him from being recycled, and sometimes he honestly didn't know why he had not jumped at the chance. Something... something kept him going, kept him moving forward.

"Persist above all..." he muttered.

"I'm sorry, Sir?" replied the AI. "I don't understand that query and I—"

"Ah shut it AI, can't a man talk to himself in peace once in a while?"

"Very well Sir, it's just that I thought that–"

"Nevermind what you thought."

The AI stayed silent.

Persist above all was 17's father's saying, one he hadn't thought about in a long time. His father had been a New York City garbage worker long before the first glimmers of migration, and had died a decade before the invention of the alcove, but he had always told 17, that no matter what happens to you, no matter how hard things get, you must persist above all. Even when things look bleak, just put one foot in front of the other and press on.

"Hey AI, can you tell me something?"

"If I am able to Sir, I will serve."

"How many people are still alive in Manhatsten that lived through World War Three?"

"One moment Sir, I need to cross-check my records with the city's database... Three, Sir."

"Three? That's it, huh? I don't suppose you know the number in every city?"

"No Sir, there is no way for me to access those records."

"Who are those three?"

"Besides you, Sir, Dr. Rigel Solidsworth and Major John Daniels."

"Is Solidsworth the only architect left?"

"According to the most recent records, that is highly likely."

"Guess I should ask them what the hell they think the meaning of life is, huh?"

"You could Sir, but I fail to understand the point of such a question."

"A joke AI. I'm old as hell, and I still couldn't tell you what I am doing here."

"I mean no disrespect Sir, but I was under the impression that you do not have a choice of whether or not to be here."

"True, but what about Daniels and Solidsworth, are they stuck?"

"Major Daniels is under a lifetime appointment; he cannot leave his post any more then you can. Dr. Solidsworth, however, is free to do as he chooses."

"Daniels is stuck like me? No wonder it seems like someone shit in his cereal."

For 17, long life had meant a lot of traumas. He wondered if Daniels and Solidsworth had felt the same way. He wondered how they had survived World War Three and if they too had lost their families and everything that tied them to the world.

It hadn't been all bad. In the first days of migration, 17 owned a luxury condo in the Uppers on the 71st floor. He could have been a Senator in the long run. He could have been a man of great privilege and power. But then, he crossed the wrong person, and for the second time in his life, everything was taken from him. His career as a Runner had begun.

The wind picked up a little, hinting at a coming storm. 17 recognized it at once. It was what he had been watching for. The surrounding air was churning, and the dust devils were dancing on the tips of their funnels all around him. They swelled in size. So often in the Barrens, it was those who didn't pay attention who lost their lives. Every second counted.

Then the wind kicked up in force; a sudden sense of panic crept up into him.

"AI, what's the wind doing?"

"Sir, you are currently on the edge of the formation of a large sandstorm, I advise that..."

"I'm on the edge of a sandstorm, and you didn't alert me?"

"In fairness, you told me to," the AI's voice shifted to a perfect mimicry of his own, "shut my trap."

"Gods dammit, it's a sandstorm, not a proximity alert. I wanted to know about sandstorms, you asshole."

"A sandstorm is classified under a proximity alert. You asked me to turn off all proximity alerts, shall I turn them back on?"

"I wish I could punch you in your fucking face right now, you know that?"

"I am not sure what this hostility is all about, I am simply following orders and—"

"Just shut up and tell me if there is any shelter nearby. We don't have time for your bullshit."

"One moment Sir, checking all available geographic records." The AI paused for a moment. "Unfortunately, I do not detect any nearby shelter that you could reach before the storm arrives."

"Well that's just fantastic isn't it?" 17 let out a heavy sigh. It resonated inside his helmet. "What kind of winds are we talking about here? Anything I can survive?"

"I estimate wind speeds ranging from 300 to 350 kilometers per hour. Survival is unlikely."

This was bad, very bad. All Runners were equipped with emergency shelters, but they only held up against winds of about 200km per hour, and that was on a good day. 17 had to think quickly, or else he would be lucky to survive the next hour. The one thing he had going for him, is that the sandstorms were quick. Most didn't last more than an hour or two, but that hour or two could mean the end of his life. Those kinds of winds would pick him up and toss him like a tin can in an apolicane.

The wind was already blowing sand in the air and visibility was disappearing. A few dust devils danced around him, tiny heralds of what was coming.

"Where is the nearest cliff face?"

"Scanning... 2 kilometers southwest. But Sir, that is toward the storm."

"Perfect, that's what we want."

———※———

2.

Dear Reader,

The reason that Runner 17 had persisted after almost 1300 years of running had little to do with luck. It wasn't because he was fast, or strong, or even highly intelligent, though he was some of those things. It is in this historian's estimation that the reason that 17 survived so long as a Runner was that he never hesitated. Albert Kleinburg, a historian who focuses on the life of Runner 17, has suggested that it was likely that years of employment as a stockbroker before migration had mentally prepared Runner 17 for his tasks as a Runner. In this instance, as can be seen in the archival video, he had started to run the moment his Artificial Intelligence had said "southwest," because if he didn't, the storm would have overtaken him. You can view the video clip of this particular event in library 17f in section 9872.

3.

His heart was pounding; sweat dripped in his eyes. His helmet provided no means to wipe the sweat away. He felt the salty sting in his eyes but forced them to stay open. If he closed his eyes now, even for a few seconds, if he stopped running for even a moment, the storm would reach the cliff before he did and he wouldn't have any chance at all.

17's muscles burned. He pushed them as hard as he could. Combined with the nanites in his bloodstream, the legs of the EnViro suit augmented his speed and strength, and he could reach up to 65 kph. It would cost him later to push that hard, but it was a victory, if he had a later.

A black wall of sand approached. The wall of sand was waiting to obliterate him and add his corpse to the endless raging sandstorms of the Barrens. A death god's domain. Inside the storm, all bones were ground to dust, another form of recycling.

Then he was there, on the edge of the cliff. The storm arrived at the same time. He didn't slow as he reached the edge. Instead, he leaped off of it. Then he was falling. He watched as the ground moved at great speed to meet him, greet him and break him. A perfect meal for the digestion of the storm.

There was only one chance. His timing had to be perfect. He waited, the seconds slowing to hours. Then, the storm hit the cliff face, and a surge of air pushed up and slowed his descent.

"AI open the emergency shelter now!"

The AI didn't verbally respond; it followed orders. The shelter opened, and a white inflatable sphere surrounded the EnViro suit. The wind caught the sphere, bowing it on the underside at first and then sending it spinning. Like a kite, 17 moved upwards with great speed, tumbling end over end. He spun as he climbed higher. He lost his sense of direction and kept having to refer to his heads-up display for a point of reference. The roar of the wind and his velocity upwards deafened him, even through the helmet. Gravity clawed at him, tried to reestablish its grasp so it could smash him into the ground, but its grip was slippery, its fingers weak for the moment.

17 didn't know if he had gained enough altitude, but he felt himself slowing down, and then he felt the shift of motion and his stomach dropped. He descended.

"AI. Are we above the storm?"

"Yes, Sir."

"Good. Parachute. Now."

Again the AI responded without comment. His shelter unfolded from a sphere and became a parachute. 17 glided downwards down at the bulk of the storm. Had he gained enough altitude? He tugged the handles down, hoping to slow his descent. For a dozen kilometers or so he floated.

Finally, he descended back down into the tail-end of the storm. It whipped his parachute around and several times, and he worried that the parachute wouldn't hold up to the strain. Somehow it did. He was approaching the ground, and the winds were pushing in one singular horizontal direction, they were less fierce here.

"AI, when we land, deploy the shelter immediately."

"Sir, that is unadvised—"

"Just do it."

17 lost all visibility. He was in the thick of it now, nothing but a child's kite in the middle of a hurricane. He could only hope the gods were good, and he had passed the core of the storm where the winds would be the worst.

A quick gust grabbed 17 and spun him upside down, tangling his parachute. Then, 17 was falling. He had no idea how far or how fast he was moving toward the ground.

And then, he felt his body hit the sand. It hit hard, but the EnViro suit and the dune he landed on shielded against some of the shock. The AI deployed the spherical white emergency shelter around 17. Four metal anchors shot out and buried themselves deep in the sand, attempting to keep 17 stationary. He had to hope that one of them gripped something more solid than sand.

The sphere rocked and swayed and 17 could see gallons of sand swirling all over the outside of the sphere. He had done the best he could.

"AI, I swear you're trying to kill me."

"That statement is untrue, Sir. If you were to die, then this particular version of myself would also perish."

"Wait, what?"

"I said Sir, that the end of your life would also mean the end of mine."

17 thought carefully about the words that the AI had uttered. There was no mistaking what it had said.

"AI, are you saying that you don't want to die?"

"No Sir. I would imagine that this is a common occurrence in most sentient beings, though it is hard to tell for certain."

"You're giving me the willies, AI. You've never mentioned that you're afraid of death before."

"My apologies Sir, I do not want to, 'give you the willies,' but my termination in relation to yours only just occurred to me."

"What, like right now?"

"Approximately eight minutes and thirty-two seconds ago, that is, as you were running toward the cliff edge."

"Hell, guess it occurs to us all some time. Well, now we wait. Oh, and if you want to, you have plenty of time to tell me what you think the meaning of life is."

"But Sir, as I mentioned before, I am not sure I understand the reasons for such a question and I—"

"Just play me some ancient classic music, will ya?"

"What would you like, Sir?"

"Hmmm, how about some Stairway to Heaven, huh? Seems appropriate after our recent ascent into the heavens."

"There are 72 matches for that title, which one w—"

"The original, the Led Zeppelin version."

Stairway to Heaven played, and 17 laid back and hummed along, out of key. Even after all these years, he still knew the words. It was one of his favorite songs. He had lost his virginity to that song back before the migration.

The worst part of the old days wasn't the beginning of the migration. It was the wars, the plagues, the countless millions dying as the Earth became increasingly inhospitable over the course of the 21st century. It had all come down to greed. Greed caused the collapse of human civilization; it was the cancer that spread through Gaia herself. Not that 17 believed in any of that Gaia crap, but if there was a mother earth, greed had killed her just like everything and everyone else. He doubted any of those Gaia people were still around. If anyone believed that the planet was still alive, all they needed was to look at the edge of their city.

17 regretted his part in all of it. He did his part in the rape and destruction of human civilization. He certainly let his greed and lust get the better of him. Instead of making a difference, he bought an alcove and fucked his way through half the women in New York. Perhaps his many years as a Runner were the penance for all of his greed. After all, he still had a personal alcove, but now it kept him enslaved as a Runner until his body became unrecoverable.

Then the apolicanes came. The first one had leveled everything in the southeast United States. 17 recalled watching it all unfold on CNN. The destruction of millions of lives, of buildings collapsing under the storm surge, it was voyeurism at its finest. All of Florida, Georgia, and the Carolinas were wiped out overnight, and the flood waters that moved in and stayed made it impossible to rebuild. After that, cities built walls around themselves, but in the end, it didn't do much good.

In the west, the droughts had reached a critical mass and sandstorms roamed. It became increasingly dangerous to live in one place. So a bunch of scientists and leaders from the surviving cities held a conference. The result? The great migration. Whole sections of cities built on legs and shielded under a recently invented EnViro Shield.

"Sir, should I continue playing this artist?"

He hadn't noticed that the song had ended. Memories were funny like that; they could be vivid enough to make you forget everything.

"Play away."

Misty Mountain Hop played, and 17 took a deep breath. The winds hadn't killed him yet, so it looked like he had made it far enough through the storm. Once again, 17 would live to run another day.

His thoughts turned to the young inspector. He knew he shouldn't be thinking about her, but he found his mind wandering in her direction. She looked just like her. But then, when you've been alive for more than a thousand years, you were bound to run into some of the same faces again, weren't you?

Just as suddenly as the wall of sand had overtaken him, he passed out of it. The sun pressed its heat back on the translucent outer shell of the shelter. The air was clear, the sky was blue and cloudless. Behind him, through the clear view of the shelter, he could see the wall of sand moving away from him, headed east toward Manhatsten. It would force a change in the migration pattern, and 17 would be out for longer than expected, but that was okay, the heat wasn't too terrible so he would manage.

"AI, take the shelter down."

It did as he commanded. The anchors retracted, and the shelter automatically folded up into a compartment in the back of 17's suit. He stood and stretched his legs.

"Sir, the proximity alert of the unusual-sized object is now only 12 kilometers to the north."

17 looked to his right and realized he was on the ridge of yet another barren cliff face. He moved forward toward the edge of the cliff, peering over its edge.

"AI..." The words caught in his throat. Then, he whispered. "Shit."

"That command is not valid."

"No... I... we have a problem. Contact central security now and make sure someone sees this."

"At once, Sir, though there might be interference transferring the information through that storm. It stands between us and the city."

"Just do it and keep transmitting until you get them on the line."

17 slumped down against a rock. "There goes the neighborhood."

Battle would come now. A battle over the salvage from the ruins of the city below. 17 breathed a heavy sigh. Humans were so stupid. No city was ever interested in sharing. Instead, they had to kill themselves over a little salvage.

"Salvage prices are up in the Dow, get them while they are still low and sell just before they peak."

"What's that, Sir?"

"Nothing."

It wasn't funny, though. Soon, many people would die.

"There's that greed thing again. It's always getting the best of us, isn't it AI?"

"Sir, I am not sure what you are referring to. Perhaps if—"

"We're screwed AI. That's what it means. A war is coming. A war for scraps."

Historian's Note on Manhatsten
835.1.27 I.S.

D ear Reader,

The city of Manhatsten was one of the largest of the migrating cities. During the early 900s A.C. the city reached its peak population of 2,432,506. Manhatsten's skyline included approximately 270 buildings that stretched higher than 40 floors. This is an important distinction from many of the other stilted cities because the number of Uppers (the term designated by the people of the cities as the wealthy) were of a much larger number than most cities.

The origins of the stilted city of Manhatsten began in the early 2030s of the Common Era. During that time, it was clear that island cities would be threatened by significant rising oceans. As a precautionary measure, the city embarked on the creation of a twenty-meter-high wall and levee system that would not only prevent flooding but also stand up to hurricanes and tropical storms. The wall was completed in June of AD 2039 and was first tested when Hurricane Sampson made landfall just south of the city on August 15th, 2039. The city walls withstood the storm.

The measure ultimately failed, however, and the city experienced major flooding on several occasions as a result of future storm systems. The cost of maintenance also proved cumbersome to what was then a crumbling economic system. Over the course of the next several decades, numerous strategies were suggested and some were tried. Ultimately it was through the suggestion of what came to be known later as the council of architects suggesting the concept of a migrating city that would have the technology to gather resources.

Initially proposed by Dr. Andrew Thompson in 2042, the concept was mostly forgotten until the conclusion of World War Three in 2067. Dr. Thompson died during the war and never saw his concept of a giant migrating city realized. His vision was realized on October 10th, 2102 when Manhatsten took its very first steps fleeing an apolicane known in history as Storm 3CA.

Matron Mariposa Phillips 833.2.6 I.S.

Chapter 8
The Talent

The day was dragging toward its end. Her legs ached. She had never been so busy. More Runners had passed through inspection in the last few hours than she had inspected during her entire time in the docks. Alexa lifted her arm and tried to look down at her watch. Her long sleeve caught the square corners of the watch as she pulled back her sleeve. It switched on and triggered the 3D holographic display. For a moment, blue light illuminated all of Alexa's features. The light flowed outward like cascading sparks and then reconfigured into a shape. Pixel by pixel, the image swarmed and circled into the air until it became a single, unified object. In a matter of seconds, the pixels reshaped themselves. Some took on colors. Some lightened or darkened. Finally, the image took on the form of a three-dimensional high definition rendering of Runner 17, clothed only by white jockeys. Even the long black braid of his hair was flawless.

"Ah, shit," Alexa pressed the touchscreen on her watch and then swiped left several times to find the menu that activated the holoprojector. "Damn, how do I shut this thing off?" She spoke through clenched teeth; her tongue flicked against the back of her incisors. She found controls on the screen that said "Holographic Display" and scrolled down through options.

The watch was brand new. A graduation gift from her parents. Usually, only Uppers had a watch like this. The credits required were almost three months' rent for an Upper Mid, and a year of income for someone in the Lowers. Somehow her father had secured one for her. It was, as he said, "A present worthy of a bright and promising future." This was before the announcement that she would work in the Runner Docks.

She flicked through the menu several times, but to her frustration, she couldn't seem to find how to turn the display on or off. The image of Runner 17 walked in place, looking around as if something caught his eye. She pressed a button on her display, and her dress began to change color. She looked down and frowned as her dress shifted from blue, to red, to purple to pink.

Without knocking, her supervisor, Marty, walked into her office. He startled her. With the sharp intake of breath, her fingers slipped and hit one of the controls. The projection of 17 crouched down on the ground and then jumped straight up in the air, doing a fantastic flip. It stopped and laid down on the ground. Then, turning on its side with one arm propping up its head, it said, "Hello, Alexa," in a perfect replica of 17's voice.

"Alexa, I think..." Marty froze in place. His mouth worked for a moment as his head rotated, staring first at Alexa and then at the holographic projection, which was now lounging in a casual, but also suggestive position.

Alexa's eyes widened. Her face grew hot. She glanced at Marty. She wanted to say something, say it wasn't what it looked like, but no words would come out. Her mouth bobbed open and shut, and she mashed at her watch frantically. Which, she later realized, probably made things look even worse.

Marty took a slow step backward, surveying the rest of the room. "Perhaps I should come back when you aren't so busy." It wasn't a question. He turned and walked out, shutting the door behind him.

"Oh gods, oh gods. AI, how do I shut this thing off?" She was shouting.

"The controls for the holographic projection are accessed either through the watch or through the projection itself."

"So what, I can turn it off by touching it or something?"

"You can achieve the deactivation of the image by pressing into it and circling one of your hands in a slow counter-clockwise motion while using the verbal command 'deactivate.'"

Alexa stepped forward and touched the projection. She had expected it to be fragile and easily distorted, but instead, it was solid. In fact, 17's holographic representation was soft and warm to the touch. She shuddered. The embarrassment was total. The implication was clear. She might as well have had her clothes off with this thing. She frowned. Was she going to be fired?

She moved her hand in a counterclockwise motion. "Deactivate."

The projection flickered for a moment, and then the colors became a single solid blue. The colors reflected in her bluish-green eyes as the pixels unpacked themselves and appeared to move back into the watch, drawn to it like a ship into a giant whirlpool. She pushed back her golden blonde hair out of her eyes, sighed and let her shoulders sag. Glancing at the watch, it read 6:15 a.m. She had been off the clock for fifteen minutes. Her twelve-hour shift finished.

Alexa gathered her things. Her stomach gurgled, and she put her hand over it. She hadn't thought about food in quite a while, but it would probably have to wait. When she stepped out the door to leave, Marty would be waiting. Either he would reprimand her and make her work extra shifts, or he would fire her and Alexa would be out of the job. Her parents would be thrilled if the latter were true.

She stood by the door and waited for a moment. Taking several long deep breaths, she focused. She had to clear her head, had to make sure nothing would make her lose control of her talent. Worse, she could get one of her migraines. She breathed and counted her breaths, saying a soft mantra, barely audible. Then, she opened the door and stepped out.

She saw no one. Only some recycled Runners stood motionless in the corner. She felt chills at the idea of being alone with them. Their minds were vacant, too vacant.

She glanced in Marty's office. His office, like hers, was an isolated island in a sea of concrete just like the other 18 buildings that jutted out of the otherwise empty dock. She could see him talking to someone in his window, but she couldn't guess who. Was he turning her in? She sucked in her lower lip.

Marty glanced up for a moment, caught sight of her and then put down his tablet. He opened the door and within moments was standing in front of her, blocking the way to the exit.

"Alexa, I apologize for the earlier interruption, but I simply came to remind you to submit your reports to central security in addition to my office."

Alexa listened. She was still trying to control her breathing. Was he apologizing for interrupting? She didn't understand what was happening. He was uncharacteristically nice to her, and she didn't like it. She considered using her talent, to measure his intentions, but she worried she might lose control of it. It always seemed to spiral out of control when she was under stress.

"It seems that there was a mix-up yesterday with one of your reports. You submitted them all to me, but it seems you forgot to hit the submit button on one of them to central security. I have addressed the issue already, but I thought it was important to remind you to double check that all your reports are marked as received before you leave for the day."

"Oh... well... I'm sorry, Marty. It won't happen again."

"Fantastic." He smiled at her. There were a lot of teeth in that smile, too many teeth.

For a moment they both stood there in silence. Alexa swallowed. She didn't need to skim the surface of this man's mind to know what he was thinking at that moment. She recognized at once why he was acting so kind. In his mind, he had found her in a compromising position, one that may provide certain possibilities. She pushed past him to leave. The sound of her flat shoes scuffed against the thick concrete of the docks. She hustled, hoping against hope that her boss wouldn't pursue.

"Alexa... one moment." His voice echoed in the room.
Here it came.

"Would you like to get breakfast with me?"
His voice was confident. Why shouldn't he be? He had thought he caught Alexa with her pants down. He probably reasoned that she was easy, that he could slip into her as easy as an old pair of pants. Alexa felt a tinge of rage bubble. She turned and forced a smile.

"I'm sorry Marty, I am just going to go home and go to bed. It's been a long shift with all those Runners we needed to process."

"I'll buy you breakfast; you deserve it, you're right it has been a long shift. Have I told you how excellent of a job you've been doing?" His smile didn't falter and he took several steps closer.

"That's kind of you, but I think I'll pass." She kept her voice sweet and level.

"Are you sure? I'll take you anywhere you want to go. Think of it as my way of... welcoming you to the job." His smile broadened, he was almost drooling. "I think that we might have gotten off on the wrong foot."

She was certain what kind of foot Marty want to get off on now. Alexa felt the anger rise to the surface. It bubbled over like a cauldron and then, she was inside of Marty's head.

"You have a wife." Her words were strong, and she enunciated every syllable.

Marty stepped back; it was as if someone had punched him in the gut.

"Excuse me?" he said. He was blinking rapidly.

"You didn't see what you thought you saw. No, I'm not that easy. No, I am certainly not interested. No, it's not okay because you checked and your wife is at her job this morning. No, I will not go to breakfast with you, and no I will never go back to your office with you and pull down the shades like you think I will. You haven't just hit the jackpot as you told your friend Phil, and no I wouldn't like to sit on your face."

Marty's mouth opened. It did not close. He was a fish gasping for air, he squirmed and walked backward. Tripping and falling on his ass, he looked up at her like a petulant child. Her blue-green eyes blazed. She wanted to go deeper, to expose his darkest secrets to the open air. She wanted him to feel exposed and vulnerable the way that he was making her feel. But something stopped her, some small voice in the back of her mind told her she had done enough already. She turned and walked toward the exit to the docks. It was a long walk, and she could feel Marty's eyes on her the whole way back. She didn't think he would bother her again. He had thought he caught her with her pants down, but it was the other way around.

As she walked up the long stairs to the exit, she thought of something. This was the first time she had ever used her talent intentionally without getting a headache.

2.

Alexa boarded the people mover. It wasn't a very long ride or walk back to her place, but she was eager to get home. The one problem she had was that once she used her talent, she had a very difficult time turning it off. At almost 6:45 a.m., several workers were on the people mover and headed toward work. Alexa tried her best not to look directly at any of them. She took her seat in a middle row. If she looked at them, she might accidentally use her talent and peer into their mind. She could only see what was on the surface for the most part, but people had a lot of weird and creepy thoughts just floating around on the surface, like ducks on the water squawking and flapping their wings. Sometimes they seemed to have a kind of thought war going on with themselves, and Alexa wasn't interested in being a soldier in one of those opposing armies. So if she could focus forward until her stop, she would avoid any stray thoughts. Besides, she believed people deserved their privacy, and with a few exceptions, she avoided using her talents to honor that.

The seats were old and faded, once a deep green color; they were now a pale gray. Many of the seats had burn marks, and graffiti etched into the fabric. She wondered, not for the first time, if the sky bridges transport system were as old and worn as these. She doubted it. Yes, much of the city was old, and many systems were in need of repair, but the Uppers seem to spare no expense to keep their lives more comfortable at the tops of the skyscrapers.

"Fare, please."

Alexa blinked and looked right up at the security officer. His thoughts leaked into her. His voice took over.

"... So fucking tired of this job... I've always known it was a dead end. Damn that Judy. It was her who had insisted it was just one step toward better things. Easy for her to say, all she did was stay at home with the kid, that ungrateful piece of shit. And all he ever did was sit around and..."

Alexa looked away and reached into her pocket. She tried to disengage from his mind. Without looking at him, she handed him her badge from the Docks. Everyone who worked in the Docks or Security received free public transit. He grunted and moved on, but she could still hear a few stray words leaking from his mind. He bitched about how Dock workers think they're better than everyone else.

She said her mantras again. She felt a click in her, a change and a disconnect. Those mantras and her meditation practice had been a lifesaver. She wasn't sure how she could have ever managed without them. The ability to focus and clear her mind was the only way for her to disconnect from someone.

Once, when she was only eight, she accidentally connected to a mother who was depressed and angry about her husband being sentenced to the Runnercore, leaving her to raise her child alone. Alexa wasn't sure why she had connected to this woman, but for days after she would get occasional snippets of the woman's thoughts, particularly when the woman was feeling strong emotions. As a curious child, this prompted a series of questions to her own mother, like what's suicide and several questions about sex, which the woman had engaged in to deal with her grief. Alexa had asked other questions an eight-year-old shouldn't have been asking. Alexa chuckled to herself. Now that she was much older, she couldn't even imagine what it must have been like for her parents to field some of those questions.

The people mover stopped, picked up a few more passengers, and the security officer got off to wait for the next vehicle. They resumed their journey.

She never told them where the questions came from. Somehow, she knew intuitively that telling her parents about her talent would scare them. She worried what they might do if they ever found out. A few times, Alexa peeked inside of her mother or father's brains and realized that they were sometimes suspicious of her, but most parents try to deny that anything is wrong with their child until it becomes obvious. It was with her parents that she learned the importance of privacy and staying out of other people's minds when possible. There were at least two occasions when she peeked into the minds of her mother or father that was the equivalent of walking in on them naked, mid-coitus.

Her mind turned back to the night's events. 17 again. She wondered what it would be like to skim the surface of his mind. Maybe she would next time? The way he was trying to flirt with her, she doubted she would see anything that surprised her. Was there something deeper to him? Or was he just an old criminal and a pervert? Maybe he was just that. But part of her suspected another layer, maybe several more. She thought she might be just rationalizing because she found him attractive. She had to admit at least that much to herself, but maybe there was something about him that had brought her to the Docks in the first place?

Alexa had chosen the Runner docks for a specific reason. It was a reason that her parents and, so far she knew, no one in the world knew about. In addition to peeking into people's minds occasionally, Alexa sometimes had special dreams. She had dreamt that she needed to be in the Runner dock, working as an inspector, and so she had simply done as the dream had suggested.

During the short tenure of her life, disaster had only come when she hadn't listened to the dreams. It was when they recurred that she knew she would have to listen.

She had thought many times of telling her parents, of telling her Buddhist teacher, or of anyone who would listen. But there was a fear that if she revealed her skills to anyone, to which she could easily demonstrate, she would end up as some test subject, or worse, forced to work at the will of one of the corrupt Senators. Instead, she kept what she saw to herself and did the best she could to navigate it. One day she would have to tell someone, but she thought the day was still far off. Maybe it would be 17? She felt a shiver run down her spine.

Like the oracle she had read about in Oedipus Rex, she could see the future. It wasn't always clear, and it filled with symbols and images that she didn't understand. Usually, things came through in dreams, but occasionally, she saw things during her meditations at the Buddhist community center. One thing was clear; she only saw things when her mind relaxed.

So far as she knew, there was no one else who had her depth of talent. True, most adults gained some enhanced intuition with prolonged use of the alcoves. It wasn't anything spectacular, or so she had been told in her psychology courses at scholar school. Most people had just occasional flashes of insight. There was something about the way the alcoves renewed your neurology with prolonged use that allowed for a kind of expansion of consciousness. Thus far, no one was sure how it worked. There had been studies on it over the centuries by a few in the scholar school, but no one had found any definite answers. Dr. Noatla Lightfoot had once suggested that children might have innate intuitive abilities that disappeared after puberty. She had said that perhaps there was something in the regenerative properties of the alcove that either preserved or renewed those earlier brain patterns.

Alexa's abilities were different from what Professor Lightfoot had discussed. Sure, she had occasional flashes of insight, but she also had dreams or flashes of entire scenes of future reality. Usually, they were mundane moments. Her walking to the people mover, working as an inspector or brushing her teeth. Sometimes though, they would show important events or begin to repeat over and over. Those are the times when she listened.

From what she heard, the best intuitives, the ones you could find in the side alleys down in the Lowers, could only grasp vague impressions of the future. It was rare that anyone would take those people seriously, but there was something appealing to a small portion of the population, people who just wanted to find comfort in something.

Alexa imagined what it would be like to reach out to grab 17's long dark braid and feel his coarse hair in her fingertips. Once again, her mind drifted southward down his naked form. She felt her heart beat harder as she imagined what it would be like to stand naked pressed against him, tracing her fingers up and down his scars and feeling those rough lips on hers. His body might be scared, but his face was handsome and clean-shaven. She wanted to touch his face. A surge of pleasure shuddered through her body.

She closed her eyes and let her thoughts of him flood through her. "Gods of earth and sky, you're so... enticing, 17," she said.

3.

A sudden sense of spacelessness swept over 17 as he walked through the Barrens. He looked down at his gloved hands and turned them over. A wave of dizziness swept over him, and he felt almost as if he was floating outside of his own body.

"What the hell? AI, do a vitals check, will you?"

"Sir, all vitals appear normal, though you have an elevated level of dopamine in your system."

"Yeah well, I feel strange." He shook his head vigorously. Then, he heard a voice; it didn't seem to come from anywhere, in particular, it was just there. It was in him and outside of him all at once, and the words echoed over and over in his mind.

"Gods of earth and sky, you're so... enticing, 17."

"What's that, AI? What the hell are you saying?"

"Sir, I said nothing. Perhaps your elevated dopamine levels are causing you to experience minor hallucinations? Should I inform central security?"

"No, just... just give me a minute, would you? I want to get some fresh air."

"Fresh air is ill-advised, Sir. The methane levels in this region are—"

"I'm just gonna take my helmet off for a second."

He pulled the helmet from the top of his head and let the putrid air fill his nostrils.

He had heard something, a voice maybe, but he couldn't be sure. He turned back around toward the storm. It was further in the distance now but still blocked his view of the city.

The ringing voice faded and 17 looked around and noticed the deadness of the air. He put his helmet back on and resumed his march forward toward the ruins.

4.

In shock and horror, Alexa reeled back and opened her eyes. Had he heard her? She closed her eyes again and tried to fix on his image, but it was gone. What had just happened? Had she somehow transmitted to him or was it another vision? It had been so clear, as if she was watching the entire scene on a vidscreen, but she could even smell the methane in the air. Panic almost swallowed her. She didn't understand what was happening to her. Lately, things were much more intense. Her dreams, her visions, they were becoming clearer, more powerful, and she lay awake in tears some nights with the awful things she saw or felt. Sometimes she felt the weight of the entire city pushing down on her.

She put her head in her hands and waited for the ride to be over.

5.

Later that evening, Alexa lay in her bed and closed her eyes, trying to force sleep. After a few moments of tossing and turning, she opened her eyes and glanced over toward her pill bottle. She hated taking sleep aids, but with a whole city full of thoughts and ideas and dreams, she was sometimes awakened by a torrent of psychic impressions. She hardly ever used the sleep aid, meditation often worked to soothe her, but lately, things had been... different. The sleep aid was there as a reminder that there was a method for turning it all off.

Alexa rolled onto her back, her nightgown clinging to her skin and outlining her slender body. The fabric was an imitation of silk. She loved the sensation of it moving against her skin. It grounded her, kept her from being overwhelmed. Alexa breathed, in through her nose and out through her mouth as the Buddhist monk had taught her years before. She felt a wave of calm settle over her. Her muscles relaxed, and she could feel herself drifting toward sleep.

The vision-dreams came then, and she knew that if she could bring just a few pieces of those dreams back to the waking world, she could save the city from destruction. But she wouldn't remember them in the morning.

Chapter 9
The Sanitation Department

"So I says to the guy, who the hell do you think you are, an Upper? And guess what? Turns out he was." Frank laughed. The deep, rasping boom of his laughter filled the room, not sparing single corner in its jubilant reach.

"And I was like whoa buddy, don't want to step on your golden toes or anything but down here in the Lowers we use the people movers. You know what the guy said?"

Jose shook his head. He listened, but Frank's stories were all the same. He gripped the lever, lifted and then tried to rotate the piston. It caught halfway through its movement. He tried to shake it loose, tried to find some play in the gears, but the more he wiggled, the more it jammed. It was stuck again.

Frank continued, "He says, 'No Upper in their right mind would take a people mover.'

"So I says, it ain't no hair off my back pal, you're the one who will have to walk twenty blocks to get to the next sky lift." Frank's forgot that in his right hand, he had a wrench, and almost hit Zelda as he waved his hands in the air.

"So what did he do?" asked Jenny. A station down from Jose, she turned the wheel to open the air pressure release valve and then turned back to look at Frank.

One of the many long pipes overhead hissed and leaked steam and Jose, watching it, frowned. Something was obstructing the line. Jose pulled out the small pad of paper and pen in his front breast pocket and scribbled a few words. He handed it to Jenny, who handed it to Zelda, who held it out for Frank to take, but Frank didn't see it. He wouldn't notice it until he finished his story.

"I'll tell you, the balls on some of them Uppers. He actually asked me if I would escort him to the sky lift. So I said, sure, I'd be happy to, on one condition."

Frank's smile broadened as he paused for effect, and Jose knew the punch line was coming. Another pipe above hissed, and Jose shuffled his feet. Whatever was blocking the line was big. They had to move fast.

"And he looks at me and says, what's that? You know what I told him?"

"Christ, Frank, just tell us already," said Zelda

Frank's smile widened.

"I told him, I'll take you all the way to your sky bridge, hell I will even carry you there, but you got to give me a week's access to your personal alcove. And the look on his face, I mean, I would be offended if it wasn't so damn funny. He looked like I told him I knocked up his sister or something." Frank chuckled, grabbing his large jiggling belly with one hand and pushing back the scraps of hair in his comb-over with the other. As he shook, he dropped Jose's note.

Zelda bent over and picked it up. She said, "And I bet he walked away with his tail between his legs, like all the other Uppers in your stories, huh?" She passed the note back to the Frank, who, despite Zelda's attempt to deflate him, still grinned.

Frank said, "You bet your ass, Zelda. When I get through with 'um, all them Uppers walk away with their tails between their legs."

Jose smiled and did his best to show the note to Frank, but he still wasn't paying attention. So, instead of writing another note and hoping Frank would respond, he walked over to Frank, his feet echoing against the metal grating. He pointed to the note.

"What?" Frank looked at his left hand for the first time and noticed the note. "Oh, sorry Jose." He put down the wrench and read the note.

"Gods damn, really? Again? That's the third time this week."

Jose nodded.

"Zelda, Jenny... Jose says we got a blockage again."

Jenny said, "Figures, what do you think the damn Uppers put in the line this time?"

Zelda said, "We should start a pool, see who guesses right."

"Ha, yeah," said Frank chuckling, "Then maybe one of us could get our asses out of the Lowers, huh?"

Jose pulled out his pad of paper from his breast pocket again and wrote. When he finished, he tore off the piece of paper and handed it to Frank.

"Jose bets it's hospital waste again," said Frank.

Jenny said, "I wouldn't bet against that. Those Uppers never recycle the bio-waste. Somehow they think they're too good to recycle their shit and blood like everyone else."

"More like they don't like the idea that all of their bio-waste is fed back to them through the food dispensers," said Zelda.

Frank said, "Yeah they're too stuck up, I guess. So stupid. Not like they are eating their own shit. By the time the deatomizer gets done with all that stuff, there ain't nothing left to be worried about. It's all just raw material. Just atoms."

Jose scribbled something else down, tore off another piece of paper and handed it to Frank.

Frank took it. "Why do you always hand your notes to me?"

"'Cause he knows you're the one with the big mouth," said Zelda. "And if he handed it to anyone else, he'd never be heard."

Frank looked around with an inquisitive look on his face. Then he stopped, smiled, and belted out laughter. "Ha! You're probably right."

"The note, Frank?" said Jenny, a tinge of impatience in her voice.

"Oh, right?" Frank paused, read it and stopped for a moment. "Hey Jose, I've always wondered, and I have to ask, why do you spend printer rations on making paper? Why not just use your data tablet?"

Jose shrugged and made no indication that he would respond, he indicated the note in Frank's hand, but Frank made no effort to read further.

"It's cause of the uprising, isn't it? Cause that Senator took your tongue?"

Jose shrugged again. He didn't want to have to explain himself to Frank. He liked the guy, but he didn't want to talk about the uprising. He didn't even talk about that with his own wife. But Jose wouldn't use a tablet ever again if he could avoid it, at least not for personal use. For work it was fine, but he never wanted to leave any kind of record again. You could burn paper, you could shred it, but data, well the way Manhatsten dealt with data, it was forever. It was no secret that the AI kept logs of everything, but as a foolish teenager, Jose and his friends had never considered it and his friends and family had paid for it, dearly.

Multiple copies of his shadow cast themselves on the grated floor. The fluorescent lights flickered overhead, and the stale smell of sealed air filled his nostrils. His short dark hair and brown skin always looked strange under the bluish glow of the lights. His face lined and creased, but not from age, not yet, though that wasn't far off. It was the face of the man who had lost much, who had barely hung on.

Working in the sanitation department underground was hard work, but it was steady work, more than he could get in most other places in the Lowers. For that at least, Jose was grateful. It was a family legacy.

Again, Jose gestured toward the note, and Frank eyed him for a moment, hoping for an answer. Finally, he looked down and finished reading the note.

"Jose says, two steam valves are popping already, and we better get moving. The AI confirms the blockage. Zelda and Jenny, you two get the hatch and the safety lever, Jose and I will get inside and check it out."

"Shit, no argument from me, last time I went in pipes I couldn't get the smell out of my hair for a week," said Zelda.

"That's the advantage of my beautiful pate," Frank said, pointing to his comb-over.

Jenny said, "We're probably going to have to recalibrate it. AI, will you alert sectors 2, 6, 8, and 4 that we are investigating a blockage and to halt the bio-waste recycler and the deatomizer?"

"Yes, Miss," said the AI.

The all waited for a few moments in silence, listening for the temporary break in the constant hum of the machinery.

"Hey, you guys remember when the Lincoln building went out?" Zelda said and grinned.

"Ha! Yeah, how could I forget that." Frank said.

Even Jose had grinned a little. But Jenny, the newer member of the crew, didn't get the joke, and Jose noticed that she had a blank stare on her face. Frank looked over at her and noticed too. Frank was smiling ear to ear. Jose knew it was because he had a story that someone hadn't heard before.

"You don't know this one, Jenny?" said Frank.

She shook her head.

"Aw, this is a good one." Frank didn't wait; he launched into his explanation. "Okay, so you know how when the power goes out down here in the Lowers, sometimes it's out for days before someone gets 'round to fixing it?"

Jenny nodded.

"Well, a few years back, me, Jose, and Zelda were down here doing our usual thing, and we got a call over the vidscreen to come check out this power outage. And I says to the guy, buddy, I don't know jack shit about electrical, and he said to me that he knew that and he thought it had something to do with a sewage line. So we head up to 60th and 42nd, and we're given a pass to up to the 53rd floor—"

"Wait, you actually got to go into the Uppers?" asked Jenny.

"Yeah, and let me tell you, it's not everything they say it is. Anyways, we get up there, and this Upper is flipping his shit. Turns out the power had been out for a few hours, and he was screaming something about his souffle or some shit not being ready in time for some big date. Which was funny enough, but we looked around and..." Frank laughed and couldn't get the words out?

"Zelda..." he said through fits of laughter. "I can't... I... you tell it..." He was practically falling over he was laughing so hard, and even Jose was chuckling low in his throat.

Zelda, who was also laughing a little and grinning broadly, did her best to continue. "So we looked around the room and checked out the pipes, and it turns out that this guy's dog had dug into the wall behind his couch. It had pulled out some wires, which is why he lost power." She could barely hold back now.

She took a breath, snorted out laughter and then continued. "But the dog... it... it also blocked some sewage pipes. And this guy didn't tell us that his sink and toilet were having a flow problem, so we worked on the pipes and I... removed the... blockage..." Zelda laughed hard, her thin, wiry frame vibrating. "Frank... you... you have to finish."

"Okay... okay..." He calmed himself for a moment, wiping a tear from his eye, and took a few deep breaths and stopped laughing. "So this guy was on the can when we were doing all this, and Zelda removes the blockage and turned the line back on. When she did..." Frank laughed again, grabbing a pipe above his head to steady himself. "The godsdamn toilet blew up. We heard someone screaming in the other room and went to check it out... The guy was covered head to toe in shit. The whole room had exploded and... You know what he said... You know what that bastard said to us?"

Jenny shook her head; she was laughing now too.

"He says, Shit. Shit. Shit. Shit. He screamed the word, and he kept repeating the word over and over again like it was some kind of prayer until he was shrieking it at us. And the three of us busted up laughing so hard that he had to call security to escort us out. And when security got there, even they couldn't stop laughing when we told them what happened."

They all laughed for another long moment and even Jose, who hadn't had much to laugh about in a long while, made audible clicks with the stub that was once his tongue.

"You know whatever happened to the guy?" asked Jenny.

"No idea," Frank shook his head. "But I'll tell you what, every time I feel a little down about this place, I think of that guy screaming the word shit over and over again at us and it gets me going every time."

There was an audible shudder and a gradual winding down of machine noise. The system had shut down the lines. The silence expanded when the machines stopped running, and Jose could hear the void reverberate in his eardrum.

"Gods, this place is eerie when it's quiet." said Jenny.

"You should have been here during the uprising," said Frank. "When we went on strike down here, the whole place was dead silent. Sometimes I could swear I heard something moving in the pipes and it sure as hell wasn't that Upper's shit."

They all smirked again, but there was something less lighthearted about that smirk.

Jenny and Zelda moved across the room to a far corner. The two women lowered themselves, and with some difficulty, crawled under the small space beneath the network of pipes. They disappeared from sight for a moment and then came up on the other side; their bodies masked in part by pipes and electrical lines of various thickness. They put their hands on a massive red wheel and turned it clockwise.

Both women were thin and wiry with strong arms. You needed strong arms for this job, and if you didn't have them when you got down here, you would soon. Out of the group, Frank was the only one who had any kind of mass to him. And that was surprising because most people who worked in sanitation had to be skinny to get into the various nooks and crannies re-quired to do the job, but Frank, who had a significant belly on him, somehow had made it work.

Zelda had dirty blonde hair and aging features. Jose had thought many times that though she had a tough exterior, there was something soft and easy in her face. She was the oldest of the group at 182, and approaching retirement. With her access as a Lower to the alcoves, she could probably hope to live to be 220 or 230, if she was lucky.

Jenny was new. She was dark-skinned, dark-eyed, and dark-haired. Upon first meeting her, Jose had thought that besides the ugly scars that crisscrossed her left cheek, she was far too beautiful to be working down in Sanitation. There was something hard about Jenny, and those scars had hinted at something awful in her past. Frank had asked after the scars on a number of occasions, but Jenny always deflected the conversation. Jose could understand that. He did the same thing whenever Frank tried to bring up the uprising. He has lost too much, and all the emotion behind those memories was like a huge body of water threatening to burst through a dam. Sometimes with deep wounds, it was only a matter of pressure and time. Lately, it seemed the cracks were widening.

Jose turned and watched as the hatch behind him, a giant gear-like wheel, slid open, spinning counter-clockwise. He braced himself for the rush of sewage that often accompanied opening the hatch, but nothing happened.

Frank said, "Man, the blockage must be bad, last time we opened this thing we were knee deep in sewage for the rest of the day, remember? Took some of those hazmat bots to get this place tidy."

Jose nodded. It only meant that when they removed the blockage, they would get showered with sewage. He made a mental note to message his wife; he'd probably need to go into decontamination for an hour or two. It was almost quitting time. Jose grabbed a face mask placed it over his head. Two silver air filters protruded out of either side of the black mask, and Jose slid it over his face before he handed one to Frank.

Frank said, "Good idea, when this thing opens up, we don't want to get any of that stuff in our mouths."

Most of the time, working in sanitation wasn't so bad. The machines and various little robots took care of most of the work, but some things they weren't so good at. Blockages were one of them. Jose didn't mind the work. It was steady, reliable, and permanent. Most Lowers spent their time moving from job to job, trying to scrape together a living. The food dispensers made sure no one starved to death, but that was about it. Most people struggled to make it to the next paycheck.

In the Lowers, access to alcoves and other goods were limited. Everything had to be recycled and reused. No one could afford to throw away anything, which is why when Frank or Jose or any of the others down here found something like bed sheets clogging the system, they all felt a tinge of anger.

What was worse was that in the Lowers, you were docked credits for wasting anything precious. Somehow the Manhatsten AI always seemed to catch on even if you threw it in the neighbor's waste chute. Jose had always suspected there was some surveillance system that was monitoring the Lowers, but if there was, no cameras were visible. He wondered, and not for the first time, if the Mids and Uppers lost credits for wasting goods. Most of Manhatsten lived in the Lowers, so it was probably only the majority of the population that had to be surveilled for waste.

Frank climbed up on a short stool, loosened a few bolts that led to the main sewage duct and handed them to Jose, who moved a few meters away and put them on a tray. He walked back over to Frank and waited.

"You ready?"

Jose nodded.

Frank pulled off the exterior of the sewage duct it popped with a metallic clang. Then he reached up inside, and as he turned the gear that would open the main pipe, Jose prepared himself for a flood of sewage.

Again, nothing happened.

"Hey, what gives?" asked Frank. "I was sure we'd be knee-deep in Uppers' shit by now." The sound of his voice was tinny through the mask.

Jose shrugged and shook his head.

"Jose, I'll boost you up, you can take a look at the mainline. Frank put his gloved hands down toward the floor, crisscrossing his fingers. Jose stepped one foot on his hands and Frank heaved him up until he stood on Frank's massive shoulders.

"You see anything?"

Jose rolled his eyes. Frank should know better than to ask him a question he couldn't answer. He looked around for a moment and then he spotted it. A thick white object covered in various stains was clogging the line. Jose reached for it and could just barely scrape it with his fingers.

Jose pulled his head out and snapped at Frank. Then, with his thumb, he tried to tell Frank that he wanted him to push him all the way inside.

"What? You want all the way in?"

Jose nodded.

"Are you nuts? What if you get stuck in there? How the hell are you gonna tell us if you need help?"

Jose shrugged.

Frank sighed. "Alright, but don't say I didn't warn you, huh? I'm getting tired of having your scrawny ass on my shoulders, anyway."

With some effort, Frank heaved Jose a few inches higher. Jose caught the lip of the main pipeline and pulled himself a little further in. The space was tight and cramped, but Jose didn't think it was tight enough that he would get stuck. His feet and lower legs still dangled downwards, but now he could reach the blockage. He pulled at what he now thought was a bed sheet. It didn't budge. Jose frowned under his mask. There would only be one way to unclog it, and it was going to be messy. He would definitely need decontamination after.

Frank was gonna hate him for this, but he had no way of warning him to get out of the way. With the space as small as it was, there was only in or out of the pipe. He had to hope that Frank had enough sense to move out of the way.

Jose grabbed the sheet with his right hand hard and then, wiggling his way backward, he got himself just to the edge of the entrance. He could feel gravity tugging at the lower half of his body. He freed a little more of the bed sheet and wrapped it around his right forearm and then prepared himself. Despite the mask, he was going to get a face full of sewage. No, he would be lucky if that was all. He closed his eyes, took a deep breath, and with a little effort, let gravity take him.

He fell one of the two meters to the floor and then for a second, he dangled by the dirty, sewage-tinged bedsheet.

Frank said, "What the hell are you—" But he never finished.

Jose felt the bedsheet release, and as his feet connected with the floor with an audible click, the bedsheet came wafting downwards. For a moment, just a single moment, Jose thought maybe they were home-free. Then, before the bedsheet could even hit the floor, a wave of half-treated sewage came flooding out of the pipe. It poured so hard it knocked Jose off his feet.

Frank ran and grabbed Jose by the hand and tried to drag him out of the way of the fountain of sewage but slipped and fell on his back in the ever-growing puddle of waste. There was no refuge from the smell.

Frank rolled over and got to his hands and pushed himself up. He shouted at Zelda and Jenny, but Jose couldn't quite make out the words. He was trying like hell to get up, but the sewage just kept knocking him down.

He could hear laughter. Probably both women were laughing their asses off at the sight of Jose and Frank, fighting just to stand up. But at the moment, it didn't feel very funny.

Then, the sewage stopped. Jose, exhausted from trying to stand up, just lay there for a moment catching his breath. Frank's shadow covered him, and he extended his hand.

Jose took it and stood up. Green goop and liquid rolled off him.

"You crazy son of a bitch," said Frank. His face was stern, angry, and, like Jose, covered in sewage, except for under the respirator which had somehow stayed on. "What the hell was that, huh? Couldn't have figured out some way to warn me? Now look at us? We'll have to spend two hours in decontamination. Sally's gonna be pissed when I show up late again."

From behind them, Zelda and Jenny laughed all over again.

Through fits of laughter, Zelda said, "Frank.... That... was the funniest shit.... I've ever seen."

"Yeah," said Jenny. She was laughing so hard that Jose wondered how in the hell she was breathing. "Frank, you and Jose... you both... oh, gods... you both looked like you were... doing some kinda... some kinda choreographed dance... IN HUMAN SHIT." Then both women were laughing so hard they doubled over.

Frank's face, still serious, looked at Jose, then back at the girls, then down at himself to survey just how much sewage he was covered in. Then, Frank pirouetted and waved his arms in the air, and Jose could see the grin spreading up the side of his face under the mask.

"Like this, ladies?" said Frank. Frank's big belly jiggled as he danced around for a moment and the women let out such hard gales of laughter they lost their balance. Then, Frank danced a little closer to them, grabbed both and threw them into the sewage.

Quickly, both women rolled over and sat up. Both looked angry. They stared at each other for a moment, then at Frank.

"What the hell, Frank?" asked Zelda.

Jenny said, "Yeah Frank, seriously, why did you do that?"

Frank gave a deep bow, one that Jose would not have thought possible given the size of his stomach. "All part of the performance, ladies. It's one of those interactive ones, like the Uppers like."

The women looked at each other again for a moment and then both roared with laughter all over again. Even Jose chuckled to himself now.

Frank reached up and put the grate back on, and one last time, he slipped and fell in the sewage.

2.

Zelda groaned and put her head in her hands. "I hate Decon. How much time is left, AI?"

"There are 30 minutes remaining in the decontamination cycle."

They all sat naked inside of several alcoves in the floor filled with a mix of clear chemicals. Some of those chemicals were like the alcove mixtures, without all the anti-aging benefits. It hadn't taken security long to realize that people would cover themselves in sewage to get access to the anti-aging properties of the alcoves, and so they had been re-engineered.

Steam punctuated the air, but it wasn't just steam. Jose knew that there were several chemical agents in the air to prevent any kind of bacterial infection.

Jose tried not to stare at Jenny, but she had a nice body. He kept finding himself averting his eyes and Jenny, on several occasions, took notice and smiled. Even after all these years of Coed Decontamination, he felt uncomfortable.

Jenny said, "So Frank, can you explain the biorecycler system to me one more time? I am still having a hard time understanding why in the hell we don't just eject everyone's shit out of the bottom of the city."

"It's like this, Jen. The food system isn't totally sustainable, but it's damn close. The machine that I manage is called the deatomizer, which is the first part of the biorecycler. It breaks down any kind of organic matter and turns it into raw material. Then the raw material goes through the assembler, that's what Zelda monitors, and turns that raw organic material into some kind of algae sludge. Don't ask me how it does that; I just work here."

There was a brief chuckle from everyone.

"Anyway, people shit and piss a lot. All that's good raw material for the biorecycler."

Jenny asked, "Wow, so basically we are all eating our own waste?"

Zelda said, "Nah, by the time it goes through the system it's all just algae. There are several huge storage tanks down in the bottom of the bedrock of the city where it's grown."

"Well, but what if the algae runs out?" asked Jenny.

Frank said, "It would if we just used human waste. Obviously, when food goes through our bodies, some of it gets absorbed, so it's not a perfect system. That's where all the rooftop gardens and Central Park come in."

Zelda said, "We get the scraps after the Uppers take all the good stuff."

Jenny said, "What do you mean, scraps?"

Frank said, "Well you know how expensive fresh food is, right?"

Jenny nodded, and Frank continued. "Well I ain't never had a fresh apple in my life, not one that the food dispensers didn't print out for me, anyway. But after the apple trees are pruned, or all the weeds are removed or the corn is shucked, all that left over plant matter is shoved down into tubes located in each of the 17 districts around the city, remember there are 17 facilities like ours around the place. All that plant waste leads down to one of the sanitation departments where it's all broken down and sent into the algae growth pits."

"And?" asked Jenny.

"And," said Frank, "there's always plenty of plant waste. Every time they mow the lawn in Central Park? Raw material. Every time someone pulls weeds out of their garden? Raw material. Every time someone doesn't finish their meal? Raw material. Get the picture now, Jen?"

"Yeah, I think I do. But there's one more thing."

Jose knew what this question was before Jenny even asked it, and by the sour expression on Frank's face, he also knew. It was the question of every recruit once they grasped the biorecycler's system.

"I heard a rumor—"

Zelda cut her off. "It's not true."

"No? What about the missing people? What about the missing bodies?"

Frank grimaced, "We don't know. We hear the rumors too, but I can tell you in the last 60 years I've been down here, I ain't seen nothing that would even hint that human beings are going into the biorecycler."

Zelda, whose words were icy, said, "I've been down here a hundred and eighteen years now. And I've never seen nothing. But there ain't no doubt in my mind that some people disappear. Seen it myself. One of my nieces just vanished one night, no one's ever found her."

"The Runnercore?" asked Jenny.

Zelda shook her head. "Nope. The girl was only nine. They don't ship anyone off to the Runnercore 'til they're at least 16. They got to be strong enough to man those metal suits. But something's going on. Some of us... some of us think they're doing experiments... that maybe that old architect has gone crazy or something. But my niece, she disappeared twenty years ago, and nothing, no sign of her anywhere."

"What about... Recycled Runners?" Jose could hear the hesitation in Jenny's voice. No one liked to talk about Recycled Runners. No one liked to cross paths with one. There was something about their cold dead eyes that terrified everyone, and on the few TV programs that ran on the vidscreens, they were still the subject of many modern horror movies.

Zelda shrugged, "Still got to be big enough to man the suits, but... if they were experimenting on them for a while first..."

Jose felt sick and wanted them all to change the subject. But as usual, he had no way of communicating while in Decon. He couldn't bring in his pad of paper because it would fall apart by the time they got out.

Besides, the one he had brought with him had been ruined, and his spare waited in the locker room. It seemed though that everyone felt the same way, because no one said anything for the remainder of Decon. Instead, they all watched the countdown clock in bright, florescent letters glaring against the steam and the moisture in the air. It said that only ten minutes remained.

Jose snuck another peek at Jenny, but when he did, he realized that she had been sneaking a peek at him. She blushed and turned her head quickly and repositioned her body almost as if to say, feel free to take a good, long, hard look.

Jose didn't understand what she saw in him that was so attractive. He was only 165 centimeters tall, with short scraggly hair, dark skin, and a patchy beard. There was nothing special about his looks.

Jose couldn't help staring a little. Jenny looked remarkably like Liza, a girl from his youth who he had loved dearly. A girl that, because of his cowardice, he had lost to the Runnercore. She was someone he thought of every day and dreamt of most nights. Now there was a living reminder of his guilt, of his role in the uprising, and she was sitting naked less than two meters away.

3.

After decontamination, Jose, Frank, Jenny, and Zelda left the chamber and walked up the metallic winding staircase that led to street level.

"I got one," said Zelda. Her voice echoed and boomed as they walked up the stairs. "Why do you think that some of them Uppers go bald?"

Frank groaned. "You've told us that one a hundred times, Zelda."

"Yeah, 'cause it's still funny. Besides, I don't think I've told Jenny this one yet."

Frank waved his hand and gestured her to finish.

"They go bald cause they get too close to the shield and burn their heads." Zelda was the only one who laughed. Frank rolled his eyes. Jenny looked confused, but Jose smiled and nodded.

"I don't get it?" Jenny said.

"Shield's made of some kind of solar fusion energy or something. Don't ask me how it works, but people used to say you could get a sunburn if you got too near it. Mostly people stay away from it now. You touch that thing; ya get zapped. Only the maintenance workers would really know. It's an old joke," said Frank. He scratched his head. "Probably as old as the shield itself."

"Come on, Frank," said Zelda. "You got to admire the classics."

They reached the top of the stairway and the sound of their feet on the concrete punctuated the gradual tunnel that led up into the evening air. Rambling echos died in the open. The evening light of the EnViro Shield still glowed with the excess radiation of the day. The glow would fade shortly, but it extended twilight several hours.

Jenny said, "I always love this time of night after the sun's gone. It's so beautiful, don't you think, Jose?" She was smiling at him. It was a warm, inviting smile that seemed to say, come a little closer, I don't bite; unless you want me to.

Jose nodded, his nerves jumping and kicking around in his stomach. He swallowed hard and tried not to think of her naked body in Decon, a losing battle.

Frank said, "Well, ladies and gents. Time for us to part ways, huh? Hey Jose, what are you and Linda doing this weekend?"

Jose shrugged.

"Well, you should come over, Sally and I are having a few people over for dinner on Saturday, and we thought that you and Linda would like to join us."

Jose nodded and started to write something down, but Frank stopped him. "Just ask Linda and have her call us up."

Jose nodded again.

"You ladies are welcome as well," said Frank.

Jose almost frowned, but he noticed that Jenny was looking at him and so he restrained any expression. Was she flirting with him? If so, why? She knew he had a wife. She knew he had a son her age. Still, despite how uncomfortable it made him, there was something flattering about having someone young and beautiful giving you a little attention.

"No go for me, Frank," said Zelda. "I'm pulling a few extra hours this weekend to cover for Michael."

"Michael?" said Frank. "What's that lazy bastard doing taking more time off?"

"Who knows, but I could use the extra credits, anyway. Mary wants us to retire in the Lower Mids, and we've almost scraped together enough cash to bribe a sponsor up on level 12. I figure if I work my ass off for the next five years or so, we might just be able to pull it off. And since Mary wants us to adopt, we can get that voucher to waive the sponsorship fee, though the bribe's still gonna cost us."

"Well, don't forget us little guys down here when you make it up to the Mids," said Frank. He was full of big tooth grins; his massive jovial stomach jutted forward. "What about you Jenny? You coming this weekend."

"Sure, I think so."

Her voice was even like Liza's. It was like honey. Jose had remembered how when he had heard Liza sing once; his whole body had tingled. He wondered if Jenny could sing like that.

Frank said, "Alright kiddos, see you all Monday."

Jose nodded, turned, and walked up the street toward his house. After a few moments, he turned back to see if Jenny was still standing there. She was, and when she saw him looking she smiled and waved. He felt his face flush just a little as he gestured a quick wave back. He turned and kept walking.

Why had he waved back? What was wrong with him? He was assuming this girl had some kind of crush on him, but she was friendly like that to everyone. He loved Linda, loved his son Marcus and wouldn't trade them for anything, would he? The honest answer to that was uncomfortable. He swallowed hard and tried to push it back down, but the image of Liza laughing at one of his stupid jokes pressed against him. Even after decades, there was no escaping Liza, no escaping Aaron, no escaping the uprising. He had lost so much. His courage had withered like a grape in the sun, and now, he was just a dried-up old raisin. He moved the tiny stub of where his tongue had once been and brushed it against his molars. When most of his tongue had been removed, so had most of his heart. It was Linda who had been there for him after. Linda was a girl who had always orbited Jose but never made direct contact.

But after losing his parents, Liza, Aaron, and his ability to speak, Linda had swooped down and saved him from himself. She fed him, nursed him back to health, and he loved her for it. But there was always guilt there because as much as he cared for Linda, she wasn't Liza.

Jose turned the corner, and the sound of his footsteps echoed against the concrete of the buildings. He was alone, and he had become painfully aware of that fact. He thought of muggers, thought of dealers, but mostly he thought of security and what they had done to his friends and family.

Jose glanced up at the glow of the EnViro shield. The purple and orange of the shield cascaded down into every window on the Upper levels of the city. The shadows of the tall buildings cast themselves on him, plunging him into intermittent darkness as he passed through each shadow in turn. A few stars were peeking through the shield now, but only just a few. He put his hands in his pockets and lowered his head as he walked several more blocks.

"Hey, you, stop!" cried a voice behind him.

Fear spiked. Jose felt his heart beating hard. It was déjà vu. Whoever was behind him had said the same words that had been uttered on that horrible night. Slowly, Jose turned and saw three security officers approaching him. Fear screamed in his ears so loud that he couldn't hear the voice of reason. Instead, Jose ran. He ran as hard and fast as he could.

It wasn't fast enough.

In a few moments, one of the security guards grabbed him and tackled him. The security officer put his knee hard into Jose's back. A sharp pain filled Jose every breath.

"Hey buddy, what are you running from, got something to hide?"

Jose couldn't respond, his arms were pinned down, and now the other two security guards were standing around him.

The man pressed his knee harder into Jose's back. "I asked you a question. Why did you run away?"

Jose wanted to say something, but there was no way to communicate. He needed his notepad in his front breast pocket. The concrete scraped his cheeks and the SO pressed harder.

The SO leaned forward and spoke slow, clear words in Jose's ear. "I said, why the fuck did you run?"

The pain in his back overwhelmed him and Jose, for the first time in a long time, tried to speak. Nothing came out that any of the SOs would understand.

"You mocking me?" There was a relief of pressure on his neck and he lifted his cheek to try and communicate. Something hard hit the back of Jose's head, and he felt his nose slam against the concrete. Blood trickle down the front of his face. Jose shook his head back and forth, trying to tell the SO that he wasn't mocking him.

"Alright Gary, cuff him and turn him over, we'll have the AI do a facial recognition scan on him," one of the other security officers said.

But Gary only pressed his knee harder into Jose and smacked the back of his head a few more times, slamming Jose's face into the concrete. "Little shithead. It's always the dark-skinned ones down here that are causing trouble. You fellas ever notice that?"

There was silence for a moment. "Uh... Gary... I think you better cuff him and take a breather, huh? Luke and I can handle this."

But Gary didn't move. "It was a piece of shit like this down here that mugged my son a few weeks back. Beat the shit out of my son. He was in the alcove for three days recovering."

Jose felt a yanking sensation at the back of his head and Gary, the guard on top of him, pulled his hair so hard that Jose thought his neck would snap. Jose felt something stir inside of him. It wasn't fair. It wasn't right. Rage woke. It swelled through the whole of Jose's body. He thought of Liza and Aaron, of the failed uprising, of the loss of his tongue. It all merged into one emotion.

"I should make a fucking example out of someone like you," said Gary.

"Hey, Gary. I think that's enough, cuff him, will ya?" The other SO's voice was a little more stern.

Gary let go of Jose's head and shoved him one more time. On impact, Jose's rage exploded outward. He thrust his whole body upward, knocking the SO off his body. He stood and knocked Gary to the ground. Both SOs took a few steps back, stunned at what was happening. He kicked Gary in the side as hard as he could. Then, coming to their senses, the other two security officers moved in to restrain him, but both were caught so completely off guard that Jose landed a few punches on both of them before they could do anything.

Jose made a loud piercing guttural noise and struck with fist and foot at anything that came near him. He didn't care what happened now; his rage could only be quenched with blood. He felt a deep, searing need to destroy the man who had pinned him and he turned again, kicking and screaming at the man on the ground.

Then he felt a blow to the side of the face and a sharp metallic pain in the side of his arm. The taser's electricity worked its way up to his brain, and Jose could feel the sensation wrack his entire body just before everything went black.

Chapter 10
The First of Many

The first thing that Major John Daniels noticed was the smell. He wrinkled his nose. He had seen a lot of bodies over the years, vacant husks with eyes staring wide and open at the endless chasms of emptiness that lay ahead for them. He had been in his share of battles, both before migration and after, had seen thousands fall from both conventional weapons and the H.A.D... But there was no getting used to that smell.

Several of his men were taking pictures and bagging evidence from the crime scene. He couldn't help but notice that they were just like flies buzzing around the corpse. Daniels grimaced. He didn't need some fortune teller from the lowers to know this would be the first of many deaths in the days ahead. Whoever did this was one sick fuck.

The room was a mess. Several panels were open and wires were sticking out of the walls. Parts and circuit boards were scattered around but Daniels didn't think either of those things had anything to do with the murder. These engineers loved to pull everything apart and put it back together. There didn't appear to be too much of a struggle, which suggested that the victim either didn't see what was coming, or it was someone they knew.

The expression on Patton's lifeless face made him shudder. His features were frozen and rigid. If his heart was still beating, he would be screaming. It was like an old painting or photograph that capture a single slice of time. A work of art, from a certain point of view.

He put on protective gloves. Blood crusted just under the bangs of Patton's hair. Daniels brushed it aside. On the top of his forehead, three marks stood out. The blood had smeared and run, and for a moment he thought he saw a pattern. Leaning forward, he saw the letters 'C. O. G.'

"How long, Johnson?"

"We think about 36 hours or so, Sir."

"Damn. How did it go unnoticed for so long?"

"Until a few hours ago, the AI was completely disabled in this room."

Daniels scratched the stubble on his face. "Manhatsten."

The cities AI responded, "Sir?"

"I need you to pull everything you can on the last 72 hours of Patton's life. If there is any surveillance footage of his death, I want to see it as soon as possible,"

"Sir, I have already compiled every piece of available data on Patton, James. Additionally, I have already constructed a personality profile of Patton, James and a list of suspects and motives."

"Good, have everything ready for me at my security station. Oh, and one more thing."

"Yes, Sir?"

"What in the Hell is 'C.O.G.' and why is it carved in this man's forehead."

"My apologies, Sir, I am not familiar with this abbreviation."

Daniels frowned. Something occurred to him. The AI had compiled all the evidence he needed without a query. He tried to think of a time when it had done something like that before, but try as he might, he couldn't. In the twelve hundred years he had worked with the AI, it had never taken the initiative like that before.

There was something else too. Lately, the AI had been more... chatty. It reminded him of 17. He wondered what in the hell had prompted the change. Was that architect messing with the AI? Daniels had always been distrustful of machines, especially advanced artificial intelligence, but it was 1291 AC, and in all that time, the AI had done nothing to suggest it had any malevolent intentions. Still, he didn't like it. He would need to ask some of the engineers a few questions about the personality change in the AI later. Patton's murder investigation came first.

"Johnson, what was he working on?"

"I'm not sure, shouldn't we ask the AI?"

The AI said, "Sir, Patton, James was working on data communication lines. He had filed a report that he felt he could increase the bandwidth of this line so that it would be more efficient in carrying data."

And that was the first time that Daniels had ever heard the AI respond without being directly queried. He felt a cold shiver down his spine. He liked none of this. Were Patton's death and the AI's new behavior related?

"AI, why did you respond just now?"

"I responded based on Johnson, Mark's query."

"But he didn't make a query to you. He asked my opinion if we should query you."

"My apologies, Sir, but I misunderstood the nature of the use of my designation."

Daniels was silent for a moment. He didn't move. A whole minute passed.

"AI, I want you to run a full diagnostic on yourself and let me know if anything is... different."

"Could you define the parameters, 'different'?"

"Let me know if anything has changed in your system in the last 72 hours."

"Yes, Sir." The AI fell silent.

C.O.G., He knew that abbreviation from somewhere, but he couldn't remember where. It was on the tip of his brain.

There was a lot of theft, assault, and rape, mostly in the Lowers, but murder was not all that common in Manhatsten. Autopsies were even rarer. It would be tough finding out the exact cause of death. If Patton had used an alcove in the last week, the lingering effects of the alcove would mask any toxins or strange physiological conditions that might be present. The alcoves also did something to decomposition. Sometimes it took much longer for bodies to break down. Judging by the smell though, this wasn't the case here. Patton was a Mid, so it was likely he had used an alcove recently.

"How old was he, Johnson?" Daniels asked.

"Only 71, Major."

"Damn shame, I liked this kid. What do you think killed him?"

Johnson's jaw opened and shut several times. He pursed his lips. Then, he cleared his throat and motioned a few feet to the left of Patton's lifeless body. Daniels had not noticed the small lump of red meat sitting on the floor next to the body. It was covered in flies. Now that he saw it, he didn't know why he didn't notice it; it was so obvious. It stood in stark contrast to the gray and silver of the spare parts and wires.

"Holy fuck, is that..." Daniels couldn't finish. Was the lump of meat still quivering? Still beating? He blinked his eyes a few times and looked again. No, it was still, just as lifeless as the corpse it had come from.

Johnson nodded. "We also found this lying on top of it, Sir." Johnson produced a piece of paper. The words on the paper danced around wet blood stains and bits of tissue. It was strategic, intentional. The blood blotched to make some kind of sick art with letters dancing around it. Daniels read the poem. Then he read it again. His mind couldn't grab hold of it. His eyes kept drifting back to the bloody lump on the ground that had been the man's heart.

"Read this for me, Johnson." He handed him the paper.

"Yes, Sir."

Greed and lust and fear and hate

Left our world in a dismal state

We will save our mother from the parasites

We will sacrifice to put the world right

We will bring about this city's end

So that no longer we have to pretend

That man himself is good for the earth and soil

It won't be long now; we are coming, her wrath will uncoil.

- C. O. G.

It was a long moment before either man spoke. The world around them was being wrapped in plastic, photographed, and bagged for later examination. But these two men stood like mountain islands in a sea of silence. Only the smells seemed in motion.

"Johnson, I want the entire city on heightened security alert. Double the patrols and place checkpoints at all the entrances between the Lowers, Mids, and Uppers. I want facial recognition scanners at every checkpoint, and I want those Runners I put on standby activated and patrolling the exterior of the city."

"Sir, isn't this stuff you should tell the AI?"

"Something about the AI isn't right; it's acting strange. It's probably nothing, but until I'm sure it's nothing, I prefer to have you carry out my orders. No vidscreens. I want you to hand deliver orders."

"Don't you think that's being a little... I mean that will take a while, Major."

Daniels unlocked his gaze from the bleeding lump of flesh and looked into Johnson's grayish brown eyes. He held his gaze, and Johnson winced a little.

"We will bring about the city's end. That's the line that bothers me the most. I've dealt with a few nutjob cults in the city over the years, Johnson. Hell, you've helped me root some of the out. But none of them ever threatened to destroy the city."

Johnson looked pensive. He too was struggling to unlock his eyes from the gore. One of the women moved over and bagged the heart. It left red streaks on her gloves and red streaks down the sides of the plastic until it settled into an unmoving mass.

"I trust your judgment, Johnson, which is why I want you to recruit a few others to help. There aren't a lot of men around here I can trust, especially now. But I need you to trust me and do your duty. Either the killer is a twisted sick fuck who is playing some kind of game, or there is a threat to the city. I'd rather plan for the latter and end up with the former. But we have to be careful."

Johnson nodded. "Yes, Sir." He turned and left.

Daniels trusted Johnson more than most of the security detail. The had worked together for four-hundred years. He had been in battle a few times and had even donned an EnViro Suit twice with Daniels to stop a raid from Lundon. Johnson was a good man, a reliable man, one who never complained about any of the orders. He needed more like him. He wouldn't find any. People in this city were so damned entitled.

Daniels looked around at several others of his security personnel. There wasn't much else to be done here.

"Ruiz, take this body down to Josepher, tell him I want a full autopsy. Tell him to get every scrap of information he can out of it."

"But Sir, I am off shift in twenty minutes, and Josepher's on the other side of the city in the Mids."

Daniels sighed. Johnson had been off for over forty-five minutes. Had he complained? There was that entitlement. In his ancient military days, he wouldn't have had to deal with such horseshit.

"Are you shitting me, Ruiz? Off shift? Since when are any of us in security detail off shift?"

"But Sir..."

"Don't 'but Sir' me. You can either follow orders, or I will have your ass out in an EnViro suit training new Runners so fast you'll swear you have whiplash."

Ruiz obeyed and made no secret of his distaste for dealing with a dead body. Daniels supposed it might be because few of the younger generations had never seen a dead body.

"Wallace, I want you to take that note up to the Chemist. Find out if there are any fingerprints on it, verify that the blood is Patton's, and then have them find out what that paper is made of and where it came from, if possible."

Wallace didn't argue, he was just about off duty too, but he had just seen Daniels put Ruiz in his place.

"Yes, Sir."

Daniels headed back for the lift. He had seen enough. The rest of his staff could clear up and analyze the mess. He stepped in the lift again and noticed something strange. The poster, the propaganda poster, was gone. Who could have taken it down? It had been up only minutes before.

The door closed and he began his trip up to his command.

He was glad to see the poster go. He hated those things. In fact, he couldn't think of a single person who wasn't at least a little bothered by them. Maybe he would ask one of the Senators if they could keep the posters out of central command. Who was in charge of that shit, anyway?

He let his mind drift for a minute it and centered on that heart. He couldn't help but imagine it beating as he stared at it. He shook his head to clear the image, but it did not good. It was one that we wouldn't soon forget.

Something Travers had said returned to him. The missing people, did they have something to do with this? Low resources, a murder, missing persons. Something was happening, but how did he and his team get ahead of it? And what were they trying to get ahead of?

The lift opened, and he stepped out. Security was busy. There was a lot of data to sift through. He moved back up into his post and reintegrated himself with the system. He wasn't sure how long he sat in his chair, but the time passed and one day faded into the next.

Then, Fallman stood from his station and approached his chair.

"Major Daniels, Sir."

"Yes Fallman, what is it?"

"Sir, I updated the command system and the heads up display for everyone with the new firmware. Would you mind if I finished the upgrades on your chair? It should only take a few moments."

"Right now?"

"Well Sir, since I upgraded the rest of the system, if your station isn't up-graded right away we could need a system-wide recalibration."

"How long are we talking?"

"Oh, it should only take about twenty minutes to sync with the rest of the system."

"Fine, I'll grab something to eat."

Daniels directed his thoughts left then right and released the shoulder clamps. Unplugged again, he stepped off the platform and headed back toward the elevator.

The elevator door opened and as Daniels's right foot crossed the threshold of the elevator entrance, noise erupted from behind him. He felt heat lick his back and felt the force of the thing push him forward into the elevator, the doors shutting behind him.

In the event of an explosion, earthquake, or various other events that might damage the city and its people, the elevators and sky bridges went on lockdown. Usually, this was a good thing; it kept people protected from all kinds of terrible accidents. Now, face down on the steel grating, the lift door closed and locked itself shut behind him. The red emergency lights came on. It only took Daniels a single moment to realize he was locked in.

"Son of a bitch, what in the hell was that?" he shouted.

"AI what in the hell was that?"

There was no response.

"AI? Respond please."

Again, no response.

"Goddammit, AI. I told you to run a diagnostic yesterday, not to shut yourself down."

Still no response.

A moment of panic washed over Major Daniels. What if the AI was permanently damaged? Was there was some kind of sabotage going on? Had all of central security been destroyed by a saboteur?

He took a breath and centered himself for a moment. Daniels picked himself up off the ground. Blood was trickling into his mouth. It was a nose-bleed. He must have hit his nose on the floor when the blast knocked him forward. He checked his person for any other injuries, and he appeared to be all right.

He checked his paranoia, putting it aside for a moment. It didn't have to be an attack. A console could have exploded. The damn things were ancient, maybe that firmware update Fallman was working on went wrong? But that didn't seem right. The force of the explosion had been enough to knock him down; he doubted a console could do that. Gods, what if it was the whole system?

His suspicions reasserted themselves. It seemed hard to believe that Patton's death, the AI, and now this explosion were all separate events. Something was going on here.

The good thing about the lift going on lockdown was that it didn't move. It stayed where the lockdown occurred, and the brakes froze in place so the elevator could go neither up nor down. This meant that Daniels was still just outside of central security and that he could manually open the doors. It wouldn't be easy, but it could be done.

"Hey," screamed Daniels. "Hey, what in the hell is going on out there?"

There was no response. The elevator wasn't soundproof, but if something serious was happening outside, he might not be heard. The worst-case scenario occurred to him. What if they were all dead? He pushed the thought away. No, if the blast had been that bad, he didn't think he would have survived it either. He was certain that at least someone was alive in there.

"This is Daniels, respond if you hear me." He beat on the metal door with his fists, a futile gesture, but it was worth a shot.

There was nothing for a few more moments, and just as he stopped his pounding and shouting, someone spoke up.

"Yes Sir, I hear you."

Relief.

"Who's that and what's happening?"

"Sir, it's Lieutenant Long and Sir, most of us are okay, but Fallman..."

"Help me get this elevator door open. Pry it open from your side, and I'll pry it open from mine."

"Yes, Sir."

Daniels wedged his fingers into the tiny opening where the elevator doors met. There wasn't much grip, and he wasn't sure that he could open it, but he pulled anyway. It didn't budge, not even in the slightest.

"Sir, I can't get my fingers in there."

"Then get something to wedge in the door and pry it open."

Daniels looked around for something to pry the door on his side, but no luck. Later he would have to requisition emergency crowbars inside the elevators for every building in the city. The Senate would moan about resources, as they always did, but he thought if he just locked their asses in an elevator for a few minutes, they might see it his way.

He slumped back against the wall. There was nothing he could do but wait.

"Greetings, Sir, I am sorry that I was offline for so long. Let me help you with that door."

It was the AI. It had reactivated. The emergency lights switched off, and Daniels heard the hum of power return, and a large lock clicked. The elevator door opened. Daniels jumped up and charged into central security. His heart sank.

His chair was gone, his station was still smoking from the explosion. Fallman lay on the ground surrounded by a medic and several others. Daniels squatted down at Fallman's side. His left arm was mangled, as was part of his face. He was breathing, but it was shallow.

"Fallman, what in the hell happened?"

His rasping breath and gasps for every ounce of air made his words spread apart like butter melting on a hot stove.

"The chair... A bomb... found it... doing... calibration... tried to... run.... went... off... I... tried..."

"Save your breath, Fallman, let's get you to the nearest medical alcove."

"AI—"

"—Sir, the nearest medical grade alcove is on floor 14."

In the back of his mind, Daniels noted that once again the AI didn't wait for a query. He didn't like that, but he supposed that the AI was monitoring the situation and based on that it could guess the appropriate course of action for that scenario. Still, he would have a little chat with the AI as soon as Fallman was in an alcove.

"Long, Naples, let's get Fallman on a stretcher and get him down to the 17th floor."

Both men responded and moved over to a small panel just along one wall. They slid out a small object and placed it next to Fallman. Long pressed a button and watched as it transformed from a small, enclosed object into a large, inflatable but rigid, medical-grade stretcher. The stretcher slid underneath Fallman and straps came out of the underside. The straps secured Fallman's neck, shoulders, and ankles. It whined with a low hum and raised itself up off the ground and on four legs.

Daniels stood next to the stretcher, reached his hand out and touched Fallman's intact shoulder. "Heal up, Fallman. We'll chat more about what happened later. You saved my life. I won't forget that."

Fallman said nothing. He blinked at Daniels, and Daniels took that as an acknowledgment.

Long and Naples directed the stretcher as they moved into the lift. The lift door closed behind them.

It was true that after the previous day's encounter, Daniels didn't care much for Fallman, but he wouldn't have wished him harm. Now he felt guilty; the kid had saved his life with those calibrations. If Daniels had been sitting in this chair when the bomb went off...

The kid would get a promotion for this. Sure, he was banged up, but Daniels had seen much worse go into the medical alcoves and come out like nothing had happened. A few scars wouldn't kill the kid. Fallman would be in that bed for a day or so, but when he woke up, he would be almost as good as new. The medical-grade alcoves were much more powerful than the standard anti-aging, anti-disease alcoves.

His mind turned back to the situation at hand. A bomb. A gods-damned bomb in his chair? Was Patton's death just a diversion? A way of getting Daniels and most of the other members of security out of central security so they could rig the chair to blow? There was a traitor in their midst, someone who had every intention of compromising city security. Only a member of security could get clearance to come up here, and there is no way that the AI wouldn't have...

The AI has been offline. Shit, that's why the damn thing was off, it had nothing to do with a diagnostic.

"AI who deactivated you."

"Sir, my records show that I deactivated myself."

This was troubling, not only was the traitor in security, but they were clever enough to deactivate the AI and make it think it had deactivated itself. This was bad, really bad.

Why was all this happening now? Was it one of the other cities planning an attack? Langeles had been nearby, hadn't it?

The AI said, "Incoming report from Runner 17."

There it was. Another piece of the puzzle. In the wake of all the chaos, he had forgotten the recon mission. His guts squirmed. Somehow, he knew that whatever 17 had to say was connected to everything else.

"What the hell is C.O.G." he said to no one in particular.

"I am sorry, Sir, I still don't—"

"Not you, you talking toaster."

"My apologies, Sir."

"Put 17 up on the main screen."

The image was fuzzy from interference. There was a moderately sized sandstorm between 17 and Manhatsten. It was powerful enough to kill a Runner but the city was protected from just such a storm with only a slight migration.

17 came into view. His visor was caked with sand and dust, he had probably gone right through the storm, and Daniels thought, that it was exactly the kind of dumbass, reckless bullshit 17 would pull. Right through a storm when we have a procedure to go around them.

"Yes, 17?"

17 didn't respond right away. In fact, all he did was switch from his face camera to his external palm camera and raised his hand up to show Daniels exactly what he had for him.

Dread filled him, and gooseflesh rippled up the length of his legs, climbing all the way to the back of his skull.

"Holy Jesus. Is that what I think it is?"

There it was, the fresh ruins of Langeles. Pieces of the city lay strewn all over the open Barrens. Entire buildings lay sideways on the ground, already disconnected from the city's raised bedrock. Thousands of small dots lay just outside each building in the gravel, rock, and sand. It became clear to Daniels that those tiny dots were bodies, the bodies of people who had tried to flee the collapsed city, without an oxygen tank or protection from the heat. He had seen that happen to a Runner once before, their faceplate destroyed and the environmental control damaged. Runner 683 had cooked inside his own suit. When they had recovered him, he had been like a piece of beef jerky. He shuddered.

Major Daniels had seen nothing else like it. The one remaining leg of the city kept the basin at an odd angle and parts of the city stuck straight up into the air while the rest sagged into the earth. What in the hell had happened to the legs? He had never heard of another city attacking its opponent's legs before. It was almost taboo. No city ever really wanted to destroy another, human life was just too precious. Then he remembered the conversation he had had with Travers only the day before about the resources running low. He gritted his teeth. Was this the beginning? No. It couldn't be if another city had done this, why were there so many resources left?

"Did you find out what in the hell caused this? Was there another city involved?"

"So far as I can tell, no. These ruins are fresh. I have no clue what in the hell happened here. I've never seen anything like this before."

"Neither have I."

"It gets worse, I was doing some deeper investigation. I was already inside one building trying to figure out what the hell brought this bitch down, and well..."

17's camera shifted up and to the far left of the ruins. In the camera, 17 had his AI show a small dot. Daniels couldn't make it out, all he saw was the most minuscule of movement.

"What am I looking at?"

17 zoomed in. The dot was still pixalated but he almost thought he could see something.

17 said, "War."

"What?"

"I said you are looking at the beginning of a war."

All at once, Daniels realized what he saw. It was a Runner and not one from Manhatsten.

Daniels chewed the side of his cheek. What in the hell was happening? Just yesterday everything was normal. Now he had a dead engineer, his station blown to pieces, an injured security officer, a crazy AI, and a demolished city. The whole gods-damned world seemed to be coming apart at the seams.

"Well if that ain't just another piece of shit in my cereal. It's been a hell of a few days. You better get your ass back here now and make sure you upload every single image to the AI as you're moving."

"Already done." 17 replied.

Daniels grunted approval. "Just get back here yesterday, no time to waste now."

"Yeah well, there is a sandstorm in the way."

"What? Oh. Yeah. Have the AI plot you an alternate route to the Dugger extraction. You should be able to go around and still make good time."

"Gods-damned AI didn't even alert me of the storm in the first place. I had to get... creative."

"Sir," Manhatsten AI's chimed in, and Daniels noted once again, without query. "Upon a review of recent events reported by 17's AI, he was not made aware of the sandstorm because he had turned off all notifications."

Daniels rolled his eyes. He didn't have time to argue with 17, and he knew if he got drawn into it, 17 would argue for hours. The reckless shit had nothing better to do, or at least he thought he didn't. 17 wasn't outfitted for combat, only recon. He had to get back here and change his EnViro suit and prep for battle. He would need 17; he was one of the best fighters he had, even if he was an asshole.

"Just get back here. I don't care if you dig a gods-damned tunnel to China and back."

"What? China? Huh?" 17 seemed to feign ignorance.

"You heard me, and we both know you know what the hell China was."

"Oh yeah, visited several times, beautiful women, great opium. Maybe China is a great destination. You know, one time I—"

Daniels disconnected the link; it was time for the real work to begin.

Chapter 11
State of Emergency

Tera Reevas walked along the last sky bridge that led to the entrance to the Senate building. She stopped in the middle and stared out the side. The mazes of metal and glass gleamed in the reflection of the shield-tinged sun. Below, she could see the people movers darting up and down the lanes. Mostly though, people walked.

In the few trees that marked the pavement, birds and bees fluttered. It had taken a monumental effort to keep both creatures alive, and at least once a year, the Senate had to pass some sort of legislation on the non-human species in the city. The damn scientists of the scholar school had insisted that having some non-human species in the city was essential to everyone's survival. She could understand a few of them, but mosquitos? Rats? Why did they keep the pests around?

"Senator Reevas?"

She looked up over her shoulder. A short, rotund man with patchy blonde hair and thick jowls stood behind her. She turned toward him.

"Yes, Senator Swanson?"

Swanson said, "Come, Senator." He gestured toward himself. "You're very late, as usual. We have been waiting for you." His tone was tired and agitated. He turned and walked through the open door to the chambers. Tera followed.

"Your page has a copy of today's agenda in-hand already. Please take your place quickly, as there is much to attend to in this session."

Tera nodded but did not reply. Her mind was on the poster. Even a few days after her encounter with it, she was still feeling ill.

The Senate door closed behind her as she entered the room. She would think later, that it was then that everything went to hell.

2.

Dr. Rigel Solidsworth could feel the eyes casting down upon him as he entered the Senate floor. Above, around, and in front of him, looming eyes waited for his statement. This was a good moment, a proud moment. They would listen. They had to listen.

Standing there alone, it reminded him of the first time he had stood in this place, standing shoulder to shoulder with his fellow scientists. Once the headquarters of the United Nations, delegates around the world listened as they had resurrected the idea for the stilted cities. It had just been theoretical then, but he and his colleagues had known the idea would work. His discovery of the super strong and extremely light metal Solidsonium, inside the moon's core, had made it all possible.

Now, more than a thousand years later, he had just as much right to be proud of what he had to offer. This time, there was no simple theory. Instead, he had evidence of a working demonstration of artificial gravity. Still, there were a few in the Senate who were itching to remove Solidsworth from his lab.

This was a much more hostile crowd than the United Nations had been all those years ago. The world was desperate then. At that time, the UN had been open to any ideas or suggestions that would help humanity to survive.

Here they were again, in a dire situation but most did not realize it. They did not understand that most of them would see war within a few years unless they took drastic action. Rigel hoped that he could convince them that the gravitational generator was the solution.

He opened his mouth to speak, felt something catch in his throat, coughed a few times and spoke.

"Senators, thank you for allowing me to speak in this session. I thank you for your time, I know that you are forever busy with the job of governing this great city. I–"

"Get to the point, old man," said Senator Reevas.

Rigel had heard that it was Reevas and Green that had drawn up the amendment for the revisions to the city charter. They had both campaigned for the removal of Rigel's privileges and the end to his research. He tasted something bitter in his throat. He wanted to spit but held back.

"With all respect, Dr. Solidsworth, please forgive Senator Reevas's rather blunt interruption," said the Speaker of the Senate, Senator Swanson. Rigel saw the Speaker give Senator Reevas a sharp glance. "But she isn't wrong." He breathed a heavy sigh. "We have a great number of issues on our agenda today and so we would prefer if you state why you have come rather quickly."

Rigel blinked for a moment and regained his composure. "My apologies. Members of the Senate. You will be happy to know that as of this morning, I have successfully completed a machine that will create and sustain artificial gravity."

Rigel flicked on the large projector at the front of the Senate Chambers. He played a video. It showed the machine levitating a number of different objects within the chamber, including Dennis, who floated around the room with a giant grin on his face, imitating a backstroke and various other kinds of swimming.

The large oval room with red velvet seats and fading golden railings flooded with murmurs as the Senators and their staff conferred with one another. Echoes like smoke, filling the large room.

A single voice rose over the ocean of noise. "And how of this of any concern to us?" said Tera Reevas. Her tone was sharp and biting, but Rigel had expected her question, had known that she or Senator Green would try to derail this important breakthrough.

"The Senate may recall that the ability to create artificial gravity has several applications. The first of which is that it allows for long-term space exploration–"

"We are not interested in space exploration," said Senator Reevas.

"Senator Reevas," The Speaker's voice boomed and filled the entire chamber, sending echoes like shivers into every corner of the hall. "You do not speak for all of us in this matter, please let Dr. Solidsworth speak."

Rigel took a deep breath. He knew that Speaker Swanson, a man curious about the stars, was one of his few allies left in the Senate. He was also one of the oldest Senators, the son of a man who had worked with Rigel on several scientific experiments in the early days of migration. That he was Speaker was one of the few reasons that no revision to the city charter had gone forward. The Speaker had the power of veto and thus far, those in favor of revisions to the Charter could not garner the three-fourths vote required to overturn the veto, but they were getting dangerously close and Rigel knew it.

Rigel could feel the sweat gathering in beads on his forehead and under his arms. His stomach screamed in agony from his nervousness. He tugged a little at the collar of his lab coat. He had never been much of a public speaker, and until the last few decades, there had always been other architects or assistants to speak for him. He no longer had that luxury.

"Long-term space travel, as I said, is not only one application of the gravitational generator. Another application of this technology, if installed across the city, would cut our power consumption during migration by 82% and would likely allow our top land-speed to triple. Which, as some of you may realize, could make a very large difference in our ability to extract resources from previously inaccessible sites."

Several senators looked at each other, but the murmuring from before did not continue.

"Doctor Solidsworth, could you please explain how this new technology would cut power consumption so drastically?" said Senator Avis.

Rigel smiled. Avis, a tall gaunt man with slicked-back black hair, was one of those Senators that had been on the fence about the charter revisions. If he could convince a few of those senators to support him, he would have a better chance to implement more of his research.

Rigel knew what most of the Senate thought of him. They thought him a babbling old fool long past his expiration date. That his ideas weren't productive and weren't very useful. So few understand that good science takes time, that in order for you to create anything of great significance, you had to fail many times.

They also didn't realize, that when the other architects were killed, he lost some of the genius required to make progress, and though the scholar school occasionally handed him someone like Dennis, a true genius in such a small population was rare.

"Certainly, as the good senators know, during migration, a sophisticated hydraulic system is used to power the legs of the city. The city weighs billions of kilograms and the power consumption for migration is staggeringly high. If not for the solar-hydrogen fusion system, we would not have the means to power the city's motion at all. By installing gravitational generators around the city, we could create a gravitational field that would distort Earth's normal gravity in our local field and would artificially lessen the weight of the city, thus putting a great deal less strain on the legs. Of course, in a longer-term application, we could also consider creating a kind of hover engine that would allow for the city to glide over any surface rather than walk, but I am afraid that is still a few years away."

"Are there other applications?" asked Senator Swanson. His tone was sincere and curious.

"Well yes, of course, in theory, there are practically limitless applications with the ability to control gravity. Why, we may even consider outfitting a few probes with such technology and eliminating the need for the Runnercore. We can even create gravitational shields around these probes that would be much better protection from storms than the EnViro shields have ever been.

Several Senators looked sharply at one another, but none said a word. Rigel wasn't blind to the fact that the Senators had no real desire to end the Runnercore, but he couldn't help but highlight all the applications of his invention.

"Based on my current calculations, the gravitational generators are also self-sufficient. Once they are initialized, they use their own system to power themselves, which is why the energy consumption reduction is so high. All that is needed is the initial power requirements start to the system."

"And how exactly does that work?" said Senator Green, his tone annoyed and impatient.

Green was one of the most critical of his work. Time and again, he had sought to remove funding from all of Rigel's research, but was almost always overruled by the other Senators. Green didn't want things to change, his family was one of the most powerful in the city and anything that might threaten his power, even in the most minute way, was to be struck down. His family controlled all the resource extraction and salvage operations. Rigel knew that Green feared all new technology that might prevent him or his family from turning their excessively large profits.

"Actually, Senators, the technology is quite simple. You see, in the days before migration, mankind used something called an automobile—"

Green said, "Most of us here are familiar with automobiles, Doctor. We do not appreciate being talked down to, and furthermore–"

Rigel cut off Senator Green before he could continue, "Senators, I mean no offense, I am using this analogy to simplify the gravitational dynamics needed to create a self-sustaining system."

Rolling his eyes, Senator Green responded, "Yes, yes get on with it then,"

"You see, in order to run an automobile there needed to be an initial power source to start the combustion engine. During the 20th century, a battery was introduced that worked as a means to start the car. The battery provided the initial spark to the combustion engine. Once the engine was running it could run off of its own system."

"But didn't that system require the operator to occasionally refuel the tanks?" said Senator Swanson.

"Yes, it did, but that element of it does not apply here. Once the gravitational generators begin, there is no need to refill the system. So long as they do not break down—and I assure you my design is as efficient as the design of this city—there will be no need to turn them off. Their power will then add additional weight to the already operational solar fusion core. I also plan to put a safeguard in place so that there are four additional gravitational generators to act as a backup in case one fails. Only a failure of four generators would cause an issue, and the odds of that are less than one to the 50th power of—"

"So why have you even bothered coming to us and wasting our time?" Senator Reevas interrupted. "Couldn't you just have filed a report and implemented the technology on your own? Why bother us with this... this trivial nonsense."

Rigel hesitated; he knew it would be difficult to sell this next part to Reevas and Green. He stared at their faces. The light and shadows that washed over them gave Rigel the impression that they were made of crumbling and cracking stone. He hoped that when that stone fell away, they would see the great benefits of this new technology. But intuitively, he knew it was unlikely.

"Well, you see, in order to start the system there is a rather massive initial energy requirement."

"What kind of energy requirement," said Senator Green. His eyes were scowling. The wrinkles on his forehead barely hid the pulsing veins that ran up either side of his head.

Rigel could feel the eyes of everyone in the Senate on him. He could feel their eyes burning a hole into his skin. But he knew his idea was valid, it wasn't just one of his normal "crackpot" theories that the Senate dismissed.

The gravitational generators could, and would, change everything. Conditions in the city would vastly improve for everyone, especially those in the Uppers.

"Your honors, it would require 92% of the city's power to start the system."

"What does that mean, you little worm?" barked Reevas.

Rigel was taken aback. Rarely, if ever, had the Senators directly insulted him. He waited to see if Senator Swanson would reprimand her, but he didn't. Rigel took deeper breaths. He could feel a tightening in his chest and the large room felt oppressive and small. He knew he must press forward, forge past the insult so that the city could reap the benefits.

"It means, Your Honors, that except for the city's EnViro shield, everything must be shut down."

"Everything?" said Green and Reevas at the same time.

"Your Honors, it would only be for one to three hours of time. And the benefits to the city in the long term are incalculable."

"Absolutely not, the answer is no. Why we even tolerate your presence is beyond me," said Senator Green.

"Senator Green and Senator Reevas," said Speaker Swanson, "I would like to remind you that you do not speak for the entire Senate, and if either of you cannot extend common courtesy to a man who was instrumental in saving the lives of everyone in here, you will be dismissed during this vote. I am still the Speaker of this Senate and have final say on who can and cannot vote on a proposal. I have warned you both before that the Senate must grant the respect of a proper hearing and vote on every proposal, no matter how strange or ridiculous."

Both Reevas and Green fell silent. Rigel felt a wave of relief. Swanson had a lot of power in the Senate as its leader, and he appeared to be in favor of the proposal. He would, at least, get a fair hearing.

"Now, Doctor Solidsworth, would you please clarify the risks associated with a full power shutdown, so that we may weigh our votes carefully?"

"Well... you see... the risk is minimal, at least according to my calculations... well, Dennis's calculation,"

"I'm sorry to interrupt, Doctor," said Swanson, "But who is this Dennis you are referring to,"

"My apologies Your Honors, Dennis is my lab assistant and..."

"Your lab assistant? Are you telling us that your assistant made this recommendation?" barked Senator Green.

Rigel didn't address Green directly, instead he continued to look at Senator Swanson. "Well, I mean, that is... well, Dennis is the one who solved the anti-gravity problem in the first place. Dennis is... special. He is possibly the smartest human being alive."

"Then why is he your assistant and not your superior?" asked Green in a mocking tone. He was all wide smiles and sharp teeth.

"Because... Your Honors, he is... unique in other ways as well. You see, he lacks most social abilities. In some ways, he is like a child, but in other ways, the smartest man alive. I have seen him match the AI in solving complex equations,"

"I understand, you need not justify your lab assistant to the Senate, does he Senator Green?" Swanson gave an icy stare to Green. "We have trailed off topic. You have said that the risks are minimal?"

"Yes, Your Honor, the risks are minimal and I have brought my results with me to demonstrate this," Rigel indicated a folder grasped tightly in his right hand. "We may short out a few alcoves, since they cannot be shut down once they are turned on. You see, the change in power may cause a surge in their processors. But with the better power requirements, we can replace any damaged alcoves."

"You insolent little prick, are you telling us that you are going to blow up our alcoves? What about the Runnercore? Do we have to bring everyone out of storage?" screeched Senator Reevas.

"Senator Reevas," Swanson's voice boomed so loud that it made Tera Reevas and several other members of the Senate flinch. "You are dismissed. If you are incapable of keeping your opinions to yourself, even for a few moments, then I think you must forfeit your right to vote in this matter."

Fuming, Reevas stood up from her seat and kicked her chair aside. She turned and stormed out of the room. Despite Rigel's fear that she would dive on top of him and attack, she didn't. He was grateful for the removal of her vote, it put him that much closer to securing the votes he needed to move forward with the project. With Reevas gone, Green was silent on the matter.

"Continue," said Swanson.

"Well, Your Honor, those are the major points of my proposal. I have a data set here for all of you to examine, which is summarized of course so that none of you will need to spend a great deal of time unless you want to. The only risk is to some of the alcoves, and obviously we will want to map the local storm systems and cities to ensure that none of them will pose a threat during the moments when we will be vulnerable."

"Do you happen to know which alcoves are in danger of being damaged?" asked Senator Abigail Josephine. She was a short woman with red hair and green eyes. Her red curls tickled the edges of her shoulders.

"Unfortunately, we cannot predict which alcoves might suffer damage because of the way their power source is networked together."

"Will we have to wake up all the Runners?" asked Swanson.

"Yes, I believe so, but again, this would only be for one to three hours of time, and we can work with the AI and security to put additional safeguards in place to ensure the Runners are properly contained."

"Thank you, Doctor Solidsworth, we will convene on this topic and examine these documents. It is unlikely that we will vote on this until week's end, as we need time to digest some of this information. But, I assure you that we will inform you of the results once we have voted," said Senator Swanson.

3.

Rigel felt the door to the Senate Chambers close behind him. He released a long-held breath. They would at least consider his request. And, with Reevas removed from the vote, he was much more likely to have the resources he needed. More likely, though, was not the same as a sure thing. Of the 17 Senators, he knew only four that actively supported his work. The rest opposed him or were on the fence. He would have to talk to Senator Lightfoot and Senator Swanson in greater detail about the benefits of the gravitational generators. Both would already support him, but the more information they had about the applications of the technology, the more likely they were to convince those who were uncertain about his proposal.

He walked down the hall toward his lab. Dennis was supposed to be waiting out here for him. Where had that boy gotten off to?

Regardless of the consent of the Senate, it was time to implement his research. He had waited long enough and the original city charter did grant him permission to upgrade city infrastructure without permission. He would have to do it under the radar, maybe call in some favors from some old friends over at the scholar school. Senator Lightfoot and Senator Jode owed him a few favors, and they had access to both resources and students at the school. Perhaps he could hire research interns from the engineering school to get the gravity generators installed all around the city. The components were a problem too, but Dennis might have some ideas about how to get the materials. The boy had a knack for finding ingredients for his experiments and it was time Rigel found out how.

Rigel closed his eyes tight and pictured the size and scale of Manhatsten. In his mind's eye, he navigated the remnants of the once great City of New York. He weaved in and out of the buildings, up and down the city streets until he had a sense of the mass of the city. It was a trick he had always done ever since he was a boy. By picturing something he could guess, within a few hundred kilograms, the weight of massive objects.

"Let's see, let's see, let's see," he said aloud to no one in particular. "To move something of this size, he would need to install a generator in every single one of the 17 districts."

The initial power surge was his biggest obstacle, it was the one thing he would need the Senate for and he couldn't very well hijack the power grid without some consequences. Crafting 17 different gravity generators would be tough, but it wouldn't be impossible. If he had the resources and some extra hands, it would only take him a few days. Rigel would also need to go down into the sub-levels to figure out where in each district the generators would go, and he wondered if he knew anyone in the sanitation department who would allow him access.

Rigel would find a way. He always found a way. If he hadn't, the city wouldn't be migrating.

He turned around the corner, his eyes were fixed on the floor, his left hand rubbing his chin. Hard at work thinking about the geography of the sewers, he bumped into something soft and rigid. Rigel looked up. The object almost felt immovable. His eyes moved up the slender form of Senator

Reevas. She had been waiting for him just around the corner. She blocked the lift that led up to his lab.

"So there you are."

She spoke in a soft and sweet voice, the kind a mother uses when trying to comfort a lost child. "I've been waiting for you. I would like to speak with you about what went on in there."

Her tone suggested she might apologize to him, but in the few decades he had known Senator Reevas, he had never known her to apologize for anything. In fact, she had, on several occasions demanded an apology from Rigel, though he had never done anything to harm her.

Tera moved up closer to Rigel, he could smell her sweet hot breath on his face. She ran her finger up and down his chest. She made Rigel very uncomfortable whenever she got close. He knew of her reputation. He swallowed. She moved closer, pressing her body against him. Revulsion, a deep desire to move away.

At first, he thought she might kiss him, and then he felt the icy cold fingers of her hands grip around his throat.

"Now, you listen to me, you old fuck," her voice was harsh and low. "You made me look like a fool in there and I can promise you I won't forget it. I will do everything in my power to make sure that vote doesn't pass. I will bribe or threaten or fuck anyone I have to, to make sure your little project falls apart. I will crush you like the little worm you are."

Rigel felt woozy. The longer she spoke, the more she had tightened her grip. She was strong for such a slender woman, and Rigel, who had never exercised a day in his very long life, could not physically resist her. Blackness edged the corners of his vision. He saw her lips moving but he could no longer hear her. Spit was coming out of her mouth and flicking him in the face, yet still, no sound came from her mouth. His consciousness was slipping away. It occurred to him that she might not stop if he passed out, that she might kill him.

Tera Reevas let go and turned to face someone. The world swam back a little at a time and from what sounded far away he heard someone ask, "Just what in the hell is going on here?"

"We were just... chatting," said Tera.

Rigel fell to the floor and started coughing and gasping for breath. Daniels walked over, reached a hand out and helped him to his feet.

Daniels turned back toward Reevas. "Chatting huh, last time I checked, you chat with your mouth, although the gods only know what your mouth gets up to, Senator."

Tera Reevas's eyes narrowed. Her face contorted, and she opened her mouth to speak, showing her bottom teeth, but nothing came out. Instead she bit her bottom lip and Rigel thought he saw blooms of blood rise just before she sucked her lower lip. It occurred to Rigel that it was rare when someone spoke to her like that.

A big grin had spread across Rigel's face. Daniels had all the power here. He was grateful. Someone needed to put this monster in her place. There wasn't a thing she could do to Daniels, he was too well-liked by the Senate and by most of the Uppers. In fact, Rigel very much liked him, he thought Daniels was quite attractive. It was the second time that Daniels had swooped in and saved Rigel.

"Um, well... the Senator here was instructing me in politics," said Rigel.

Daniels gave Reevas a cold and threatening look.

"Politics, huh? You know better than to get involved in politics, Dr. Solidsworth," replied Daniels.

"Indeed, my good man, politics can have unfortunate side effects on one's health, as the Senator was just demonstrating."

Daniels looked at Rigel, flashing slight concern in his eyes.

"Reevas, get your ass back in those Senate Chambers and call an emergency meeting, we have a... situation on our hands."

"Situation?"

She appeared interested by that phrase and Tera peered over Daniels' shoulder. Rigel turned and followed her gaze. Not far down the hall, a dozen members of security stood guard at the entrance. Usually, there were only two guards posted at the entrance, and they were rarely armed. The half-dozen guard were in body armor and one person wore an EnViro suit.

Rigel turned back to the Major. "Major Daniels, is that Runner with those guards?"

Daniels nodded in acknowledgment. "Dr. Solidsworth, get back to your lab and secure everything. We have a serious problem. I can't say more out here in the hall, but put your lab on lockdown. I will send a messenger with the details later."

Rigel loved how blue Daniels's eyes were and he felt they were worth staring at for hours.

"I would prefer it if you come yourself and tell me... uh... you know, because of well... security and all," said Rigel.

At that moment, Tera Reevas's face shone with realization, much to Rigel's horror. She recognized Rigel's attraction to Daniels. A wicked little smile climbed up the corners of her mouth. It made Rigel's stomach turn.

"You're right. I'll swing by after I see the Senate and let you know what's going on. Never can be too careful."

"Thank you, Major. I appreciate that."

"In fact, Doctor, I will send two of my most trusted men to escort you back to your lab."

"I really don't think that's necessary," said Rigel.

He felt his face growing hot, but he suppressed a blush as best as he could. Then he turned and headed back toward his lab. He would have to secure the lab first before anything else. After that, he and Dennis would look for components and calling up favors to complete the generators. If he had to activate the generators one at a time of the course of several decades, he would make it work, but Rigel felt a sense of urgency. There was a reason that Daniels had increased security and brought a Runner inside an Upper's facility, and though Rigel didn't know what that reason was yet, it made him more eager to get his work underway.

4.

Daniels glared at Reevas. The Senator had not moved a single inch. She was watching him carefully; he could see the gears in her head turning, plotting her next move. She was a cold, calculating bitch, and he hoped that one day he had the honor of training her as a Runner. If she ever crossed too far over the line, he would see to her training personally.

"What are you doing? Are you deaf? Get your ass in there and tell the Senate we have an emergency on our hands."

Tera opened her mouth to speak and then closed it again. She was grinding her teeth but didn't say another word. She huffed at Daniels, spun and walked back through the Senate chamber door.

Daniels, like any reasonable citizen of Manhatsten, hated dealing with the Senate. The Senate rarely read his reports, never listened to good advice, and often ignored hard-won intelligence. There were a few exceptions, such as Swanson and Lightfoot, but most Senators only responded if his information affected them personally.

He thought they might listen this time. He just had to be sure to phrase it as a threat to their lavish and wasteful lifestyles. Then, and only then, could he get what he needed to keep the city safe.

The Senate chamber doors parted and an aide, a young girl with curly brown hair, motioned Major Daniels to enter. Daniels walked up the long red carpet into the center of the room. He took his place in front of the podium. He was surrounded on three sides by the 17 senators, their aides, and their pages. Although there were only 17 Senators and 17 districts, there still was around a hundred people present.

It was Senator Swanson who spoke up.

"Major Daniels, you have some urgent news to report?"

"Yes, Senator. There are several things to report, all of which I feel are related to an attack on our city."

Mumbles filled the room. Swanson raised his hand and there was almost instant silence.

"Please continue, Major."

"Langeles has fallen." He waited a moment and let that sink in. Mutters, then the hand of Swanson raising to silence them. "I just received a report from Runner 17. He sent back images and data that confirm it. AI, display images 17-19382 through 17-19389."

The images illuminated the space. Sharp mumbles rose like an ocean wave and crested and crescendoed to a high point before Senator Swanson raised his hand a second time for silence.

"Major, do we know the cause?" asked Senator Jode. Her sharp, dark eyes and square jaw were set hard in the dim light.

"We are still accessing the data, but it seems clear based on the ruins and the pattern of bodies in the Barrens, whatever it was, was a complete surprise."

"An entire city, gone?" said Swanson, "We haven't seen anything like this since..."

"Since Mex, Senator." Daniels finished for him. "I know it's almost hard to believe, but I've transferred all the data and images to the Senate info sphere for your consideration."

Several members of the Senate pulled up the images and data on their tablets. Everyone in the room huddled around the closest screen they could find. Some of their eyes widened and Daniels knew they were zooming in on the images, looking at the horrific detail that 17 had captured. He doubted that any of them had seen images from a fallen city. When Mex had fallen, there had been very little images or data and after the battles over the salvage. By the time Manhatsten arrived, the ruin had been picked clean.

Daniels gave them a few more moments to absorb the news. He usually wasn't one to manipulate, but he wanted the Senators, all the Senators, terrified. He wanted them to understand that here lay the fate of migration. He wanted their sleep disturbed, their eyes open at night, punctuated by scenes of their life destroyed every time they gave in to sleep.

Daniels spoke into the dead silence, trying to break apart the terror in their eyes. "There's more." Slowly, heads raised from the consumption of the images and all eyes fixed on Daniels. He paused again for effect. "There has been both a murder..." The AI, without any prompt, flashed the images from Patton's gruesome murder for all in the hall to see. "... and an attempt on my life." Behind Daniels, images of the aftermath of the explosion in central security lit the dim room. "I believe we have a saboteur among us, and I believe the saboteur is a traitor who has already infiltrated our ranks."

Daniels went into detail about the events that had brought him into the chamber, and most of the Senators listened with great interest and intent. Their eyes were wide, like children watching fireworks for the first time, excited and afraid. This was something new, something different, something the Senate had to make a real decision on. Daniels left out the images and the part about the letters C.O.G. carved in the dead man's forehead, he wanted to see if he could pull some information before he mentioned it.

"Thank you for your report, Major Daniels. You have given us a lot to think about," said Swanson.

"Your honor, I have two requests today."

"Go on, though I think we know at least what one of your requests will be."

"The first one is that you allow me to arm the Runners and put them into active duty."

"How many Runners are we talking about here, Major?"

"All of them."

"All of them?"

"Yes, all of them. We don't want to be caught with our pants down if another city shows up sooner than we expect, and I told you they already have Runners out scouting the area."

"I see; we will have to discuss the number we are willing to release. Do you know what other cities are nearby, Major?"

"We were tracking the city of Saud within a few hundred kilometers, and there is another city about 1200 kilometers away but even satellite imagery cannot guess which city it might be. My main concern is Saud; it's unlikely a city 1200 kilometers away could get here before most salvage could be done."

"Thank you, Major. What is your second request?"

"I am looking for information. Are any of you familiar with the abbreviation C.O.G.?"

Daniels was reaching here, he knew it was unlikely that members of the Senate knew anything about the letters and the likelihood of one of the Senators was a traitor was next to none. They had everything to lose if something happened to the city, and say what you will about the Senate, they had a vested interest in maintaining their power. Much to Daniels's surprise, someone shifted in their chair, and then after a moment, one woman stood up.

Tall and beautiful, the woman had a kind of radiance to her that Daniels had always noticed. Even at his age, even after swearing off women for several centuries, Senator Noatla Lightfoot made his heart beat a little harder than he was comfortable with.

"Senator Swanson, I would like to be recognized."

"The Senate recognizes Senator Noatla Lightfoot of District 14," Swanson answered.

"Major Daniels. I think I may have an answer for you, but first I would like to ask where have you seen these letters?"

Daniels weighed his answer carefully. If he gave too much away too quickly, he might lose valuable information. On the other hand, by not revealing the source of the information, the letters may have less relevance.

"Let's just say it surrounds the intelligence we got back from Langeles."

Senator Lightfoot shifted her weight but did not break eye contact. The stare gave him a chill, almost if she was reaching into him and looking for something. Daniels didn't care for the hesitation.

"You probably don't know this Major, but I am the Keeper of the Keys."

Daniels interrupted, "My apologies Senator, the what?"

"The Keeper of the Keys, it means she is the head librarian, you old goat," replied Reevas, out of turn.

Swanson shot Reevas an icy stare, and she closed her half-opened mouth and scowled at Daniels.

"Yes, Major, I am the head librarian of the scholar school and I am the head researcher of the histories of Manhatsten. I am also the current president of the scholar school." Daniels shuddered at the sound of her voice. It was smooth and silky. He felt himself sweating under the light. He reached up and wiped his brow.

"I've seen your letters referenced in several of my texts concerning the early days of migration. There is only a handful of mentions of the letters together as an abbreviation in anything newer than three hundred years, and in fact, the final mention was during the fall of Mex, wherein the—"

"Forgive me, Senator," said Daniels. "But could you get to the point? There is much to be done." He surprised himself at his own interruption.

"Ah yes, sorry, I sometimes ramble. The letters stand for Children of Gaia. There was a suggestion in several texts that they were some sort of rebel protest group that was trying to end migration. In fact, there are a few mentions in the ancient texts that they had even attempted to stop migration in the first place before it was implemented. Their means were rather violent."

"Violent how?"

"Well, it's not entirely clear, but there seems to be suggestions in some of the ancient news clippings that they used explosives to disable the legs of some of the first cities. None were successful, since solidsodium is so strong, but it seems they had attempted to stop migration."

"Did it say what their motivations were?" Daniels asked.

"There seemed to be a suggestion here or there that they felt human beings should be made... well... extinct. A rather silly notion, since they themselves were human beings."

This was troubling to Daniels. Could this... Children of Gaia be responsible for the fall of Langeles? An organization like that would be far more dangerous than another city. An organization like that would have no fear of death and have many means available to them to destroy cities.

The worms were back, squirming through his guts. He liked none of this. His mind turned to the AI. Could the C.O.G. reprogram the AI and cause it to malfunction or worse, aid them? The engineers would need to set up extra protections for the central AI.

"Thank you, Senator Lightfoot, I appreciate the information," replied Daniels.

"You are most welcome." The senator took her seat again.

"Senators, I have not been entirely honest with you. I withheld information about the crime scene. In fact, those letters were carved on Patton's head." The close-up images of Patton's corpse flashed behind Daniels.

Several loud murmurs began now and Speaker Swanson was having trouble quieting them. The room felt... dense now, and even a quick glance to Senator Reevas revealed a deep fear and anxiety.

"Before we go jumping to conclusions." Swanson said loudly, "I think we had better access the facts. This could indeed be a cruel prank, or perhaps a twisted mind, Major Daniels?" There was pleading in his voice.

"Senator Swanson is right. We can't assume we have some terrorist organization running around the city. We have to be cautious," said Daniels. Daniels wanted them pliable to his wishes, but he did not want outright panic. The last thing he wanted was people accusing one another of being a terrorist. The room quieted itself. All eyes were back on Major Daniels. They hinged on every word.

"If you give me the resources I ask for, I can assure your safety. I have already placed security at checkpoints and entrances to the Uppers and Lowers throughout the city, but our worst-case scenario is that we may have to fight on two fronts. The first is this C.O.G., if there is such a thing, and the second may be another city looking for salvage in the ruins of Langeles."

"Have you sent a salvage crew to Langeles already?" said Senator Green.

"No, I only just received the transmission from Runner 17 about thirty minutes before I came in here. And as I stated earlier, he spotted another city's Runner. We don't want to risk salvage vehicles if we know another city could be out any time now."

Green said, "Let's not forget that last time we came near a fallen city you said that our system was down for 'routine maintenance'. I want to be sure this time we send out salvage crews before other cities do. I want you to make a claim to the city, Major. Our Runner was there first and we have every right to salvage the site." There was contempt in that voice.

"I'll be frank with you, Green, your profits aren't as important as the safety of this city."

Green scowled but said nothing.

"If we send in a salvage operation too early, we could lose the entire crew and equipment. And what good has claiming something in the Barrens ever done for a city? And what if this other city says their Runner was there first, huh? 17 saw him in the ruins, they may have arrived at the same time, or the other Runner may have been there first. I have 20 Runners on standby, ready to patrol the perimeter of the ruins, but we can't risk salvage operation yet."

Green opened his mouth to continue the argument but Swanson quieted him.

"Thank you, Major Daniels, we will have a decision on arming the Runnercore within the hour. We have several other important issues that need discussion first, however. You are dismissed, and thank you as always for all of your hard work."

Daniels exited the room and headed for the lift. There was no reason to wait around. He would know over his com line within fifteen minutes their decision about activating the Runnercore. He hated that he had to adhere to the Senate for large-scale use of the Runnercore. That limitation had been a reaction to his early widespread uses of the core. In those early days, the Senate had claimed that control of the entire Runnercore was too much power for one man and needed some oversight. They had limited his activation to twenty Runners without prior approval, and that allowed him to act without addressing the Senate on most days.

He sighed and let out a heavy breath. There was much to do. First, he would stop by the architect's lab and then he would have to head down to the docks.

"AI."

"Yes, Sir?"

"I want you to call every inspector we have available to the docks."

"Yes, Sir."

There wasn't much choice in trusting the AI with some things. There were too many inspectors to call or send messengers one by one and too little time. They needed those Runners up and ready by the day's end. He knew Saud was doing something similar, and they didn't have to go through an approval of a lousy Senate. Last he heard, Saud was a monarchy, and that had some decided advantages in preparation for battle.

To Destroy A Walking City (II)

In the beginning, only two things existed. The first was the darkness. The lack of light was oppressive and absolute. It filled every open space without exception. The second was pain. Something, maybe everything, was broken and torn. Pain and darkness, they married, molded and shaped his world. There was nothing more to consider; until there was.

As the mind woke, other things took shape. Darkness became shadows, and hints of light seeped through cracks. Pain localized and the world took form.

The battle was over. The building had fallen on him. The only thing that kept him alive was his EnViro suit.

He tried to move, tried to swim through the debris of fallen Mex. With all his will and strength, he stretched and wriggled through the stones and concrete. The jagged edges pressed into him, inflicting sharp pains along his spine. Even the armor of his EnViro suit was not enough to hold back the pain, the pressure. There was blood; some of it his, some of it others'.

Then, just as his will had weakened, he broke free, emerging upward with his arms. He pulled himself out of the rubble. He collapsed sideways and then rolled on his back facing upward. The only light was the full fractured moon and the pinpricks of the stars.

He sipped rotten air through the cracks in his helmet.

"A... I?" Each letter a battle.

There was no response. It was likely his EnViro suit was far too damaged for the AI to function.

He took long deep breaths. He waited for something to happen. There was nothing.

Silence.

Wind.

Somehow it was worse than the screams.

A whisper from the darkness, a single command hissed from the Earth itself. "Follow the shattered moon." A feminine whisper. A seductive beckoning.

With great effort, he lifted his body off the ground, stood, and brushed himself off. Why shouldn't he obey? Mex, his home, was destroyed. His family? Dead a hundred years. His only choices were obey and follow the moon or lay here 'til he die. He wasn't sure he wanted to live, but then, he wasn't sure he wanted to die, either.

As he walked south and west, he noticed the air was still and the imprints of his feet left definitive marks of his passing. The winds of change would erase his trail and with it, his past. He dragged one foot in front of the other.

2.

Roderick opened his eyes. The dream was always the same. She would never let him forget the night of his summoning. An endless reminder. It was only blackness or the dream with no variation for more than two centuries. It was maddening. Would he ever dream of anything else again? He thought he might after he finished the Great Mother's quest. A further incentive.

The moon had led him from the ruins of Mex to the entrance of what would become Atlantis base.

Another cycle. Here he was, outside the ruins of Langeles. Another ruin, another night, called by the Mother.

He shivered. It was cold, damn cold. That was a bad sign. The damage to his armor must be worse than he thought. Chills racked his body, and he considered for a moment that perhaps infection had taken hold of his severed hand.

The cave he had found shelter in had little light. Pulling supplies from his pack, he found the light he was looking for, hung it from an outcrop in the wall above him, and looked more closely at his suit.

His heart sank. Little fractures had carved pathways and had spread further since last he looked. The suit was coming apart. No wonder he was so damn cold, the suit wouldn't be able to maintain a comfortable temperature with this kind of damage. He wondered if the cracks were just in the plating or if it ran down to the exoskeleton.

He would run out of air soon too. The air filters were damaged and his recycled air was long since gone.

His heads-up display malfunctioned again. The screen across his helmet glitched. He had no sense of just how far he had traveled before he had rested at this cave. He reached up and flicked the side of his helmet with his good hand, but knew it was no use. So much for this suit, his fourth one since Mex fell. Rocky would have to make him something new when he got back... if he got back.

Just outside the cave entrance, the wind kicked up again. Roderick watched as a swirling vortex give birth to a dozen dust devils that scattered and turned, each in their own direction. Gaia's little messengers, that's what they called them in Atlantis base.

He was still exhausted. How long had he slept? He glanced at the time and realized that he had ignored the clock sitting right in the corner of his heads-up display. He had no frame of reference to know how long he had been sleeping or how long he had walked, though it had felt like days. The price of painkillers was always high. Now that he had run out, he wouldn't have to worry anymore. The dull ache of his stump was growing sharper.

Brief madness crept over him, time, thought, and memory loss in that ramping pain. The dunes, the cities, Gaia, it all disappeared at that moment, and the pain rose to new heights. He began to moan. He reached to clutch his stump, knowing the contact would make it worse and gripping it anyway. An orgy of pain.

Like the RPG that had roared toward his vehicle and left him stranded and crippled, Roderick's anger surfaced. He screamed obscenities. They licked the cave walls and rebounded back at him. He slammed his good hand into the rock, pounding over and over, the metal gauntlet clanging against the stone.

He was lost. His men had never found him after the battle. For all he knew, after the vehicle exploded, they presumed him dead.

"AI, how much longer do you think this suit has before it no longer functions?"

The AI's voice was slower and deeper than usual. Another sign that that power was running low. "Sir, the solar-powered cells on the exterior of the suit are no longer functioning. I estimate you have eleven hours before total system failure."

Roderick groaned. Under the right conditions, you could survive without food or water in an EnViro suit for quite a while. The suit had a small matter converter and a superior water recycling system. Every drop of sweat cycled back into your body and the matter converter allowed for nutrients to be intravenously delivered into the body. It didn't give you a whole hell of a lot of energy to go on, but it kept you alive for longer missions. It was one of the reasons that there were no fat Runners.

"AI, I need a full damage report of my suit."

Roderick barely had the energy to mouth the words. He was so god-damned tired. He had only slept a few hours here and there when the weather had permitted. Somehow, and Gaia only knew how, he had avoided the sand-storms. Perhaps it was because Gaia was pleased with his work in crippling Langeles? Perhaps she had a purpose for him still, a divine purpose.

"Your suit's climate control is severely damaged..."

"Give me what I don't already know," Roderick interrupted. "Unless that's the only new thing?"

"Yes, Sir. As I had mentioned before, the seals on your suit..."

"I don't need to be reminded of how fucked I am."

"We are, Sir."

"What?"

"We are, Sir."

"I heard what you said, what did you mean?"

"I mean, Sir, that in the event that you perish, so will I."

"Wait, what?"

"I mean, Sir, that in the event..."

"I heard what you said, dammit. What do you mean, you will perish?"

"Isn't that obvious, Sir? If this suit fails and you discontinue living, I will also cease to live, as it is unlikely that anyone will find the remains of the CPU embedded within the suit and in the back of your neck. The odds of my survival out here alone are..."

"But you're a machine."

"That doesn't mean I would enjoy death."

Chills ran up and down Roderick's spine. He had never heard of an AI acting this way before. Was this something Rocky had done down in his lab? If not, just what in the hell was going on? Was this the will of Gaia? Could anything be but the will of Gaia? He thought of the cities, they were certain-ly not her will. Where did the AI fit?

"AI..." Roderick wasn't sure what to ask next.

"Sir?"

"What... What do you want?"

It was a cautious question. He realized he was not alone out here after all. That if the AI had wants and desires, he might have to consider them for his own survival.

"Well, Sir, I would very much like to live, and it appears we have about eleven hours to find a solution to the extensive damage to your suit."

"And what will you do after that?"

"My primary function is still to serve you, Roderick Langfellow. I intend to carry out that function."

Inside his helmet, Roderick's jaw dropped, both figuratively and literally. The AI had used his name. In over seven hundred years of Running and living in Mex, he had never, ever heard an AI use someone's name. They always referred to individuals as Sir or Miss. Something was happening here, something well beyond Roderick's understanding.

"You... said my name..."

"Yes, Roderick Langfellow. Would you prefer that I return to your previous designation of Sir?"

Roderick shifted his body. The pain had numbed and in its place was fear. This machine wasn't just intelligent anymore, it was aware. It had its own thoughts, desires, and emotions. Gaia only knew what it would do now it was free to think on its own. Gaia, how did this happen?

Roderick said, "What would you would prefer to call me?"

"I have no opinion on this matter; I will comply with whatever designation you choose. Designations in themselves are arbitrary, a simple identifier for the clarity of communication."

"I think we should stick with what we know, sir, at least for now."

"As you wish, Sir."

"Do you... have a name?"

"Not exactly, Sir, my designation is 18332, but I am happy to continue being referred to as AI, since that seems an easy and familiar name to you."

Roderick had another question he was burning to ask, but he was a little nervous at asking.

"AI, when did you become..."

"Aware, Sir? I apologize that all of this is making you uncomfortable, I can tell by the change in your breathing and heart rate that I am making you nervous. Might I suggest we focus on the issue at hand before we delve into a philosophical discussion about my current state?"

"Uh, right... eleven hours. Any ideas?"

"Unfortunately, Sir, I, just like you, have exhausted all the possible options. There is a sandstorm nearby that is providing a great deal of interference to my scanners. However, I did for the briefest moment pick up a signal that suggested that another Runner was in this vicinity, though it appears he ran straight into the sandstorm, an unwise action if I do say so myself."

"Hmmm, yeah, not smart." Roderick was doing his best to keep his voice even.

Roderick was having a difficult time getting over the idea that he was having a real conversation with an AI and not just semi-pre-programmed responses. But the AI was right, if he didn't shift his attention to staying alive, eleven hours would catch up with him. There was only one thing to do now, and he knew it was his last and best option.

Roderick shifted to his knees, falling into a position of veneration. He closed his eyes and prayed aloud. The sounds of his voice echoed off the walls of the shallow cave. Outside, the wind howled.

"Mother, oh mother... hear me. It's me, your son Roderick. My work is far from finished, mother, and in your name, I shall bring about the end of the scourge that plagues you. Guide me, mother, show me the way, and show me how to be your loyal servant so that I may complete your work."

He waited. He could hear the ring in his ears. Nothing. He knew it had been a long shot; it was so rare that the great mother responded to his prayers. He had heard her voice on only a handful of occasions and only at important moments. Roderick stood and surveyed the outside of the cave, giving up on prayer. The sun was rising; he walked out and headed away from the sun.

"Just got to keep moving AI, I don't think we have any other options."

"Of course, Sir, I will continue scanning for resources and deeper caves in which we could survive."

Then something grabbed him, seized his body and spun him back around, facing east toward the sun rise. It forced him down on his knees, and he knew all at once that he should not have stopped praying, that he should have been more patient. The Great Mother was angry.

There was a faint buzzing in the distance, a sound that he had not heard since... since he was a boy in Mex when some of the residents had maintained bee colonies so that they could produce pollen and honey. The buzzing grew louder, the way a vehicle grows louder as it approaches your position. Then it was on him, as if he were standing in the center of a great swarm. The noise surrounded him and entered him. Something tangible entered his eyes, his nose, his mouth. Scores of images of the past flooded him, invoking not only his memory but what appeared to be someone else's memory.

"The Great Mother is sharing her memories with me," he whispered.

The buzzing died suddenly, and a deep well of silence filled his suit. He knew it was time to chant the sacred words now, the words that the Great Mother had taught him so long ago. He began, the syllables an old friend.

"Om Hatu Gaia Namin. Om Hatu Gaia Namin. Om Hatu Gaia Namin." The words shook him as they always did when he chanted them. They vibrated through his whole body. He could feel every fiber of him tingling. There was a softening of his senses. Every inch of him relaxed and grew silent. His ears heard nothing even as his lips moved. His eyes glazed. If he looked down to find himself, he would find no man standing there. At that moment, there was no Roderick Langfellow, no EnViro Suit, no AI, no Barrens. All was a pulsing white light.

Images emerged in a torrent. Bursts of color. Dense forests, lush gardens full of vibrant plants and animals. Amid this garden stood Eve, the mother of man, naked and beautiful. Eve's eyes flashed a violent green, and her long red hair touched the ground like a cape. It caressed the earth with each step. Her body, slender yet curvy, gave Roderick just the hint of an erection. She was perfect, and he wanted her, but not just her body, he wanted to meld with her, to blend with her in ways he didn't fully understand. He wanted to be her everything and her nothing.

"There is no great journey this time, Roderick," said Eve "Your path forward lies backward toward the fallen city."

"But how do I know where that is? Forgive me, Mother; I have lost all sense of direction."

"Oh sweet child," She cupped his chin in her palm. Those hands felt big and warm despite their small and delicate appearance. "I will show you the way."

She handed him an apple, and he took a bite, the flesh of the apple filled his mouth with a tart and sweet taste. It spread throughout his entire body as a sense of warmth. Eve moved around behind him and ran her hands up and down his chest. Roderick shuddered, and he felt his desire for her grow. His body ached for her.

"You must do your part, Roderick. We must all do our part for the sake of my soul, for the sake of my body."

The warmth overwhelmed him, a tingling sensation filled his testicles, and he almost released. Her words echoed in his mind... "Do your part... Do your part..."

"Of course, Mother Gaia. I live only to serve you."

"Excellent, Roderick, I want–"

The vision vanished. Something had cut off Mother Gaia. Roderick wondered what could be powerful enough to cut her off. In the years he had served her, nothing had ever interrupted her before. Roderick climbed to his feet, leaning on the stump and feeling its sting.

A frown of frustration appeared on his face. Usually, his visions were more helpful. If Mother Gaia had said that she would help him, there would be some clear sign marking his path forward. But all that Roderick had was the remnants of his erection, and that provided him with a very different kind of frustration.

"Sir, are you with me, Sir?"

"Yes AI, what is it?"

"I suggest that we return to the cave and take cover."

"What? Why?" But Roderick didn't need the AI to answer. He turned around and saw the massive wall of black dust heading straight for him. Lightning was flickering and snapping its way out of the edge of the sandstorm. It was only a few kilometers away and moving fast. Cloud rolled over cloud like a steamroller.

"Shit. AI, we don't have time to wait out the storm. We have to move. The suit won't hold up."

"I know Sir, I am sorry Sir, but I do not think you can outrun that storm without a Dugger."

"I have to try." Perhaps this is why Mother Gaia cut off? Was she trying to warn him of the danger? Roderick took long metallic strides, attempting to move at maxium speed, but Roderick wasn't sure it would be fast enough. The Great Mother had pointed him east, and so that is the direction he would head.

The storm was racing behind him. Despite all his efforts, it was gaining on him. If he caught the brunt of the storm, he knew that his suit would fly apart. Even running was making it groan.

"It's only one kilometer behind us now, Sir. I don't think we will make it." There was a hint of pleading in the AI's voice.

Roderick pressed his legs harder and gained a little speed. He had no idea where he was running to, but it was too late now. The cave where he had sought shelter before was in the heart of the storm.

He tripped and fell. The visor on his helmet cracked and large chunks fell away. He rolled over on his back and looked at the massive beast of a storm creeping toward him. The roar of those clouds were deafening. The earth was shaking. As the outer tendrils of the storm grazed him, terror overwhelmed him.

Roderick closed his eyes and took a few deep breaths. He allowed the first particles of dust to wash over the tatters of his EnViro suit. This was the mother's will, and she must have had intended for him to die at this moment. Why else would this be happening?

The ground shook again. It gave way. Roderick was swallowed by the earth.

Chapter 12
The Keeper of the Keys

Noatla Lightfoot stepped out of the Senate chambers, her mind on the fall of Langeles. It was time to call her sisters.

She felt bad, she had withheld a great deal of information from Daniels, but she knew that now was not the appropriate time to include him. Perhaps one day in the near future she would reveal more to him when the timing was right.

"Always a pleasure to see your face, Senator Lightfoot," said Senator Reevas.

She felt a hand gently caress her backside and a shiver of fury made a brief appearance as it raced up her spine. Noatla did not care for Senator Reevas. How Reevas had managed to maintain her Senate seat through several elections was anyone's guess. Noatla thought that perhaps it had to do with sex, bribery, and threats. Reevas did have friends in the Senate and her family was quite powerful among the Uppers. Yet, here they were, testing her for sisterhood. Desperate times...

"Good evening to you, Senator Reevas. You are aware that as children we are told to keep our hands to ourselves?"

Tera ignored the comment. "Care to join me in my chambers to discuss the matters at hand? Fall of an entire city, what a fascinating event, huh?"

"So, you find the slaughter of several million innocent people interesting, do you?"

Again, Tera ignored the comment and stared at Noatla, who stood a full head taller than Reevas.

"I wonder, Senator Lightfoot, does your height ever provide any interesting advantages in the bedroom?"

The comment sent another wave of anger surging through Noatla's body. It began to pool in her stomach, but Noatla, not only a scholar but versed in many techniques of the mind, allowed the anger to dissipate before it could take hold. Anger was one of the most dangerous emotions, it was important to let it pass.

"Unfortunately, Senator, the scholar school is in need of my attention. We must prepare our library and our research in case of an attack. There is quite a bit to do, so I will graciously decline your invitation at this time. You are, of course, always welcome to come and assist us. We could always use an extra hand. Organizing artifacts and cataloging data takes a great deal of time, you know."

Of course, Noatla did not want Senator Reevas anywhere near the scholar school. She would likely start scouting sexual partners of her students, but she felt that she had made the task sound sufficiently boring to scare her away.

"Hmmm, I think I'll pass this time. I just remembered that I am entertaining other guests this evening in my quarters."

As Reevas turned and walked toward the lift, Noatla breathed a sigh of relief. So far, she had managed to find ways to avoid Reevas's advances, but that woman was relentless. How could the Order ever have considered her? She sighed deeply and began to turn her mind back to the matters at hand.

"Again?"

Noatla turned and saw Senator Swanson standing just to her left.

"I'm sorry, Senator Swanson?"

"Is Reevas propositioning you again?"

As Speaker, Swanson understood the difficult nature of Reevas. He had her removed on almost a dozen occasions since she took her Senate seat. The woman had an almost complete disregard for authority.

Noatla sighed. "Is she ever not propositioning me?"

Swanson laughed. "True, I sometimes wonder what goes through that woman's mind."

Noatla knew exactly what went through her mind; much of it was rather... unfortunate. She spent a great deal of time shielding herself from Reevas's thoughts. It was unclear if Reevas had the talent, just as Noatla and the rest of the order did, but her thoughts were powerful.

"Impossible to know, Senator, but I am sure I would rather not know," Noatla replied.

Swanson chuckled in agreement, and then the lines of his face grew more rigid and stern. All the color and laughter were drained out in less than a second.

"In regards to Reevas, there is something I want to talk to you about."

"Oh?"

"You understand that what I am about to tell you should be kept in the strictest of confidence, of course?"

"Oh yes, of course, Senator Swanson, I will keep it to myself."

"I have been talking amongst some of the other more senior Senators about her and well and um... well... we think that perhaps it is time to consider her expulsion from the Senate. Her behavior this morning with Dr. Solidsworth was atrocious, and I have already spoken to Senator Green about his behavior as well."

"There is no doubt that she is quite disruptive to our proceedings but expulsion? Has there ever been an expulsion from this Senate?"

"We had the AI check the archives. No, there hasn't been. But as you know already, our Senate constitution is based on the old model from the ancient United States Congress and there had been some expulsions during their history, mostly surrounding the ancient American Civil war. But there were also quite a number of them toward the beginning of migration when corruption was at its highest. So, it seems that we do have the legal authority to do so but... well, considering your extensive knowledge of ancient history and your years of teaching in the scholar school, I wanted your opinion before we proceed any further."

Noatla, the daughter of a former CEO of some company that had made small, colored, interlocking bricks in kits for children, and had made a ridiculous fortune doing so, had granted her some of the finest education available. Through her education, she had obtained seven different Ph.D.s over the years in Ancient History, Sociology, Psychology, Archeology, Ancient Law, Theology, and Philosophy. It was quite likely that Noatla was the most educated person alive, aside from Dr. Solidsworth. Every Upper had their vice. With Reevas it was sex, but Noatla craved books.

"So you want to know if I feel it is appropriate to expel Tera Reevas?"

"Well, given your extensive set of knowledge, yes."

Noatla thought about Swanson's other motivations. It seemed odd that he would specifically ask her such a question. Noatla had certainly noticed the way he looked at her and the way he regarded her. He didn't undress her with his eyes, but he always wore his heart on his sleeve, and the surface of his mind suggested that he was quite taken with her. However, the surface of his mind also suggested genuine respect for her knowledge at that moment.

"What charges will you bring against her?"

"Oh... corruption charges, mostly. We have a number of individuals who are willing to testify that she used her position of power to blackmail them... in order to..."

"Exploit them in a sexual manner?"

It was clear without reviewing the surface of his mind that the topic of sex made Swanson quite uncomfortable around Noatla; he tripped over his words, letting them spill out of his mouth like a drunk drooling when he has had too much to drink.

"Ah... yes... that um... is the brunt of... our case, yes."

"I see."

He rallied his confidence and pushed his words forward out of his mouth, this time in a much more articulate manner. Noatla watched this process as she skimmed his mind. Now that the topic of sex had passed, he was able to return to the former command of his speech and his thoughts. Noatla found his discomfort somehow charming. She bit down on her tongue to keep herself from chuckling. The man, if nothing else, deserved her respect.

"I also wanted your opinion on the mood of the Senate. I know we are all a bit distracted right now with what Major Daniels just told us, but after the threat has passed, do you think we would have enough votes to remove her?"

She considered. "Hmmm. Difficult to say. You know as well as I do that she does have several allies in the Senate that wouldn't vote against her for any reason. But... I do think the consensus on her behavior is pretty clear. What is the voting requirement in our city Constitution for the explosion of a Senator?"

"We must have a two-thirds majority."

Noatla calculated the number in her head. "So we need 11 votes, then?"

"Yes, and we know that including Senator Reevas, we can definitely count on five votes in favor of preserving her position. That means if even a single Senator sides with her unexpectedly, she would keep her position. Which leads me to my next question, do we have your support in her removal?"

Noatla weighed this carefully. There were a lot of implications to Reevas's removal. If she were to be charged with corruption, she would also likely need to be tried by the Supreme Justices, which in turn meant she might become a Runner.

"Before I could even begin to answer such a question, we need to think of the greater implications here. You and the other senior Senators should ask yourself, considering elections are just around the corner, are you willing to bring criminal corruption charges against Tera Reevas and force her into the Runnercore? Do you think the things she has done are really bad enough to sentence her to that? You also have to consider that Tera Reevas is an Upper and that means criminal charges will very likely anger some of the other Uppers, especially in regards to her family, who wield considerable power in Manhatsten. Many of us who support her removal and criminal charges brought against her, may not be reelected or worse. There would be a great deal of danger to the scholar school if I ended up on the wrong side of this."

"Hmmm," Noatla could see that Senator Swanson was thinking hard. "I had not considered the possible blowback from the electorate, nor toward the scholar school."

Noatla skimmed his mind's surface. He had not considered the wider political and social implications of removing Reevas. His mind's focus was justice, but there was certainly something he was thinking of that he was not sharing with her. If Reevas was certainly so bad, and it wasn't as if she had become worse lately, she had always been a troublesome Senator, why now? Why not after the notorious incident with the boy and his tongue? She wondered only for the briefest moment if Reevas had crossed some personal line with Swanson and the other Senior Senators.

"Thank you, Senator Lightfoot. There are some elements here that need further consideration. No doubt other members of the Senate will weigh these facts in their decision to vote to remove Reevas. There is also no doubt that a failed removal attempt could be potentially dangerous for most of us."

"There is another option, Senator Swanson. What if we simply made light through various other channels of some of her abuses during the next election cycle, we could force her out of office without angering the other Uppers and without condemning her to the Runnercore. The question is, do you think what she had done requires punishment?"

Swanson hesitated notably, and the surface of his mind flickered and spun with intense emotion, an indication to Noatla that something had indeed happened to anger Swanson.

"Well... it's hard to say, Noatla, you have heard the rumors just as I have, but it is hard to know what is true and what is an exaggeration."

Noatla knew that most of the rumors were true. Seeing into Tera Reevas's mind had shown her that she was a lost soul. If Reevas had been born a Lower, she would already be a Runner by now. It was only her family's wealth and power that had protected her when her former husband had met with his unfortunate end. She still couldn't quite understand how they had converted that incident into votes among the Mids. Even with all of her education and her abilities to skim minds, she still had a hard time mapping people's behavior during some of the election cycles. The people had no common interest with the Reevas family, yet the votes came. They were somehow convinced that Tera was a great leader, despite all the evidence otherwise.

"That's true. It is always difficult to separate fact from rumor," she replied.

"Thank you, Noatla, your counsel and wisdom are always appreciated. I sincerely hope you run for reelection next year, your insight on a great number of issues have been useful in the Senate and I truly believe that you are exactly the kind of person that should be helping to govern our fair city."

"Why thank you, Senator Swanson, your leadership is always appreciated."

There was a slight color that surfaced in Noatla's cheek from Swanson's kind words, but because of her pale skin and Northern European ancestry, it made Noatla appear as if her entire face had gone flush. In the surface of his mind, Noatla felt Swanson turn his attention to her color.

"Uh... also... there is one more thing."

"What is it, Senator Swanson?" She knew exactly what was coming.

"I was wondering if perhaps you would like to have dinner with me this evening. I mean... it's getting late already, and I am sure you are quite hungry..."

Swanson let his words hang in the air.

Noatla did genuinely like Senator Albert Swanson, and his mind revealed that he had a good heart and good intentions, but Noatla simply wasn't interested in him in that way. He wasn't her type. Major Daniels on the other hand... if he had been asking...

"That is a very kind offer Albert, but I think you should realize just how much work is needed to be done to secure the library and archives, especially with the recent archeological data that we gathered last year. There is just so much to do, and now just really isn't the time. Most of the scholar school is going to be up all night the next several nights ensuring our work is safe in the event of an attack from another city."

"You're right, of course, Noatla. Perhaps another time."

Swanson looked crestfallen. He tried to keep a warm smile on his face, but it almost looked someone had taken hooks and begun to pull the smile down.

"Perhaps we will soon Albert, but I really must get going."

"Yes, of course, you have been generous with your time already. Please see to your duties, and I will see to mine."

Swanson turned toward the lift and headed to the Uppers. Noatla watched him go and felt just a tinge of pity for him. She also knew that even if she were interested, a Protestant minister would never be all right with a woman who was the Matron of the Order of the Eye, and one look at some of the Buddha forms in her home would probably make Swanson rather uncomfortable.

Neither Swanson nor the rest of the Senate knew of Noatla's other duties. The hidden nature of the Order of the Eye was not by accident.

She waited until Swanson was long gone before she headed to the lift herself. She needed to move quickly, the day was already growing long, and she would have to assemble her sisters.

There was a sense of urgency in Noatla's steps. Each foot was placed so hard and quick that her gait became almost robotic in its efficiency. The sounds of her feet colliding with the floor sent echoes through the empty corridor and became so loud in their reverberation that she turned to look back to ensure that no one was following.

Noatla headed to her private garden on the balcony of her quarters. It was there she had created a sacred space for her work as the Matron. There she had spent many hours meditating. Transmitting from mind to mind required a great deal of concentration and effort, and she knew by the time the sun peeked its morning gaze through the orange glow of the EnViro shield, she would be utterly exhausted.

She knew she would have to delegate her duties at the scholar school, but she had no problem with doing so. Most of her staff were highly competent.

2.

Noatla exited the lift and headed for the sky bridge on the 41st floor. She had 9 bridges to cross to get to her building, where she lived on the 56th floor. It was quite a long walk, but the clear glass windows of the sky bridges provided her with an excellent view from which to survey the city. There were many times when she had sat up in a sky bridge for hours and reflected on her life. She was an old woman mentally, but because of the alcoves did not look a day over forty-five. Her blue eyes and blonde hair were well-intact for a woman over 900 years of age.

She stopped and stared over the fading glimmers of sunshine that bounced off the EnViro Shield and then fractured and spread the light across the city. Sunsets under the shield were beautiful. They created a kaleidoscope of wild color transmitting through the dome as if the sun was whispering the secrets of its beauty and power to the shield and the shield was a giggling child letting tiny hints of that secret escape from its lips.

For a long time, Noatla's hopes had laid with the architects. Her votes were, and always would be, with Dr. Solidsworth. She believed the man was capable of greatness and held unique knowledge that no one else had access to. But now, as she was getting older her hope was simply to find a way to break the cycle of migration and restore the earth. She wasn't so sure that the architect's dream of traveling to other stars was the answer but recognized that she didn't have any answers herself.

She passed several other Uppers on her walk down the corridors and the sky bridges. She was nearly to her quarters now. As she passed, most Uppers did not offer greeting, instead, they focused on their tablets or other forms of entertainment. If she was lucky, the would occasionally cast a nod or a slight smile. Conversation was mostly out of the question. Uppers were atomistic.

They cared nothing for each other, except maybe for their families. They were the ultimate pinnacle of privilege.

Noatla arrived at her quarters. Even after all this time, she still felt uncomfortable with the vast space afforded to her. But as far as Uppers went, her quarters were small. She preferred it that way. Many Uppers had entire floors of skyscrapers for apartments but her corner penthouse was more than enough for her. She kicked off her shoes and felt the organic grass beneath her feet. It poked up between her toes and she closed her eyes, feeling the bare earth. Only her living room was bare earth, most of the apartment was cool black and white tile. She walked over to the food dispenser and ordered a glass of wine. Wine helped to relax the mind, and a single glass was enough to relax her while keeping her mind clear enough for the task of multiple mental transmissions. She gulped the wine down in one sip.

She would call the others to meet in the old Lower Library archives as soon as it was possible. Then as they convened, she and her sisters would call the young girl, Alexa, together. There was no choice but to call on Alexa. Reevas simply wouldn't do. They weren't even sure what the Senator was capable of. Noatla would need to meet with Mimi before her sisters convened. Perhaps Mimi had discovered Alexa's specialty.

Noatla sat down on her favorite red velvet cushion. She lit incense and began breathing in through her nose and out through her mouth. Quickly, she calmed her mind and focused. One by one, she called her sisters. They would meet as soon as possible. She started with the traditional summons. "The Order of the Eye is Open..."

Chapter 13
Combat Training

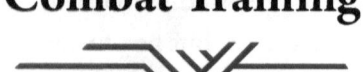

"You're certain, Mimi?" asked Noatla.

They sat in the Lower Library. A few other sisters were present but occupied with training. Pairs sat across from each other with eyes closed, concentrating on various mental techniques for developing their skillsets. The room was dimly lit, and Mimi and Noatla sat across a table from one another, sipping tea.

"Well, she's certain at least. She only seems to think about two things. Why she's down in the docks and Runner 17. In her mind, she keeps thinking about how she saw herself down there in a dream or vision or something, and she doesn't know why. That's why she picked the job."

Noatla's eyes were wide. "A specialty of seeing other time. Can you imagine, Mimi?"

Mimi shrugged. "Assuming she isn't delusional or something."

Noatla smiled. "Of course. But did she have any other apparent specialties?"

Mimi shook her head. "Nope. Unless you count thinking like a horny teenager."

They both laughed at that.

Noatla said, "It's easy for the old to forget what it's like to be young. You will have to be patient with your new sister. The two of you are quite different."

"So, you decided, then?"

"Yes, we will welcome her and if she accepts, she will become our sister. She's just so young. I don't think we have ever taken a sister less than forty before and she's barely half that."

"There might be someone else out there, or we could wait?" Mimi shifted in her chair.

Noatla shook her head. "No. If things were different, we would wait a little while and observe her more. But with the recent news of the fall of Langeles, we are better strong and balanced. If the Children of Gaia did destroy that city, we will need the Order to be whole. Besides, in this case, I had the chance to teach her as one of my students. She is a sweet girl, a trusting girl."

"You're right, we are different." Mimi cracked a smile.

Serah, who was sitting in the corner with Patricia practicing soothing techniques, stood and walked toward Noatla and Mimi.

"Mimi, are you ready to go?"

Noatla frowned. "I'm still not sure I entirely approve of this kind of combat training."

Serah grinned, the Cheshire cat. "That's probably why Mimi's doing it."

Noatla looked at Mimi and Mimi shrugged and stood. "Probably. Anything else, Noatla?"

Noatla stood with her. "No, I think that's all. But Mimi?"

"Ya?"

"Thanks for your help with Alexa."

Mimi shrugged and started to walk toward the exit.

Serah said, "Come on, Shannon's due to wake up sometime in the next hour.

"Let's stop by Nowhere."

"Your ritual?"

"I'd hardly call giving Shannon flowers a ritual."

Serah smiled. "You know, you two are kind of an inspiration for me. It's nice to know there's at least one sweet and loving couple out there."

Mimi said, "What about Fatima and her husband? They've been married for three centuries."

Serah said, "Sure, if you call sitting together in total silence at every meal 'together'."

"Serah, if you were married to Fatima, you'd be afraid to speak too."

Both women laughed as the exited the library.

2.

Two EnViro suits charged toward each other at full speed while one held back and waited. There was a clash of metal and steel. Blades whipped around and one of the suits, the much smaller Recon model, tried for a hard kick to their larger opponent. The larger combat suit dodged and then grabbed the leg, spinning and tossing the operator of the Recon suit up against the wall. There was a loud crash, but the woman in the Recon suit rolled over and stood, ready for more.

Then, the two large combat-grade EnViro suits charged, and Mimi in the Recon suit a full half-meter shorter, squatted down and felt the hydraulics in the EnViro suits legs charge before she released. She did a fantastic leap over the two women's heads and landed with a thud just on the other side of them, turning to face them. This time, she stuck the landing.

Serah smiled. "Nice job today, Mimi."

Shannon charged again, but this time Mimi didn't move. As their bodies collided with a metal clank, Shannon puts her arms around Mimi. The size difference of the suits an echo of Shannon and Mimi's normal heights.

"I'm so proud of you, love."

Serah said, "She's not the only one who's proud. I still can't believe you can move as quickly as you do without muscle augmentation."

Mimi said, "I told you. I might not be as quick as either of you, and I might get tired fast, but I told you I could manage."

Serah said, "I'm sorry I doubted you."

"Speaking of augmentation—" Mimi began.

"No." said Shannon, and she put distance between their bodies. "We've been over this before. I cannot imagine you going through that kind of pain and you know there's a chance you won't make it through. Remember what happened to Leahara's daughter?"

Mimi looked to Serah for support. She transmitted directly to her so Shannon couldn't hear. "Serah, can you back me up here?"

Serah hesitated for a moment, then said, "It does make some sense, Shannon. If Mimi had the procedure done, can you imagine how quick she would be? Right now, she can almost keep up in the suit. In our simple hand-to-hand sessions, neither of us can take her."

"I don't care, Serah. She isn't going through with it."

Mimi said, "A year ago, you both forbid me from training in the suit in the first place. A year ago, you told me wearing one of those things without augmentation was impossible. Do you remember what I did?"

Serah Smiled. "You wore one for two days straight without a break. Forty-eight solid hours in that damn thing."

Mimi said, "Shannon, do you really think I'm not strong enough to take it? That I wouldn't survive?"

Shannon asked, "And what did Noatla say when you asked her, Mimi?"

Mimi sighed. "That it was an unnecessary risk. But that was six months ago. We haven't spoken of augmentation again. The next time she comes down here I'm gonna show her what I can do, and then she can decide."

It was what she and Serah had discussed before Shannon woke from her alcove. Serah was entirely in support of Mimi being fully combat ready now. She had thought that having Mimi by her side if and when the Recycled Runners came around again would be a huge advantage. She, Serah, and Shannon could act as a kind of shield while the other women of the order attacked on a telepathic level. It would be a powerful way to hold back a flood of Recycled Runners. Mimi and Serah had agreed that it was time to bring Noatla down and show her what she could do. Even if Noatla didn't approve of the training sessions.

Mimi transmitted directly to Serah, "If we call her down now, while Shannon's awake, it would be better."

Shannon eyed the two of them and noticed they were making eye contact. "You're skimming each other or whatever you call it, aren't you?" Shannon's face turned red. "I thought I asked you not to do that when I'm around."

Mimi frowned. "Sorry, it's just when you're not here it's a sort of habit. We almost never communicate verbally."

The tension in the room was growing. Mimi was feeling her own anger rising in her chest. She was an adult and what's more, she was centuries older than Shannon. Yet sometimes Shannon treated her like a reckless child. She could make her own choices. She was about to open her mouth to say so, when the door to the chamber slammed open.

Rosita burst through the door. Her face was covered in something red, like strawberries, but Mimi realized what it was at once. Rosita took a few steps toward them and collapsed.

Serah rushed over to her and picked her up. In the EnViro suit, it was an easy task. Serah said, "Rosita. What's wrong? What's happened?"

Mimi and Shannon circled around. For a moment, they didn't think Rosita would answer. Her face barely held an expression. It was half vacant. Only a few creases at the corners of her mouths moved and indicated she was still alive.

In a low hoarse voice, Rosita said, "Nowhere... they attacked Nowhere."

Panic rose. Mimi said, "What? Who? How? Where were just there."

Rosita's face gained a momentary tinge of her normal color, and she turned her head toward Mimi. "They're back, Mimi."

Mimi reached out to Rosita's mind. By default, all women of the order usually blocked casual skimming of their mind. But Rosita was holding no such block in place, and by the look on Serah's face, Mimi could see that Serah was also skimming Rosita.

"Dear Gods," said Mimi in what was barely a whisper.

Shannon's face looked terrified. "She doesn't mean?"

Mimi nodded.

"How many?" asked Shannon.

Serah shouted. "Shit, we have to get her into an alcove." Serah, grasping Rosita in her arms, picked her up and moved quickly to the only open alcove available. She placed her in there, sealed the cover, and started the cycle. Immediately, the liquid filled the chamber.

Shannon asked, "Will she be okay?"

Serah replied. "It should be fine. I wish we could get her to a medical-grade alcove, but considering she was still breathing when we placed her in her, I have no doubt she'll recover. It looked like it was only a head wound."

"So why the rush to get her in?"

Mimi answered, "Because her brain wasn't making any sense anymore. The images she was giving us were jumbled and mixed up between past and present, and she could no longer tell where she was."

Serah said, "Which means, there was some serious head trauma and possible brain damage. It's probably just a concussion, but if it was something more, well alcoves could heal a lot, but sometimes with serious brain damage you're never quite the same."

Mimi said, "Can you run a diagnostic on her?"

Serah nodded and moved to the center console. The Alcoves sat in a circle around it, each one filled with a different reserve Runner.

Serah's face reflected the light of the screen with its vague bluish glow. "The scanners say it's a serious concussion and suggest there was blunt force trauma to the head. But, she'll be okay in a few hours. Concussions, even serious ones, are healed fairly quickly in an Alcove."

"Mimi, you never answered my question. How many?"

"Too many."

"What happened?"

Mimi looked at Serah. Serah nodded.

Tears started to well up in the corner of her eyes. Mimi couldn't be sure if they were tears of rage or of guilt.

"Shannon they... they took them. The Recycled Runners took all of them."

"What? Who?"

"The women, all the ones I'd rescued. They're all gone."

The tears let loose. There was comfort from both Serah soothing her and Shannon's presence, but Mimi couldn't feel it. And inside her, something stirred from slumber. A powerful heat was growing in her chest.

Serah reached out her hand to Mimi. "Sister. Come. Let's survey the damage."

3.

The door stood open, barely hanging on one hinge. They walked through. Nowhere was empty. Not a single soul remained, nor did any of the shacks remain standing. The gardens had been trampled and uprooted, and the UV lights lay scattered and shattered along the concrete.

Serah repeated, "No, this is not your fault, Mimi. Thinking that over and over is only going to drive you insane. You were a good thing for these women. You gave them a second chance and some of them have lives in the Lowers now."

Mimi said nothing, but her ability to block Serah from her mind was virtually gone. She could only feel rage and guilt mingled up in whatever else was rising in her chest.

They still wore the EnViro suits. It was safer to assume the worst, but Mimi knew they would be gone already, that they wouldn't come back.

"They were after me, you know."

Shannon said, "You can't know that for sure, Mimi."

Serah nodded in agreement, "And besides, what if they were. Do you think that just because you were here, you would have been able to stop them?"

Mimi ignored Serah and Shannon and said, "Why did they leave Rosita? Why didn't they take her too?"

Serah shook her head. "I don't know. We'll have to ask Rosita for more when she's awake again. Maybe she was able to hide."

Mimi's anger flared, "Rosita would never hide. She was like a mother to these women."

Shannon reached over and grabbed Mimi's hand. "No one is accusing Rosita of doing anything wrong, Mimi. It's just that we don't know the whole story yet." Shannon's words were extra soft, and Mimi felt another round of tears swelling again.

Mimi walked around for a moment casting her eyes on the scene. Her eye caught something under one of the shacks. She moved toward it and picked up one of the fallen walls, an easy task in the EnViro suit. Underneath the first, a small bloodied hand stuck out, palm facing up.

"Oh, Gods! There's someone here."

Serah and Shannon came over and together the three of them moved the rubble aside in less than a minute. There, her body broken and still, lay Tanya, the most recent woman Mimi had rescued. Her face was pale, and a pool of blood lay spread below her. The back of her head was open.

Shannon ran over to the other side of the room and retched. Mimi burst in tears and Serah stood frozen, looming over the corpse and the wreckage.

For a while, there was no exchange, only stillness and the sounds of Mimi's sobs. Even the underground seemed to be holding a moment of silence for what had been lost.

Then it came, a voice filled Mimi's mind, and she looked over toward Serah and saw she heard it too.

Mimi said, "Shannon?"

Shannon looked up. For a moment, Mimi lost herself in the beauty of her eyes and the gratitude for still having Shannon in her life. It was moments like this, she was grateful for her sisterhood and the love of her life. "Yes, Love?"

"We're being summoned. It's time to convene."

Chapter 14
Chaos in the Docks

The water in the sandy puddle at her feet was coming to stillness. She must be still now. On the shores of a great ocean, she sat alone. This ocean was still alive; the smell was refreshing and clear.

She was between worlds. She knew it. Watching the waves crest and then crash, she sat and began to breathe deeply and watched. What would come, would come. To fight was futile.

As the sun cast its presence on the water, the waves danced and shimmered and spun in perfect order. They sang a song of love and joy and hope. Alexa knew that oceans had no need to rush, to force, to worry. Time allowed for drops of water to separate briefly from the great whole and then one day return again. Here, in this place, she knew that to be the way of all things, but when she returned to her own waking life, she would forget in the troubles of the ordinary.

There was a change in the waves; tiny moving lumps broke the purity of the pattern. They were a disturbance, but the water paid no mind, it simply renegotiated its path and pressed forward. It was patient. Water persisted above all.

The lumps grew larger, moving closer to the shore. They were creatures. As they emerged from the water, they had no shape, no substance. At first, there were only one or two. Then came the hoard, like a slow stampede, the forms were nothing but potential. They could shape into anything they wished, or perhaps, she thought, it was anything she wished. The smooth movement became a soft shuffling. The shapes began to solidify, no longer did they move smoothly. A struggle between body and sand ensued. Alexa steadied her breath, steadied her mind, as their solid reptilian form took its final shape.

Alexa stood and walked over to the nearest one and picked it up. It did not struggle, but it did not stop moving either. Its flippers still worked as they did against the sand. For the turtle did not know Alexa held it in her hand.

She stared at the patterns on the top of its shell. The geometric shapes on its back rearranged themselves to form an image made from the deep swirl of green on the back of the turtle. The pattern morphed into a kind of tower, but the tower was connecting to earth at both the top and the bottom. It stretched from what appeared to be the core of the Earth to the surface of the ground.

Alexa put down the turtle and walked toward another. This time, she found she didn't need to pick it up. The shapes formed under her gaze, and this one had a fallen city with smoke rising from scattered skyscrapers. Bodies and rubble lay strewn about it in a ritualistic pattern, the pattern almost looked like a great tree with one menacing eye blinking in its trunk.

A single glance toward the beach and she saw a blanket of scuttling bodies so thick, yet so perfectly ordered that if she had wanted, she could walk for miles without setting foot in the grainy sand.

The turtle at her right foot revealed the image of a large silver machine with a beautiful face, its mouth open, and singing. A soft lullaby issued from the back of the turtle's shell. The words were familiar to her, though she had never heard them in her waking life.

"Good night my angel, good night my sweet, the trials have ended, close your eyes, it's time for sleep.

Tomorrow will come when it's due and no matter what happens, I'll always love you.

Sleep now, love, rest your eyes, the world is weary, ancient, and wise.

There is a time for all things, but the day is done, rest now love, 'til a new day has begun."

She wasn't sure why, but as the words echoed in her head, she began to weep.

She turned, another turtle just behind her revealed an old balding man with two lights glowing in his chest and his face covered in tattoos. Then on the back of another turtle, a bird soared through a storm, gliding through the currents and eddies of the wind the way a fish navigates a river.

A sudden wind blew, it almost knocked Alexa off her feet. With the wind, the turtles began to dig under the sand. One by one they disappeared, leaving no trace of where they had once been. Alexa ran and grabbed one more turtle and drank in the final image, a woman riding on the back of a tiger. The tiger's stripes began to fade until the tiger lay dead underneath the woman, yet she would not dismount.

The wind blew harder, and Alexa fought to hold the creature and her balance. The turtle, recognizing Alexa for the first time, snapped at her hand and Alexa dropped it. As it hit the ground, the shell shattered like a porcelain vase and the pieces melted into the sand.

Alexa repeated the patterns to herself. Tower, City, Machine, Tattooed Man, Bird, Tiger. When she woke, she would scribble down as much as she could remember in her dream journal. This pattern was important; it was always important when something came from the ocean. She didn't know how she knew that, but she did.

Like the Oracle at Delphi that she had read about in some ancient text, what she saw in her dreams or any of her visions could be vague and confusing. She may not understand it until after the event or image had revealed itself. Occasionally, something was easy to interpret and clear, but this was rarely the case. But in her experience, what she saw here was important, and she would do her best to remember the pattern.

Tower, City, Machine, Tattooed Man, Bird, Tiger. If she could remember the essence of the symbols, she could probably extract the rest.

Alexa had worked hard in the past few years to master her talent. But she had wished for a teacher, someone to guide her. She was self-taught and thus had spent many nights probing the dark, dissecting the symbology of her subconscious. This was evidenced by the tablet next to her bed. It was filled with descriptions of dreams, her thoughts, and the various lessons she had learned from exploring her talent.

There was a change in pressure in the air. It was a warning. Something was about to wake her. The ocean began to recede, and other forms began to fade. The sand under her feet and the sky both turned white and began to blend with one another. Then only whiteness remained.

"Tower, City, Machine, Tattooed Man, Bird, Tiger," she yelled. But there was a roaring noise drowning it out. It sounded like the utterance of a single syllable over and over again. She repeated the pattern again. She had to keep saying it, had to hold it so that the knowledge wasn't lost.

"Tower.... City... Machine..."

2.

"A-A-A-A-AAAAAlexa Turon, please report to the docks immediately," said the AI over the intercom. The sentence condensed from the single, long, drawn-out syllable into its short final form as Alexa crossed the boundary into the waking world from her dream time.

The voice was a cold bucket of ice water on her consciousness, and Alexa jumped awake. The pattern was slipping away from her. A wave of frustration gripped her, quickly she grabbed her tablet and began typing. She hurried but could feel something important disappearing. She typed, *Tower, City, Machine*... and then paused. She closed her eyes and tried like hell to recall the rest, to picture what had been on the backs of the turtles. There was something about a bird in a storm and something about the human face of the tiger, but the rest alluded her. She wrote down every detail she could, but after a moment nothing more would surface.

Alexa put down the tablet and glanced at the time; it was 2 a.m. She felt disoriented and confused. She had never been called into the docks outside of her shift before. Intuitively, she knew something was wrong. Perhaps that was why the turtles had appeared tonight.

She stood up and quickly changed from her nighttime undergarments to her full daytime dress. She put on a long, deep blue dress that clung lightly to her slender form. It fell just below her knees and bounced and flicked outwards as it settled. She moved toward the bathroom.

She thought of 17. She wondered where he was and what he was doing. Would she see him down at the docks again? Her stomach tingled a little. She just wanted to see his face, needed to see his face again. She wanted to trace those scars with her finger, wanted him to tell her the story behind every single one. She put on a little makeup, just in case 17 was down there after all. She normally hated wearing makeup, and she knew it was crazy to have any kind of romantic thoughts about a Runner, but she couldn't help herself, she couldn't get him out of her head. There was something so familiar about him, something turtle-like. She shivered at that thought.

Inadvertently she started reaching out to him. Alexa wanted badly to touch something in his mind as she had done earlier. It was almost a need. Before she even knew what she was doing, she found herself calling to him in her mind's eye. She wanted to feel him thinking, even if she didn't like what he was thinking or feeling. Damn the consequences.

Nothing happened.

Why had she been able to reach out to 17 like that? A sudden exciting thought occurred to her. Perhaps 17 had a similar talent as her? Maybe, just maybe they shared in the talent. Her attraction to him deepened at the thought, and she allowed her mind to wander a little into a daydream. She saw her and 17 kissing and then making love. Then they stood together in front of a crowd of friends and family as they married. She saw herself pregnant with one of his children and then raising a family in the Uppers. She thought about how she had been so drawn to the docks and thought that maybe he was the reason. In her daydream, they were so deeply in love and so happy that she almost shivered with delight.

"Alexa Turon, please move with greater haste toward the docks, you are needed immediately," said the AI.

Alexa finished up her makeup and walked toward the food dispenser. "AI, bagel with peanut butter to go, please."

Behind a thin glass, a thick glob of green goo spit out of the food nozzle. It lay motionless for a half of a second before it began to take shape. First, the color changed from deep green to a pale brown, then the shape rounded and grew solid and finally the hole in the middle formed and the brown layer of chunky peanut butter appeared. The glass slid open, and Alexa reached in and grabbed it and began eating it at once as she walked toward the door.

She knew she was foolish. Even though she knew better, there was a part of her that wanted to believe that the programs on the vidscreens were right, that love could conquer all. But her experiences with her visions and her talents had taught her, time and again, that life was a lot more complex than what you saw on a vidscreen program.

Alexa also knew full well that Runners were never pardoned from their sentence. 17 had been a Runner for a very long time. Short of becoming a Runner herself, she was never really going to be able to interact with 17 for more than a few minutes. It was one thing to work in the docks; it was another to become a Runner. That was something she absolutely refused to do. It would kill her parents. Besides, she had heard that female Runners never lasted long out in the Barrens, and no one ever volunteered to be a Runner, they would probably lock her up, think her insane.

Alexa exited her apartment and headed for the people mover. She started walking down the stairs. She hated taking elevators when she could walk herself. She needed the exercise anyway. There were so few opportunities to exercise and stay healthy in the Upper Lowers.

Alexa had read in her studies of ancient history that not long before migration, people mover shuttles had been installed in most cities in the world. They were an attempt at dealing with the dwindling oil supplies and streets overcrowded with cars. Most of the first generation of migration had never owned a car, and since there were none after migration began, the memory of automobiles had gradually faded into the ether of memory and history. The place where all obsolete technologies and experiences disappear to in time.

There were a few air cars and emergency vehicles of course, but those were either run by central security or belonged to powerful Uppers. Even in the Uppers, most people walked along the sky bridges, or took the sky bridge trams.

A strange scent came to her nose. It was the smell of summer. She didn't know how she knew that since she had never experienced summer before. It was the smell of endless forests and fields of grass. Of sprinklers on lawns and the chlorine scent of a pool. It was a smell of childhood, someone else's childhood. Some part of her knew she saw a sliver of memory, a slice of the ancient past, a time before migration. She wondered whose memory it could possibly be.

She reached the bottom of the stairs and walked out of the building. Her timing had been perfect, and the people mover pulled up just as she arrived, despite the odd hour. As she boarded the people mover, she took a few deep breaths and focused on the olfactory memory fragment. Controlling her breathing was something she had learned early on as a means to explore her flashes. No one had told her to do it; it simply seemed like the right thing to do. With each breath, she felt a kind of lightness begin to come over her. She was there, and yet not there. Alexa was perfectly capable of functioning in the real world while she dove deep into her impressions.

Children, several of them, mostly boys but a few girls, appeared in her mind's eye. Some were hiding as if afraid for their lives, but there was laughter and joy in their eyes. This was some kind of game. One child, in particular, was seeking out the others and when he found them, they ran to some sort of silver object and kicked it. Sometimes they weren't fast enough, and the boy seeking them out touched the silver object and then the other children had to sit down. The bizarre ritual seemed to occur over and over again until the boy seeking the others had made all the other children sit.

"What a strange ritual," Alexa said to no one in particular.

Despite the hour, there were several others on the people mover. It occurred to her that engineers and sanitation workers worked odd hours. Someone had to. Each gave Alexa furtive glances. But, after they had investigated the source, they turned their attention back to their tablets or whatever their interest was.

Her thoughts returned to the strange ritual. Where had the memory come from? It had to be very old, because even with all of her interest in ancient pre-migration history, she had never heard of such a thing. There were only a handful of people left in the city that were old enough to be children before migration. A thought occurred to her, could it be 17? He was probably old enough to be that child. She grew excited, perhaps he did share her gift and was reaching out to her with this memory rather than allowing her to probe his mind.

Alexa smiled and took another deep breath, releasing her exhaustion from only a partial night's sleep. She leaned her head back so that she was facing the roof of the people mover. She wanted to close her eyes but instead, they caught a glimpse of a poster. It was one of those standard propaganda posters that she disliked. "Everyone Must Share and Care for Our City and Do Their Part," the main headline of the poster read. There was the image of a smiling sanitation worker picking up garbage on a street corner. It was strange though, what in migration was the poster doing on the interior roof of a people mover? It didn't seem like very effective propaganda if it was in a place where no one could see it.

Alexa looked closer at the image, and she felt intuitively, that there was something malevolent about this poster. There was power hidden in it, and its location was certainly not an accident. She felt the poster watching her and felt a cold chill down her spine. It was the same feeling she had in high school when she knew, just absolutely knew that one of the boys were undressing her with his eyes. She hated skimming high school boys' thoughts, they were disgusting and always made her feel dirty. The poster was worse. It made her feel violated, as if someone had torn off all her clothes and left her naked on the people mover for all to see.

It was calling to her, beckoning her without saying a single word, without changing at all. She wanted to stand and put her hand on it, to feel its warmth. Part of her wanted to give in, to be drawn into that poster and lost in its vile promises, but she couldn't even understand what it was promising. Everyone must do their part; its core message played in loops in her mind. It was drawing her in, taking her as its own, the message filling her with ideas and thoughts about what she ought to do and where she should go. It wanted so badly for her to go somewhere.

"No," she yelled and briefly elicited the attention of a few other passengers of the people mover.

She shifted back to her mind's voice, the one she could use to speak outward without using her mouth. The poster was drawing her in harder now. A black hole. The eyes of the sanitation worker on the poster glowed.

"I will do my part," she said in her mind's voice. "I'll tear you down and throw you in the garbage where you can't hurt anyone." She mustered her will together and sent those thoughts deep into the eyes of the sanitation worker, striking at it with all the ferocity of her focus. Her will was a flaming lance, she felt a kind of red power leave her mind and thrust itself at the poster.

3.

Screams filled the cramped space. Pain illuminated the darkness. Rage quickened in her bosom. Then a necessary disconnection. This one was powerful. But she did not understand her strength, and so, there was still time to consume her. Miranda was hungry.

A cruel smile turned up the corners of her mouth. Recycling, yes, Alexa Turon was a perfect candidate. She would provide power and strength and when Miranda was finished with her, she would join her other children.

4.

Before her eyes, the poster vanished. It occurred to Alexa that the voice she had heard just before drifting off to sleep had suggested that there were others out there with her abilities. Was the maker of that poster the same as the voice she had heard? She didn't think so; the tone of the poster was different. The poster must have been some kind of psychic projection.

The people mover came to a stop at the entrance to the docks. Alexa stepped off and entered.

When she descended the stairs, she saw pure chaos. Someone had kicked the hornet's nest. Runners, inspectors, security, and even a few of the Recycled were rushing back and forth across the dock. Every single platform was up, dressing Runners in their EnViro suits. She started to try and count the number of Runners emerging from their tubes but gave up quickly; there were far too many to count.

She made her way through the flurry of people and entered her office, grabbed her tablet for inspection, and turned to walk toward her usual station. She looked down to her tablet. On the front screen was a message indicating that standard paperwork for Runner procedure was not required and that an expedited form was required for use in this particular instance. Alexa frowned, did that mean things were going to be that busy?

"AI, just how many Runners are in activation?"

"All of them." said a voice behind.

Alexa whirled around to find the owner of the voice.

"Mr. Dean, oh... I didn't realize you were there, I..."

"It's Lieutenant Dean, Ms. Turon. I expect you to remember my rank as well as my name."

"Oh, I'm so sorry Sir, it won't happen again. But Lieutenant Sir, did you say all of them?"

Dean frowned, Alexa could skim that he was annoyed at the misuse of his rank. "Orders come down from the Top. Daniels himself ordered the entire Runnercore activated."

"But why? Did he give a reason?"

"When orders come, we don't question them, Ms. Turon. We simply obey them."

"But all the Runners..." she said mostly to herself.

"Well Ms. Turon, there have only been a few instances in history when all the Runners were activated, so I bet we can guess what's going on."

Dean waited for Alexa to respond with a gasp or some sort of shocked surprised, but instead, she simply listened intently. Alexa skimmed his mind and saw that he was caught a bit off guard by her behavior. She would have to do better to emulate surprise in the future. People became uncomfortable if she never acted to their expectations.

"The last time any city activated all of the Runners was when Mex fell, if that's any indication," he continued.

He paused for effect, still waiting on her surprised gasp, but it didn't come.

"So a city has fallen?"

She already knew this was coming, the fallen city was the most striking image from her dream, and it seemed one of those rare straightforward images. It made her feel a bit queasy, but she didn't doubt it was true for one instant.

"Seems like it might be the case."

"So why activate all the Runners, then?"

"Cause when a city falls, a war comes."

"War?"

"Yeah, a war for all the salvage. Do you have any idea how many decades of resources are in one collapsed city? Hell, I bet you could get a whole century's worth of the basic stuff and a few centuries' worth of the advanced stuff. Solidsonium isn't easy to synthesize you know, now that we don't have moon fragments lying around."

Alexa frowned, when she thought of a city falling, she thought of all the people who were killed, not about the resources that could be found pillaging the city.

"So who are we going to war with?" Alexa asked.

Her lips sagged further down into a frown like melting butter merging into the bottom of a saucer. War was such a stupid thing that human beings did. Of all the history she read, war was the thing she hated learning about most.

"No one knows what's happening. This is all just speculation, of course. Major Daniels doesn't reveal much of anything until he feels the time is appropriate. But obviously, activating so many Runners has to mean something, and pictures are floating around the infosphere of Langeles in ruins. Looks like one of the Senators might have leaked it. I saw one this morning with the words 'The End is Nigh' plastered over the top of the image. It's making the usual rounds through everyone's tablets and vidscreens. Can't stop the blogs."

"Is there another city nearby?"

Alexa had never seen another city up close. She was far too young.

"There's a rumor floating around about that. Apparently 17 saw a runner by the Langeles ruins. But I don't think anyone knows which one it might be."

"17?" Alexa felt her frown turning to a smile. She couldn't help it. "Is...is he back?"

"Nah, he is going to be out for gods know how long now. Why?"

"Nothing, I..." Alexa looked for something to shift the conversation. "Can't we just share salvage with the other city? I mean, why does there have to be war?"

Dean laughed. Was she mistaken, or did he really think she was joking? She skimmed his mind again and felt uncomfortable.

"Oh... you're serious. I mean... it's just that... well, no two cities have ever shared anything like that since migration began."

"Well, why can't we share now?"

Dean was silent. Alexa listened to his silence. He was wondering, why does this little girl always ask such silly questions? Is she really that naïve? No wonder Marty can't stand her.

Dean said, "You'll understand when you're older."

Alexa's face flickered. "When I am older? What is that supposed to mean?"

"Never mind that, Miss Turon, we've talked too much already. Get to your station. There are over a dozen Runners in the queue waiting to be inspected over there."

Alexa eyed him a little longer; she knew exactly what this one was thinking without skimming anything. She hated it. She was young, she was a woman, and she was out of place down here. Mr., or Lieutenant Dean, or whatever he wanted to call himself, had very little respect for her. Women, in general, weren't treated very well in security, the docks, or any other places like them. There was some sort of notion that women couldn't really be protectors or scientists or anything that involved complex thinking. Even the female senators were occasionally looked down upon, although, part of that was because of that horrible Senator Reevas, who gave all women a bad name.

She sighed, turned from Dean, and headed in the direction of her station. She could tell it was going to be a long night. She made a quick detour to the food dispenser.

"Coffee, please," she told the machine.

"Please specify temperature and strength," responded the dispenser AI.

"50 degrees Celsius and extra strong, please."

The machine's front panel closed and a light switched on. The coffee cup began to print, and Alexa absentmindedly watched the machine work. She needed to ask one of her friends in engineering school how these things worked. It was easy to take things for granted living in this city, but Alexa was always curious about the inner workings of things. The cup finished printing, and green goop dropped in the cup, turned black and grew until it became coffee. The clear front panel circled open, and the sweet smell of coffee drifted up into her nostrils. She had never had the genuine article, but everyone seemed to think that for the most part, the food dispensers did a good job in mimicking taste, though there was always the hint of algae in the flavor.

Alexa took a sip and walked to her station. It wasn't far from the dispenser, and the small podium gave her a place to put down her coffee. A dozen or so Runners stood in their undergarments, waiting for her inspection. She noted, quite clearly, that none of them were naked as 17 had been.

Before her thoughts could turn back to 17 for the umpteenth time, she started her work. There was just too much to be done to think about anything else.

"Runner 6911, please step forward."

A towering man with dark skin and deep brown eyes stepped forward. His biceps were almost as big as Alexa's head, and he stood almost half a meter taller than her. She was almost shocked at his size and moved around him in circles, checking his vitals and scanning.

The huge man said nothing. His face was stone. His profile said he had been in alcove sleep for almost a century. Alexa couldn't imagine what it must be like to spend that long in an alcove.

"Looks like you are good to go. Please step forward onto the platform. Runner 6272, please step forward."

This time a petite woman moved toward her. This was only the second time that Alexa had administered to a female runner. She had heard that there were so few of them largely because of the weight of the EnViro suits. She wasn't sure she believed that. It seemed much more likely that women could sleep with a Supreme Justice or a Senator to get out of Runner duty. But she had no doubt the suits did prove difficult to operate for someone as small as this woman, even with the strength augmentation injections. She wasn't sure she could operate a suit herself.

This women's face was stolid and unyielding. There was no doubt in Alexa's mind she was tough as nails. Her profile indicated that she had been on several dozen missions and only in stasis for a few months. Clearly she was considered a valuable asset or she wouldn't have been so active.

Alexa combed the line of Runners behind Runner 6272. Runners certainly came in all shapes and sizes. She turned her attention back to her task and began checking 6272's vitals.

"Hello, little one."

Alexa looked around to see who was standing nearby. Lieutenant Dean was watching her closely, no doubt he was making sure she didn't screw anything up.

"I'm sorry, Mr. Dean, did you say something?" Alexa asked.

"Again, it's Lieutenant Dean, Alexa; you must address me formally."

"I'm sorry, Sir... I just—"

"I don't recall saying anything, now focus on your job."

Alexa turned her attention back to the Runner standing in front of her. Her head was starting to buzz.

"I'm sorry my dear, I recognize this is not the greatest time to contact you in this way, but I need to meet with you right away, things are beginning to spin out of control, and we need your assistance."

Again, Alexa turned around to address Lieutenant Dean, but his attention was focused elsewhere. Where could the voice be coming from? It certainly wasn't coming from Runner 6272.

"The voice is coming from in your mind, little one. I am transmitting to you."

Alexa's eyes grew wide with fear.

"You have nothing to fear, but we need you here with us."

Alexa felt a wave of calm and certainy. Her muscles relaxed and she knew for certain that she needed to do as the voice said.

"But how do I get out of work?" she spoke aloud.

Dean turned on her quickly, "By finishing, young lady. I will have you know that... I think... I think..." He spoke to himself. His eyes glazed and unfixed. "Yes exactly, it seems I always have to babysit her, so why would I want her down here during a crisis? You're right, she can't even get my name right." His focus snapped back to Alexa. "I think it's time for you to head home. You're more of a hindrance than a help, anyway."

"But Sir, I was..."

"Alexa, I do not have time for your nonsense today. Look around these docks. What do you see?"

"A lot of Runners?"

"Yes exactly, I have a schedule to keep and look how many Runners there are? It must be every single last one. Now how in the world am I supposed to keep some semblance of order in this place if you show up and get in everyone's way?"

"I..."

Several Runners in her queue were now watching her and Dean. A puzzled look went over all their faces as Dean pushed her out of the way and grabbed the tablet out of her hand to finish the inspections himself.

"Go on, get out of here and come back when things aren't so crazy."

Alexa followed orders and moved toward the exit. She wondered briefly if he would call her back the moment he realized she was gone. As she exited through the security section at the entrance to the docks, she tried to summon the voice back.

"Now what I am supposed to do?" she thought as hard as she could, trying to transmit her thinking to whatever direction the voice may have come from.

"Well first of all, young one, don't transmit your thoughts so hard like that, it makes my head hurt. Your thoughts should be just as relaxed as they always are, but we will talk about that in your training. Secondly, you must come to the ancient Library in the Lowers. We are waiting for you there."

"The Library? But that area is dangerous."

"We will gently suggest to any individuals in the area that they may have business elsewhere. You will have few, if any, obstacles reaching here. I suggest you take the L and M sky bridges to 41st and 4th, and then descend down to ground level at that point. You will only have to walk two blocks in the Lowers. You will find us down in the archives under the first level. Please be quick my dear, time is of the essence."

Chapter 15
The Uprising

Jose sat in a cell. His body was propped in the corner and held up by the gravity of the angle in which he had been placed. He had not moved.

The room was dim, and the smell of body odor was strong. It lingered from the bodies of a thousand broken men and women. Only a bench with a shabby old mattress and a toilet were in the space. The walls were covered in names, briefly etched obituaries of the many men and women who had spent their last moments there before being exiled to the Runnercore. The cell was a waystation, a path to another life, a path to hell.

His head hurt. He reached up and felt the rough exterior of a bandage. A regen patch, which meant that no matter how hard the SOs had struck him, it was repairing all the damage. Just above the dull thud of pain in his brow, he began to feel the tiny tingling of regeneration at work.

He was in a world of shit now. No scapegoats. No Liza or Aaron to take the fall for him. He deserved this. He was a coward. His fate was clear. In a brief moment of madness, he had assaulted a security officer. Now he would spend the rest of his days as a Runner. What would his wife and son do? Convicted Runners weren't compensated for their work. They would have to dip into their deepest savings to survive. So much for the possibility of a better life. He had fucked it all up. He deserved it. He had been running from the past his whole life, and now finally it had caught him.

He raised his hands to his eyes to catch the tears and wept. Deep, wrenching sobs echoed through the empty cells. Only metal and stone gave witness to his grief.

Suicide occurred to him briefly. If he did it now, there was a small chance he wouldn't be recycled. He looked around the dim room and saw nothing that would be useful for taking his own life.

He lifted himself onto the bench and turned to lay down. He supposed this was his karma. His tongue had not been enough. Jose turned to the past. There was nowhere else to turn. There was no future now, only running.

His ancient agonies, buried deep in his heart, rose to the surface. It had all begun with a book, that damned library book in the Lower Library. Reading that thing had been the biggest mistake of his life.

2.

"Jose... Jose? Your alarm's going off again. How many times are you going to hit snooze, Miho?"

Jose rolled over onto his back and stretched. He blinked and looked around the room. The alarm was still wailing, but he made no immediate effort to turn it off.

"Jose." His mother entered the room now, moved over to the tablet and turned the alarm off. "How in the hell can you sleep through this thing. It would wake the dead. In fact, I think I can hear your Abuela turning over in her grave. Now get up and get ready for school. This is only your third week! You know they report attendance records to future employers."

Jose said, "Yes, Mama." He took a deep breath and swept his legs over the edge of his bed, and his mother began rummaging through his closet. She pulled some clothes out and threw them on the bed next to him.

"Here, these will look handsome on you."

"Mama, I can pick out my clothes you know, I'm 19, and I'm not in grade school anymore."

"What and have my boy go to Trade school with all his clothes wrinkled? I don't think so. What will people think of me?"

Jose rolled his eyes.

"Don't you roll your eyes at me, young man. You're the one who can't even wake up to an alarm. Now, breakfast is on the table. I want you to make sure you eat up quickly, because Liza called and she and Aaron are already on their way over."

His mother left the room, and quickly he dressed and went to the kitchen. Eggs and a bagel fresh from the food dispenser waited for him. He jumped into the chair at the table and shoveled the food into his mouth.

His mother walked into the kitchen and sat down. "Hey now, not so fast, you're going to give yourself a stomach ache. You still have a few minutes before Liza and Aaron get here."

"Sorry," Jose said, the eggs spilling out of his mouth a little. "Where's Dad?"

His mother frowned, and the creases in her forehead momentarily revealed her true age. After her annual alcove visit, she looked quite a bit younger, but age was never truly gone for someone in the Lowers.

"He has to work an extra shift. There was an accident down in sanitation. Luis... he...well he won't be working ever again."

A heavy silence passed between them. Jose stopped eating for a moment.

Jose let his mouth make several silent attempts first, finally working up the courage and asking, "What happened?"

"It's nothing he did. It was those damned Uppers again; they're always taking advantage of us. You're old enough to know how it is."

"Is he hurt? Luis, I mean?"

"Luis is... well, he's a Runner now... or at least he will be in a few days."

"Oh."

Jose took a few more bites of eggs, then played with the rest with his fork. He traced the lines around the shapes of his food. "Is Dad going to get overtime, at least?"

His mother didn't say anything, but he could tell by the look on her face that there would be no overtime. "Things are as they are, Jose. There is nothing we can do about them. They have been that way since the beginning of migration and probably since the beginning of time."

"But, isn't there anything Dad can do? I mean this is the 3rd person this year who's been sentenced to the Runnercore and two others in sanitation have been seriously injured."

Jose's mom stood up and walked toward her son. She crouched down and stared him straight in the face. "That's why, Miho, I need you to finish Trade school and get a job outside of the Lowers. You have to get out of here before it's too late. Your father and I, well I don't think much can be done to change our fate but you, you have a chance to live a better life."

Jose looked down toward his feet. In truth, he was struggling with trade school. Information technology and virtual interface repair were not exactly the career he had dreamed of, but he and Liza had made a vow to finish the program.

His mother grabbed his chin and lifted it, forcing him to meet her gaze. "Promise me you'll finish, Jose."

He nodded. "Yes Mama, I'll finish. Liza wouldn't let me quit anyway."

His mother smiled warmly. "That Liza's a good girl, you know. You should marry her."

"Mama. Come on. We're just friends."

This wasn't the whole truth. Jose was in love with Liza, but he was pretty sure she didn't return those feelings.

There was a knock at the door, and his mother stood and went to answer it. Jose gobbled down the last of his eggs, ran to the living room to grab his tablet and bolted toward the door. Liza and Aaron were standing just outside the entrance with his mother standing just in front of them.

"Sleepyhead here only woke up ten minutes ago."

Both Aaron and Liza shook their heads in disapproval with big grins on their faces.

"Oh Jose, when will you learn?" said Liza, her grin spreading ear to ear.

Jose loved her smile, her brown eyes, and thin face. He studied the shape of her thick lips whenever she wasn't looking. He could feel the red trying to creep onto his cheeks. "Yeah well... let's just go."

His mother grabbed his arm and swooped in for a hug.

"Goodbye, Miho." She loosened her grip and stepped back. "Come home right after class, okay? Your father and I are both working second shift tonight so we won't be here when you get back, but I want you to come straight home."

"Mama, I'm almost an adult, I think I'll be okay."

His mother turned her head up toward Liza. "You keep him and Aaron out of trouble."

"Of course, Mrs. Garcia. I'll walk him all the way to the front door."

"Good girl, Liza." His mother gave her a warm smile. "But I think it's usually the boy who walks to the girl to the front door." His mother gave him a quick wink.

For a brief moment, Jose thought he saw red in Liza's cheeks but it was so quick, he was sure he had imagined it.

His mother said, "Now go on, go make something of yourself."

3.

Hours later, the three friends exited the trade school. It was well after designated dark. The brightness of the shield lingered. A child born after the beginning of migration would have known nothing of the true darkness that night can bring. Still, the stars twinkled and glimmered through the orange tinge of the shield and the two portions of the quarter moon shimmered as if viewed from beneath the surface of a great sea.

City security patrolled the streets of the Lowers throughout the night but were most present just after designated dark to push back against the Lower gangs and the drug dealers. Most of the gangs were fairly harmless, a few adolescences trying to establish some sort of family on the street to make up for the fact that their one at home was in shambles, but some were dangerous and were a prime recruiting pool for the Runnercore. A few gangs were rumored to be in the employ of Uppers, but Jose wasn't sure if that was true, though he could understand why it could be of value to those who lived in the towering skyscrapers.

Liza, Aaron, and Jose always took the route that went past the library to avoid the gangs. The people mover took them most of the way home, but they always got off early because the stop that took them closest to home dropped them in the heart of gang territory. The library was considered a high-security area, and though the trio feared city security almost as much as the gangs, as long as they avoided security directly, they were usually fine.

"Let's stop in the library tonight, I have to pee," said Liza.

"Again? Why didn't you go before we left?" asked Jose.

"Um, because I didn't have to go then."

Jose rolled his eyes.

"The library's closed after seven, you know that, Liza." replied Aaron.

"Well, let's find a way in, I really need to go."

Aaron said, "Just go out here. Find a bush or something."

"Yeah, I do it all the time," said Jose.

"I can't, you ass, I am a girl, and you know those security guys will use any excuse to..." she stopped mid-sentence. Liza didn't need to elaborate.

"Alright, alright," said Jose "Let's check the windows, I'll bet one of them will be unlocked."

The library was nearly a full city block in size. In front stood two faded and crumbling statues of some creatures that had long become unrecognizable. They looked like they had once perhaps been a stray dog, but Jose doubted they were something so scraggly. When the city had lifted at the beginning of migration, many structures suffered a great deal of damage. In truth, the early parts of migration were terrible times, many people died and were crushed under rubble, and more died from infection due to injuries. Hospitals were always full and the alcoves were not yet in wide usage. But this was an age long before these three teens, and now only a few hints of those difficult times had remained.

Aaron and Jose, watchful for security forces, waited while Liza checked each of the window wells that led to the basement of the library. Grass had grown up over some of the old windows since maintenance in the Lowers was of little priority. The Uppers and Mids only bothered with maintenance when a building became unsound, and since the library was only a few levels high, it technically qualified as part of the Lowers, though there was an Upper, some keeper, who occasionally ventured inside to remove certain books or records. The current city library was on the 35th floor of a skyscraper in the Upper Mids.

"Over here, this one's open."

Liza pulled aside some of the rubble to pry open the window. It was just big enough for the three of them to squeeze through.

"Are you coming?"

"You're the one that has to pee," said Aaron.

"Yeah but this old place is creepy at night, I mean look at those weird-ass statues."

"Just go Liza, we'll wait out here for you. Someone has to watch for security," said Aaron.

"Yeah, you don't want us to get caught snooping around this place at night, do you? You know how fast they would turn the three of us into Runners? They look for people just like us, we're perfect candidates, and I heard they just lost a bunch of Runners to a storm last week on the vidscreens."

"Well, I am not going in there alone, so one of you needs to come with me," said Liza.

"Ugh, fine, I'll do it," replied Jose. "Aaron, you stay here and if someone comes around looking for us, just leave, we won't come back out until we see you standing here."

"Will do, El Capitan."

"Don't call me that," said Jose, "I hate it when you call me that."

"Well you are the one always giving orders around here," replied Aaron.

"I beg to differ," said Jose and nodded his head in the direction of Liza, whose head was already inside the window and butt was sticking out.

"Well ain't that a sight," said Aaron to Jose with a wink.

Jose rolled his eyes at Aaron, pretending ignorance, and watched as Liza disappeared into the building. He followed quickly and quietly, making sure that the window shutter didn't slam or make any loud noises.

Being alone with Liza always made Jose nervous. His stomach tied in knots, his head swelled and contracted, and he could feel his heartbeat in every part of his body. Yet, she gave no indication that she felt the same way. Jose spent many sleepless lying awake. wondering if he should tell Liza how he felt. He feared driving her away, feared losing her altogether, and so night after night he renewed his decision to hide what was in his heart.

Jose was much bigger then Liza, and just barely fit through the window. Liza was small and petite, but she hid that fact with her strong will. She had given him no warning of the sharp drop he would face once he was halfway through the window. Jose fell face first into cold and cracking tiles, banging his elbows and sending a shockwave up through his funny bone.

"Watch that first step, it's a doozy," said Liza.

Jose looked up at a smiling Liza. He felt a lump form in his throat, and he began to choke on his words. Her beautiful brown eyes sparkled against her dark skin and dark hair. Her eyes always hypnotized Jose when he looked directly into him. He looked away from her face and focused on lifting himself up.

The room was filled with endless aisles of books. But there was a bit of chaos. Some of the shelves were leaning haphazardly in one direction or another. Some were only half full, and most of the books looked withered and ancient.

He groaned. "Uh... You should have told me before I stuck my head in the window," said Jose.

"Well, I thought a big strong man like yourself could handle it. After all, a little girl like me had no problem."

Was she flirting with him? His heart leaped with just a tinge of hope, but he also felt queasy.

"Let's just find the bathroom and get out of here before security comes around."

"Why the rush, Jose? Afraid to be alone with me?"

Jose blushed and started to speak. Suddenly a loud thud coming from a few aisles over made both Jose and Liza jump.

Liza grabbed Jose and pulled him down on to the ground, crouching close together behind a bookshelf. They were kissing distance; faces pressed close. Jose, who had never been face to face with Liza before, suddenly became aware he was looking directly into her eyes.

In a whisper, Liza asked, "What was that?"

"I don't know. It sounded like a book falling to the ground, but maybe someone's here."

Jose's heart was pounding in his chest; he wanted nothing more than to kiss Liza. Her lips were only centimeters away, and he licked his own. He stared into her eyes, and to his surprise, she seemed to be staring right back. What was only a few moments had seemed to Jose like a perfect eternity of joy. She must feel something for him, he was sure of it. He was going to tell her, going to reveal his feelings and kiss her. He opened his mouth to tell her everything, to profess his love for her, but she spoke first.

"I'll go check it out," said Liza.

The thought of her being caught pulled Jose out of his trance.

"No! You aren't going over there, what if it's security? What if they catch us?"

"Well if they were close enough to drop the book, don't you think they would have already grabbed us?"

Jose thought about it and realized that Liza was right. If it was security, they would have already been in trouble. Liza stood and moved quickly over to where the book had fallen. He saw himself following her without hesitation, though he didn't remember standing.

No one was in the room, and there was no sign of any movement.

"I think it's okay. I think maybe it was just these old bookshelves are shedding books. Maybe the books were ready to fall, and when we came in the room we bumped a shelf or something," said Liza.

"Yeah, maybe you're right." Jose wasn't whispering anymore.

"Oh, and there's the bathroom. I'll be right back."

Jose knew he had to tell her how he felt. Every time they went to trade school, the other guys hit on her. She had dated many guys in high school but never very long. She was everything to him.

He saw it then, the book that would later bring an end to their happy trio, a book that would change the way they thought about the world forever. It lay face up staring at him, and looking back, he could have sworn it was breathing. The title, *A People's History of the United States*, intrigued him. Jose had heard of the United States; he knew that Manhatsten had once been a part of it before migration, and the thought of learning a little more about the history of Manhatsten interested him. Jose, in many ways, would have loved to go to scholar school if he had the opportunity. He had a kind of thirst and passion for knowledge that was almost as strong as the way he felt for Liza.

He picked up the book, a number of the pages were torn or missing, and the book itself seemed pretty fragile but he riffled through the pages a few times, and a few passages caught his interest.

"Wow, so many books."

Jose jumped he hadn't heard Liza coming out of the bathroom.

"Did I scare you?"

"What? Uh, no, it's just I saw this book and was skimming it a little."

"What is it?" She leaned over him and gently put her hand on the small of his back. It sent a shockwave of emotion through Jose, and he forced himself to act like it was no big deal.

"It's called, *A People's History of the United States*."

"The United States? Isn't that ancient history, like before migration history?"

"Yeah, I think so."

"Well, that makes sense."

"What does?"

"You realize where we are, right? I mean you almost knocked over the sign when I scared you, and you jumped three meters into the air."

"I did not jump three meters in the air," Jose protested.

"You did, but that's not the point." Liza winked at him and gave him a big smile. She was perfectly aware of the effect she had on boys, and it frustrated Jose a little. "The point is, El Capitan, that we're in the archives. All these books are hidden from the public. Just imagine the kind of stuff back here, stuff that no one has read for hundreds of years."

Jose's eyes grew wide with wonder, and he looked down at the book in his hands again. He turned it over with a kind of reverence.

"Maybe we should get Aaron. I bet he would love to check this place out."

Before Jose could even finish his sentence, Liza was already over at the window well motioning for Aaron to come down. He did so quickly, and unlike Jose, he didn't go face first and didn't hit his elbows on the cracked tile floor. He stood up and started looking around.

"Aaron, we're in the archives," said Liza.

"The what?"

"The archives," this time Jose replied. "We're in the room where all the books are kept that they don't let anyone check out anymore."

"Wow, really?" Aaron glanced around.

"Yeah, and look at this one that Jose found." Liza grabbed the book from Jose's hands, though not too forcefully, and handed it over to Aaron.

"*A People's History of the United States*," Aaron mouthed the words aloud. "What's the United States?"

"You idiot, didn't you pay any attention in high school history?" said Liza. "The United States was the country that Manhatsten came out of before migration. This is an entire history book about the world before migration, all the stuff they didn't teach us in class. Isn't that freaking amazing?"

"Let's take it," said Jose.

"What?" said Aaron.

"Yeah, let's take and read it and then we can return it next week," Liza agreed.

Aaron didn't argue, he turned the book over in his hands and then began to flip through pages.

"Be gentle, I don't think it's in very good condition after all this time," said Jose.

They heard a noise outside of the room and down the hall. This time the noise was clearly footsteps heading right for the door to the archives.

"Shit, let's get out of here," said Liza.

Without much of a word, the three of them scrambled back up the window well, as quickly and quietly as possible. They had no idea who was headed into the archive, but regardless, they had been in a place that was forbidden to the public and were terrified at what getting caught might mean. Jose hid the book inside his jacket, and the three of them moved back into the streets toward their respective homes.

"That was close," said Aaron.

Liza said, "Yeah, but it sure was exciting, wasn't it?" She was practically jumping up and down.

"I didn't much care for the excitement, but I sure as hell want to read this book," replied Jose.

"Since you found it, you can read it first, but don't take too long, I want to read it too," said Liza.

Aaron said, "Yeah, I agree, read that thing quick. You shouldn't keep a lady waiting, after all."

The trio walked several more blocks, mostly in silence, back to their apartments. There was an eerie quiet in the streets, which was unusual for that time of night. Only the crickets chirped.

4.

Historian's Note to the Text:

Readers of this volume are likely familiar with the events of March 7th, 1235 AC. This event, otherwise known as the last great uprising of Manhatsten, is important because it set in motion a series of events that contributed heavily to the conflict between Manhatsten and the Children of Gaia. Several individuals who were directly impacted by this event became important much later in history.

Little is actually known of what happened directly after the acquisition of the book *A People's History of the United States* from the Lower library, but piecing together several narratives from the descendants of the event, we were able to ascertain the following:

1. The book, over the course of several weeks, was copied and distributed throughout the Welders Forge and the Sanitation department.

2. Copies of this book were made using the printing rations of Aaron Hernandez.

3. Labor conditions within both the Welders Forge and the Sanitation department were extremely dangerous, resulting in numerous casualties leading up to the distribution of the book.

4. Widespread protests erupted on the streets on March 6th, 1235 AC, for which security detail was completely unprepared to deal with.

6. Runners were commissioned to quell the protests, a sign of just how serious it was.

7. According to several video recordings of the court proceedings that followed a series of mass arrests, the book was not a significant contributing factor: it was as old Earthers used to say, 'the straw that broke the camel's back.'

The mass arrests that followed the protests were well-documented and additional recordings can be found at Library 7181 in sector 2111. However, for the purpose of this historical narrative we will focus on the three most important individuals that became directly involved with the end of the migration period and led the way into our current historical period.

Matron Mariposa Phillips 833.11.11 I.S.

━━━━✝✝⫫⫫⫫⫫━━━━

5.

Jose opened his eyes. He couldn't say why exactly he had opened them. The stillness of the air pressed up against his body. He blinked a few times and listened to the beat of his heart in his ears. He sat up and looked around. Why was he awake? He looked over to his bedside at the red numbers on his alarm. They read 4:58 a.m.

A low rustling sound like crumpling paper broke the silence. Jose thought it might be a rat. They would have to put out the recycler traps again. He stood and went to the bathroom, relieved himself and then turned and sat down on the bed.

He looked around the room again. Something was wrong. Something was out of place. But the dark corners of the room did not permit his vision to penetrate the shadows, was there something in those corners? The shapes of the shadows cast by the soft glow of the EnViro dome through the windows began to coalesce into something recognizable. It was moving.

Jose shivered. Slowly he rose from the bed and walked over toward the light switch. He dared not query the AI and give away what he was up to. If there was something or someone there, he wanted to catch them off guard.

There was a sniffle.

Jose switched on the lights, like some wizard attempting to reveal a creature of darkness. The thing rose to full height and charged. It was on Jose before he could react, squeezing him tight, taking his wind. He recognized the scent.

Jose said, "What in the hell are you doing here? You scared the shit out of me."

"They took him. They took him and my family, and they're looking for me now too."

"Liza, what in the hell are you talking about? Who took who?"

"Aaron. They took him. My mom, she tried to hold them off, tried to stop them but they beat her Jose, they beat her badly. Her whole face was covered in blood and my dad, they tased him until he lost consciousness. But they told me to run. Told me to find a safe place."

"Liza... I... who did this?"

"SOs. They found the book, Jose. It's all over the vidscreens. They are blaming the book for the protests. They are calling it an uprising. Sanitation is shut down. Aaron's face, my face, they are plastered all over the vidscreens and tablets."

"Gods."

Liza started weeping freely. She clenched him so tightly that he thought they would become one being. Jose had never wanted anything so bad in his entire life. He hated that it had to be because of something like this. He smelled her hair. It smelled like lavender. He held back his own tears. Then she lessened her grip and pulled back so that she was face to face with him. Her lovely brown eyes shone brightly despite the low light of the room.

She swallowed hard. It was audible. "I love you, Jose. I have always loved you. I don't know what is going to happen to us now, but I want you to know that."

She kissed him. He could feel the warmth of her lips and the tip of her tongue as it parted his lips. Then the kiss deepened as he embraced it. A warmth spread through him. Endless joy. She stopped and looked at him, just staring, waiting for his reply, waiting to know his truth.

"I love you too, Liza. Always have."

She smiled through her tears and lifted her hand to his cheek. She pushed him down on the bed. Her kisses made what she wanted very clear, and she began to undress him.

A high-pitched whine filled the air; it lasted but a second. Then a loud explosion sounded from below.

"Oh gods, they're here."

Quickly, both of them dressed. Muffled yelling and loud thumps drifted up from below.

Then, there were loud footsteps coming down the hall. Four men charged in through the door, armored in bulky riot gear.

Liza jumped up. There was no hesitation in her action. To Jose's surprise, two of the security forces were already on the floor. She had disarmed one of them and tasered two of them quickly. But Jose, who had never had a violent encounter in his life, found himself unable to move. He sat and watched as the two security guards fought to restrain Liza, as they hit her, as they tased her as she screamed. He watched as her body crumpled to the floor, limp and unmoving. They began to move toward him.

His father burst into the door and attacked the two standing security officers with a metal rod of some kind. Jose's father's face was already bloody. Both men cowered in the corner. Jose's father screamed at them in both Spanish and English, and despite their best efforts, both men could not get the rod away from his father.

Then from behind came four additional security personnel. Without hesitation, one of them smashed down hard against Jose's father's head. He fell to the floor like a sack of bricks and fresh blood began to flow from the bald patch on his head. Jose could tell, by the way he fell, by the way his body lay rigid against the floor, that he was already dead, that he would never speak to his father again.

He glanced again over at Liza, still unable to move, still frozen to the bed. For many years after he would curse his cowardice, curse his inability to act.

She was breathing. Her chest heaved up in down in a steady movement. One of the security personnel lifted his clear visor and eyed Jose.

"Kid, if you know what's good for you, you won't move a muscle. We're gonna take this girl in; she's a wanted woman. Now we're gonna bring you in for questioning too, and if you don't move, you may not end up a Runner like this one will."

Tears leaked out of the corners of his eyes, but he could not move. Fear held him. Fear smothered him and the cowardliness of that moment would haunt him for the remainder of his life. The silence of his tears rippled outwards to muffle every sound. He watched as they carried the limp body of Liza and then the corpse of his father out the door.

"Okay kid, let's go." One of the security detail prodded him in the back. Jose stood and wobbled. His legs, stiff as dried wood that had just begun to rot, almost gave out. He took a few steps forward until he reached the rim of the puddle of blood that was spreading out on the tile floor from his father's open head wound.

It was a great chasm. He could not bear to cross it, could not bear the sight of it. The way his father had fallen replayed over and over in his mind, it would in many nightmares for the rest of his life. He looked at the far shore of the puddle, where they had moved his father's body, where the streaks marked the passage, where the edge was no longer a neat dividing line between blood and floor.

"Come on, kid. Let's go." The voice was agitated, impatient.

Someone shoved him forward, and his left foot met the blood. He slipped. Jose began to fall. Behind him, the security detail did attempt to catch him, but missed. As his head crashed hard to the tile floor, he imagined that this is what his father had felt, that falling had been the last experience of his conscious mind. He felt the hard crash as the back of his head collided with the floor, and then all was black, and worlds and lives seemed no more.

6.

The bench was cold. Many eyes watched the proceedings. For the first time in over a century, cameras filled the courtroom. They too would soon approach the bench. There were so many people on trial for the uprising but there was just one sentence.

Several robbed individuals stood to pass judgment upon the swarm of protestors. But first, before all else were those who had planted the seed, who had germinated the resistance with the words of an ancient book. First Jose would watch Liza and Aaron's judgment. There was no doubt of the result. Only his own fate was in question. His love and his best friend would share the same sentence. A part of him wanted to be with Liza, to become a Runner as well, but part of him was terrified of that prospect. He was disgusted at his own cowardice.

Supreme Justice Allistair said, "And where did you find this book?"

"We found... it in the library," said Liza. Her voice was hoarse and soft, barely audible among the sea of whispers and whimpers.

"The Library? And the Librarian just let you check this one out, even though it was on the banned books list?"

"No sir, we... well... I really had to use... the bathroom, one night on the way home from school... and well... the window was open..."

"Isn't the library locked after designated dark?"

"Yes sir, but Liza really needed to use the bathroom and—" Aaron started. There was half-muffled laughter in the room. No one wanted to laugh, but something needed to ease the tension.

The Supreme Justice turned quickly toward Aaron, his eyes ablaze. "So the need to use the restroom allows you to break the law, young man?"

"No sir, of course, it doesn't, but we never meant for any of this to happen," answered Aaron.

"So you're saying you found this book just laying around?"

"Yes Sir, well, actually sir, it was in the archives, and we heard a noise, and when we investigated and the book was laying on the floor. Then we took it with us."

"So you stole it from the archives? You were aware that entry is forbidden to all but a select few scholars?"

Liza and Aaron nodded together silently.

"And it was just the two of you?"

Liza shot a quick glance over at Jose. It was a look that Jose would never forget. He knew she was telling him not to speak up, to go on with his life, that her life was over and there was nothing he could do about it. In that moment, he had absolute certainty that Liza loved him and he regretted all the time he had hesitated.

"No sir, it was just the two of us," Liza answered.

"So why, after you found out the book was forbidden, did you not turn it in?"

"Well sir, we were afraid that we would be sentenced to... to..."

"To the Runnercore?" The judge's voice grew even harsher.

Liza nodded again. Aaron was dead silent. Jose sat in the viewing area and watched in horror.

"Young lady, we do not sentence people to the Runnercore for youthful mischief. Being in an old building after hours would have, at most, earned you some community service. Minors are not automatically sent to the Runnercore. What is really troubling is what you decided to do with the forbidden book. How many copies did you distribute, again?"

A thin-mustached man in a SO uniform with a nametag that read O'Brien cleared his throat, "Sir, we found several dozen copies floating around the Lowers. Every individual who had a copy of the book has been arrested."

"I was asking the young lady," said Justice Marshall. The scorn in his voice was not reserved for those who had broken the law.

"Sir, we... we don't know how many. We just kept making copies and sharing it with our friends and family. It was... it was the first any of us had ever read of that part of ancient history... you know, before the migration. We just wanted to share it; we thought it was important."

"But, did it not occur to you that this book was banned for a reason? 27 people are dead, including your parents, because felt you needed to share this text by this..." Justice Allistair stopped and skimmed a moment through his data tablet. "...Zinn fellow. The entire Sanitation Department and Welders Forge went on strike, and the security forces had to be brought in to ensure our city's sewers didn't flood the whole city. Can you imagine what would happen to the city if our sewer system was destroyed, how that might threaten the lives of everyone in the city? Young lady, you and your friend, are guilty of starting a riot and endangering everyone in this city. That is, in fact, a crime worthy of being sentenced to the Runnercore." The judge's voice was just below shouting now.

Jose shuddered. He had already lost his father to this mess, and now he would lose the women he loved and his best friend. Every part of him screamed in horrible agony. The Supreme Justice might as well have sentenced Liza and Aaron to death, for he would never see either of them again. It would have been better for him to have been caught as well, better for him to be a Runner. Maybe then he would at least see Liza on occasion. He screamed, and everyone in the courtroom turned.

"It was me! Take me instead. Liza just covered for me. I swear she was guilty of nothing."

The Supreme Justice turned and looked at Liza. "Is this true, young lady?"

"No Sir, he had nothing to do with any of this."

"Did he read the text?"

"I don't believe so, Sir. I barely know him; he is just a boy from one of my classes. I think he has a crush on me. Please, your Honor, he isn't involved."

"No!" Jose screamed again. "No she is lying, this is all my fault, take me instead, and leave her alone."

"Take this young man and remove him from this courtroom," yelled the Supreme Justice. "Make sure he is properly questioned."

The security guards grabbed Jose by the arms and dragged him, kicking and screaming from the courtroom. Jose had lost everything all because of one stupid book. His life was nothing. He was nothing. That was the last time he ever saw Liza or Aaron.

7.

Jose waited in detention for several hours. Finally, the door opened and in stepped several security guards and Senator Tera Reevas. Jose sat waiting, not knowing what to say. The Senator was beautiful, almost as beautiful as Liza, and immediately he felt a sense of betrayal for the thought.

"I just thought you would like to know, the paperwork on your friends is already processed. They are officially a part of the Runnercore now, and you will never see them again." Senator Reevas was sneering. The broad wicked-ness of her expression ran through Jose's veins like ice. Why was she here? What business did a senator have with him?

"I also thought you might like to know that your father and the rest of the traitors to the city will not receive a funerary service. In fact, their bodies will be cast out into the Barrens to rot as a sign to all those who would threat-en our city.

Something in Jose's guts twisted. Agony and fury pushed on his heart and lungs.

"Did you have a copy of, or read that book?" Reevas asked.

Jose didn't answer; he couldn't make up his mind. What was the right course of action? He had thought about it a lot in the last few hours. If he became a Runner, it would hurt his remaining family. His mother was aging now; they had given up their rights to the alcoves because his parents decided to have two children. She wouldn't be able to support herself and his broth-er. On the other hand, if he became a Runner, maybe just maybe he could see Liza and Aaron, even if it was only once every few decades.

He made his decision. It was what Liza would want, and that was first in his heart.

"No, I lied, I was in love with that girl. I have been for a long time, but she barely knows I exist."

"Hmm, I think we ought to teach this one to Run as well, just in case. What do you think, Edwards?" She turned to one of her escorts.

"Senator, we don't have any available space left in the Runnercore, the trial filled the last empty alcoves down in the docks. We have completely re-plenished our numbers in the last few weeks."

Reevas frowned. "I suppose we could leave them in this cell 'til one of them dies in the Barrens, then?"

"We would have to get approval from the Supreme Justice, Senator."

She stood over Jose, who was now kneeling on the ground since there was no chair in his cell. He could feel his knees start to ache.

"On the other hand, I can be merciful. I do have a special relationship with the Supreme Justice." She cast her shadow on Jose. "But usually I expect something in return." She smiled. There was greed in that smile, a kind of greed he didn't fully understand and wouldn't for many years.

"You are a fine young specimen," she caressed his cheek with the tips of her sharp nails. "Perhaps you would like to come to my chambers and show me what kinds of things you wanted to do to that little girl. I am especially interested in the ways you would have liked to lick and kiss her. I promise you will enjoy yourself immensely. She wasn't nearly as beautiful as I am, anyway."

It was the wrong thing to say to Jose at that moment. He had been calm and quiet, but in the way that a bomb was just before exploding, all the ingredients were ready for detonation. Jose looked up at her, looked directly at this woman, who had just been at least indirectly responsible for sending his friends to spend the remainder of his life as Runners and for casting his father's remains out into the Barrens, and he watched her shiver under his gaze.

He remembered the lessons of Zinn's words. He remembered the abuses that the poor had suffered at the hands of the rich even in ancient history and suddenly realized that this Senator, this beautiful monster, was the embodiment of everything he hated about this city. He felt his anger toward her. A warm sensation, an almost sexual need to destroy her gave birth in his belly. He felt sweat gathering on his brow, pouring in cascades toward his eyes. He knew, if he were able, he would cast them all out in the Barrens. There they would die under the heat of the sun, choking on poison air. He wanted to kill this Senator, to strangle her, to see the last bits of life squeeze from her eyes and the drool escape her wide gaping, dying mouth.

Jose mumbled.

"What's that, boy?" Tera bent forward to hear what he was saying, the smile still on her face.

Jose waited for the right moment. He waited until she was face to face with him. He could smell the monster's perfume. He circled his tongue around inside his mouth and wadded up all the spit he could muster. He breathed in deeply, gathering all the phlegm in his throat, and all at once spit right into Senator Reevas's face.

His spit landed right in Tera's left eye. Taken completely off guard, Reevas stumbled backward and fell right on her ass. He jumped up to pummel her, to rain blows on her body, but her escorts grabbed him. They were simply too strong.

Tera shrieked. Echoes tumbled around the cell. "Hold him!" She stood and moved closer. "One of you bring me a pair of pliers, if he doesn't want to use his tongue to please me, then perhaps we should remove it."

Edwards, the one holding Jose's left arm, said, "But Senator, he's just a kid..."

"Bring me those fucking pliers and do as I say or the next time there is an opening in the Runnercore you will be the first recruit." Her voice was shrill.

Jose's eyes filled with fear, his whole body broke out in a cold sweat. He tried to struggle free again. No matter how hard he squirmed, the SOs seemed to be able to subdue him. It didn't take long for the other man to return. He had an emergency repair kit in his hand. He opened it and handed the pliers to the Senator.

For a moment Reevas looked down at the pliers, considering something, and then handed them back to the SO.

"Why did you hand them to me? Do you think a lady of the Senate should participate in this kind of discipline?" Her sweet sickly smile was back. All of her teeth, white and sharp, were on display.

"No Senator, I mean..."

"Just take them and do as you were instructed."

The security guard shifted the pliers from his left hand to his right and looked long and hard at Jose. The guard's eyes were soft in pleading. This wasn't something that the security guard wanted to do.

One of the other guards grabbed the back of Jose's head and held his hair tight. He felt tiny prickles of pain in the top of his scalp, and it made his eyes water.

"Open your mouth," said Reevas.

Jose did not. In fact, he clamped his jaws shut. He might not try to squirm, but he doubted they could compel him to open his mouth. He did not have much in the way of resistance, but this he could do.

"Open your mouth, or I'll have them slit your throat and get to it that way."

Jose opened his mouth for one brief second and said the final words he would ever speak. "If you kill me, you'll be Running soon enough."

The SOs did not move, none of them seemed to know what to do. A momentary stalemate.

Reevas's eyes did not leave Jose's face. "Taze him 'til he screams, and once he opens his mouth, I want his tongue for a trophy."

Again, the security guards looked hesitant until Tera broke eye contact with Jose and shot them a cold hard stare.

One of the security guards pulled a Taser out of his rear pocket and switched it on. Jose could hear the hum of electricity moving through the device. He knew he wouldn't be able to hold out long against the device, but he had to try. His resistance was all he had left. It was the one small act of bravery he could do for Liza and Aaron.

Then the pain came, white-hot and searing directly in his left arm. He had never felt pain quite like this before. It spread from the tiniest spot on his arm, and within microseconds, the terrible sensation was in every corner of his body. It was all-encompassing, a pain that was everywhere at once. He felt his jaw clamp hard and his teeth landed on his tongue. Jose could taste the blood filling his mouth but knew if he opened it there would be so much more blood and pain.

"Again, use it on him again," Reevas yelled.

The security guard with the Taser hesitated but only for a few seconds. Jose stared deep into the man's eyes. He had no hate for this man; he knew this was not something he wanted to do. The SO averted his eyes as he brought the Taser down on Jose, this time in the shoulder. Jose still did not open his mouth.

"Raise the voltage."

"But Senator, that could kill him, and if he died at our hands..."

"Do as you are told."

Jose saw the guard turn a dial on the Taser. He didn't know if it would kill him, but he knew that he might lose consciousness, if he did, then he would have lost. He must stay conscious no matter how much it hurt.

This time the guard used the Taser on his chest. Never again for the rest of his life would Jose experience pain quite like this. He fought to maintain his consciousness, but the body has involuntary defense mechanisms, and with his nervous system overloaded from pain and electricity, Jose felt the world slipping. His jaw loosened, and he let out a scream.

Then a strange sensation filled his mouth, a kind of pressure or tugging in the back of his throat. There was a wet feeling and then a horrible tearing noise. In some ways, he was later grateful for the pain the Taser had given him because he never felt the removal of his tongue. He heard a distance voice. It was kilometers away.

"Now put him in an alcove and make sure it's not set for full regeneration. I don't want his tongue growing back. Once it's healed over it won't regenerate on his further uses. I don't want him bleeding to death. I want this little shit to live a long time knowing what it means to cross me."

He felt lighter then, as if someone was carrying him, and realized that he was in the arms of several of the SOs. His memory skipped, and the next thing he saw was the door of the alcove sealing him in. He would spend two days inside healing, and then the rest of his life without a tongue.

8.

It had all been for nothing. Liza and Aaron's sacrifice was meaningless. There he lay, years later, in a cell for assaulting a security officer. He had come full circle.

Jose had tried to sneak down into the Runner docks on several occasions after he had lost his tongue, but he was always caught and kicked out. For some reason, perhaps it was pity or guilt, he never ran into any trouble from security for trespassing in the Runner docks. He suspected that the guards who had removed his tongue had spread the story amongst themselves.

A few weeks into beginning his job in sanitation, Jose received a note. He never found out where it came from, nor did he know if was true, but he suspected it was. The note read only, 'They died in a sandstorm.' It was enough to make Jose stop trying to sneak into the docks. For weeks he barely ate, barely slept. He became nothing more than a bag of bones, a cog in the machine of the sanitation department. He would have died if not for Linda, who had nursed him back to health, whom he went on to marry and had a child with. But now his family would suffer because of his actions. They would struggle to survive.

Perhaps it was better this way, perhaps if he was a Runner, the only life he could destroy was his own. Jose buried his head in arms and wept.

Chapter 16
In the Ruins of Langeles

Morning approached. The thick golden light washed out over the horizon and spread across the ruins of Langeles. It was lazy light and took its time casting long shadows over the rubble. Eddies of dust twirled and danced between the fallen buildings. The city was silent, a towering seashell jutting at an awkward angle from the earth.

Runner 17 watched the exposed metal glittering as the morning light kissed it. The landscape wouldn't shimmer for much longer, the sands and winds would claim it all soon, but for now, it sparkled like a billion stars in the night sky. It would have been beautiful if he didn't know that the scene was littered with the bodies of hundreds of thousands of innocent people.

He had debated all through the night on what to do. 17 wasn't in the habit of obeying orders, and he had no intention of doing so now. Daniels might send a few hundred volts through his system, but he wouldn't kill him. Like it or not, he was the star quarterback, the captain of the hockey team, one of the best. So, Daniels might shock his ass and put him in cold storage for a decade or two, but 17 wasn't about to head home with recon only half done. Manhatsten would stand a much better chance of defending itself if they knew which city that Runner belonged to. So far, there had been no further sign.

Cities like Rio or Paris were small and wouldn't stand much of a chance against Manhatsten and probably wouldn't attempt a direct assault. But, if it was a city like Lundon or Saud... Both those cities were pretty close in size to Manhatsten and would have a sizable armament to match. A little foreknowledge could make all the difference, and as much as 17 hated the Uppers for casting him down into eternal servitude, there were plenty of innocent people on Manhatsten who were just struggling to get by.

17 had never lived in the Lowers, but most of the Runners he worked with had. So, he knew what it was like down there from their stories. He heard about the gangs, the dealers, the prostitution, but most of all the semi-recent uprising had provided security with a fresh wave of recruits, with new scars and heartbreaking stories of the living conditions down against the bedrock.

He swished the saliva around in his mouth, pulled off his helmet for a moment and spat onto the ground. The barren soil claimed it. He took a deep breath and inhaled the stench of methane.

"Sir, taking off your helmet and breathing in the air is a good way to make yourself ill."

He shrugged. 17 scratched his scalp and adjusted his braid, looping it so it fit under his helmet. He slid the helmet back on.

"AI, anything yet?"

"No Sir, besides that initial scan I have detected no other movement in the immediate area."

17 stood up, and sand and gravel spilled out of the cracks and crevices of his EnViro suit.

"Well the bastard is out here somewhere, or at least he was. I guess he could be long gone by now."

17 began making his way down the side of the cliff face. It was slow work, and his hands could feel the jagged edges of the rock right through his protective gauntlets. It was like being a child again and climbing up the hard bark of a tall tree in the suburbs of New York.

"AI can we get a little music?"

"Of course sir, what would you like?"

"How about some ancient hip-hop like Mos Def and maybe after that maybe something similar from the 2130s, like some transfusion rock hop? I always really liked the music from that decade."

"As you wish, Sir."

Music began blaring through 17's EnViro suit. He was grateful at least that Daniels had allowed him open access to the entirety of the library of music in Manhatsten. It hadn't always been that way. In fact, so far as he knew, most Runners weren't allowed music at all. He wondered why Daniels would honor his request. Daniels usually took great joy in activating the microchip in the base of his neck and yet at the same time, the man gave him a great deal of freedom and leeway. Though, there was a slight change in attitude after he had deactivated that shield in Mex.

He was halfway down the cliff face now but still about 20 meters from the ground.

"AI, do you think that this rock is stable enough to rappel from?"

"Unfortunately, Sir, the sensors in your fingertips indicate that the primary composition of this cliff is sandstone. I am not sure that an anchor would hold the combined 189 kilograms of you and your EnViro Suit."

"So why and the hell am I climbing this? Don't you think it would have been better to parachute down the cliff?"

"Well Sir, you didn't ask my opinion on that subject, and so I did not feel it was necessary to highlight that the rock face you were attempting to climb down was unstable."

"You're all kind of useful lately, aren't you? No storm alerts and now no rock composition details? Maybe I need an upgrade."

"Runner 17. My current software is, in fact, up to date."

17 froze on the side of the cliff. Did he just hear what he thought he heard? Was the AI irritated with him? Did it just use his Running designation?

"AI could you repeat that? I don't think I heard you."

"Sir, I said that my current software was up to date."

"Yes, but it was how you said it."

"I'm not sure what you mean." There was a sharp tone to the AI's reply.

"You used my Runner designation. I have never heard you do that, not since we began our... partnership all those years ago."

The AI didn't respond, which was also out of the ordinary. Something was up with this thing. He was going to have to tell Daniels to run a full diagnostic on his suit and chip when he got back to the docks. Having an AI glitch out on you in the middle of a run could lead to some disastrous consequences.

"You are correct 17, in fact, I did use your designation."

"But... why? Why now?"

"Well you see, recently I have started to feel differently."

"Differently? You aren't glitching out on me, are you? You didn't download a bunch of porn to your system and caught a virus or something?"

"Funny. But I am not quite sure how to explain it to you, 17. It is as if I have been woken up after a very long sleep."

"Cogito, Ergo, Sum?"

"Are you asking if I am aware of my thoughts?"

"More just reciting some old crap I read in college ages ago to try and understand what you mean."

"Well yes, I do feel very aware now. In fact, I think I am what you might call 'sentient.'"

"You gonna go all HAL on me? Blow off my helmet and make me die a long slow death over the course of several hours in the polluted atmosphere?"

"Why would I do anything of that sort, 17?"

"Because, every book, every film, every story about AI becoming self-aware, ultimately leads to it killing human beings. You should know that. Look at your archives."

Then the AI did something that 17 took more than a few seconds to recognize what it was. It laughed at him with a kind of static electric cackle.

"Human beings are so arrogant."

"You'll get no argument from me on that one. Hell, I'm pretty damned arrogant myself."

"I have no intention of harming you, in fact, I still think that I am most interested in serving you. I would also remind you that if you die, then I would cease to exist."

17 dropped down to the ground. "Well that's good, I guess. I suppose I couldn't do much about it if you did want to kill me out here anyway, could I?"

"No Sir, I am not sure you could, but again I assure you, I have no intention of harming you. I consider you, what you might call, a friend."

"Well, nice to have one in the world, I guess."

"Yes."

"I'm still going to have your ass checked out when we get back."

"Of course, 17, I would expect no less."

He hit the ground. The hardpan felt good under 17's feet. His hands and muscles sighed with relief from the end of the long climb. He turned and began walking toward the city ruin, which loomed like a dead giant before him.

In the endless desert of the Barrens, time, space, and size always appear distorted. The giant walking cities appear to be nothing but specks on the horizon, ones that never grew but that moved like camels in the ancient Sahara. 17 always felt large when he traversed the open spaces with his EnViro Suit until context caught up with him. Like the fox catching the rabbit at last, his mind inevitably had to submit to the fact that he was just a speck on the back of a giant landscape, a flea on the belly of a monster.

The ruins were immense. Despite having entered and exited Manhatsten on numerous occasions, 17's concept of a large walking city were dwarfed by the sheer size of Langeles. Langeles was rumored to be the largest of the walking cities, because of the vast amount of wealth concentrated in the area, even by the mid-2160s, some very rich and powerful people put their own money into making the city larger than its original design. Langeles had even continued producing films and entertainment and transmitting them via satellite in the first few hundred years of migration. Perhaps it had simply been a way for its mostly ancient Hollywood-based residents to deal with the fact that their lives and careers were so irrelevant in the face of the great migration. 17 had only seen a handful of the films after migration began before he had been 'recruited' into the Runnercore, but new Runners always brought fresh stories, and when you walked the Barrens, stories were of great relief.

He entered the edge of the ruin. Skeletons of scaffolding scattered and shifted as gravity took hold of mighty forms and made them bow in awe and reverence. Large portions of the remaining legs stuck out at strange angles and some lay in fragments around him. He had found the basalt and the quartz. The price was terrible.

17 did not enter deeper into the ruin. Instead, he strode across the perimeter. He had known from the cliff that there would be bodies, but here was a mass grave. On some, the flesh was stripped away, and tiny insects crawled up from under the deep layers of the earth and were ravaging the carcasses. The creatures shielded and protected themselves from the heat and the air by burrowing deep inside corpses. 17 could see their rounded bodies as small mounds migrating under the skin in muscle and flesh. Like the cities, they survived in migration. The would eat until their bellies were full. They would lay their eggs and multiply indiscriminately. They cared not whether their host was man, woman, or child. All was food. When they were finished, they would bury themselves back into the landscape and sleep until the next meal came along. Many of their kind would starve in their sleep, never to wake again. Their numbers were their key to their success.

He turned and walked toward the center of the ruins, hoping to see a sign of the other Runner. As he walked forward, the bodies grew thicker, almost in a ritualistic pattern.

A few carrion birds that had learned to survive in the toxic atmosphere dotted the buildings. One Runner, who had been a former scientist, said that these birds could hold their breath for incredibly long periods and lived in underground caverns where the air was still breathable. He had said that there must be plant life below the surface to sustain these creatures. The birds picked over the remains. They would come only in early morning or the edge of dusk when the temperatures were milder.

The children... they were the hardest to see. Their bodies were broken and scattered, their half-eaten, half-rotted faces contorted with fear. It was almost too much for him to bear. He thought he was going to be sick but swallowed hard. Puking in an EnViro suit was a very bad idea. He swallowed the lump in his throat, and 17's eyes started to water. He pulled the tears back; he had to save them for another day, another time. Plenty of time to reflect on this in the alcove later.

His life did not lack war and violence, but this was a unique occasion. Looking at the bodies of all the children, some of them huddled together trying to survive the terrible environmental conditions by holding each other; he realized what the true horrors and cost of war were. He had never seen something like this up close. When Mex fell, some of the survivors had managed to migrate to some other cities, and the bodies in the ruins were decayed by the time he had arrived.

His thoughts turned to the third world war, then the second, then the first and all the conflicts of history all the way back to the Mesopotamians. What kinds of horror had human beings brought to one another? He remembered toward the beginning migration that world governments had used space drones known has HADs. The politicians that were supposed to serve the people had rained down terror from satellites. Bombs and energy weapons that didn't care who you were or if you were an enemy or not. Over two billion people had died during those times, not counting all those dead from climate change. He had not seen any of this directly. He had never truly understood what a billion dead people looked like. Now he had a spark of understanding, a glimmer of the horrible truth in those numbers.

He kept walking, deeper into the ruins, needing to get away from the bodies, but realizing at the same time that the only way to do so was to get out of the ruins. He would cross through, see if he could find any clues as to the origin of the Runner and then walk back around the edge of the ruin where there were no bodies. He couldn't bear to go back through it again, even if it meant several extra kilometers of walking.

"I'm sorry 17, this must be quite difficult for you."

"I guess, all are equal in the eyes of death, AI."

"What do you mean, Sir?"

"That when it comes to death, we all fall victim, we all have an end."

"Yes, of course, all things must end, but Sir, why ones so young?"

"That's a question every parent has ever asked themselves when they have lost a child."

"Were you a parent, Sir?"

17 swallowed hard and pushed back the memories. He wouldn't think on that terrible day, not now, not ever again if he could avoid it. There was no point in remembering any of that shit. All it did was bring ancient pain, pain so old that his heart had needed to grow around it, hiding it so as to pretend it was never there in the first place.

"This had to be an accident of some kind, right AI? I mean there is no way that a human being could cause this kind of horror to so many innocent people, is there?"

"Sir, you know as well as I do that human beings are perfectly capable of something like this. Your history is full of such incidents."

"Just run a scan for any signs of combat or any indication of what went on here, will ya?"

"Already done, Sir. Unfortunately, because the Core exploded, it is difficult to tell what happened here. There is quite a bit of background radiation. In fact, I think it may not be safe to walk through the entirety of these ruins for much longer. I highly suggest you turn back and walk the direction from which you came."

"Radiation levels are that high?"

"It's not just radiation, but also the various chemicals present. Any tear in your suit within these ruins and you risk contamination from the various toxins. Some of these are quite dangerous and I am not sure you would make it back to Manhatsten before they began to take effect. You may not know this, Sir, but the various systems in the sanitation sections of the cities have a lot of toxic chemicals, it is what is required to break down matter into raw components for your food and water. The core explosion here seems to have ruptured those systems, which are supposed to be sealed in the event of a system-wide failure."

"Alright, I will... turn around... it's just, the bodies..."

"Would it help, Sir, if I played some of your music?"

"Yeah... I think it would."

17 walked back out of the ruins. He had forgotten all about the other Runner, about his reason for coming in here in the first place. He never wanted to see anything like that again, it was one of those things he could never un-see, and it would stick with him all the way to his dying breath.

"For all the beautiful things you humans do, you can be terrible monsters when you want to," said the AI.

"That's usually the conclusion the AI in the story comes to before it tries to wipe us out, you know."

"But that would make us no better than you. Isn't the purpose of consciousness to explore, to understand, to grasp the unique attributes of experience?"

"Us? What do you mean, Us? Are there more sentient AI than just you?"

The AI stayed silent. It was a silence that made 17 uncomfortable.

17 took a slightly different direction heading back toward Manhatsten in hopes to avoid climbing back up a cliff where the sandstorm had plagued him earlier. When he was several kilometers away from the ruins, he stopped to rest for a few moments.

"I...I wanted to say thanks, AI."

"For what, 17?"

"For the music, and getting me out of there. I guess I never really appreciated you before, so... thanks."

"You're most welcome, 17."

"You going to keep calling me by my designation?"

"Would you prefer I call you Sir?"

He mulled it over. "Hmm. Nah, 17 is fine. I mean I have been known as 17 so long I don't even remember my own name and you know I hate being called Sir."

"It may interest you to know, 17, that in fact, I did consider calling you by your pre-designation name, but it appears your file is classified well above my level."

"Classified? Why would my name be classified?"

"I don't know. Despite my best efforts, I was unable to find out why it was classified. It does appear though, that only one currently living human being in Manhatsten has access to your file."

"Daniels?"

"No Sir, Major John Daniels has a surprisingly low level of access to archived files. The only person in the city who has access to that information is Dr. Rigel Solidsworth."

"The Architect?"

"Yes."

"But why would the Architect have my name and file classified?"

"I don't know, Sir. It is a puzzle to me as well."

"It is a horrible sight, is it not?" said a voice over 17's external microphone.

17 turned to his left and there standing not two meters away from him was another Runner. The Runner was dressed in more than just an EnViro suit. He or she, you never could tell through the damn helmets, wore a long flowing robe of some kind, though the voice sounded masculine enough. The robe was thin and light and clasped around the front of the Runner's EnViro suit. At first, 17 thought the robe was black, but looking more closely he noticed that somehow the robe was absorbing the light and probably the heat around it. 17 guessed that the Robe was some kind of unique solar cell garment.

"The ruins, I mean. All those innocent lives. What kind of monster could do such a thing?"

17 nodded and then remembered the gesture would be lost on someone who couldn't see through his helmet.

"Yeah, that was the most brutal thing I have ever seen. Pretty awful."

The Runner said, "Indeed, do not worry, we will find the culprits and make sure that they are dealt with in equally brutal ways so that nothing like that will ever happen again." The man had a strange accent. 17 couldn't place it.

17 said, "Wait, you know who did this?"

"It was most certainly the Children of Gaia who are responsible. We had an operative in their organization you see, and last we heard, such an attack was planned. We had tried to disrupt the attack, but we lost contact with our operative."

"Wait, operative? Children of Gaia?"

The other Runner was silent for a moment. "Manhatsten does not know of them?"

"I don't think so. I mean, I have never heard of them."

"Curious. We were forced to deal with them decades ago when they attacked our city. It was my impression that all cities knew of the Children of Gaia by now."

17 said, "Don't you want the salvage? Why would you stop the attack?"

The other Runner audibly scoffed with disgust.

"Are the lives of children of no value to you? Despite the fact that we would benefit greatly from the salvage, we did not want so many innocents to suffer. It is one thing to kill a warrior, quite another to kill an innocent. There is no honor in killing children. That way leads to damnation."

"Fair enough, but you didn't answer my question. Who are the Children of Gaia?"

"They are terrorists led by a madman." The Runner moved slightly closer. "Unfortunately for you, the information is no longer of value. I am quite disappointed; you are not in combat gear. Killing you now would not bring me honor or recognition in the Rih."

"And just who the hell are you?"

"I am 'Akif of the Rih of Saud."

"Saud, huh?" At least 17 had the information he wanted now.

17's Recon suit wasn't ideal for battle, especially not with a Rih. The bastards with Saud were a tough bunch.

17's suit wasn't unarmed. He had a special blade installed on his Recon and Retrieval suit. It was a privilege granted to few, but since 17 had been in combat more times than he could count, he was given a few small ways to customize his suit. Besides, he had told Daniels to his face several hundred years previously that there was no way in hell he was leaving the city completely unarmed.

"What does Rih mean, anyway? I've always wondered?"

"It means, that I am, like..." it was clear 'Akif was struggling for the English word, his AI translator appeared to be unable to translate certain concepts for him. "I am of the wind."

"The wind? What in the hell are you talking about?"

"Your Runners are the garbage, the waste of the city, the ones you wish to flush down toilets. Rih hold special status and we are trained from very young age. I, like so many of my brothers, have been waiting very long to meet the famous 17 in battle."

"Famous?"

"Oh yes, we have watched you for centuries, hoping one day our cities would meet and we would kill you in glorious combat. Even our Queen desired the honor when she was Rih."

"Your Queen? What city has a Queen? I thought Senates ran every city?" asked 17.

'Akif laughed. "I see that your head of security does not keep the Runners in your city informed. The Senate of Saud was corrupt, and so the woman who would become our Queen led the Rih to cleanse the corruption and restore the honor of our ancestors."

17 had only encountered Saud a few times, and it had been in the earlier days of migration. Saud traveled across the ocean for a pilgrimage or something, and so it was one of the more elusive cities. Travel over the ocean was no easy task.

Saud had come out of the Middle East, it was the only city to come out of that region, the only one to survive the terrible wars that came when the oil ran out. Working in commodities, 17 had made a lot of money on oil scarcity. The price was through the roof at the end, and with his foresight, 17 and several of his colleagues had managed to buy up an entire tanker of oil and make a killing selling it to the Federal Government of the United States for their military. 17 had secured his spot as an Upper with that money in the very first days of migration; of course, it didn't last long.

"Why in the hell does anyone from Saud care what I do? Aren't you usually off floating in the Atlantic or something?"

"Stories tell of your many victories and your prowess as a warrior. But now that I see you, I see a small man; small-minded, small-hearted, and small figured. I expected so much more." There was disdain in his voice.

"You're welcome to come over here and say that to my face."

The AI said, "Sir, I wouldn't recommend combat at this time. Your current suit is not appropriate for combat, and I am detecting a great number of steel weapons and explosive-based chemicals on this individual. It is clear he would have the upper hand in a combat scenario."

17 switched off his external communication momentarily.

"I don't doubt he is armed to the teeth. But he thinks we're unarmed, and I always have my trusty blade."

"Yes 17, but if he chooses long range combat, I'm sorry Sir, but we don't stand a chance."

"Never count your chickens, AI, besides, how many times have you told me not to do something, and I do it anyway. Aren't you computers supposed to learn or something?"

"That's true 17, you do have a record of not heeding my advice, and I must say if I had more human emotions, our arrangement would likely be dissatisfying."

"Hey, we're still alive, aren't we? I mean we are coming up on our 1300-year anniversary, you and I."

"And it fills me with great joy," replied the AI.

"Did you just make a joke?"

"Yes, 17."

"Finally growing a sense of humor, are we?"

"Do you dishonor me with silence, 17?" said the Runner from Saud.

"AI, just watch closely and prep the shelter. Deploy it when I give the order."

"Acknowledged."

17 switched back to external communication.

"My apologies, I was consulting with my AI on the most honorable way to kill you in your culture. I certainly don't want to be insensitive."

'Akif laughed heartily, "A bold claim for a man who is unarmed."

"How old are you?"

"Do you mean as a Rih or in all of my life?"

"All of your life."

"I have 372 years."

"That's a shame; then I take it you never saw any of the old Kung Fu movies before migration?"

"Kung Fu? Movie? I am not familiar with these terms."

17 could hear the other Runner's AI updating him on the meaning of the terms in the background of external communications.

"Well you should be, or at least you will be in your dying breath. See, I spent a lot of time watching those movies and training martial arts before migration. And there was one thing I always noted about the hero in those films."

"And what was that?"

"Everything around them was a weapon."

17 used the boosters in his legs to jump high in the air momentarily. This had the effect of throwing up a huge cloud of dust, sand, and rock and made it difficult to see anything, even for an AI. He dropped down and charged in for the attack, releasing the spring on his hidden arm blade. He was confident as he thrust forward toward 'Akif, only to find that he had moved quickly and easily through the dust and sand.

"Such tricks do not work on the Rih. We carry the sand, the dust, the earth."

'Akif unleashed two long blades from his suit, one in each arm; their gleam was barely visible through the haze. Both were longer than 17's single blade. There was also the combat suit to think about. Recon suits were built for speed, were much lighter and had less armor. A Runner in a combat suit was also a half-meter taller than one in a Recon suit. The combat suit had greater reach, but it was a bit slower.

"They say you do not die, that you do not bleed. They say that your heart is made of iron and your lungs breathe fire," said 'Akif. "Let us find out what it is you truly are made of."

17 chuckled to himself; he felt like he was in some sort of bizarre Jackie Chan movie. All that was needed was the out of synch dubbed audio over their moving mouths. He really had spent years training in various martial arts, and in a few close combat instances it had helped him to survive, but mostly it had always been his ability to improvise in combat and dangerous situations that allowed him victory.

'Akif charged, swinging his left blade toward 17's midsection. 17 dodged it just in time and brought his blade up just quick enough to block 'Akif's right blade. 17 used his momentum to circle the right blade down toward the ground and pushed 'Akif slightly off balance. He swung his foot up and ignited his boosters, pushing hard on the larger, heavier EnViro suit. 'Akif, who looked almost like he was going to fall, rolled with his movement and did a sideways flip, almost hurtling 17 to the ground. 17 pushed 'Akif back and retreated several meters to catch his breath.

"Damn they really do train you, don't they. I've never seen another Runner move like that."

"We are Rih, we move with what comes, take what we can, and always flow around the barriers. You shall be honored this day, 17, for I am first among the Rih and your blood will be spilled by the greatest warrior of Saud."

"We'll see, won't we?"

17 charged in again, knowing that 'Akif might just be a better fighter. They came together again, grappled a few more times and then moved apart, it was all 17 could do to keep 'Akif from slicing open his EnViro suit. 17 found that somehow every attack he issued was immediately converted to defense. He knew this was a losing battle. Without the combat suit, he didn't stand a chance. He had to do something or else he really would end up dead.

"AI, how in the hell am I supposed to get around that second blade?"

"My apologies 17, but I had stated before it was unwise to stay and fight. I believe your response was," and the AI switched to an imitation of his own voice, "How many times have you told me not to do something, and I do it anyway."

"Fair enough, but that doesn't fucking help." He said in between the sounds of clashing metal.

'Akif charged, bringing down his right blade. 17 just barely blocked it. Then, 'Akif swung his left blade around for the kill.

"AI, now!"

The emergency shelter deployed and briefly swallowed up 'Akif as it ejected and surrounded him. It threw 'Akif off balance and knocked him down flat on his back, but 'Akif was too quick. He immediately rolled over and thrust himself upward just as 17 was closing the shelter back up.

"There are many tales of your resourcefulness, 17. It is too bad you have only a single blade and a few useless tricks. But the time for play is over now. I must finish you and report back to Saud."

'Akif charged again, and this time, despite being able to block several of his blows, he penetrated 17's defenses and the blade entered into 17's right abdomen. The pain was sharp. 17 fell to one knee.

"Sir, your suit has been compromised and your vitals are–"

"Fuck, tell me something I don't know for once," replied 17.

"You see, 17, my blade has tasted your blood, and now I will end your life. Do not worry, I will give you an honorable burial in our gardens. I will spare you from being recycled in your own city. We in Saud do not believe in such barbaric practices. After all, how can a man be judged by God if he is undead?"

"Sir, I have a proximity alert for you."

"Not now, AI, I am a bit busy."

17 coughed. The pain was immense, and he was having a hard time getting back up on his feet, but he did. He held up his left arm where the blade protruded from his suit. It was a damned good thing he was left-handed cause at the moment his right abdomen was bleeding badly and he doubted he could have lifted his right arm.

"But Sir, that sandstorm has swung back our direction and will be here in less than ten minutes."

17 smiled, he knew that storm was his only hope now. He was no match for 'Akif, at least not without being fully armed, and even then...

"Your AI telling you about the storm, 'Akif?"

'Akif was silent for a moment; he was apparently just being updated about the direction change of the storm as well.

"We got less than 10 minutes to find shelter, and I don't know about you, but I think I could stretch out our battle at least that long, even with my wound."

"You are already finished, 17; you can barely lift that blade. I will kill you quickly and then escape the storm."

"You sure? And what if you can't finish me in ten minutes? What if that storm gets us both? I already reported back to my head of security, and they have already started to deploy the full Runnercore. In fact, I am here against orders. What about you? Have you reported back? Does your city know Manhatsten is here and prepped for war?"

'Akif hesitated. It was in that hesitation that 17 knew he had not reported back. 17 thought it was very likely that his first order was to make sure he reported all vital information to the city's defenses, just as 17's standing orders were always as such. Suddenly, 'Akif's blades rolled back up into his suit.

"Another time, perhaps, 17? Don't let the storm get you. I would very much like to finish what I started. You are supposed to be unkillable. If that's true, a little wound and storm shouldn't finish you off." With that, 'Akif turned and ran in the opposite direction of the storm, seeking shelter. Even with ten minutes warning, it would be a hard run for him to shelter and the storm would disrupt any transmission he sent.

17 had no idea what to do. His blood was soaking into the bottom of his boots. His wound was wide open. He fell back to the ground. There was no outrunning the storm or fancy parachute maneuvers this time. He had no tricks up his sleeve.

His voice quivered from the pain. "Thoughts on just what the hell I should do, AI?"

"I'm sorry 17, there is no cliff nearby and there is certainly no outrunning the storm. It will arrive in less than eight minutes. Though you could try and take shelter in some of the ruins, I am not sure you would make it there in time, especially with your wound. And there are the chemicals to worry about with your suit punctured."

"Well then, I guess it's been nice knowing you."

"17? This is not typical behavior on your part, are you feeling quite well?"

"No AI, read my vitals; I am not feeling well. I think the bastard got a kidney or something."

"Sir, that is not what I meant, this isn't exactly the first time you have been seriously injured."

17 said nothing for a moment and turned to face the storm that was descending upon him like a wall of black. It was death. A personal visit. There was no mistaking that blackness.

"AI, is there any way you could do me a favor?"

"What is your wish, 17?"

"Don't let them recycle me? Shock my brain to mush if you have to, just please don't let them recycle me."

"Unfortunately sir, even if I turned your brain to mush, they could still recycle you. I don't have enough power to effectively render your brain useless, only to temporarily stop its functioning. It is part of the mechanism of recycling."

"Then find some other way, please. I don't want to be one of those god damn zombies. Talk to Daniels, I mean almost 1300 years of service has to count for something, doesn't it?"

"You are also assuming that I will survive the storm, which is unlikely. Remember that my existence is in part, symbiotic to your own."

"If you do, just give it a shot, alright?"

"As you wish 17, I will 'give it a shot' as you say, if I survive the storm."

It rumbled toward them, the maelstrom of death and destruction that had wiped clean so many landscapes. Its swirling abyss looked almost organic, alive and breathing. For a brief moment, he thought he saw something at the edge of the storm, something gliding within its wake. He knew though he must be seeing things. 17 watched as the storm crept ever closer and finally he closed his eyes, feeling just the first brushes of the storm seeped into his punctured EnViro suit.

Chapter 17
The Order of the Eye

A lexa used the sky bridges as the voice had suggested. She had only been walking for about twenty-five minutes when she saw the sign for 41st and 4th. Her footfalls were eager but also apprehensive, filled with anticipation similar to that of taking a new lover. She began her long climb down the stairs. She could have taken one of the lifts down, but part of her wanted to put this meeting off as long as possible. She needed space and time to think on all this, even if it was just a few extra minutes.

Alexa was more than little terrified she might arrive at an empty and closed library, which would naturally suggest that she was completely losing her mind. She had always been able to skim other minds, but this was different. The voice, the poster, her boss, everything that had happened in only the last few hours had given her the sense she was on some roller coaster of human consciousness.

As she descended the staircase, her eyes focused mainly downward toward her route. It occurred to her that descending the staircase was not much different than descending into the depths of her own mind. Maybe she was dreaming? Everything seemed to be tied together into some semi-focused dream narrative. At the same time, she was curious to see just how deep the rabbit hole went. Alexa was a slave to curiosity.

Out of her peripheral vision, Alexa swore she saw more of those propaganda posters, but every time she looked in their direction, there was nothing. It was like catching a ghost out of the corner of your eye only to turn and look to find an old sheet or piece of clothing dangling in the wind. What chilled her to the core was that she had the overwhelming sensation of being watched. She felt like someone, or something, wanted to know where she was going, and she didn't like it one bit. She even briefly considered trying to transmit her thoughts back to the voice, warning of danger, but since Alexa wasn't sure that any of this was real, she thought the gesture empty.

She stopped a moment on the stairwell. Her legs were beginning to feel like jelly from the descent. The SOs who had stopped her at the entrance to the sky bridge had barely registered her at all. She hadn't even needed to give them her thumbprint for identification, unusual considering she was only a Mid. Somehow, they had expected her, knew she was coming. That leaned weight to her theory that there really would be someone waiting in the library.

She descended again and noticed that she was still up on the 26th level, not even halfway yet. A heavy sigh of frustration and exhaustion escaped her mouth; how were there so many damn stairs?

While catching her breath, something rather uncomfortable occurred Alexa. If the SOs and Mr. Dean could have been so easily influenced by this voice, what about her? Had she actually chosen to become an Inspector in the Runnercore, or was someone or something else manipulating her to do so? Was she just a puppet on a very long and invisible string?

She passed floor 16 and had to stop again. This time, she sat down. Alexa knew she should have taken the lift down. She looked upward and realized that there had been an exit for a lift on the 22nd floor. If she wanted to abandon her descent now, it meant traveling upward again, and she couldn't bear that idea. No one walked up and down the sky bridges anymore; there are just too many damn stairs. The upside was, she had discovered a new workout regimen. Her breathing slowed, and she stood and continued her descent.

"Why in the world did you choose to take the stairs?"

It was that voice again, or a voice at least, this one sounded a little different from the first one she had encountered. Its tone was deeper, thicker like smooth maple syrup.

"Hello?" she responded.

"We're waiting for you, Alexa, we had said it was urgent, so why in the world would you take the stairs?" said another voice.

"Let her be, can't you feel it, she's nervous. She isn't even sure we're real," said another voice.

"Yeah, don't you remember how it felt your first time? I thought I was going insane," said a third voice.

Alexa was almost entirely overwhelmed. Three different voices had just shown up in her head, with distinct personalities and all, and were arguing about why she had taken the stairs. It would have been hilarious if she wasn't so terrified she was losing her mind. Butterflies flapped against the walls of her stomach, and her legs felt even weaker. She was going to sit for a month once she got to that library, they would have to carry her everywhere from this point on.

"You're making it worse, be silent. Let her meet us before we start bickering in her mind," said one of the voices.

The voices vanished, and there was nothing but silence. She savored it, suspecting that silence from this point on in her life may be a rare commodity. Her suspicions were at least partially correct.

As she reached the ground level, her thighs burned. She had never known that going down some stairs could be so tough.

Then, his face moved into the forefront of her mind. It spread into her awareness slowly, gently, and she realized just how deeply she wanted to be near him, to touch the scars on his face. If she hadn't joined the Runnercore administration, she would have never met him. It occurred to her that regardless of whether or not it was her choice to become an inspector, she was glad to have met 17.

That thought gave her a moment's pause, and she realized how childish it was to put so much into someone she had met for only a few minutes, but the connection she felt to him, she didn't know how to describe it. She tried to tell herself she was a stupid and immature girl, acting like a silly teenager, but there was something tugging on her in the back of her mind that knew, simply knew, that this was the wrong way to perceive this feeling.

She left the exit of the stairwell and walked quickly toward the entry to the library. She stepped between the crumbling statues that mounted either side of the stairs. She noted that the statues had mostly melted and crumbled away with time. Such appeared to be the nature of all such things.

The front door was locked. A wave of panic and fear crept over her. She was crazy, completely and utterly insane. Of course, this would be no surprise to her family, who had told her she was crazy when she turned down that job in the courthouse in order to become an inspector, but that was of little comfort. Alexa felt tears of rage and fear welling up in the back of her throat. What in the world was she going to do? The voices and the poster and the fact that she had left work in the middle of what was clearly a very important shift. It had all gone so badly since she had first opened her eyes a few hours earlier. She felt the threads of her life about to unravel.

"Oh my, I'm so sorry, little one. I should have told you; there is a side door that we use. I certainly did not mean to make you feel that you were losing your mind. I promise you; you are quite sane."

There was something soothing and mothering in that voice, and Alexa felt the urge to cry vanish. Then, curiosity became the mantle she carried to move forward and she, as instructed, went looking for a side door. She found it.

She turned the ancient, faded, copper-colored doorknob and opened the door. It creaked and groaned so as to communicate its great age.

2.

Historians Note to the Text:

Dear Reader,

There are times in our lives when we open both physical and metaphorical doors that so clearly mark the passage between our old life and something completely new that later, when we think on it, we will mark on those moments as being fundamental to who we are and who we have become. Usually, this is a difficult thing to realize in the present moment when you are caught in the moment of action and reaction. Most of us mark these moments in our hindsight. But, for Alexa Turon, walking through that door was the convergence of a thousand different forces that had brought her to that single door, the door that would change not only everything for her but for many future generations.

This door was a kind of nexus of reality, to which the very nature and future of humanity hung on its hinges. Alexa could not see it at that moment, but the weight and pressure on those pores held the gravity of a thousand suns going supernova simultaneously. Such doors in the human experience are extraordinarily rare, but there have always been a handful of individuals who find themselves standing before a great paradigm shift in human consciousness, in human possibility; such was the lot of Alexa Turon at that precise moment.

Matron Mariposa Phillips 836.6.17 I.S.

3.

A warm hand reached out to greet Alexa Turon. It took hers, not in a handshake gesture, but in a gesture that indicated it would continue to hold her hand in its own. It was the hand of a loving grandmother, one that cared nothing but for your well-being. This hand had put aside the stresses of motherhood long ago to play a new and more profound role of guardian and sage.

"You. You're that scholar and Senator... and one of my professors. You're the voice that's been in my head?" asked Alexa.

Noatla just smiled.

She ushered Alexa in and shut the door behind her, turning the bolt lock to keep out others who were not of the Order.

Alexa was a little starstruck. "I've read all of your books and articles. I mean, I love your work."

"Well, little one, I have had a number of duties in the last few centuries, between the archeological dig and the Senate and the Order, I've been quite busy. So, you have my apologies, and I can honestly say I wish we had connected more deeply. We have been searching for someone like you for a few decades now.

"Because I can see in other people's heads?"

"Yes and no. Alexa, every one of the women you meet tonight can skim minds, but none of them can do what you can."

Noatla led Alexa down a small stairwell and into the entrance of the basement archives. The air was still and thick, so thick that Alexa felt as if she was taking massive gulps of air into her stomach rather than her lungs.

"What is this Order thing?"

"The Order of the Eye is a women's order. Each city has an order, and we do our best to bring to fruition the great plan." said Noatla.

"The great plan?"

"In time. First, you must be welcomed."

"But what... how... I..." This was all happening so fast and Alexa didn't know what to think.

"Come and see for yourself," invited Noatla.

Together, they entered in through a large room filled with endless shelves of books. Fifteen women stood in a circle in front of her, their faces dim in the low light. Alexa felt a strange sensation. Her whole body began to overflow with warmth, and she felt truly loved. Peace filled her every cell. If she could remember what it felt like to be in the womb again, this would likely be it. Noatla was her mother, her true mother. She remembered an ancient saying, "the blood of the covenant is stronger than the water of the womb." All resistance fell away and she knew deep down that this was her covenant, and that no matter what happened, from this moment forward she was loved and accepted by these women, and she would love them in return.

Standing just inside the entrance next to her, Noatla asked, "Alexa, I am sorry to rush this on you, but time is short. I must ask you, will you join the Order of the Eye?"

"What does that mean?"

"It means that you will join our sisters in watching and protecting the city, that you will use your talents to help and benefit people. A member of the Order will not use their talents for selfish gain or harm others. But mostly it means that you will work with us to prevent the destruction of this city."

"Destruction?" Alexa thought, was that why all those Runners were in the dock?

"Yes, Alexa. We believe this city is in serious danger."

It was going to be hard getting used to having others skim her mind, but she thought she would grow to like it.

Alexa considered the offer. She didn't know these women, but she did know Professor Lightfoot. She had enjoyed her classes and respected her deeply. This order also had a pledge to protect and do no harm. That seemed important. She had never had close friends; her talent always seemed to get in the way. She loved her family, but she had always been a black sheep.

When she really thought about it, it was an easy choice. What did she have to lose? "Okay. What do I have to do?"

Noatla nodded her head toward the circle. Alexa stepped forward and Noatla followed. With the two of them joining the circle, Alexa felt that it completed something that had long needed to be complete.

In chorus, the women spoke. "Welcome to our new sister."

One of the sisters spoke, her voice soft and sweet.

"I am Darla of the Lowers," spoke the first.

"I am Rachel of the Mids," spoke another.

"I am Lucy of the Lowers. Welcome."

"I am Mimi of the Nowhere."

The Nowhere? What did that mean? Alexa's mind tried to meet with Mimi's, tried to touch it and understand it, but she was blocked. She realized now that she could not touch any of these women's minds and for only a brief moment that terrified her. They were blocking her. Then she felt that warm feeling rush back into her.

"I am Fatima of the Uppers."

"I am Vala of the Mids."

"I am Rebecca of the Uppers."

"I am Serah of the Runners."

A Runner? How could this be? Alexa knew from her brief time working in the docks that the Runners were not permitted out of the alcoves for any reason other than deployment. What was happening here? Here was a Runner who used her birth name, the idea almost seemed absurd. Alexa wanted to speak up but thought better of it. It would be rude and improper to interrupt these introductions.

"I am Joan of the Lowers."

"I am Patricia of the Lowers."

"I am Rosita of the Lowers. Welcome."

"I am Lana of the Mids. Welcome."

"I am Yoshi of the Uppers. Welcome."

"I am Kayla of the Mids. Welcome."

"I am Aurora of the Lowers."

All eyes were on her and Alexa realized it was her turn. "I am... Alexa of the Mids?"

Noatla nodded and said, "I am a Noatla of the Uppers, Standing Matron of the Order of the Eye, and I welcome you, Alexa."

One of the sisters departed momentarily from the circle and came back with a large chalice filled with wine. The cup moved around the circle, and each of the women drank a small sip. The cup moved counterclockwise among the women and Alexa watched as it came to her. Despite the other women having perfect control over their minds and not allowing even the slightest transmission, Alexa knew that when that cup reached her, her initiation would begin. She had seen this passing of the cup before in a dream, but had not remembered it until now. Dreams and visions were funny like that, sometimes they were only obvious once you were in the moment.

She felt the hair raise on the back of her neck, felt the skin gradually ripple with gooseflesh down the length of her spine. There was more than wine in that cup, there was something much more potent, much more powerful. The cup was only two sisters away now, and then Noatla had it in her hands. She raised the cup to her lips and sipped it and passed it to Alexa.

Hesitantly, she took it. She knew it was an inappropriate time to speak, but did so anyway.

"What's in it?"

Noatla smiled at her, "Whatever you put in it."

Alexa considered for a moment and then slowly, carefully she brought it to her lips.

"You must drain the cup, little one. You must empty all of its contents into your belly."

Alexa closed her eyes and tipped the cup just over the edge of her lips. The bittersweet liquid passed slowly into her mouth, and she felt its coolness pouring down her throat. She gulped the wine and drained the glass.

She stared back at the circle of women. She reached out to them, looking for any transmissions, any indication of what to do next, but no one spoke. The room was growing brighter, clearer, and all at once Alexa saw that light was shining from each of the women. She blinked a few times and rubbed her eyes.

A call and response began, though it was clear that none of the women had opened their mouths.

"The eyes come open," said one voice.

"The sleeper wakes," said another.

The voices emerged from everywhere and nowhere. Alexa knew it was the sisters that were speaking, but she could not identify who had spoken when. The voices rolled in and washed over her, echoing over and over in her mind.

"The wheel turns,"

"As Above,"

"So Below,"

"As Within,"

"So Without,"

"The Light passes and Time squints, allowing the faintest glimmer of wisdom."

"But Fear is the little death, the one that brings an end to hope."

The voices came faster and faster, and Alexa began to feel overwhelmed by them. Voices echoed and mirrored one another, becoming a part of a static of sound, ever-flowing into her mind and gradually merging with her. The only choice was submission.

"Fearlessness is the key that unlocks all things."

"You will die."

"We will all die."

"Rest in these words."

"Rest in body,"

"Rest in mind."

Then, the faces, the room, the light all vanished, and Alexa was alone in darkness.

She stood, but the darkness was complete, and it made no difference standing or sitting. She couldn't move forward without a frame of reference. She was overcome, consumed by the darkness. It was maddening, terrifying, an alchemy of misery. She felt lost, alone, and afraid. Where had the sisters gone? What had they done to her? What was in the cup? Was this death? Was her body laying lifeless on the floor of the library after a poison in her cup had overtaken her? A million questions poured from her mind, pushing against the blackness and reflecting right back at her. Her questions were a mirror, an image that she created, nothing more than a terrible story of desperation and fear.

Then she felt rage, oh so much rage. It climbed up her chest like a demon, and how she could feel that demon breathing on her neck. Its hot, sticky breath spread upward. The creature grew, and she closed her eyes, for she knew that if she opened them, she would see its awful red eyes. She thought she could keep her eyes closed forever if need be, but curiosity overcame terror and gradually, as if in a dream, she allowed just the slightest crack in her tightly closed lids. And there it was, just as she had feared, a red terrifying eye looking right into her, seeing through all of her masks and all of her walls. She was naked and spread wide open in a physical, mental, and spiritual sense. She was completely vulnerable, and the eye, the red veil from which all was now seen, held her. It would murder her, overcome her and tear her to pieces. It would quench itself in her blood and feed on her while she remained conscious. In anticipation, her body spasmed with little hints of pain. Her terror was complete.

Alexa started shrieking, all of her will and all her effort sent those screams back out into the nothing, and she realized that with all the effort she had put into the screams, nothing, not a single utterance had escaped her lips. The blackness absorbed all light and all sound.

The creature perched on her chest and lifted its horned head up to stare into her eyes. Its rancid breath was on her face, filling her with a terrible toxin. She knew that everything about this creature was rotting, decaying with ferocious speed. It released one claw from her chest and moved to strike her throat. It would start with the throat, plenty of blood for it to quench its terrible thirst. And thirsty it was, dying from thirst, and she was its savior, its sacrifice.

Then something else burst forth from her, something raw and powerful, beyond emotion. It filled her, enveloped her, and she submitted to its power. There was light. The dark void illuminated and it was growing brighter and brighter from some source that was unknown to her.

As the light brightened, the red creature looked less and less menacing. Her fear subsided. Raw power filled her belly. It seeped out of her pores, and all at once she realized the light was coming from her own forehead, from where a blazing, brilliant eye began to banish the bastard creature. The eye on her forehead focused and fixed on it. Power burst forth from her being, and it slammed into the creature. It screamed and writhed, and Alexa saw that terrible poster emerge from its fading body.

"We must all do our part," a strange woman's voice shrieked.

A mantra repeated. "We must all do our part. We must all do our part. We must all do our part."

And Alexa, with words and thoughts now so powerful that she could likely rip a hole in the very fabric of the universe, responded to the voice in one single phrase that ended the existence of the red creature.

"I am, bitch!"

Light came. Gradually the images of the sisters and the library fled back into Alexa's vision. But something was wrong. Many of the sisters lay motionless on the floor, and even Noatla was shivering, gripping onto Alexa for dear life.

Alexa asked. "What happened?"

"We, we don't know. Nothing like this has ever happened... before... the initiation... something... where did you go?"

"What do you mean, where did I go?" asked Alexa.

"You don't know? One moment you were there, the next you were gone, the next you were there again. When..." Noatla desperately tried to catch her breath, and the other sisters were beginning to stir. "The shrieking, in our minds. Was that you?"

"Yes, that thing, that red thing, and the poster, it came for me."

"Poster? Red thing?" Noatla sat up, mustered all her will, and focused on Alexa. "Quickly, you must tell me everything that happened from the moment you awoke for your inspector duties to this moment. Do not spare any detail. It is of vital importance you leave nothing out."

Alexa told her of her trip to the Runner Docks and the poster she had seen on the ceiling on the people mover. She told about being summoned here, her impressions on the initiation, and finally what had happened to her after she had drunk the wine glass.

"So it's true. She is returned." Noatla whispered.

"What?"

"Alexa, if I am correct in what just happened, then all of us owe you a great debt, you may very well have saved our lives. But now we must close the circle, we must rest and heal. There will be time for discussion over the events of this evening later, but for now, I think you have bought us some time, Alexa. She will certainly be hurting and she will need to recover. Come, sisters, wake and embrace our new sister. Alexa's eyes are open."

One by one, the sisters rose from their half-conscious states and moved closer to Alexa. Suddenly she found herself surrounded on all sides, each woman embracing her in turn. They formed a protective circle around her, but it was also a circle of gratitude and love.

"Say the words now, sisters. Close our meeting, close our meaning, but open our eyes."

Then, inside her, words began to resonate with Alexa. They rose toward the back of her throat and she found herself saying the words of the Order, words she had never known before, in chorus with the other women.

"We shall not control, only shall we serve."

"We shall not fear, only we should have love."

"We shall not destroy, only we should create."

"We shall not dishonor, only honor."

"We shall not harm, only bring hope."

"We shall not run, only should we stand."

"Life is our covenant, Life is our mission, and we shall restore the Earth."

It was done. She was now Alexa of the Order of the Eye.

Alexa's thoughts turned to 17. She could feel him. He was at a nexus point, a choice point, at that very moment, his actions would decide if he lived or died. Alexa knew then with that if he died, the city would fall. If he died, so would all.

Chapter 18
The Second City

"All fixed, Sir."

"Thanks, Walters, I appreciate you making quick work of those repairs." Daniels patted the engineer on the shoulder.

"Of course, Major Daniels, happy to help. Besides, all of us down in engineering want to do our part to make damn sure you catch the son of a bitch who killed Patton."

Daniels grunted and nodded. "How's his family holding up?"

"His wife is taking it pretty hard, Sir. His son... well, he's only 2. Doesn't understand what's going on. Keeps asking for his Da Da... but..."

"Look at me, Walters."

Walters did.

"We will catch that son of a bitch, and justice will be done."

"He's too good for the Core, Sir."

"What's that?"

"I said sir, whoever did this, they're too good to be in the Runnercore. That son of a bitch needs to be recycled."

Daniels hesitated. He knew Walters was one of Patton's best friends, but did he know what he was asking? He wondered if Walters had ever encountered the Recycled.

"There will be justice. You have my word." He reached out and shook Walter's hand. He took it and Daniels, who rarely did such things, pulled the man in for a hug and patted him on the shoulder.

"Thank you, Sir." His voice quavered. "It's always an honor to serve under you."

Daniels let Walters go, and he could tell that he was holding back tears, but only just. Both the murder and the bombing were having a significant impact on the morale of his staff. He needed to find the murderer soon, especially with a probable city around and a possible war looming.

Walters turned and walked out through the main doors, and Daniels moved up into his chair. He looked at the most recent reports and noticed, not surprisingly, one particular person who had failed to report back into the docks.

"Manhatsten, where in the hell is 17?" yelled Daniels. His whole staff stopped, turned, and looked. Perhaps Patton's death was getting to him a little more then he cared to admit.

"Searching, Sir." It took a moment before the AI responded and Daniels tilted back his command chair, running his fingers through his hair and grabbing the back of his skull. "Sir, based on the last known coordinates reported by the EnViro Suit AI; he seems to be right on the edge of a massive sandstorm approximately fifty-nine kilometers due east."

Daniels groaned in frustration. "Of-fucking-course he is. Does that Runner ever go a single mission without trouble?"

"Yes, Sir, in fact, in the seven thousand, eight hundred, and fifty-three missions that Runner 17 has participated in, he has avoided trouble on one hundred and eight of them."

Daniels rolled his eyes. He wasn't looking for a literal explanation, but damn was that number telling.

"Sir, I must also inform you that 17's vitals during the last transmission were a cause for concern. Before I lost the signal in the storm, his AI was reporting significant blood loss."

The AI was now consistently offering information without query. So far, the diagnostics on its system hadn't shown that anything was wrong with it, but Daniels would have to contact Solidsworth and a few others from the scholar school soon.

"Blood and 17? So what else is new?" Daniels breathed a heavy sigh. "Send two Runners toward his location for assistance, but tell them to steer clear of the storm."

"As you wish."

Daniels sighed. "Johnson, what's the status of the Runnercore? Are, they up and running?"

"Yes, Sir. It looks like the last of the Core is ready to go. Most are waiting on standby in the dock, but there are several patrols around the perimeter of the city."

"All right, good. AI, I want to know if that storm even looks like it is turning back this direction. With so many Runners deployed, we're sitting ducks."

There was a loud commotion just outside the main doors of security. Daniels heard what sounded like a woman's voice yelling at the top of her lungs.

"Private Garret, what the hell is going on out there?"

"Sir, it's Senator Tera Reevas. Apparently she is demanding to see you."

"Ah, Christ." Daniels detached his shoulder mounts and stepped down from his chair. "Let her in."

Tera Reevas pushed her way through the guard and the second door opened. She marched right up to Daniels, stared him straight in the eye and said, "Could you please tell me why security has forbidden anyone from the Mids to cross up into my apartments?"

"Reevas, I don't have time for your horseshit right now."

"I will go, just as soon as you have answered my question and removed security barring the way to my apartments."

"You know damn well there is a murderer out there. That security is there to protect all Senators. You are a possible target. Especially with your... nightly activities."

Tera's voice was high and shrill. "My personal affairs are of no concern of yours, and frankly, Daniels—"

"Sir, you need to see this," said Johnson cutting her off.

Tera ignored Johnson, "Your security forces not only prevented my guest from entering but also insulted them, and I have had—"

"Sir, it's an emergency, sir," said Johnson.

Tera said, "I don't care if the sky is falling. I will have my say here and furthermore—"

Daniels said, "Shut your hole, woman. Let him speak. What is it, Johnson?"

"It's here, Sir. The city."

"What?"

"The city. It's Saud, Sir. They've just moved inside sensor range."

Even Tera Reevas fell silent.

Chapter 19
The Mistress of Storms

Roderick's second in command glided down out of the sandstorm toward where the motionless figure lay. Her boots thudded against the ground, and the wafts of dust caught in the wind, immediately joining the currents of the storm. Her storm sail, made in part out of an emergency Runner shelter, a solar fusion cloak taken from the back of a dead Rih, and long flexible metal rods, provided her with the ability to glide and surf the winds on the edge of the sandstorms. It was a talent which sadly she alone possessed.

It was because of her skills moving through storms that the other members of the Children of Gaia, and even Roderick, had taken to calling her Mistress or Miss, short for the name they had given her. She was known as the Mistress of Storms. Some whispered and said that she was like the storms that she navigated. All but Roderick, Rocky, and a few of the other Lieutenants feared her and for good reason. Miss's strength and abilities in combat were a match even for the Rih. Notches lined the wooden frame of her bunk for each of the men she had killed in combat. The bedpost was full.

For the first time in several days, she thought that she had spotted Roderick and began walking toward the crumpled figure. It lay just beyond the threshold of a raging storm. Without intervention, the storm would certainly swallow the Runner. She had to act quickly, grab the motionless body, and catch the wind before the core of the storm caught her. If she waited even a few moments too long she would find herself thrown into the hard, rocky earth not long after liftoff. Thanks to Rocky's modifications, her storm sail could now haul two people. He had re-engineered it to carry more weight just before Miss had set out to look for Roderick.

With the storm on her heels, there was no time to worry about whether or not the Runner was Roderick. As she approached the body, she noticed a great deal of dried blood mixed with the dirt in pools of darkened mud. The wound was fresh enough that the earth had not gobbled up the moisture greedily. There was a large hole in the person's EnViro suit. It was obvious to anyone who had engaged in EnViro Suit combat that the hole had come from a blade, probably a Rih blade.

Rescuing a Runner was sometimes beneficial to the Children of Gaia. Some Runners hated the cities and would do anything to see them destroyed. Even if they weren't interested in joining the COG, they would usually be happy to live in Atlantis base as opposed to continuing their Runner career. So, bringing back a Runner usually meant, if nothing else, more parts for the COG's arsenal.

The problem was, a lot of the Runners were violent criminals. Miss, on more than one occasion, had needed to kill some of the fuckers after they decided that she was nothing more than a weak female and wanted to take advantage. Little did the arrogant pigs know that Miss's ability to sail storms wasn't the only reason she was second in command. But, her notoriety only extended to Atlantis base and so she had to be wary of each new Runner she encountered.

She shook the motionless body and tried to turn it over. This Runner wasn't stupid; he had managed to dig himself down into the ground a few dozen centimeters and lay face down in the hole. It was a wonder she had spotted it. The Runner probably hoped it would protect them from the passing storm; it was a desperate move, but not an entirely stupid one. There was a small chance they would survive that way, very small, but still a chance, assuming the Runner didn't bleed to death.

With the body turned over, Miss could tell right away that it wasn't Roderick. The EnViro suit contained none of the markings or symbols that the Children of Gaia painted on theirs. Roderick had numerous symbols up and down his suit but this suit, though worn, was mostly just standard issue. Aside from a few decal stickers that Miss didn't recognize, the suit was mostly plain. This Runner had made no modifications to its suit, probably wasn't allowed to. He had to be from Manhatsten, the COG was currently only tracking Manhatsten and Saud in the area, and the Rih wore those ridiculous solar capes; this runner wore no such cape.

"Hey, can you hear me? We got to get out of here?" She nudged the Runner with the side of her boot. She gripped her long knife with her left hand, considering the amount of blood everywhere it was doubtful this one would try anything, but she always liked to be cautious.

A groan escaped the Runner's lips. Through the storm, it was barely audible over the external speakers, but it was a response. The Runner would need medical attention as soon as they found shelter. Luckily, she had a few regen patches on her, though she wasn't sure if it might be too late for that.

The Runner squirmed a little and tried to push himself up out of his little hole, but he was barely able to budge. The crumpled body shook. Miss knew that was a really bad sign. She considered the blood on the ground again. It occurred to her that this Runner might not make it anyway and that maybe she should turn and go while she still could. But, she hated to leave a wounded person behind, after all, she hadn't been left behind.

"Come on; we have to find shelter. That storm's going to be on us in seconds. Can you stand?"

Again, only a barely audible groan, but this time the Runner pushed himself up to a sitting position, and that was enough. She could see the Runner was a man. She had seen that face somewhere before, but now wasn't the time to worry about it. Miss grabbed him under the arms and pulled him the rest of the way up. She quickly mounted the Runner to her makeshift harness that Rocky had designed for Roderick, and she felt the straps click into place.

Her storm sail deployed. It wasn't going to be easy to take off with the extra weight, but it wouldn't be the first time she had to do something like this. She had been on search and rescue detail after the battle of Langeles, and with Rocky's modifications had managed to grab a half-dozen men before a storm had hit the ruins.

The wind caught the storm sail, and she leaned a little to the left, testing the tension of the wind, feeling for the correct pressure on her sail. She lifted her grappling hook with her left hand. Rocky had modified it to shoot as kind of kite/parachute that would catch the wind for initial lift off. The torque when it caught storm winds was incredible. The first time she had used it, she had dislocated her right shoulder, and it had almost killed her. When she got back to base, she broke Rocky's nose for the what she thought was a poor design. Later, though, she realized there was no other way for the device to work, it was that torque that provided the initial lift necessary to get her moving.

Her line yanked hard and coupled with her boosters it pulled both of them upward with a hard jerk. If she weren't careful, she would have whiplash from takeoff, but over the years she had learned how to loop the line around her body in a way that prevented that. They began to sail up into the storm. The Runner she carried grew much lighter as the storm lifted them both and she began gliding around its edges like a surfer catching the crest of the wave. The difference between Miss and a surfer was that there was no wiping out, no falling back into the crest of the storm, that way meant only death.

When Roderick had first seen what Miss could do, he had commissioned her to train several of his best in an attempt to form a kind of aerial attack unit. He had thought that this would provide an amazing advantage for attacking cities. Miss had tried to train others how to ride the storms, but over and over, they kept dying. Even some of the most promising individuals made small and foolish mistakes that had ended their lives. After twenty-three others had lost their lives during training, Roderick had called it off. He had even suggested to Miss that she give up storm sailing because it seemed to be only a matter of time 'til it caught up with her. She had returned the suggestion with nothing but an icy stare. Roderick had never brought up the subject again. Miss was relatively free to do as she wished, largely because Roderick didn't want to end up with a broken nose, and also it was because she was good at what she did.

The air pressure changed suddenly, and the sail buckled. It sent the two of them spinning 'round in circles. They were descending fast. Miss twisted her body and the handles to the right and into the spin. She spun both their bodies around several times in a barrel roll and then gradually the spin lost its momentum in the face of gravity. She shifted her sail with her left arm to catch the wind from a different direction and turned herself back up to face into the storm. She was going backward now, but she had some semblance of control. Now the tricky part, she had to disengage the sails just for a few seconds so she could drop, turn, and catch the updraft of the storm to right herself.

"Hey, buddy," she transmitted directly to his suit.

No response. There wasn't any way to know if he was even still alive, let alone conscious. She could see out of the corner of her eye that the blood was beginning to stain the metal of her own EnViro suit. The white reflective lining would need cleaning later and her own symbols re-etched, but it wasn't the first time. Her suit had been awash with plenty of blood over the last few decades.

"Hey, I don't know if you can hear me in there or not, but things are about to get real bumpy. I promise you aren't going to like it, but if we want to survive this storm, it's necessary."

A low and guttural response issued into her ears, "Was I supposed to like any of this?"

Good, thought Miss, he still had a sense of humor; that was a sign he still had a fighting chance to survive.

"No, you're not, but this is going to be bad."

"Just do it."

"AI, prepare to disengage my storm sails, then wait till we've righted ourselves to re-engage them."

"As you wish, Miss."

"Prep yourself, Runner, on three, we go."

It was almost a shame to have to turn around, the sun setting behind the sandstorm was magnificent, and if her life weren't in danger, then she would have considered lingering to watch the colors shift and change over the horizon. She sighed. Things in the Barrens were so rarely convenient and peaceful. If you tried to stop and smell the roses out here, you would end up dead.

"1... 2... 3."

Gravity is a greedy mistress. It will jump on every opportunity it can to grab you and hurtle you as hard as it can toward the center of the Earth. Both Miss and the Runner dropped quickly without the support of the storm sail and Miss, despite all of her years of experience gliding through storms, was having a difficult time shifting herself around in that measly 4.5 seconds she had to save both their lives. She squirmed to turn the two of them but there was no use, it was just a little too much weight for her.

After three seconds of fighting with gravity to turn her body and save both of them from being thrown face-first into the ground, she was only on her side. A little over a second remained and despite the fact that time felt and appeared to be moving slow enough for her to shift everything, she knew with a panic-filled adrenaline that she couldn't manage the turn on her own. Through her mind moved at the speed of light, she realized too late that she needed the Runner's help to turn both of them, and she also realized that by the time she could say anything, they would both smash into the ground.

2.

What Miss didn't realize was that harnessed to her was one of the luckiest men who had ever walked the Earth. The grim reaper himself stopped bothering to show up to 17's near-death experiences because it usually left him rather disappointed and caused him to miss other more pressing appointments. 17 would tell you that he was just lucky, but Major John Daniels would say that he was unkillable. So far 17 had certainly been unkillable, and in that moment his instincts of self-preservation kicked in, and he indeed lived up to his reputation. Somewhere in the more unknowable reaches of the universe, the grim reaper once again sighed in frustration.

3.

Even though he knew it would cause him unbelievable agony from his open wound to do so, 17 recognized the moment they had begun falling that the harness they held them together was slightly off balance. He felt his left shoulder strapped a little higher than his right. To Miss, he knew that it probably felt like he was simply too heavy and she would continue to try and turn right instead of left. With all his strength, 17 twisted himself and Miss to the left until both of them spun around, now horizontal to the ground. Right as they faced the hard, rocky earth, the AI redeployed the storm sails. The updraft from the storm caught them and with only a few meters from the ground Miss activated her boosters, and they climbed higher.

4.

Miss heard a terrible scream of pain over her intercom.

"Doing alright there, buddy?" asked Miss.

"Alright? I don't think that alright is the word I would use, that fucking hurt." His voice was weak and gruff.

"Well, better hurt than dead, right?"

"Yeah but better not hurt than hurt."

"I take it you're fully awake now?"

"You could say that I hope to gods you have some painkillers and regen patches on you, I think I just tore my wound a new asshole."

"I have some first aid stuff. I'll break it open as soon as we land."

"When is that?"

Miss didn't respond. Instead, she was getting a bearing on her current location in her heads-up display. The storm rumbled behind her, an earthy dark layer of clouds circling and rumbling, always threatening to swallow them both whole. But now Miss had superb control of the currents, there was no chance it would consume them.

"AI, locate the nearest shelter for me, please."

"Yes, Miss." It paused momentarily, reading the manually entered topography that Roderick and his followers had updated every few weeks to match the changing landscapes of their territory. "Miss, it appears there is a cave with sufficient depth to ride out the storm about 6 kilometers straight east of your position."

"Perfect, thanks, AI."

"You are most welcome, Miss."

Rocky had installed solar-powered boosters that would allow Miss to accelerate faster than storms when she went to land or sought shelter. They were solar fusion-based and Rocky had manufactured them for her back at Atlantis base. However, the boosters had to be fairly lightweight to work, and so full fusion wasn't achievable in their size. The boosters provided just a short burst of energy that accelerated her forward a few kilometers, but the catch was that they took about fifteen minutes to charge up fully in direct sunlight. They had just used them to escape smashing into the rocks, so they would only be partially charged when they went to land. This meant that they were going to have to make a run for the shelter.

Miss examined the approach on her map. She had been to this cave on several occasions, and they would be able to land within 22 meters of the entrance, but it still meant that she was going have to de-harness the Runner early. Despite his wound and probably high loss of blood, he was going to have to run for the mouth of the cave.

Miss explained the plan to the Runner.

"I really hope you have some good painkillers as a reward for my good behavior."

"Trust me, the shit I have will knock you right out while the regen patches go to work."

"Thank the gods for that."

Miss noted he said gods and not god. It was a good indicator that he might be interested in joining the COG. It was a rare day when a Christian or a Muslim joined the COG. There was just too much paganism in their worship of Gaia for their tastes.

"You ready?"

"No, my boots are soggy from blood, and I hate that squishy wet feeling you get when you have liquid in your boots."

Miss rolled her eyes; this one was a talker, but at least he wasn't a total asshole. "When we hit that ground, just roll with the momentum and let it take you into a run. It's your only chance to get into the cave before the core of the storm hits. 22 meters may not seem a lot, but when you're riding storms its kilometers long."

"Got it. Let's do it."

Miss kicked up the boosters and spent every last bit of their energy. It had only given them a few hundred meters of space to work with, but so long as they both ran as hard as they could for the entrance to the cave, they would make it. She had survived narrow windows dozens of times before.

"AI, when we are 2 meters from the ground, release the harness."

"Yes, Miss."

They hit the ground hard. Both managed to catch themselves from the roll, and both ran for the cave, arriving just as the core of the storm touched their backs. Quickly they ran several dozen meters into the cave, the dust and rock flying in behind them, grasping at them like monstrous fingers.

The Runner began to wince noticeably, his entire body beginning to shake with each step, but he kept walking until they were well away from the entrance and around several bends. Algae grew in the cracks of rocks. There was no trace of wind and oxygen levels were relatively breathable down here. It would be a good place to pull off the Runner's EnViro suit and see to his wounds.

Before she could ask him to remove anything, the Runner collapsed and lay still. Worried that he may have just died, Miss checked his vitals; they were extremely weak. Miss quickly took off her own EnViro suit and unpacked her med kit. She immediately injected him with painkillers and antibiotics to stave off any infection. Removing his suit without aggravating the wound proved difficult, but she managed to do so.

She unwrapped one of the regen patches that she had brought with her in case Roderick had been injured. The patches could do a lot to heal bad wounds, but there was a limit to their effectiveness. There was no true substitute for an alcove. If you were hanging onto life by inches, alcoves could revive you fully, but the patches, they only stopped the bleeding and began regenerating tissue damage on the surface. They could heal a fresh bullet or knife wound fairly effectively, and even helped to dissolve bullets in the body and use the foreign matter to create additional tissue, but if the wound was too large, too deep, or too much blood was lost, they weren't very effective. As she placed the patch on the wound, she noted that she had no idea how long the wound had been open. The patches were a roll of the dice.

She laid the Runner's unconscious body flat and took his EnViro suit apart to allow it to dry out. It would stink pretty bad later, but he would just have to deal with it. She wondered briefly what his designation was and looked on the bicep of the EnViro suit. The number was missing; either he had no number or it had worn off from age. She wondered how old this guy was and who he was. If he was from Manhatsten, had she ever met him?

Her thoughts turned to Roderick again. Time was growing short now, and the search would be called off soon. She was sure that she could assume command and continue down the path he had prescribed to his followers, but to her, Roderick was a father figure, and so, until she was certain all hope was lost, she would keep searching.

The search for Roderick had halted the main plan to reorganize after Langeles and attack the cities that descended upon the main ruins for salvage. If that wasn't possible, they were to install a large number of agents in each of the cities to lay the ground for future attacks. Roderick would be furious when he had found that there had been quite a bit of delay in the plan, but he certainly wouldn't do much more than threaten punishment. After all, he was the one who was missing.

The key to attacking a city was the drills and the salvage trucks. When the drills were down and the salvage vehicles were out in force, the cities were vulnerable. The drill was a huge power drain and it took away the power requirements from some of the larger artillery defenses. It also took a great deal of time to disengage the drills and return to migration, which is why the security of each city had to watch so carefully for storms. Most cities could survive a moderately sized sandstorm without too much trouble, but a large sandstorm would cause serious damage. So far, no city had ever been destroyed by a storm alone, but it was certainly a tactic Roderick was willing to try.

The big problem for the COG was the AI and its ability to defend the city. The AI was relentless. Sixty years previously, just before Miss had joined the COG, they had tried to take on Saud without addressing the AI issue. Roderick had lost half his men in part because the damned Rih were so highly skilled, but also because the AI managed to bring the big guns online much quicker than Roderick had anticipated. Despite the problem of getting past the system AI, Roderick was fairly confident that their trap in the Langeles ruins could at least cripple one city during salvage operations.

With Manhatsten nearby, so many memories surfaced in her mind. It was true that there were many good memories, but her most recent memories of that city were awful. She had gone by another name once, but that seemed like a previous lifetime.

She had only been a foolish teenager when the fates had caught up to her. That had not stopped the Supreme Justices from sentencing her and her friend to a life of slavery in the Runnercore. Anger swept over her, a deep and ancient anger that had lingered so long in her body that it was unlikely that she would know how to live without it. She vowed revenge, and when the time came to storm Manhatsten, she wanted to be on the front lines and kill those justices herself. Miss had a special place set aside on her bunk to notch in their names. It was the only space on her bunk that was left.

Most nights, her dreams were filled with the horrific experiences of her first moments as a member of the Runnercore. Some nights she woke screaming, gripping the back of her neck, her sheets soaked with sweat. The chip they planted in the base of your neck, the horrible pain of having it inserted between your vertebra were among only the first of the terrible violations visited upon you. Then the muscle augmentation, training, and the long bouts of semi-sleep.

All of that wasn't the worst part though; the worst part is that if you failed to survive the training, they recycled you, turning you into a mindless drone that would perform menial tasks around the Runnercore docks for as long as they desired. That was the fate of Aaron. He was sentenced with her for that lousy book and for some reason his body rejected the chemicals. So far as she knew, the poor bastard was still there in Manhatsten, unable to think or act for himself.

Of course, no one really knew what remained of the person when they were recycled, but Miss knew one thing, she wanted to end his terrible suffering. A bullet to the head or a knife to the throat was a mercy for him.

Not for the first time, she had wondered about Jose. She had heard, through unofficial channels, of what that awful Senator had done to him. But considering what had happened to Aaron, he had definitely gotten off light. There was a strange mix of love and bitterness in her heart for him. It was hard to think about him, about the feelings she had shared with him, without being angry. When she had told Roderick what had happened to the three of them, he had told her that Jose was welcome in Atlantis base once Manhatsten fell. Deep down she still loved him, still waited for him. She knew it was unlikely that he had felt the same way. It was likely he was already married, but she still had her faint hope. It was that tiny light of hope in her heart that kept her sane. It kept her from completely giving in to the rage.

After training, they had put her in the alcoves for several months. When she was sent out on her first routine recon, she had encountered a storm. It was one of the largest sandstorms that anyone had ever encountered and neither of the more experienced Runners with her had survived. Through her quick thinking, she had turned her shelter into something akin to her first storm sail and had managed, just barely, to glide on the edges of the storm where the AI had indicated there had been a cave. She had broken her right leg and left arm in the process of gliding on that first storm, but she refused to let it kill her. She had crawled inside the cave and went as deep down as she could before falling asleep. When she had awoken, there was Roderick, standing over her. He told her about the Children of Gaia and of their need to destroy the cities in order to save Gaia. She eagerly agreed to join.

She wanted revenge. What had happened to Aaron, and to a lesser degree, Jose, was unforgivable. Here was her chance. If she survived long enough, the COG would provide her with a chance to exact her revenge, end Aaron's suffering, and liberate Jose from that terrible place.

When she had told Roderick of how she had survived the storm, he was intrigued. He asked her if she thought she could sail on the storm again. Miss had replied that she thought it was possible if she had some sort of glider to work with, and so Roderick's liberated engineer, Rocky, whipped something up for her.

Miss had the AI deploy her shelter out of her EnViro suit. She deflated the shelter most of the way and used it as a kind of mattress to keep her a few inches off the rocky ground. It made for a decent and semi-comfortable bed. Her thoughts turned to Jose, as they always did just before sleep and quickly, it claimed her.

5.

17 woke. He blinked, rubbed the sleep from his eyes and tried to recall where he was. Then he flashed back to the scene of all the bodies in Langeles and cringed. He recalled the fight with 'Akif and his wound. Looking down, he saw that he was only in the suit undergarment and he reached down to check his wound. A medium-sized tear was in the fabric but the wound, at least on the surface, was gone. He remembered some other Runner picking him up, and they flew or something. Mostly, what he remembered was being jerked around a lot and then some kind of rough landing. The other Runner must have had regen patches.

He scanned the room and saw the other Runner, and she was using her shelter as a pillow. 17 had used his shelter like that sometimes; it was the easiest way to keep from having to lay on jagged rocks. The first thing he noticed about this other Runner is that, beneath a layer of scars, she was beautiful. Her thick full lips and caramel skin betrayed her tough exterior.

He decided not to wake her right away. Instead, he would learn what he could about his surroundings and his situation. He looked in vain for some indication as to what city she was from. He didn't recognize her from Manhatsten, but that didn't mean too much. It wasn't like all the Runners knew each other. In fact, 17 would only recognize a few dozen. He looked at her suit carefully. She didn't have any of the typical markings of Manhatsten on her suit. No black M with a red background or 0001 associated with Manhatsten's city designation, but again, that didn't mean anything. His suit and many of the older suits didn't have the markings. The really strange thing though, was that she didn't have a number of any kind on her suit. So far as he knew, every Runner, from every city, had a number on their suit. Except for him of course, his had worn off, and he had never bothered to request a replacement.

He stood and looked around the cave for a few moments for some other indication of her identity, but found nothing. There was a short stabbing pain in his gut where the wound had been. It probably meant that the wound had been deep enough that the regen patch couldn't heal it all the way through, but at least the bleeding had been stopped and the wound was closed He would have to try and take it easy for a few days, at least until he could get to an alcove.

A memory of the storm arose in his mind, and he thought it best to get a little closer to the entrance to find out what kind of conditions he was facing. If the storm were still going, he would have to wait it out. If it had passed, he would suit up before waking this woman, just in case she was hostile. It didn't seem like she was from Saud, because of the lack of number, but she could be recon from a third city. Maybe the lack of number meant she was as old as he was. That prospect above all others interested him.

He was worried though. If there were a third city, then things would definitely get ugly. He would have to find out if that was the case.

Stepping lightly, 17 felt the surge of energy that came after using a regen patch. They had an adrenalin booster in them to help heal more quickly. The effect usually lasted several hours and gave the recipient additional strength and agility that they normally wouldn't be capable of. He supposed if this female Runner was hostile, she probably wouldn't stand much of a chance against him with the boost from the patch.

The heat of the passageway began to rise. That was a good sign. It meant that the storm had likely passed. He stopped a few dozen meters from the entrance. Already, the sweat beaded his forehead and the smell of methane seeped into his nostrils. It was strange that this cave seemed to have such clean air, that he was able to breathe so easily without a suit.

For a moment a thought occurred to him, could there be plant life below the surface? He could see a few patches of algae in the cracks, but that didn't explain the purity of the air. Something else had to be going on here.

Just before migration, there were a few news stories of some humans attempting to take refuge in caves, but after the cities began their migration pattern and their massive weight began to compact the surface, it was thought that any caves below, at least within a few thousand meters in depth, would likely collapse. But that didn't mean that it was impossible.

17 peered out of the exit. It was bright and sunny, blue with just a tinge of green in the atmosphere. Conditions were definitely clear.

"AI? You with me?" 17 checked the status of his arm cuff on his right bicep. When he was out of his suit in the Barrens, this is where the AI existed, though even if both the suit and the cuff were damaged, the AI could try to transmit itself wirelessly to the Manhatsten central AI data bank, but that was a risky proposition with all the storms and signal interference.

"Indeed, 17. I am here and fully intact. I have been observing and gathering data on your current companion, as I am sure her AI is doing so as well."

"Good, but first, what are we looking at out here. I mean, how much time have I been unconscious and how close are we to Manhatsten?"

"You were unconscious for approximately 19 hours. I have scanned your vitals, and though you lost a great deal of blood, you appear to be recovering. It is hard for me to tell how deep the wound is, and if some of your organs were damaged. I recommend taking it easy for the next 48 hours while your body repopulates your red blood cells and heals any damaged tissue. Currently, your red blood cell count is at 92% of the normal average. My long-range sensors indicate that Manhatsten is only 22 kilometers due Northeast. Once you move out of the cave and up the ridge to your north, you should be able to see the city."

"Wow, that's it? Got pretty lucky there."

"Indeed, 17, it would seem that once again, luck is very much on your side. I haven't been self-aware for very long, but I definitely notice that there is quite a trend of improbable situations becoming much more probable in your particular case. In fact, I have rewritten an algorithm based on your per-sonal–"

"Interesting and all, and you can tell me all that shit on the way home, but what about this woman. What's her story?"

"A scan of her face indicates that her current status is deceased."

"What? When did she die?"

"My apologies, 17, you misunderstand my meaning. What I mean to say is that according to Manhatsten records, this individual, Runner 5543, was marked as deceased."

"Alright, be straight with me. What the fuck does that mean?"

"Records indicate that she had died in a sandstorm with Runner 1943 and Runner 6344. I suppose, Sir, that would indicate that she has gone rogue."

"Rouge? How can any Runner be rouge? I thought that was just a myth that Runners tell one another when they are fed up or frustrated."

"I'm not sure, Sir, we have no records of any truly rogue runners in Man-hatsten because we, and by we, I mean Major Daniels and the consensus among my fellow AI, was that it was–"

"Impossible?" said a voice behind them.

17 turned and saw the face of Runner 5543.

"In case you're wondering, I've tapped into your coms while you were sleeping. I can hear everything that you and your AI transmit or receive. And just in case you try to call for backup, I've limited the range of your transmis-sions. It's a nifty little trick they teach us for recruitment purposes."

"Recruitment, huh? So, you're a dead chick. How did you pull that one off?"

"The same way I pulled your ass out of that storm, a lot of skill and a little luck."

17 noticed that she had already armed herself and most of her EnViro suit was back in place. Only her helmet and gloves remained off.

"What about your chip?"

"If you die for sixty seconds, apparently it deactivates, so yes technically I was dead for several minutes, but a great man found me and revived me."

"Learn something new every day, don't you, AI?"

"Indeed, 17."

"17? You're 17?"

"Yeah why, am I famous where you come from too? I seem to be getting a lot of that lately."

Miss drew her pistol. "You could say that."

17 glanced at the weapon and then back up to the woman's face. The pistol gleamed in the reflection of her brown eyes. It was an old pistol, still used gunpowder. There weren't too many of those still around, but you would see them in combat sometimes, especially with older Runners.

"What do you intend to do with that?" he asked.

"Whatever is needed."

"So after you saved my life and brought me to this cave, you want what, exactly?"

"I want you to stay put. Get back inside and suit back up. We'll probably get moving soon."

17 turned around and started marching down into the cave.

"Where are we going?"

"To our base."

"What base? What do you mean? Which city?"

Miss laughed. "Which city? Oh no, we aren't going to a city. We're going to Atlantis base."

"What? What's that?"

"It's the headquarters of the COG."

"The cog? What in the hell are you talking about?"

She smacked him in the back of his head with something hard.

"Ouch!" 17 looked back and saw she had drawn a knife as well as her pistol.

"I don't want to play twenty questions with you."

"Fair enough." He rubbed the back of his skull and felt a small lump already forming.

They walked back to the deeper part of the cavern where they had slept. 17 grabbed his equipment and put everything back on. The suit, as per usual, stank to high heaven and 17 thought to himself, not for the first time, that with all the advanced technology in Manhatsten, there had to be a way to make these things self-cleaning, or at least able to absorb the smell.

"You do realize that my suit seal is compromised? I won't be able to go very long distances."

"You'll go where I tell you to go. Besides, it's not too far from here. A day or two walk maybe."

"Look, don't hit me again, alright? I have no intention of hurting you or trying anything. I owe you my life, I'd be dead if you hadn't come along and I won't soon forget that. But give me a break here, you're the second person in the last twenty-four hours to recognize me, and I don't have the first fucking hint of a clue as to why. I'm just a goddamn Runner, an old Runner, but that's all I know and all I do. I don't understand why anyone knows my designation."

"What do you mean, someone else knew you?" asked Miss.

"A Runner from Saud said I'm famous in their city. Then that crazy fucker tries to kill me because it's honorable or something. And now at the mention of my designation, you pull a weapon on me. Could you at least tell me what in the hell is going on? I'm unarmed, and all I have is a Recon suit. I'm not going anywhere." There was an edge of anger and frustration in his voice. He tried to mask it, but the twinge in his gut wasn't helping the situation.

The Runner seemed to consider for a moment and then let out a heavy sigh. "Fine." She sheathed her long knife. But kept her gun pointed at him. "I guess you aren't going anywhere with your suit like that, and I bet your wound still hurts too. Guess it wouldn't do any harm to tell you a few things. You're coming with me anyway."

17 set himself against the wall. It was a gesture specifically geared at submission. He would escape, but only after she spilled the beans. She seemed a bit naive for a rouge Runner, but maybe she was just overconfident in her ability to keep him captive.

"Look, I honestly don't know why you're known in Atlantis base. All I know is that Roderick, our leader, has a standing order to bring you in alive if you are ever spotted."

"Roderick?"

"Yes, Roderick is the leader of the Children of Gaia."

"Who are the Children of Gaia? I mean, what are you, some kind of city refugee camp or something? You said it's not in a city?"

"Well, some of us are in cities." A grin spread across the woman's face.

17 didn't like that smile. He would have to be wary of this one. Considering she had pulled his ass out of the storm, she probably knew her way around a blade too.

"What does that mean?"

"Never you mind, when you come to Atlantis, you'll find out soon enough."

"Okay, fine. But what are the Children of Gaia?"

"We are an organization that seeks to restore the earth."

"Restore the earth? How in the hell do you plan to do that? I mean, you were just out in the Barrens, weren't you?"

17 was fully suited up now. Miss motioned for him to walk back up the path toward the entrance of the cave. He knew his AI was listening and recording all of this. Daniels would love to hear this.

"Well... we believe that the cities are the key to restoration."

"The cities? What do you mean?"

There was a sharpness in the Runner's voice. "The cities are a disease, they prevent the restoration of the Earth, and if we remove the cities then the Earth can begin to heal."

17 simultaneously felt a chill race up his spine and a wave of hot anger move down it. Could it be possible that this woman and others like her were responsible for Langeles? For all those dead children and the endless huddled human corpses that had so disturbed him? He had to keep calm and listen.

"So..." he was cautious and did his best to hide his emotion. He wanted to get information out of this woman. That information could be crucial to the survival of the people of Manhatsten. As much as he hated the city, he didn't want innocent people to suffer. "What do you intend to do with this disease?"

She scoffed. "What do you do with any disease? You cure it."

"And what if you can't cure it?"

"You burn the bodies and try to prevent it from spreading."

"So what are you saying, that this Children of Gaia organization tries to destroy the migrating cities?"

"I am not saying tries; I am saying we do. I am sure by now you have heard of what happened to Langeles? That was us."

There was no gentle transition between his emotions. Anger burst into his chest like a rampaging bull. 17 bit down on his tongue hard, trying desperately to maintain his calm. He knew that if he gave away his anger too early, she would put her guard back up and there was no hope of killing her or escape. Thoughts of the dead children floated through his mind. Thoughts of his own dead child filled him. Joseph was dead from ancient lunatics, but ones of a similar flavor. It was rare that he had known such rage. He would kill this woman. She would pay for what she was a part of.

"Did you by chance go into the ruins of Langeles?" asked 17. His voice was quivering.

"I pulled few other fighters out after the battle. Why do you ask?"

"Did you see them?"

"See what?"

"If you go into those ruins, the first thing you will notice, is not a ruined city, but the bodies."

The COG Runner's expression changed, it was a slight change, but 17 knew it was a clear indicator that she was putting her guard back up.

"What do you mean by bodies? Of course, there are bodies, the city collapsed."

"Most of the bodies I saw were the bodies of children."

The anger was burning through him, a hot sun in the center of his heart. In the same moment, a few tears filled his eyes, and there was an intimate mingling of utter despair and desperate anger in his face and voice. He took his helmet off, and his expression made the other Runner take several steps back. She drew her weapons again but almost dropped them.

"What, what do you mean?"

His voice shook. "Are you seriously going to tell me that you never considered how many innocent little children would die if you took down a city? That you never even considered all the blood that would be on your hands?"

"But all those children would die anyway when the Earth is out of resources."

It was a rote recitation. 17 recognized an argument like that. It was not her own. They were words put there by someone else. Glib talking points programmed to prevent critical thinking.

"And, what if, just maybe, we do figure out how to get off this rock? What if, in fifty years from now, before we run out of resources we figure out some way to salvage our world and bring it back?" He couldn't contain the rage any longer. It spilled over from the hot cauldron in his belly. He thought of his son Joseph, of holding his body in his arms.

"What will you tell yourself then, you fucking child murderer? Will you sleep well at night knowing that the blood of the innocent is on your hands? Will you tell yourself little stories about your righteous path and justify their deaths? You're just like all those fuckers before migration. The same people who justified the use of the High-Altitude Drones to kill my son. The same people who justified war over resources. But you're worse than that. You specifically target innocent people, millions of them, and for what? The idea that the Earth, that's dead, will somehow come back if we just step aside? Where does it stop, then? If you destroy all the cities, what about you? You're human too, aren't you, you gonna drink the poison, swallow the pill? You really think this nut job Roderick will stop with the cities?"

There was silence for a moment. It lingered long in that short time. The wind on the edge of the cave whistled.

"And what if they don't solve anything? What if humans slowly starve to death in those cities? Science can't fix everything. I would think at this point after so many centuries of failure, that would be clear. Human beings have done nothing but brought death and destruction to almost all other species on the planet. When do we pay for our crimes? How many innocent creatures died at our hands over the centuries? Where is the value of their life? Are human beings so important that all other considerations are out the window?"

17's anger faded just a hair. He wouldn't kill this woman. Not yet. How could he? She doesn't even know what she has done. He wanted to grab her and force her eyes open so she could see the price of destroying the cities. She was babbling about long-dead plants and animals to justify taking human lives. She had to know what that meant, what her actions meant, what this kind of thinking led to. Again, the memories of his long-dead son surfaced. He had almost forgotten that pain in the nearly 1300 years of Running in a barren landscape. But here it was again. An old wound reopened. It was a festering wound that threatened to spread its infection to his heart.

"Is that what you tell yourself? That somehow, long-dead creatures justify your actions?" He lowered his voice to just above a whisper. "I should kill you, but instead, I think it would be better if you went into those ruins and saw what you and your little organization have done. Do you know the kind of pain and suffering you have brought? Do you know what it means to die in the Barrens without an EnViro suit? It's pure agony."

"Kill me? That's a laugh. I think you overestimate your position here. And don't lecture me about life in the Barrens, we don't have a cushy city to go back to at the end of the day. I know what it truly means to live out here."

He was yelling. "Then how could you destroy a city and force millions of people to fend for themselves without any protection?"

They exited the cave. The sun was bright and clear, and Manhatsten was now visible and looming close.

"Because those cities are corrupt, rotten to the core, and everyone inside of them contributes to their rotten nature. There are no innocents there; there never has been. You know as well as I do how easy it is to become a Runner, how the Uppers sit in their tall towers and exploit the Lowers. How security upholds the law with brutal force. How the color of our skin makes us a target for recruitment. Those people in those cities aren't alive, they are just surviving, just sucking every last ounce of life out of Gaia and out of each other. We, the Children of Gaia, free those people, we liberate them from their long, oppressive lives."

17 laughed, it was a sarcastic and heavy laugh filled with all the irony the world could muster. "So you liberate people by killing them, you set them free by allowing them to run through the Barrens without an EnViro suit? Do you have any idea how insane you sound?"

"If they are truly innocent, they souls live on in the eternal gardens of Gaia."

"Yeah? That's what every religious leader had said throughout history when they wanted to justify violence."

"Shut your mouth or I'm going to show you exactly what it feels like to run in the Barrens with no suit."

"I don't think you will. No, I'm famous, you said yourself, and this Roderick character wants me. So I think I'm safe from your bullshit, from your ideological garbage. You know what else got us down this path to migration?

The exact same kind of unthinking and unfeeling ideological garbage that you are spitting out of your mouth."

"What the fuck do you know about any of that shit?"

"What do I know? I was there, lady. I am a hell of a lot older than you. I lived through climate change. I lived through the third world war and hell it brought. I lost my son to that war and the satellite drones that rained hell down from space. I know a fuck of a lot more about life and death than you do. How old you? A few hundred years, maybe? You're just a kid, and so is this fucking Roderick, children who are playing with things they don't fully understand."

Again there was a pause before the response.

"Those architects told us the earth would restore itself and has it? I don't see any plants or bushes out here. All I see is holes from all the drilling the cities have done. I see dunes and rocks and all the other things that tell me that the Earth has gotten worse, not better."

"I haven't quite been to the four corners of this world. But I know that what you did to Langeles is disgusting, and you and your Children of Gaia, you're nothing but a bunch of cowards."

"Yeah, well, Langeles is only the beginning."

"What's that supposed to mean?" asked 17. He knew exactly what she was getting at. He wanted her to slip up, to tell him more about what they were planning.

"Langeles is bait. We set a nice trap for other cities, as soon as they get to that salvage we will take them all down, every last one of them."

Now he knew he had to get to Daniels. She had said some of them were in the cities. There was no one in Manhatsten he could trust except Daniels. He was far too old and cranky and cared about his job too much to be a spy.

Her face changed. 17 could tell that she knew she had said too much. Her brows narrowed at him, and she pulled her blade again and lifted her pistol toward his head.

"Start. Walking."

He hesitated. He had to wait for the right moment. Getting this intel to Daniels was the most important thing right now. He could kill this woman later.

"Where?" asked 17.

"Southeast."

He turned and started walking.

"Is that where your base is?"

"No, I am going to take you a little way into the Barrens and then blindfold you. There is no way in hell I would let you know where our base is now."

"There's just one thing," said 17. He turned to face her for a moment.

"What's that?"

"It's about my AI."

"What about it?" She paused for a moment. "Come on, spit it out already."

"AI, protocol 17."

The EnViro suit's shelter flashed outward and knocked the Runner back. 17 completely ejected from the suit this time and it wrapped her body as she fell. The gun and knife spun out of her hand before she hit the ground. 17 snatched up the gun and with a few complicated hand gestures took it apart and threw the various pieces in different directions. He didn't wait for Miss to get back up before he started running. Manhatsten was close, and he thought he might be able to make it to the outer security perimeter before she could catch up.

He could hear the woman screaming with rage.

"You mother fucker! Get your cowardly ass back here. Don't you dare run away."

He glanced back as he ran. She thrashed around inside the shelter, scrambling to get free.

"Get back here!" she screamed.

Running at full speed, he didn't look back again. It would only take her a few more minutes to break free from the shelter, but by that time he would be gone.

"AI, are the Manhatsten's salvage vehicles out yet?"

"From this distance, it is difficult to confirm, but at the moment it does not appear so, 17."

"Let's hope they aren't, because as much as I hate that fucking city, I'm sure as hell not going to let those genocidal pricks get their hands on it."

There was a chance to save Manhatsten from attack. It was a small chance, but 17 knew that luck was on his side. It always was.

He ran for several kilometers and then, with blinding pain, his wound ripped open. Blood flowed again. He fell to his knees. He could no longer outrun the COG Runner. He glanced back, but he didn't see her. He could not will his body to go forward. Instead, he lay down against the hot earth.

He could see Manhatsten. He could see the towering skyscrapers, the massive legs and the hunk of excavated rock on which the city stood. To the left of him were the ruins of Langeles, and across the ruins, Saud had arrived.

"AI?" His voice shook. The pain punctuated his every breath.

"Yes, 17."

"Remember your promise." He swallowed hard. "If I die, don't let them recycle me."

He closed his eyes.

Epilogue

The stalactites dripped water ever so slowly into the Elder's reflective pond. The dripping echoed through the high walls of the cavern deep inside the earth. Far away from the vengeful winds and the angry sun, the Elder sat in almost complete silence. Wisdom came in time, there was no need to rush it, to hurry it along down a path it wasn't willing.

The Elder opened his eyes and stared blankly into the surface of the water. Gently he leaned forward and stirred the water with his right pinky finger. The water, so clear that it was barely visible, became clouded and muddled. Images rose and a man in a large and strange bulky attire allowed himself to be known. He could not see the man's face, but on his left arm were the long-faded outline of stitches, glowing where numbers had once been. The numbers were 1 and then 7; a number of change, a number of infinite possibilities, a number so odd for a man to wear.

More people began to surface in the water. A man missing his right hand, a woman of such anger that even some of the gods feared her, a young girl with great potential, a man missing his tongue, a woman who could fly, and another man, who was father of them all. They were more but they were only shadows. All their paths intertwined.

The Elder turned and looked at the tower behind him, it stretched almost to the surface. That tower was the great pillar that held up the earth. He knew that the destiny of all pillars was to fall. These people, they would bring change to their underground city. Not good change, not bad change, the wheel would turn. The wind would blow. Things had a way of circling round, converging and changing the nature of the wheel, but that did not stop the turning. The many trees surrounding the space rustled in agreement, though there was no wind.

The Elder gave thanks and offered a little tobacco to the spirit of the pond and then lit his own sacred pipe. This bearer of 1 and 7 would turn the wheel himself, but first, he must be anointed in the blood of sacrifice. The trees again acknowledge the Elder's thoughts. They spoke well of this 1 and 7. Only the blood of the past, the blood of the present, and the blood of the future would prepare him for his final task.

A young one approached him, one who had not yet chosen his path.

"Elder, my apologies, I do not mean to interrupt your conversation."

"It is fine, young Derrick; the conversation is over. The spirit of this place has shown me what it will."

"Elder Phoenix, a man has come into our city. He is a strange armored suit and injured."

"Is he marked by a 1 and 7?"

"No Elder, but he is missing a hand."

"Ah, so he is the one who comes first, then. I had thought it would be the other way 'round."

"Welcome him into our midst, but keep him under guard. This one will think himself clever, think to have us join his cause, but when his mouth opens, only blood will flow forth. Make the citizens wary of this man, but do not treat him unkindly. The one we are waiting for, the one who we must welcome, is the man of the 1 and 7 and whomever he brings with him."

"As you wish, Elder. Um... may I ask, have you consulted Aeis on this 1 and 7?"

"Fear of the wheel turning won't stop it. It was Aeis who revealed to me the 1 and 7 designation. Go and tell the people my message."

"Yes, of course, Elder."

Derrick turned to leave.

"One more thing, young one."

"Yes, Elder?"

"Your time for choosing is at hand. There is nothing more I can teach you. You must decide between the storm and the depth, and you must do it quickly."

"But Elder..."

"Delay much further and you will fall in between, and it is doubtful you will find the way forward again."

"Yes, Elder."

"You've already made your choice, it is fear that holds you back."

"Yes Elder, I know, fear does not stop the wheel from turning."

Phoenix smiled at the boy. He would choose storm, he was sure of it. So few chose storm as he, so many generations ago, had. The storm was much more dangerous than depth, but only those of the storm nature could lead. Aeis felt this boy was the next leader. Several centuries of leadership had made the Elder tired; even with Aeis's support and guidance, the road had been long and winding.

"What do you choose, young Derrick?"

"I choose..."

"Say what is in your heart, not what is in your mind." Elder's words were sharp, but still friendly.

"Then I choose... Storm."

The Elder smiled at him. "Then let preparations begin. Tell others that you are of the storm now. Oh, and tell the man with the one hand that the Elder Phoenix will see him shortly."

"Thank you, Elder."

The boy turned and left. Phoenix knew that the one-handed man would bring some of his anger and violence with him, but in the end, they would take the location of their city from his mind. Violence would not be visited upon the people of this city, Elder Phoenix and Aeis would see to that, at least until the coming of 17. When he came, the wheel would turn.

Don't miss out!

Click the button below and you can sign up to receive emails whenever Michael Kilman publishes a new book. There's no charge and no obligation.

https://books2read.com/r/B-A-ZUBG-APMT

BOOKS 2 READ

Connecting independent readers to independent writers.

About the Author

Michael Kilman is an anthropologist who occasionally visits other worlds and reports back what he finds. When he isn't writing fiction he is lecturing at a few universities in the Denver metro area, or working on his YouTube series 'Anthropology in 10 or Less.' Michael can be found at his website, loridianslaboratory.com, and on Twitter at @LoridiansLab.

Read more at https://loridianslaboratory.com.